The Predators

Gil Hogg is the author of *A Smell of Fraud*. He is a lawyer who has practised internationally and now lives in London.

The Predators

by

Gil Hogg

ARAMIS
BOOKS

Aramis Books
13 Stockleigh Road
St Leonards on Sea
East Sussex TN38 0JP

NOTE: ARAMIS BOOKS LTD DOES NOT ACCEPT UNSOLICITED MANUSCRIPTS OR OTHER MATERIALS

First published in 2001

Copyright © Gil Hogg 2001
All rights reserved

ISBN 0-9540215-2-5

The right of Gil Hogg to be identified as the author of this book has been asserted in accordance with the Copyright, Designs and Patents Act 1988

All characters and incidents in this book are fictitious. Any resemblance to actual persons, living or dead, is entirely coincidental.

This book is sold subject to the condition that it shall not, by way of trade or otherwise, be lent, resold, hired out, or otherwise circulated without the copyright holder's prior consent in any form of binding or cover other than that in which it is published and without a similar condition including this condition being imposed on the subsequent publisher.

A CIP catalogue record of this book is available from the British Library

Typeset by
David Chaproniѐre, Streatham, London

Printed and bound in Great Britain by
Bath Press Ltd, Bath

Acknowledgements

The author is grateful for the assistance and advice of friends in the FBI who naturally wish to remain anonymous.

Chapter 1

It was dusk when the man in the washed-out blue overalls and baseball cap, with a pair of work-gloves hanging out of his back pocket, moved up the drive of Jackson Bray's house in the deeper shadow of the trees.

He was empty-handed, with wide, heavy shoulders. A man used to hard work. A seam of short silver hair was visible at the back of his cap. His grim face was weathered to a crust. He stepped purposefully, without a backward glance for the flaring red clouds over Lake Oneida.

The house he was approaching was half submerged in trees, the windows reflecting the dying sun. The nearest neighbours were beyond shouting distance in their comfortable homes, tucked in folds in the hills.

It was an expensive area of large architect designed properties, tailor-made to the requirements of wealthy homebuyers. They bought the privacy of half a dozen wooded acres—and the seclusion.

The man marvelled at how vulnerable people like Bray were, so far from anywhere or anybody with all their expensive possessions. You only had to look at the house to know what was inside—carpets, silverware, rugs, paintings, ceramics, jewellery.

The man wasn't a thief or a burglar—but what pickings if he were.

You couldn't help noticing that those who lived around here were at the mercy of any weirdo who happened to drift by, twenty miles from the nearest small town.

Of course Bray would have a gun, maybe several. In this part of upper New York State, the residents weren't backwoodsmen. They were retired business executives. Sure, they could use a gun if necessary, but they weren't the kind of people who greet a stranger at the door hiding a Winchester Repeater behind them.

The visitor wasn't worried about Bray's armoury. Bray would never get a chance to use it.

He could hear the howl of a chainsaw. Bray was working in his woods, cleaning up after the autumn storms.

The man had planned thoroughly. Jackson Bray's wife was away, with the two children, spending a school vacation week with her mother. Bray's cleaning woman worked only in the mornings. The Brays didn't keep a dog. Bray himself had returned home from his office at WayCom Inc in his gleaming new Mercedes 300SL SW an hour before. Bray was alone.

The intruder looked very much like a tradesman, called in to do a small job on the plumbing or the electricity wiring. He had a superb feeling of being in control of the situation, although he could not know precisely what would happen in the next thirty minutes. That was the exciting part.

He would let events develop in their own way. He could cope with any move Bray might make, and it was a charge to guess what Bray might try to do, and how he himself would react.

Dealing with Bray was going to be pure sport.

★ ★ ★

Jackson Bray found it a comfort to work with the chainsaw. The scream of the saw masked the thoughts—fears—that beset him. The soft way the blade sliced through the heavy green maple wood gave him a sense of accomplishment. He was cutting through the thicket of troubles around him.

The girl was definitely on to him. He hadn't had a moment's sleep from the time he realised that. She'd hacked into his confidential PC diary, clever bitch.

Who *was* she? A nosey colleague, or some kind of plant put in by management to see whether anybody was selling secrets.

He had told his contact that he couldn't supply further information until he was sure about the girl. Christ, he could be caught in the act if she was a plant.

When he told his contact—the woman—she didn't reply, didn't say anything at all. Nothing. She just stopped the car in which they were driving while he talked, and let him out. He felt like he'd shat in his pants, and she was too polite to refer to it.

And then he'd lost his nerve, decided to give up before the FBI got him, turn himself in, get a plea bargain. He put his whole life on the line and *called the FBI*.

Twenty years of comfort and respectability and a nice family and a wife he still cared for. He had gone into a callbox and junked all that comfort and pleasure. In a few seconds. Churned his life into a hell.

And he chickened out on the call too. Couldn't go through with it. Hung up the receiver before the FBI agent came on the line. What the fuck was he doing?

He knew the technology backwards. He had spoken to the FBI operator. He would have been routinely taped. It would take the FBI about half an hour at the outside to identify him, because the FBI were listening to WayCom, and were sure to have voiceprints for everybody on the project.

It was only a matter of time before the FBI came sniffing after him. What he was going to do had thrashed inconclusively in his mind for twenty-four hours.

The pulsing and whining of the saw seemed to diminish the anguish, transmuting it to the deep cuts torn into the flesh of the tree.

He was glad Clara and the boys were away. He'd think it out tonight, alone.

★ ★ ★

The call was taken by Darren Lenz, a trainee at the FBI's callbank in Washington DC.

Caller: "I want to speak to somebody handling security on secret government technology."
Lenz: "Security on what? Will you say that again, caller?"
Caller: "Security on secret defence contracts, dammit!"
Lenz: "Right, sir. Your name please?"
Caller: "No name."
Lenz: "OK, sir. Can you tell me what kind of defence contract? You see, I have to plug you through to the right department, and I need to know—"
Caller: "Information technology. The contractor's name is WayCom Inc."
Lenz (after searching his infoscreen):
"I'm putting you through to Agent Gerstein ... Caller? Hullo, caller?"

★ ★ ★

Agent Gerstein called WayCom's lawyer, Mike Hayden in Washington.

"A guy tried to make contact, called us, about the security of WayCom technology, Mike. An inconclusive call, but we got a voiceprint."

"Who is he?"

"Jackson Bray, a computer engineer on STELA 2. Same guy Mariette Stevas thought might be on the take."

"Bray. So Mariette was right. How do you want to play it, Al?"

"We don't have anything on him. Maybe you should talk to him first. He's your client's employee. Softly. You know the line: tell us everything, buddy, or you're finished. Let me know how you go."

★ ★ ★

Two men faced each other amiably, in the office of the head of intelligence of the National Security Agency, in the Defense Department Building on New Jersey Avenue, Washington DC.

Hayden stretched in the old hide chair. The leather, polished by countless well-clothed bodies over the generations, creaked when he moved.

He could feel Byron Cerillo's influence like a charge in the air they were breathing; it seemed to emanate from the dark mahogany panelling, which once graced the office of the first Defense Secretary, Thomas Jefferson.

Byron Cerillo, the head of intelligence, plump in middle age, with a gleaming olive dome, sat behind the desk, in his slightly elevated chair, in command.

There was some parallel between him and the late J. Edgar Hoover. Although utterly different in appearance and style, Cerillo, more than any man alive, had knowledge of the deeds and misdeeds of others. And he was feared for it.

Both men listened carefully to the strangled voice on the tape. A recorder on the desktop replayed the call.

"Sounds overwrought, doesn't he?" Cerillo said. "Our suspicions that the STELA 2 technology is being stolen and sold seem justified."

"Not on this tape alone, but we'll take a close look at Bray," Hayden said.

Cerillo's arresting feature was the way his eyes moved; they glowed brown-black, luminous and unblinking. His dark glance dominated the otherwise comfortably rotund body.

"Mr Hayden, your client, WayCom, is going to lose the contract if the technology is leaking away to foreign governments. They should be screening their staff, watching them like a hawk."

"Why do you think Bray went off the line?" Hayden asked, avoiding an argument about whether WayCom were doing their job properly. There was a reserve between the two men which reflected the conflict between their interests."

"You can think of the possibilities as well as I can, Mr Hayden. One, somebody stopped him. Two, he changed his mind, got cold feet. Three, he wanted to start an investigation without getting involved. Four, it was a mischief-making hoax."

"I'd be inclined to go for two or three. He wants a investigation. He's an IT man, so he will probably know there's a risk of identification, but he doesn't care. He's confused, under some kind of pressure."

Byron Cerillo studied the lawyer, and in a distant way rather envied him. Cerillo thanked God for the gift of a superb brain, but couldn't help feeling short-changed in the personal appearance department.

Hayden, in contrast, although he always looked a little rumpled, had a nicely cut suit and a tall, lean frame to show it off, and what irked Cerillo, the kind of short, vigorous brown hair—grey streaked at thirty-five—that would never thin. Cerillo passed a palm over his own smooth skull.

"I'll buy that," he said.

"And I'll see Mariette," Hayden added.

Mariette Stevas, who worked for Cerillo, was the undercover agent they had placed by agreement in WayCom's STELA team.

"She might have more on Bray. She dropped to him, which was nice work," Cerillo said, evidently impressed. "I hear you're friendly with her."

"So what?" Hayden snapped.

"So nothing, Mr Hayden," Cerillo said, the big eyes dwelling on him with slight amusement. "I just like to understand the relationships between the players in a game like this, the interconnections ..."

Cerillo carried his position as a leading government mandarin lightly, and with a touch of sardonic humour—but Hayden could sense the arrogant edge. Cerillo had to hint that he was watching *everything*, and Hayden wasn't going to be drawn into talk about Mariette that had nothing to do with business.

Hayden chilled out. He looked at his watch and calculated how long it would take to get to Syracuse.

"Before you go, there's somebody I'd like you to meet," Cerillo said.

Cerillo led Hayden along a windowless corridor of the Defense Department Building, and punched the keypad on a locked door. They went inside.

The room, with its gleaming rubber floor, was bare except for a row of five armchairs along one wall. The overhead lamps were bluish and harsh.

Hayden sat down. He was looking through a glass screen into a spacious, well-lit office; it had a thick grey carpet, and streamlined cream-coloured workstations moulded to suit the positions of the half dozen or so operators.

The forefront of the room was occupied by a woman who faced Cerillo and Hayden over her desk, fifteen feet away. She was about thirty, tanned, and wore no makeup. Her long fair hair was held back by a black headband. She had a friendly smile, but her black and white check St Laurent jacket with its high collar gave her a formal appearance.

Cerillo settled his corpulent body in the chair beside Hayden.

"Good morning, Mr Cerillo," the woman said in a voice that was full, warm, difficult to place in any particular state or city.

"Mr Hayden, good morning," the woman added, to Hayden's surprise.

"Mr Hayden, this is Stella, our new security officer. You see she already recognises you. She's concentrating mainly on the WayCom contract."

Hayden examined the scene, puzzled. "Uh-huh. Hi. You've seen a file photo of me? I didn't realise you had one."

"I certainly remember your photograph, Mr Hayden. I have your career history."

"What do you have on Jackson Bray, Stella?" Cerillo asked.

Stella had a computer screen before her, shielded from their sight. She was picking up information from there. On her side of the glass panel clerks were moving around, studying PCs, word processing, handling streams of printout, talking.

"On the question whether Bray can be suspected of espionage, he has a bank account at Banco Nacionale, Cayman Islands, not notified to the IRS, and his general style of life is beyond his salary. His recent call to the FBI implies that he knows that espionage is active, and perhaps that he is implicated. Let me analyse the call for you—"

"No need to do that," Cerillo interrupted.

"That's useful to know, thank you," Hayden said, and paused. "Oh, just one question, Stella. Can you remind me who won the Masters golf at Augusta last year?"

Stella was unperturbed. "I like to keep to the job, Mr Hayden. This is a security briefing."

The words came back in the same tolerant tone.

Stella out-stared both the two men calmly, a half-smile on her face.

★ ★ ★

"She had you fooled for a while, come on, admit it," Cerillo said when they were back in his office.

"I wasn't sure at first. She's eerie, isn't she? Even smart enough to try to hide her ignorance."

Cerillo was in a communicative mood. "It's dangerous to talk in front of her as though she wasn't there. In a primitive way, she has a kind of common sense. She is Space and Terrestrial Experimental Learning Autocomputer, STELA phase 1, in one of its numerous forms. Naturally, we call her Stella."

"And the room, her staff, her own rather immaculate appearance?"

"Virtual reality. There's nothing there except circuitry. Amazingly lifelike, but a sideshow as far as we're concerned. WayCom wanted to impress us, show how you can set a robot up. All we're interested in really is the capacity of the artificial intelligence. Stella to us is just a small black box."

Cerillo said Stella could engage in a firefight with an enemy aircraft, and probably outthink a human pilot in combat situations.

"In civilian life, and in her STELA 2 form, she should be worth billions. She's far cleverer than the chess playing computer—but of course still short of the judgements of the human intelligence."

"And she has access to the NSA database for all her reasoning?" Hayden asked.

Cerillo had control of the world's most sophisticated surveillance capability, with links throughout government in the US to the FBI, the CIA, Interpol, and Europol. And he could, if he wished, combine these sources with the US's military and diplomatic intelligence.

Cerillo rocked his egg head. "She does. And more."

"Who's the genius behind this, Mr Cerillo?"

"It all started around 1950 with a British scientist, Alan Turing. I guess you'll have heard of him. STELA 1 itself is the brainchild of Gino Luchinelli—you've met him at WayCom. He's the most advanced brain in semantic, as opposed to syntactical, programming. You understand the difference?"

"I understand the principle, but that's a long way from understanding how they do it. Under normal syntactical programming, the computer has a set of rules, and works out results from them. The PC can be programmed to express the result in any language. In semantic programming, the computer has an understanding of the meaning of actual words—"

Cerillo leaned forward over his desk confidentially, clasping the plump fingers of both hands together in front of him. The pools of his eyes grew larger, and darker.

"It is complicated. But you know, human beings will always be cleverer—and much more evil."

★ ★ ★

Hayden flew to Syracuse. He stayed at the Marriott overnight. At 6 am he drove out to Lakeport in a rental car.

He approached the area where Bray lived through gently undulating wooded hills, developed with spacious luxury homes.

He steered up the steep drive to the dark-timbered, split level home, with wide windows and patios overlooking Lake Oneida.

Nobody answered his knock at the front door, and he could detect no movement within through the long windows which lined the terrace.

He walked around the side of the house. He passed a silver Mercedes SW parked in the open car port. The other car space was empty.

He tracked across the flowerbeds, to the back door. It was open. There was a faint mist of dampness on the tile floor, as though the door had been open all night.

He called out Bray's name.

No answer.

Hayden had no right to enter the property. But on impulse he stepped inside. He called Bray's name again.

He moved through the kitchen with its wall of tropical fishtank, across thick beige carpets, through a stylish reception room, and a mahogany laden dining room.

He looked quickly into each room as he passed. There were children's bedrooms with neatly made beds, posters on the walls and toys on the dressers.

One larger bedroom had a king-sized double bed: on the undisturbed bed-cover lay a suit, an office shirt and a tie. Beside the bed, a pair of black lace-up shoes.

Bray had evidently changed his suit upon returning from work, but not waited to hang it up, or throw his shirt in the laundry-basket.

The house was empty.

Hayden returned to the kitchen door, curious, and stood looking out at the woods: fine oaks, beeches and maples. And the fresh smell of a damp but sunny morning.

The door of the tool shed across the lawn was open. Hayden went over and looked in at an array of tools and gardening equipment.

On the floor, by the door, stood an open four-gallon gasoline tin, half full, and a funnel. Bray or somebody had evidently been fuelling a gardening machine.

Hayden took the paved path into the woods. The trees shushed slightly above him and showered a few drops of moisture.

He had walked fifty yards, when a flash of orange colour caught his eye through the foliage: it was a garden tool of some kind, and he stepped toward it.

Then he saw a larger indistinct grey shape resting on a bed of leaves.

He stepped closer—a human figure crumpled beside the tool.

Bray lay on his back beside the cut bough of a maple tree, his face grey-white, a paper mask, smooth, almost unrecognisable to Hayden, who had seen his photo a number of times.

The dark eyes were open, and the expression was strangely calm, earnest and attentive.

Bray wore a cotton workshirt and jeans. His right leg was at a curious angle to the rest of the body; it had nearly been amputated at the groin. The thigh-bone had been severed, and a section of it protruded, with a string of torn flesh, and blue-white muscles.

Beside the body was a blood-flecked chainsaw. One of Bray's hands rested on the handle of the saw, as though it was an affectionate pet. The ground around Bray was darkly saturated, but on his jeans, and on the pine needles, the spray of blood showed red.

Hayden bent close to the still mask of the face, reached out to touch the throat to see if there was a pulse, and then withdrew his fingers before touching.

A fly buzzed. Bray was long dead.

Chapter 2

Vance Wayman's office was in a glass building like a huge bug, set in parkland a few miles outside the city of Syracuse.

Hayden checked in at the desk at 8 am, and Rosemary Delmer, Wayman's PA, came to meet him. He followed her to Wayman's office.

Vance Wayman welcomed him, but always with a critical eye, as though looking for a weakness.

Wayman was in shirtsleeves, and wearing only socks on the carpet, trousers held up around his podginess by broad scarlet suspenders.

Wayman was a legend on Wall Street. And a hero to many. His early career as a wheeler-dealer on the street was shrouded in myths. He had started as a ladies' fashion salesman. He was a deal-maker with only the most basic formal education.

Over fifteen years, he had brought the Wayman Computer Corporation from a small-time component manufacturer to the cutting edge in both software and hardware. He had done it by a series of corporate mergers and takeovers, hiring and firing, selling or junking the parts he didn't need.

He had a reputation for savagery cloaked with charm. To those who were on his side, Wayman was a near-visionary in his ability to stay ahead. To those who were against him, Wayman was a destructive force who had consigned tens of thousands of careers to the dumpster.

"This is bad news, Mike. I'm very upset. Maybe it was an accident."

"No chance."

Wayman had no time to dwell on the dead man, and little interest in the macabre details. "Bray selling us out? Who in hell to?"

Wayman was thinking of the forthcoming Senate Committee hearing on the STELA 2 contract. It wouldn't look good.

"We don't know anything yet. Cerillo is saying you could lose the contract."

"The wind has changed in Washington. They don't like me."

"Why?"

Wayman held up a hand, and rubbed the thumb across his fingertips, the money sign. "I dunno. New alliances. More profitable liaisons. I dunno."

"You don't think you're at fault at all?" Hayden asked the question dryly as though this was an impossibility.

"I believe our project work, and our security systems are the best of the best. Follow up on Bray. You'll find we examined his underwear with a microscope. And get Cerillo to send me a check for what the NSA owe me—before STELA 2 is complete, and starts running for President," Wayman added grimly.

The tall, tinted windows of Wayman's suite looked out from the seventh level front of the building across to the vast car park. Beyond the parking lot, were trees and parkland; it was WayCom territory as far as the eye could see.

"I like to see my staff arrive," Wayman said, waving an arm toward the glass. "I'm on the horn or dictating to my secretary, I watch."

Wayman at first glance looked pudgy and nondescript, but he had magnetism; there was an irrepressible spirit about him. He was smooth skinned, with a short nose and fleshy, cherubic features. In his early forties, the surplus flesh was beginning to thicken underneath his chin. The lines on his forehead were deep. His scalp gleamed through a coating of slicked-down fair hair.

Hayden sensed there was something else. Wayman was that rare chief exec, a busy man who always seemed to have time.

Wayman pushed up the sleeves of his white shirt to reveal pallid, meaty forearms, and leaned his butt against his desk, facing the windows.

"You know, Mike, I once had a room in the St Francis Boys' Home in the Bronx. Looked out on a brick wall a few feet away. If I put my head out the window, all I could see was a crack of light a hundred feet up, where the wall hit the sky. This place is kinda different."

"Yeah. This is no boys' home."

Hayden followed Wayman's stare. He could see the cars had started to arrive in a solid stream; they looked like candies on a tray at this distance, gradually building up patterns of colours as they parked.

Buses brought disabled workers from Abbey Forks, five miles away, but most of the staff arrived by car, and walked from the parking lot toward the security barrier at the front entrance. Some looked up at the mirror-glass walls of the building.

"They know I'm up here, but they can't see me looking down at them."

Vance Wayman seemed to draw strength from the lines of

employees flowing toward him, nourishment flowing into his bloodstream.

"I put WayCom together, Mike. And I fight every day to keep it together."

Hayden watched groups of young men and women moving toward the security barrier, white, hispanic and black. The men were mostly in dark suits and white shirts, with hair that picked up lights from the sun. The women wore brighter clothes, often smart slacks.

He saw a black Cadillac sedan swing into the underground space beneath the building.

"A company car. I turn a blind eye to the drivers' scams. They fiddle the gas, skim a percentage for private sale. Sometimes they use company cars as hirecars! I don't do anything. See the big woman in white?" Wayman said.

Hayden observed the nurse, in a white uniform, walking in a crowd of suits, heading for the medical annex.

"The medicos and nurses dish out Valium and Prozac and brandy like cornflakes and milk. They certify sick leave as though every day was Christmas day—"

Wayman pointed. "That guy there, six and a half feet tall, hair cropped like a sergeant-major?—catering boss."

Hayden couldn't miss the two hundred and fifty pounds of him.

"His staff get free flowers, fresh vegetables and fruit, with the odd chicken or ham thrown in. They think I don't know."

Wayman wasn't a purist about theft. "In my world, if you're a waitress, you go home with a fresh steak in your bag."

"You mean fiddling is endemic, and the STELA 2 people, like Bray, are doing their bit?" Hayden asked.

"I mean it's a highly imperfect world, Mike. As Charlie Hayden's son, you ought to recognise that."

There it was again, the Charlie Hayden effect, scraping across his consciousness like sandpaper.

Hayden didn't respond. He had come to quite like Wayman. Or was he mesmerised by the man?

"You know your daddy was quite a power on Wall Street. Charlie Hayden. Taught me a few things. Ha ha!" Wayman said.

Hayden had faced this leering comment, or the like, many times before. He had built a hard shell around it. But underneath the shell, he squirmed.

Wayman stuck his thumbs through his suspenders resignedly, the boys' home kid getting some juice from the problems of those who were more privileged.

"Your old man was just unlucky. Everybody's stealin' and he got caught."

Hayden's eyes were shrouded. "I'm not my old man."

"I like you," Wayman said. "I gotta legion of Ivy League dildos doin' my mergers and acquisitions, Mike. I hired you *because* you're Charlie's son, not a polished plate Yale man. Because you can swim in the DC slime. Don't forget it. Don't let me down. Protect me from those bastards in Washington."

Hayden gave a cracked smile, and looked away, out of the windows.

He saw Gino Luchinelli, technical boss of STELA 2, bulging gut, untidy thin hair, in a sports jacket and white slacks, coming across the lot with a dog; it was a boxer on a leash. The dog barked at the crowd, scattering them.

"What will the asshole pull next?" Wayman complained. He mumbled that he provided a creche for children, sports facilities, a manage your own time system, and a raft of health benefits, but the staff always came up with a new demand. Next thing, there'd be a request for kennels.

"Of course Luchinelli *is* different—he knows he can get away with murder, and he's always doing it," Wayman conceded.

"You think he's loyal?"

"Yeah. He's a boffin. Only interested in his work. Pay him in peanuts, and he'd do it the same."

"Uh-huh," Hayden said, unconvinced. "Well I won't waste your time looking at the view." He was terse, still rankling about Charlie Hayden.

"Business, huh? Business, not philosophy. OK." Wayman grinned.

Rosemary Delmer swung the door open instead of speaking to her boss on the intercom. The way she stood there, hand on hip, told them it was important.

"The President's aide is on the line, and he wants you to pick up the phone. The President will be on the line in a moment," she said, as though the President called every day.

Wayman clamped his teeth. The long climb from the St Francis Home, working day and night had taken its toll—headaches, bad dreams, stomach pains, an ever-present imprint of concern on his face. Tension. Laughing was a rictus movement.

But there was a charge of adrenalin in running a big corporation which overcame the pain, and made it all worthwhile …

He reached for the phone as Hayden was ushered out.

Chapter 3

Jed Olsen and his daughter Sherry were amongst the select few to be hustled through the security at the VIP entrance to the White House, for the reception on the South Lawn.

It was an early autumn afternoon in Washington DC. The leaves of the cherry trees were thin and grey, but the air was unseasonably warm. The sky, penetrated by the needle of the Monument, was light blue, and cloudless.

Sherry was eighteen, and not yet a victim of fashion. She wore a simple Laura Ashley floral dress, with a full skirt, low heel shoes, and a wide straw hat with a pink ribbon.

She was just beginning to accompany her father to official engagements like this, and she didn't feel all that poised. Especially as she knew she was going to meet her mother, who was now Mrs Vance Wayman.

It was really wacky to partner your *father*, and meet your *mother*, who was partnering someone else—even if your mother was your best friend.

"Can we make sure we say hullo to Mother and Vance as soon as we get inside?" she asked her father, anxiously.

Sherry was on difficult ground; she knew her father disliked Vance Wayman, and he didn't like her mother much either. She couldn't figure why wrinklies got so screwed up about relationships.

"Sure," Jed Olsen said agreeably. And he meant it. The Washington crowd needed to see that his relations with Diana and her husband appeared to be open and amicable—even if they were closed and bitter. Having lost a wife who was a society icon, the last thing Jed Olsen could afford to do, as a matter of pride, was to look sour about it.

In a few moments, with Sherry's pushing, Jed Olsen had been dragged away from important people he'd sooner have stayed with, and they had joined Diana and Vance Wayman.

The four stood—not close—cardboard-stiff grins on their faces, in an exclusive square, keeping out the photographers, and newsmen, and other guests who pressed past.

Sherry hugged her mother, and Vance Wayman. "Oh God, you look terrific," she said to her mother. The first words spoken amongst the four.

Diana Wayman smiled affectionately at her daughter. "Thank you, darling. Blame Versace," she said.

She was a slender woman, slightly taller than her husband, with long flowing honey hair. She glistened in the sun in her cream broad-brimmed straw hat, and light tan suit. She had a presence.

The two men barely gestured to each other, and didn't speak, shake hands, or allow their icy eyes to make contact.

Wayman was unremarkable, a thickset, fortyish businessman in a grey suit with thin hair and rimless glasses—he was almost indistinguishable from half a dozen other men in the crowd, and completely outshone by Jed Olsen.

Olsen was ten years older, well over six feet tall, athletic, with a strong-boned open face, a high forehead, and a fountain of thick grey-blond hair which he wore rather long in natural waves.

Wherever Jed Olsen went he created a stir with his gracious, presidential manners. Most people here knew who he was, and those few who didn't, would be curious. Like his former wife, he had a presence, an aura. He looked like *somebody*—and he was somebody. He and Diana had been one of the most brilliant couples in DC a few years ago.

After a few moments of inconsequential chat between the two women, the two pairs parted.

Sherry immediately took her father's hand, and disregarding the other guests, swung round to face him. She stood on her toes, pressing against him, and looked up into his blue eyes with the sunlines around them.

"Daddy, why do you always have to *show* you dislike Vance?" she whispered.

"I didn't think I was," Olsen said, smiling for the crowd.

"It sticks out a mile."

His expression hardened. "Well, he took your mother away."

"Oh, come on Daddy, you and Mom were finished long before Vance came on the scene. You had your girlfriends—"

His own daughter was saying this to him on the lawn of the White House with the President twenty feet away. He could smell the milky heat of her cheeks, she was pressing so close.

"OK, OK. Miss Know-all," he hissed, nodding agreeably to nearby acquaintances at the same time. "I trusted Vance Wayman once, and he robbed my business of its brains, set us back ten or more years—"

"Business, shit! *You're* the one who's always saying it's a game, and the best person wins. What's to be so sore about?" Sherry shook her head in disbelief.

"We'll talk about this, Sherry, but not here."

Olsen spoke in a low voice, out of the corner of his mouth, and turned away from the gush of youthful frankness—it was like a jet of cold water. He moved smoothly into greeting a senator and his wife.

Jedadiah Adams Olsen III began to work the crowd with his daughter, like any politician, allotting a few moments to each according to the importance of the person.

He knew many by first names, and he had a good memory for personal details—a new baby, a recent bereavement, an over-exuberant dog. Anything to tug a heartstring, and remind of loyalty.

The Olsens were an influential dynasty; they had maintained a place in East Coast and national politics for three generations. They had old money from the turn of the nineteenth century, produced by the earliest business machines—typewriters and cash registers. Jed Olsen was more than a handsome figure in this crowd.

The formal part of the proceedings was about to begin, and guests were finding their way to the rows of chairs arranged around the presidential podium.

Jed and his daughter moved to reserved seats near the front. All the heavy artillery of the press and TV were there in force, pointing their mikes and lenses at the platform and, where necessary, elbowing the guests aside, or insolently placing trolleys bristling with camera equipment in front of them.

"How's your mother, Byron?" Jed Olsen asked Byron Cerillo, as he took his seat.

The head of intelligence at the NSA was beside Olsen, sun glinting on his dome, the searching eyes hidden by Raybans.

"Well, thanks Jed," Cerillo nodded, flattered by the personal remark. The passing mention of his mother was a reminder that pricked deep into Cerillo's past.

The Milstein family—relations of the Olsens—had taken an interest in the precocious only son of their Italian immigrant housekeeper. A Milstein family trust had helped with the boy's school fees. Byron Cerillo had well justified the charity which took him through high school to Yale.

Cerillo's gratitude to the Milstein family was immeasurable.

"I see Wayman is here, trying to make out with the President," he said.

"The President may be the only friend Wayman has. Men like Wayman don't make many friends," Jed Olsen said, caustically.

He brought his mind back to the ceremony: the President stepped on to the platform, with his chief of staff half a pace behind. The crowd quietened.

The President welcomed Lieutenant-Colonel Sharon Armiston, one of the USAF's top guns, and the colleagues of her flight. He explained that Sharon's flight was credited with destroying more attacking Iraqi planes over the Gulf than any other.

The President had lost a little weight, and his colour wasn't as high as usual. The sun shone on his glossy black helmet of hair—dyed, Jed Olsen insisted.

The President raised his arm to the applause—the Commander-in-Chief showing off his fighting force.

The flyers had their brief moment of fame, three men and two women, clever, almost nerveless pilots, superbly fit, and at the height of their form. They waved to the crowd, and the cameras. Sharon Armiston said a few carefully crafted words—how proud of their unit they were, and how honoured they were to meet the President.

"Sweet sound-bite. Coast to coast stuff," Cerillo whispered.

Olsen snorted. "The President touts for these moments like a dog begging for biscuits."

"How many planes did you knock out personally, Colonel Armiston?" the CBS reporter asked, pitching with practiced accuracy into the millisecond of silence which followed Sharon Armiston's words.

Sharon Armiston's reply was cool and immediate—and carefully prepared: "We rate all kills as flight kills. Often they involve more than one aircraft. We don't have personal totals."

The reporter accepted the reply without realising how smoothly rehearsed it was, and without understanding that he had touched on a major piece of public misinformation.

Byron Cerillo leaned close to Jed Olsen and said, confidentially, "You can see the Pentagon brass giving approval, but they know it isn't true. Most of the latest Gulf kills have been made by pilotless aircraft. STELA 1 technology. We don't want to talk publicly about it at the moment. We're happy to let Sharon share the glory with her team, until we make more progress."

Olsen had already heard this. He couldn't contemplate the success of the STELA technology without a surge of annoyance, because, but for Wayman, his own company, Fairford, would have developed STELA.

It was a story that had never ceased to trouble him, and it submerged the press activity around the pilots as he watched.

After the Second World War, the Olsens' Fairford Systems Inc left cash registers far behind, and became a world leader in mainframe computers, headed only by IBM; and then again, successfully made the leap to microprocessing. Fairford and the Olsen clan seemed to be set fair to continue their domination—only to be eclipsed by a tubby little nobody with a shiny scalp, and misty—shifty—eyes behind his spectacles: Vance Wayman.

Olsen looked past his daughter, along the row of seats at the profile of his ex-wife, the straight nose, tbe invitingly sensual lips. A proud and beautiful woman as he'd always appreciated; but what had he missed about her?

How *could* she be so obviously captivated by an oleaginous creep like Wayman after all these years?

It wasn't that he missed Diana in a deeply personal sense—it was actually true, as Sherry had said, that long before their separation their relationship had begun to fall apart. It was the thought that she was now Wayman's possession that needled him. Anybody but Wayman.

It made his intestines writhe, to be sitting with his daughter, while her mother was a few yards away, with the man who had done so much to harm him.

Jed Olsen's private vow to bring the loud-mouthed, illiterate street-trader down was the only thing that made scenes like this bearable.

Olsen dragged his attention away from the pair, and spoke in a low voice to Cerillo. "I hear things are going forward for the Senate Committee enquiry into STELA 2."

"Sure," Cerillo said, quietly. "Wayman will get a hard time."

"What are the chances that the Committee will recommend termination of the contract?"

"I'll be surprised if they decide anything else," Cerillo purred. "That's a personal confidence, Jed."

"I understand, Byron. Thank you. You have evidence?"

The question was asked in a faint, almost careless monotone, but it was a vital question to Jed Olsen.

He turned, his eyes fanning casually over the assembled crowd. He contrived a look of ease. One or two senators and congressmen, a general, the head of the CIA, noticed him, and inclined their heads respectfully.

If his company inherited the STELA 2 contract, the artificial intelligence technology would make it a world leader for decades, but even more than that, the satisfaction of besting Wayman ...

Cerillo went on in his ear, "Wayman's cost overruns are huge and unacceptable. The FBI are looking at whether there have been security breaches—"

"And there's the small matter of who Wayman paid off to get the contract," Olsen said.

"If you come up with evidence on that, Jed, it will be like gasoline on the bonfire. The Senate Committee will roast Wayman alive."

Olsen contemplated Wayman's indictment for bribery. Nothing in Olsen's life would give him greater pleasure; it would be exquisite.

"You know, Byron, at Fairford we haven't stopped our research. I doubt there's anybody else in the US—the world—to match us."

Cerillo didn't reply directly, but removed his glasses for a moment, his huge eyes fixed on Olsen's, and for all the intellectual rigour that was packed behind them, Olsen could detect a quiver of servility.

He put his hand lightly on Cerillo's arm. "You're doing a good job, Byron."

Olsen spoke judgementally to the NSA intelligence chief, as though he was already President, and Cerillo was working for him.

Chapter 4

Hayden's meeting with Mariette Stevas was in the crowded car park of a shopping mall at 10th and Lakeview in Syracuse.

He had driven to the park after his meeting with Wayman. Perhaps he chose the place for a meeting because it was so unthreatening on a bright, chilly day, with lots of shoppers parking, and loading their cars.

He waited, and after quarter of an hour he felt a nudge at the passenger door, and Mariette slid into the seat beside him, and closed the door. The interior was filled with her perfume.

She shook her dark hair back, and pacified it with her hand. She looked very young, and open-eyed, and although there wasn't a ripple on her brow, she looked worried. A young hotshot trying to prove herself. A new NSA recruit hoping to make a career in intelligence work.

She was about eight or ten years younger than him, and it seemed like a lifetime. He couldn't understand why a middle class kid with a Vassar background would want to go into this work. She was seeing the soft side of it at the moment, but it had a hard side, a dark side.

She leaned over and rested her lips on his cheek.

He had, what would you say, seduced her? The older man, scuffed at the edges, ex-married, and the kid wanting to live it up, wanting to know. He had asked himself whether it was wrong. But no, he couldn't see it was. He was free. She was free. OK, she was a working acquaintance, but so what? Their liaison didn't compromise his work, or hers.

He was fond of her. She helped to soothe the bruises he was still suffering from his former marriage.

They talked quietly for a while. She told Hayden that she had been watching Carl Leman, the Financial Controller on the project. He was very nervous and distracted, but she had nothing specific on him.

"Occasionally he takes an afternoon away from the office which doesn't seem, from his diary, to be a regular business meeting and I've tried to follow him, but nothing more serious than a visit to the dentist."

"OK. I'll have a look at our file. He might be ripe for closer surveillance."

When Hayden explained Jackson Bray's call to the FBI, and his murder, Mariette glazed over. An exhaled breath and silence.

"Jack Bray *dead*? I can't believe it."

"It's a high-stakes game, Mariette. What's the matter? I know you knew Bray, perhaps liked him. Are you so surprised?"

She swallowed and shook her head airily. "No. Of course not—"

But she was.

"Well?" He looked at her indulgently.

"Mike, there's something I *intended* to report … I think Bray might have been on to me. He might not have been really sure, but I guess he might have suspected I was after him."

"What happened?"

There was a note of incredulity in his voice, because he was confident that the chances of her being identified were very slight.

"It was so stupid, I hacked in to his personal diary, and he must have been aware that somebody who was unauthorised was getting in there. He put in a program to trace the visitor. Very smart. Then he came to me. He said it was nice work, doing that, being able to get through the firewall, and how did I do it. I said it was just a little trick I'd taught myself—"

"Yeah, but how did you explain *why* you were looking at his schedule?"

"I said I was interested in what he was doing because I thought he might take me to dinner. I tried to laugh it off."

Mike Hayden gave a sceptical sigh. "And of course he never bought it."

Mariette Stevas's even teeth bit her lower lip before she spoke. "Maybe. Half and half. He was kinda flattered I think that I was chasing him. Or might be chasing him."

"When did this happen?"

"Three days ago."

"Three days. Time for people to do some thinking, and make a move. *You* may have panicked him into that call to the FBI. You should have told Al Gerstein or the NSA."

"I was going to report, it's just I haven't seen Al in a week."

Hayden tried to assess the risk to Mariette if she stayed on the job. His eyes strayed across the peaceful mall.

The NSA had got her a legitimate post as a junior computer

programmer on the STELA 2 research team. Only Cerillo, Vance Wayman, Hayden and the FBI knew about her. *Until Bray realised.* It had been a perfect set-up for her to watch the team from the inside. She might trap a rat; she might not.

Mariette had watched every member of the team, but fixed on Jackson Bray some weeks ago, a clever but bitter computer engineer who had been passed over in the lottery of executive promotions.

And the NSA had followed up Mariette's reports with an investigation of Bray's affairs. His phone and personal computer had been tapped. His questionably high life-style had been uncovered, and an intercepted e-mail had revealed the undeclared foreign bank account.

Even before the killing, it looked as though Mariette could have the right target—but for her to obtain actual evidence that Bray was selling secret information about STELA 2, and identify who was buying it, might have taken months.

Mariette was looking at him questioningly, enduring the silence. "What do you think, Mike?" she asked, finally.

"I see it like this. Bray was our man, or one of them. He suspected you were on to him, and felt threatened. Maybe he had other pressures, He might have realised he was being bugged. He panicked. He made that call to the FBI thinking of leniency. Remember what he had to lose. He was in his forties and looking at a quarter century in a Federal pen. He would have had to stop his activities. He was probably forced to tell his buyers that things were getting hot, They would have had to drop him cold, and if they suspected he was going to squeal—well, they had to silence him."

"Go that far?" Mariette looked around at orderly middle America getting on with the day, toting bags full of fruit and stores, kids eating ice-creams, women pushing baby-carriages, two senior citizens leaning on the bonnet of an old Pontiac, passing the time …

"Yeah. Don't be fooled by the polite, laid back atmosphere at WayCom. I see a red light. You'll have to speak to the NSA about getting out. I think you should go now. Drop everything, and get back to DC."

Mariette pouted, unwilling to accept Hayden's view, and shook her head in disagreement. "No Mike, I know I messed up. OK. But surely we don't have to abort the whole mission, I mean—"

Hayden persisted gently. "Bray's buyers may have other agents in WayCom beside Bray, whom they want to protect. They might feel you're a threat."

"Shit!"

Mariette was thinking of the computing work that she genuinely enjoyed. Her task watching the STELA team was a search that overlaid her formal duties, and absorbed the rest of her waking hours. She had worked so damn hard. It was a neat assignment that would boost her career if she could have spiked Bray or one of his colleagues ...

"Look, Mike. I think we should let it coast for say a couple of weeks. See how people react. It could be a golden opportunity to get more information. Hell, nobody's going to come around the corner with a thirty-eight in their fist. I may be able to salvage something out of the wreck—"

"Officially it's up to Byron Cerillo, but I'm concerned for you, girl."

Mariette slumped. "I feel such a failure." Her voice went up a note, and started to waver.

She was also thinking of the wrench of walking out on the friends she had made at WayCom, and her gem of an apartment in Cypress Drive. She was deflated, and Mike Hayden seemed to her to be thinking like a guy who saw a gun barrel aiming from every dark corner.

He relented a little. "Don't blame yourself. These things happen. Get instructions what to do from the NSA as soon as possible."

She nodded curtly. "Yes, Mike."

"Let's go out tonight and have dinner," he said, as she slipped out of the car.

"My place at seven," she said, miserably.

He watched her heading across the parking lot, weaving between the cars, her head hunched down, and the wind blowing her hair.

Chapter 5

Heidi Stoller parked the hire-car in the cramped car park at the offices of Fairford Systems, thirty miles from the parkland surroundings of WayCom.

The premises were caught up in Syracuse's industrial sprawl; there were no lawns or gardens, only a desert of car parks, and a head office building of five levels in greying concrete, built in the 1930s, fronting acres of red-brick buildings.

This site, which had been the centre of the world, or near enough to it, in 1970s computing, was like a prison, Heidi thought. It was flat, and surrounded by a double chainlink fence fifteen feet high, topped by razor wire.

Fairford had a jazzy glass complex in Silicon Valley, but this, their head office, and main research laboratories, remained a continual reminder of how Fairford had flagged over the recent years.

Heidi entered the lobby, and was shown immediately to the executive floor. Her visits were rare, and low key. By choice she never used the company jet to fly from New York, or the company limousine from the airport, although they were at her disposal.

As she swept along the corridors, she had a brief glance at some of the thousands of young—there didn't seem to be anybody old—men and women, neatly dressed and groomed, concentrating mesmerically on their PC screens.

On the executive floor, the rooms were high ceilinged, with tall doors of dark wood—all closed—and thick dark green carpets. Doors opened, and she was shepherded through to the office of Jed Olsen, the chief executive officer.

Heidi Stoller, cold-looking when her face was immobile, now had a small smile, her ash-blond, straight hair drawn back and tied in a pony tail. She put her arm affectionately on Olsen's shoulder as he stood to greet her, and then settled herself on a couch near the window with a glass of Perrier water.

Jed Olsen left his seat and came over to sit with her, while a secretary performed the coffee ritual. A lock of greying fair hair fell boyishly across his forehead. His easy expression betrayed none of his concerns.

Heidi opened her briefcase, withdrew a thin file, and held it toward him.

"Jed, I've pinpointed the three or four more WayCom people who are key to the STELA 2 project. Luchinelli, we know is eccentric and hopeless, and most of his immediate helpers are brilliant, but unreliable. You could get trouble tangling with them—"

Olsen scoffed at the unpleasant reminder. "Luchinelli, and his cronies! That cow Stiegwitz. They're not going to help us."

The memory was all too clear for him, and came flooding back graphically. Ten years ago, he had formed a partnership with a high-flying New Yorker, whose computer company was growing like poison ivy.

One of their projects had been to exploit artificial intelligence—the development of a computer so powerful, and complex, that it could perform many of the functions of the human intelligence.

It had been obvious to both Jed Olsen, and his new partner Vance Wayman, that the leader in AI would eventually lead the world in computing. The prospect was of vast rewards, and almost frightening market power.

Olsen had despised the uncouth Wayman from the first moment he met him, but Olsen knew raw talent when he saw it. Wayman was going to be a serious competitor, a dangerous one.

He had felt instinctively that a competitive war with Wayman would be long and costly. The best way to deal with Wayman, and his upstart company, was to take him in like the foundling he was, give him succour, encouragement, respect, bankroll him, absorb him into the Olsen empire. Use him, and neuter him. That way, Jed Olsen and Fairford would stay on top.

That was the simple plan. And so it began.

What Jed Olsen hadn't realised until too late, was that the upstart, the foundling, far from being grateful for the patronage and support of Olsen, began to betray him from day one of their partnership.

Wayman had gathered all the know-how about AI that he could, wooed Gino Luchinelli and Flora Stiegwitz, the two chief scientists on the project, and numerous other key people, engineered a dispute with Olsen, and decamped with his prizes.

It had been a humiliating setback for Olsen, and his public image had suffered.

And Wayman took Diana Olsen with him as an additional trophy.

Olsen had responded with a flurry of lawsuits, but they could accomplish nothing; some of them were still on the books. For every claim there was a counterclaim. Luchinelli and Stiegwitz were the key people, and they now belonged to Wayman.

Jed Olsen's skin crawled when he recalled the endless flow of smartass remarks he had endured from Wayman in their business meetings. Society dinners when he had to watch Wayman using a knife and fork like offensive weapons. When he thought of the white-bellied Wayman romancing the bikini-clad Diana on the deck of their yacht, in Maine ...

Heidi Stoller had completely lost Olsen's attention.

"Jed, I know Luchinelli won't help us. Are you with me?"

"I was thinking—"

"The best mark is Steve Reilly, the thirty-nine year old coordinator of the project. He has a PhD in mathematics, He knows a lot about the technical side. Tough, learning fast, and going places in management. A practical problem solver. Good record. He's vulnerable and he's got STELA 2 at his fingertips. If you get him, you could really advance your own work on AI."

Jed Olsen opened the file. Anything that might best Wayman was worth looking at. He glanced quickly at the two sheets of paper, savouring, as he did so, the strong scent of the Columbian coffee he insisted on having in the office; it relaxed him.

Heidi watched him like a lizard watching a bug, confident he would buy.

"Reilly is vulnerable?" Olsen asked.

"He hasn't been doing as well at WayCom as he thinks he ought to. Debts. Matrimonial problems."

"He hasn't been there long," Olsen said, pointing at the curriculum vitae.

Heidi smiled. "You know these aces want instant gratification—a raise today, promotion tomorrow."

"You think he'll play ball? He'll have signed a confidentiality agreement. He'll have agreed not to work for a competitor for a year."

"Sure. All the usual drawbacks. But I think he'll play."

Heidi Stoller was sure of herself. She waited patiently, uncrossing and recrossing her long legs in their silk tights.

There was a pause while Olsen weighed it up. The will to beat Wayman burned blindly inside him.

Jed Olsen had the nucleus of an AI team under Peter Haffner, the one top scientist who had remained loyal to him. Haffner had been fed with secret information from WayCom as a result of Heidi's efforts, and Olsen reckoned they were not far behind WayCom at a fraction of the cost. The temptation to undermine Wayman further, and boost his own team was almost irresistible.

"He's an impressive guy. *If* he will play," Olsen conceded.

Heidi sensed this was the moment: "I move on Reilly then?" She straightened from her casual pose and reached for her file, slight amusement around her thin, well-shaped lips.

Olsen nodded slowly in agreement. For a second, the sunbed tan of his face had as many lines as a cart-track.

Chapter 6

Hayden drove back to the Bray house at Lakeport after his meeting with Mariette, satisfied that he was right to be forceful with her about ditching her undercover role. As the lawyer on the case, he could perhaps be distant. He wasn't responsible for her, and neither was his client, but he cared for her.

He couldn't help thinking that they were on a crust that was very thin, innocently natural on its face, but the slime beneath was deep, and crawling with predators—and Mariette was in danger of going down.

The Bray driveway was crammed with tech vehicles and FBI sedans. Al Gerstein and a team from the FBI field office, with the local sheriff, were finishing off their investigation of the crime scene.

A uniformed cop stopped Hayden in the back garden. Hayden flashed his ID, and explained he was a lawyer representing Bray's employers. The cop alerted a man in dark plainclothes who was addressing others.

The man broke off, and came over to Hayden. He was sallow skinned, long-faced, hulkily strong, with deep vertical lines beside his mouth, and a lick of black hair.

"Hullo Mike," Gerstein said, baring broken teeth.

Hayden moved with Gerstein, past the crowd, deeper into the wood. Crime technicians were taking photographs and measurements. The body had been removed.

"What do you make of this?" Gerstein asked.

Hayden found it hard to make anything coherent out of the greed—if it was greed—that led a prosperous, healthy, presumably sane executive to get himself capped. Maybe it was the way Wayman said it was: people were dishonest if you gave them a chance. And the amount of money you had to start with didn't matter. The relatively rich, or the rich, always wanted more. Charlie Hayden, with millions in the bank, and a reputation as one of the solid, reliable men of Wall Street had been dishonest. You couldn't cloak what he did with legalities, although his lawyers tried.

Charlie suppressed market sensitive information about a stock while he persuaded others to sell to him at a low price. When the suppressed information became public, the shares hit the roof. Charlie aimed to pick up a quick couple of million bucks. He actually screwed up his whole life—and in a sense the shit was still falling on his son.

Hayden confined himself to the facts: "Seems to be set up to show the saw slipped, cut him, he fell, and bled to death."

"*Looks* like the scenario, doesn't it?" Gerstein said. "But there's a tank full of gas on the saw. Somebody switched the gas off. Otherwise the saw would have run on and used the gas. Bray couldn't have cut the power. And the position of the saw in relation to the body, bearing in mind Bray had a leg severed at the groin, doesn't add up to an accidental fall. I'd say somebody cut him, and then set it up, took time while Bray bled into oblivion."

"When did it happen, Al?"

"Doctor says last evening. He can't be more specific yet. Bray's wife was away with friends for the night. Children also away. Decided to do a little tree surgery after work. Too good an opportunity for the killer to miss. House seems untouched."

Hayden backed away quietly. Most of his cases involved piles of papers, and intellectual arguments, and the manias of living persons. He didn't usually get to see the bodies, but he knew there were sometimes bodies out there.

"Our forensic team will scope the house and the woods. We'll let you know what we find, OK? Looks like it could go down in the books as an accident. We'll have to find other evidence for my theory to become official," Gerstein said with a rueful grin.

Hayden told Gerstein about Mariette Stevas.

Gerstein showed the concern of the father he was. He regarded Mariette as a kid, and had always been nervy about her role.

"However good a fit she was, the NSA should never have put a tenderfoot in. I always said it. Now her judgement shows it. She doesn't really understand what she's playing with. The NSA gotta retire her. I'll see Byron. She can't help us any more."

"Make sure Cerillo does that, will you, Al?" Hayden said.

Hayden and Gerstein made an examination of the house, including Bray's writing desk, in an attempt to find who Bray had been dealing with.

They had been poking around for five minutes when Gerstein said, "Jesus. Wait a minute. Something *is* missing."

Hayden was beginning to think so too. "No computers. Not

even ones for the kids."

"Only the work stations and the power plugs. Somebody lifted them."

"It figures," Hayden said.

They found nothing of importance.

Hayden hurried back toward his car. He walked quickly down the drive in the sunshine. The beech trees had the heaviness of early autumn, with a sprinkling of gold leaves. A bundle of pure white clouds were piled up over the lake. A great day with a stain on it.

★ ★ ★

At the car, Hayden used his cellphone to call Marietta's cellphone, and her apartment, and got no answer. He called his contact at WayCom's offices, Karen Bridges, their security chief. After friendly preliminaries, he said, "I'd like to come and see you about Jackson Bray—on the STELA 2 project."

Karen Bridges said sure, and they fixed a time to meet in the WayCom cafeteria for a sandwich. She didn't ask why, because she knew the FBI and the NSA were always nosing around the STELA project, concerned about security, and Hayden was there to protect the WayCom interests.

Hayden pointed the rental Buick toward the commercial park outside Syracuse, where the futuristic glass and steel building housing the WayCom HQ and research laboratories was located, in a green landscape of lawns, and stands of beech and oak, And in the distance on a clear day like this, the blue line of the Adirondacks.

Hayden left his car in a visitor's slot, checked in at the front desk, and went up to the rooftop cafeteria a few minutes early. He took his jacket off, loosened his tie, and sat at a terrace table in the sun.

He had a view over the surrounding lawns, and woods. He thought about Bray, who might have been relaxing on this same floor now, enjoying his pasta, and a beer.

The staff were starting to come into the restaurant areas—there was a whole range of eateries to choose from. Le Moyne House was the head office and principal think-tank of WayCom, with a couple of thousand employees.

He opened the copy of *The New York Times* he had picked up at the hotel. A page he had noticed while he snatched a cup of coffee in the lobby that morning showed one of WayCom's regular corporate image ads. It was a whole page, designed to suggest how stable, prosperous and competent WayCom were—a reassurance to investors in the financial markets.

WayCom were world-wide, capitalised on the New York Stock Exchange, with 150,000 employees spread around the globe.

Hayden had seen plenty of spreads like this placed by the corporation in the past, and they all had the same theme. This one was entitled "WayCom—a new hi-tech world". It showed a group of serious young people, male and female, black, Hispanic, white and Asian, studying a design on a computer screen.

You were meant to get the impression that at WayCom the culture was friendly and informal, that bosses sat around chatting with their staff, producing brilliant solutions to which everybody on the team contributed.

Hayden knew that WayCom had spent a fortune with consultants trying to change its culture from the old-fashioned command style, to something like the team method of their Japanese competitor, Mitsuko.

WayCom had knocked down the walls between offices, and made people sit together in the open spaces. Senior executives talked about *communicating*, and went around in shirtsleeves with loose ties, to show they were at one with the staff.

At Syracuse, they had abolished separate dining rooms related to rank and created, amongst others, the pleasant space where Hayden sat. Superficially, the effect of the changes was agreeable and unifying.

But Hayden's experience was that WayCom was still, at heart, a command structure where information was guarded jealously.

The people at WayCom lived in their particular jungle, and they had to react to it. A waitress in the cafeteria might steal a steak to take home, but what, Hayden asked himself, made a man like Bray want to sell out?

From the talk Hayden had heard, nobody at WayCom, from the humblest WP operator upwards, seriously believed in the fairness of the panels and committees which seemed to assess the worth of an individual. Career path analysis, aspiration interviews, and annual assessments, were all regarded with a certain scepticism.

But WayCom would still have been described by critics as a good employer.

Hayden had taken time to absorb the advantages of this corporate life. He had spent a lot of time at WayCom over recent weeks.

As a lawyer employed by a Washington firm, most of his time was spent in cramped city offices in artificial light, at meetings where there never seemed to be enough chairs, or enough space for his elbows at the table. Here, the staff enjoyed space and a laid-back work style.

In one sense, this was a desirable place to be, to have a career. High skills were required. People were well-paid and had a lot of fringe benefits. The company provided pensions, medicare, sport and music and drama, it loaned money, subsidised education and training, and ran free nurseries for children. WayCom was a vast all-embracing provider. A big nanny.

Hayden tried to think where the malignancy in this affluent organisation might be. He tried to visualise what was gnawing at the kind of high calibre executives who would betray WayCom.

He listened to the pleasant babble of conversations. The staff at the nearby tables all looked cheerful and innocent, well-dressed, sounded as though they were enjoying their jobs. Then he had an image of Bray's rancid face in death. Suddenly the day didn't seem so benign. Under the warm surface there were cold undercurrents.

"Hi, there! Fixing your tan?" she said.

It must have looked like that. His shirt cuffs were undone and slightly rolled, beginning to reveal his tanned forearms covered with soft hair.

"Just enjoying."

Hayden gave her a real smile, but he wasn't enjoying, and he'd ceased to notice the sun. He didn't feel like the pastrami on rye with mustard, and a cold orange juice, that had been on his mind at first. He settled for a black coffee without explaining, and so did Karen Bridges.

Karen sat opposite without speaking, her startling green eyes searching him, the sun catching fire in the frizz of her ginger hair. They already knew each other. They met at law school. NYU. It was Hayden's second law school. He dropped out of Yale at the time of Charlie Hayden's indictment, spent a year on the beach near Carmel, and then hooked up with NYU.

Karen was also friendly with his former wife. There was a slight abrasion between him and Karen—two people who knew a lot about each other, learned from others, and hadn't quite agreed how friendly they should be.

After the coffee she walked him to her office which by its size, the view from the picture window, its soft leather furniture, and rich carpet, identified her as an important executive.

"I inquired about Bray, Mike. I have his personal file, but I expect you know all about him already. What's happening?"

"Bray is dead. Killed in what looks like a chainsaw accident in his garden last night. I guess you'll hear about that."

"That's terrible," Karen said, but she was as calm as Wayman about the death.

She looked puzzled. "You suspected him of security breaches? Better tell me. You know I can't do my job with you holding out."

"I'm not holding out. There's nothing I can tell you. We have no evidence. Bray *might* have been involved."

He explained the call to the FBI.

"You think the chainsaw wasn't an accident?"

"I'm sure of it."

He asked Karen to arrange his admission to the secure STELA unit. He was allowed open access to WayCom staff.

"Are you going to tell me what you're doing there? "

"Just routine, talking to the people."

"Who? You're talking to suspects about security matters for which I'm responsible, and you don't level with me. I'm fucking *responsible*, do you get that?"

Karen grated on his nerves.

"I'll tell you when I have something. I'd like to talk to Carl Leman and Mariette Stevas." His tone was bland.

The mention of Mariette's name fired her instantaneously. "Mariette Stevas? You can talk in bed, can't you, or are you too busy, lover boy?"

"You've got a nice mouth, Karen. I always thought that."

But she was reminding him that she too commanded a lot of surveillance resources. She had connected him with Mariette.

"And you let your dick get in the way of your duties. *I* always thought that."

He ignored the not too veiled reference to his marriage. "What problem do you have with Mariette?"

"I know she's an NSA plant. It took me about a week after she started to make sure. I do my job. I'm in charge of security, remember?"

★ ★ ★

Hayden was let into the secure STELA 2 unit. He found that Mariette Stevas wasn't there. Her supervisor hadn't heard anything to cover the absence.

He questioned the two or three people who worked at stations near to Mariette, but they knew nothing of her movements, and hadn't seen her since the previous day.

He took the liberty, and opened the drawer of Mariette's desk. He saw a flask of perfume, and a personal notebook. In a lower drawer, a sweater and a pair of soft moccasins. He was certain she had never returned to the office after their meeting.

He had a pulse of coldness, and then tried to dismiss it ... but Mariette wasn't the kind of operator who goofed off for the afternoon without telling her supervisor.

To make Hayden's visit to the secure unit entirely unproductive, the man Mariette had named as a further suspect, Carl Leman, wasn't there either. He too had disappeared from his desk without his secretary knowing where he was.

★ ★ ★

Instead of waiting for their date, Hayden drove quickly to Mariette's third level apartment in Cypress Drive, after leaving the WayCom offices.

It was a quiet area, the streets deserted around the apartment block. He interrupted the porter's television viewing, and asked him to call Mariette's apartment.

There was no answer.

He walked up three flights of stairs, and used the key she had given him. The door was unchained, and Hayden went inside.

The place had that empty feeling. There were just two main rooms with polished wooden floors and rugs, a large lounge, and a bedroom. A small cooking area was tucked behind a bar at the end of the lounge. The place was neat, and bright, with a view of the treetops in this leafy neighbourhood.

Hayden scanned the articles in the rooms quickly to determine whether Mariette had been home since their meeting—whether, in spite of their date, she had checked out.

No sign of lunch, or hot coffee in the kitchen. The bathroom towels were dry. In the bedroom, a pigskin manicure case was on the dresser, a full rack of dresses in the wardrobe, a canvas travelbag underneath.

There was a rag doll on the pillow of the neatly made bed. It was a bed he'd slept in a few times. He had spent some wonderful evenings here with dinners they cooked between them, and a couple of bottles of wine.

In the bedside table drawer he found the spare set of car keys.

In the lounge there was a book Marietta had been reading, and a writing case.

The apartment was full of the kind of items he would have expected her to take if she was leaving.

Hayden came down in the elevator, grim-faced. The porter indicated the area reserved for residents' parking, and Hayden searched the lot in vain for her pea green Volkswagen Beetle. He told himself there was no reason for undue concern.

He went back to his hotel, showered, changed his shirt and suit, read through the encrypted e-mails and reports from his assistant, Cathy Ong in Washington, and the FBI, and set out in the hire car for Mariette's apartment in time for their date at seven.

On the way, he stopped at a liquor store and bought a bottle of Southern Comfort. He picked up a bucket of ice from the machine in the foyer at Cypress drive. He went up and let himself into the apartment.

The moment he opened the door he knew that nothing had changed since his earlier visit. Mariette wasn't there.

He sat in front of the bottle, at Mariette's dining table, sipping and waiting, listening to water running in the pipes, and the occasional muted voices of other tenants of the block as they came and went.

Nine o'clock seemed to arrive very quickly. The bottle was half full, the ice in the bucket melted. It was dark, and quiet.

He wiped his forehead with the palm of his hand. He called Gerstein.

Gerstein groaned. "We'll put out a make on the car. Nothing else at the moment. She may turn up."

Hayden gave him the details, and afterwards tried to believe, against the odds, that Mariette was well and free. He did not sleep well in his bed at the hotel.

Chapter 7

As Heidi Stoller eased the hired Series 7 BMW sedan through the traffic in downtown Syracuse, she mused over the problem of Carl Leman. It was a problem she had to solve herself. She couldn't lay it on anybody else.

She had a Charlie Parker CD on the player. The music, and the soft insulated movement of the car, made her thoughts run smoothly.

Heidi met Carl Leman about every six weeks, to collect papers and tapes. She'd noticed that something was wrong with him over a period of perhaps six months, although it had become more marked recently. Leman had become nervous and uncertain, and the quality of the information he provided was falling.

She had set today's meeting at Cavendish Square. The autumn breeze suited her temper; it was cutting. She pulled the BMW alongside the sidewalk at the park, and Carl Leman was waiting. He was huddled in a long coat, with a baseball cap pulled down over his forehead. He slipped in the passenger door.

A small black cartridge on the seat by Heidi's side showed a pinpoint of green light, telling her that Leman wasn't wired.

She pulled away immediately without speaking. She drove around the commercial district until she was sure nobody was following, and then parked in a side street.

She turned to him. Carl Leman could hardly meet her eyes, and his puffy face with its small steel-rimmed spectacles was unnaturally waxy. His short, grey hair spiking out from under the baseball cap, was whitening. He was under forty. He looked fifty plus, and ill.

"What's the matter, Carl? The material I had from you last time is no help. I hope this lot will be better." Her voice contained only quiet concern.

He reached in his coat pocket and handed her an open paper envelope containing three computer disks. The veins on the back of his hands were swollen.

Heidi held the envelope slightly away with her fingertips, as though it smelt unpleasant. She was wearing transparent surgical gloves.

"What is this?"

"A paper of Luchinelli's on semantic programming, and computer graphics on the performance of the chips."

"OK." She reached into the glove compartment and removed a thick white envelope. Then she looked out of the windshield into space, but held the envelope out towards him.

He took the envelope immediately, and it disappeared into his overcoat.

He breathed heavily making a mewling sound. "You don't seem impressed. I can't get the stuff so easily now. There's a new technical coordinator. Remember, my job's finance. Questions can be asked if I'm burrowing into technical files. The machines log the entries."

"Oh yes, Reilly." Heidi already knew about the new technical coordinator.

Leman was surprised. "Yeah, Reilly. New from Mitsuko in Japan. He's watching everything. You know about him?"

"Uh-huh. He worries you?"

"You know everything that's going on, don't you?" He showed alarm.

In the confined space of the car she could smell his sickly, soapy odour. "Pretty well," she said, casually.

She knew his temperature had shot up, and something was coming.

He exhaled sharply, and looked straight ahead to the cars parked down the street. "I want to quit."

She tried to keep the chill out of her voice. "You can't just quit, Carl."

"I've about had it, I can't take much more"

They were parked by a small memorial garden with a traditional Native American woodcarving, created from sycamore trunks, depicting the settlers advancing against the indigenous tribes. People were always in strife.

Heidi didn't show the contempt she felt for this high-ranking businessman who was behaving like a hurt child.

"You can't take much more, huh?" she responded mildly.

"It's got too much for me. My hands shake. I can't do my job properly—"

"It's taken nearly three years, and let me see—nearly two million dollars," she reminded him. Her tone was sugary.

"I know. I know. But it's a strain. I can't go on and on. Do you think I can go on like this *forever*? I can't face my wife. I can't go to church. I've done enough …"

The mention of church particularly needled her. She wanted to call him a miserable, cowardly creep, but she softened.

"Carl, I need you. And you enjoyed having the money, didn't you? Are you thinking you've got enough stashed away now so you'll weasel out, and live happily ever after?"

"No. It's got me down—"

"I didn't know you were religious."

"I've turned more and more to God over the last year. He's the only consolation I have."

The derision Heidi felt did no more than ripple her brow for an instant. "What do you think will happen, then?"

"I don't think I can be of any use to you any more."

She stared at the pathetic sack crumpled on the seat beside her. This was an officer of WayCom Inc with a multi-million dollar budget, and hundreds of staff, an intelligent man trained with all the expertise of Harvard Business School, a prize-winner in physics at MIT.

"You haven't been any use for the last three months or so. But I've paid, Carl."

"Can we call it quits?"

There was a whine in the words.

"My instinct is to say no we can't. We're at a critical stage now. We need everything you can get us."

She spoke calmly and reasonably, placing her hands on the steering wheel, admiring them under the thin covering of the gloves with a passing thought. She had slender, long, smooth-skinned hands, and wore a blue diamond solitaire ring on her right hand.

He paused, still staring ahead at the traffic, and breathed through a wire mesh in his chest. Heidi could tell he was working up to a punch line.

"I feel like going to the National Security Agency, telling them everything."

The words were alarming to Heidi; they showed how far off-base Leman was.

The smell of him was more like blood and disinfectant, as though underneath his coat he was wounded, and bandaged, and about to haemorrhage. Heidi felt a touch of nausea.

"That wouldn't be wise, Carl. You'll wind up in the pen." The harsh note crept in.

"Don't you understand the *pressure*?" He turned his dog-sick eyes to her. "I need to get this business off my chest before I can begin to live."

She gave a low, derisive laugh. "You'll begin to live all right, in a Federal prison."

Heidi looked away in disgust. She didn't believe he had the guts to go to prison—but he wasn't rational. His follies had turned molten inside. He was a volcano threatening to erupt.

She decided to deal with him delicately. She turned to him again and spoke softly.

"You haven't done anything yet, have you Carl. You haven't talked to anybody?" She put the question when he had his dreary eyes on hers.

He flinched, and looked away. "Of course not. I've wanted to. But I haven't actually ... *done* anything."

In that instant, she was sure he was lying. It was only a question of how far he had gone. She had to be decisive.

"OK, Carl. Let's leave it this way. You think it over, and meet me in a month. If you still feel the same, it's all over. You can walk. You won't need to worry any more."

"OK," he said, dazed, unconvinced that she could be so reasonable.

Heidi tried to make light of it. "Loosen up a little, man. Take time. And remember you owe me something."

"I couldn't turn you in," he said, two rivulets creeping down his cheeks. "I don't even know your name! We've been meeting all this time. Talking. The woman-with-no-name, that's what I call you in my mind. I don't know anything about you, who you are, where you come from. Nothing. I don't even know where the material I give you is going."

He had spoken to her as though she was some kind of friend, despite her anonymity.

"If you talk, how can you avoid telling about me, whether you know my name or not? The FBI or the NSA will want to know your contacts, who paid you."

She realised Leman would be no match for the FBI or the NSA interrogators. They would squeeze him like a tube of toothpaste, and as easily. He was gutless.

"Don't be a fool, Carl. The game is over as soon as the National Security Agency know you've been selling secret WayCom data. They'll crucify you. Twenty years. A long crucifixion. Wait. Do as I say."

Carl Leman climbed out of the car slowly, like an old man with arthritis, giving her a haunted glance as he did so.

He stumbled into the memorial garden in a trance, clasping the deep pocket of his coat, which contained the payoff envelope, protectively.

Heidi spurred the BMW away, burning rubber.

She had a clear sense that something drastic had to be done to stop Leman talking. The sooner the better. Leman knew little enough, as he said, but it might just be enough to lead to her, to destroy her.

She conned the car through the downtown traffic easily, with Ella Fitzgerald on the stereo this time.

She had always known that the likelihood that her sources would eventually crack was high. Only split personalities could play Leman's role effectively. It required a special duality to appear to be a reliable senior executive, trusted with company secrets, but at the same time sell them to a competitor.

The best operators were those who had an angle—who hated their company, or the big chief, or had some other weird crusade—obsessives. She sensed Leman wasn't like that. He was a weakling who wanted to send his kids to private schools, and fly first class to see Paris art galleries, and she guessed he might have some other expensive weakness. Now his weepy conscience had corroded him.

Heidi let the Beamer out a little on Medway Drive, sixty, seventy, and turned up the CD. She thought she could handle Leman.

Chapter **8**

Being Charlie Hayden's kid was a cross Mike Hayden carried, and one that defined the way he was. When Charlie Hayden was indicted for stock fraud, and sentenced to prison, Mike flipped for a year.

In the space of about a week when the news of the indictment and arrest broke, and the national newspapers and TV screamed with righteousness, the foundations of Mike Hayden's privileged existence crumbled away.

He paid the tab for his rooms, and with no more than a quiet word to a couple of friends, packed as much of his wardrobe as he could carry in the saddle-bags of his Harley-Davidson Gold Star, and took off from the Yale campus for California.

Hayden hung out on the beach near Carmel, sold the Harley and his flashy clothes, refused help from his married sister, and worked digging clams and night service at a junk-food bar. In daytime, he concentrated on getting good with a board while he thought it through.

To his sister, what had happened to their father was a tragedy about somebody else with a different life. Julie had a new name, and was submerged in Ohio with her husband and three children.

To Hayden, it was loss of faith in a hero. Their mother was dead. Hayden's few telephone conversations with his father were full of silences. Charlie Hayden was unrepentant. It was the Vance Wayman line: *Everybody was doing it and I got caught.*

"So you want me to feel sorry for you?" Hayden had said.

When he finally graduated from NYU, the usual offers from prestigious firms weren't there. Nor were Hayden's applications successful. Being Charlie Hayden's son meant you weren't wanted in a top corporate practice.

Hayden could have taken a job with one of the smaller firms, or gone to another city but, like staying in California, it seemed like running away. Instead, he did two years as a street lawyer in New York.

Then Hayden was invited to join a firm in Washington specialising in consumer and environmental cases—the members were all people of around his age who wanted to do complex legal work, but were disenchanted with the boring side of mergers and acquisitions, and bond issues, and didn't put the dollar first. Hayden joined them, and he hadn't regretted it.

The Charlie Hayden effect hadn't gone away, probably would never go away, although it had faded on the legal horizon.

Hayden's apartment in Georgetown was on the top floor of an old brownstone—you could get out on a sheltered roof terrace with potted palms, see Washington sprawling along the Potomac, and hear the planes moaning overhead.

The apartment had a bachelor's kitchen designed by his ex-wife, where every cupboard could be reached without moving too far from one spot—cooking wasn't high on Hayden's list of priorities unless he was entertaining Mariette. The living room was comfortable with deep couches, a solid oak table and dominated by tall, crammed bookshelves. The books, a few law books aside, were mostly fiction.

There was a silver framed photograph of his ex-wife's dog, an Irish setter. He still got along with the dog. No kids. The marriage had been a campus romance that became a tie for two overworked professionals, and ended with a lot of rancour.

The rooms were untidy, because Hayden's cleaning woman dusted around everything, as though any casual article left anywhere, including an empty ketchup bottle, was a relic of religious significance.

The evening after Hayden returned from Syracuse, he had dinner with his assistant, Cathy Jean Ong, a petite Chinese girl known to everybody in his firm as CJ, at Morton's on Prospect Street. They had lobster and avocado with chilled vodka shots, and sparkling water chasers.

He and Cathy were friends. She was a computer nerd with a classy degree from Fordham Law School. They were both workaholics. But in the little leisure they took together, he was expanding her knowledge of western dishes, while she remained the authority on oriental cuisine.

Afterwards, they walked along M Street, to the Barnes & Noble bookshop to browse, and then retired to Hayden's roof terrace. They sat in the dark, wrapped in anoraks against the chill. Hayden sipped cognac. Cathy stayed with sparkling water.

Cathy had seen the psychological profiles produced by the FBI for the whole of the STELA team. She was sure the profiles identified the possible suspects, but of course proving that some of these clever people were breaking the law was next to impossible—unless somebody cracked.

"I reckon we might have got something from Bray if we'd heard earlier from Mariette that he'd figured somebody was on to him. And maybe this guy Leman remains a possibility," Hayden said.

"Well Leman is right up there at the top of the suspect profile. But remember, Mike, he's only a possible suspect. This kind of profiling rules out a lot of people, and enables us to concentrate our efforts. But Leman may be whiter than white."

"I'll talk to Al and agree how we tackle Leman ... I want to know what happened to Mariette."

Cathy noticed he wasn't saying he wanted to *find* Mariette. There was a tacit but grim anticipation that Mariette might not be alive. And Hayden's attitude had changed almost imperceptibly. From being a calm protector of Wayman, he had become more aggressive, and less patient. She understood why, and sympathised. "It's tough—about Mariette—but don't lose your objectivity, Mike."

His mouth narrowed angrily. He met the meditative Asian eyes of his friend. And then he laughed dryly, and with difficulty. "OK, OK, you're right."

But what was in Cathy Ong's mind was who was determined enough to kill for the technology. Bray had been murdered. Mariette had been abducted, and perhaps more ... Who?

"There's no mileage in it for corporate officers, however powerful," she said.

Hayden conceded. "But that's when you stand and look at it from way back, CJ—"

"You mean up close it's more about personal motives?"

"I think so. Bray called the FBI. Suppose he was going to spill. That could threaten somebody's freedom. Suppose Bray tipped his buyers off about Mariette. They feel threatened. How do you eliminate these threats? Perhaps the only way to be sure is to kill."

"When you put it like that," Cathy agreed reluctantly.

Hayden said he thought a foreign government might kill for this technology. "The STELA know-how is revolutionary. It's vital for national defence. Nuclear defence systems. Whichever power has it will be in a league of its own. Plenty of people have died passing atom bomb secrets, why not IT secrets?"

"So you think a foreign government is getting at WayCom?"

"It's my best bet," Hayden said. "They may be using all sorts of intermediaries—must be—but ultimately, yes, behind it all, a foreign government."

"Don't get in the way, Mike."

***

Cathy Ong worked closely with the FBI over the next few days to find some leads from the Bray death, and the Stevas disappearance. She churned every detail they knew, rechecked every member of WayCom's STELA 2 team, bugged each one, sifted all the accessible telecom traffic into and out of WayCom. But nothing.

Hayden accepted Al Gerstein's judgement, that the Bray killer was an opportunist who might have killed a dozen ways, but managed to take advantage of Bray's tree work, and the absence of his family.

The killer left no trace or prints. It wasn't a casual, bumbling killing. It was a neat professional job that looked like an accident. The coroner's verdict on Bray was open.

A search of Bray's affairs had been under way before his death, and what was now revealed was big sums in overseas trusts, and holiday villas in Nice and Brittany, worth more than he could have saved from his earnings, all concealed from the IRS. But there was no lead to who the paymaster was. Hayden couldn't get any further. He had to leave the Bray estate to the tender mercies of the IRS.

Mariette Stevas seemed to have vanished without trace. Her apartment yielded no clue in an FBI examination. Attempts to track her car from the car park of Fraser's Mall, where she met Hayden, failed.

An image which kept coming back to Hayden was her figure, hunched in disappointment, threading between the cars as she crossed the windy parking lot, after their meeting.

***

Hayden went to see Mariette's parents. He owed her and her family at least that. He presented himself as a work colleague and friend, not a lover. He somehow didn't want that complication, nor was it necessary.

The parents were an elderly and well-off couple in Providence, RI. They received him with warmth, and courtly manners, unable to detect the depressive realism beneath his charm.

He had afternoon tea with home-made scones and English raspberry jelly, and admired their garden. He realised they knew little of the risky world in which their only daughter had been hoping to make a career.

He did not dash their hopes that she might be alive, because they were his hopes too. He came away feeling a grey malaise in himself, and a hardening resolution to pursue the case.

Chapter 9

Heidi Stoller and Jed Olsen settled in the pale sun coming in on the window seats, and Olsen's boardroom cook served chicken sandwiches, and sauvignon blanc. The pair were at ease together.

"How are you going to get to this man Reilly?" Olsen asked.

"Better you don't know, Jed."

"OK. I appreciate your caution. How did you get on to him?"

"Ruth Charlton."

Olsen had heard of Ruth Charlton from Heidi. She was a headhunter in a prestigious firm who had built a profitable business on the side by finding employees who would rat on their employer, and selling them to a competitor.

"Let's not talk about that," Heidi said.

Heidi Stoller was something between a friend and a working ally of Jed Olsen's. Nobody knew more about Olsen's deep dislike of Vance Wayman than her.

Heidi Stoller had sighted Jed Olsen long before he was aware of her. After all, she was one among many computer experts, and he was chief of one of the US's oldest if not biggest IT companies.

Jed Olsen liked her. He liked women. He had a voracious appetite, some would say, but after the conquest, his sexual interest usually waned.

He often found it easier to work with a woman he had made love to—conquest wasn't an issue then. This is how it was in his attitude to Heidi.

She was a shapely thirty-six year old, who could change from unnerving chilliness to exude warmth and sex appeal in the space of a moment. She had a decisive air, intent on her business. Olsen no longer wanted to bed her, and she felt the same.

They had met at a weekend house-party at the Milsteins, in Palm Beach, when she had been in the US for two years, and she was prospering as a software consultant in Manhattan.

He had pursued her in New York, in the weeks that followed. First, lunch at Giambelli's, then cocktails after work at Regine's, then dinner at the Ritz-Carlton's Jockey Club, and finally a suite at the Plaza.

Heidi herself had been under no illusion about his pursuit; she encouraged it subtly.

He was the archetypal ram. He had aimed his genitals at her, and he meant to have her. The affair would be short, but profitable.

Jed Olsen could be a useful friend—and he was sexually attractive. There were trimmings too—he gave her, amongst other baubles, an emerald necklace from Van Cleef & Arpels, and professed a depth of feeling for her, which was endearing, even if it wasn't true.

Heidi had responded warmly, not caring that he might be pursuing other women, at the same time, with similar blandishments. To her, it was common sense to have a liaison with one of the most prominent men in the computer industry.

As soon as Jed Olsen perceived that Heidi could be useful to him outside the bedroom, which was in the first days of their relationship, he began to make enquiries about her.

He went far beyond her small New York consultancy. He spent many thousands of dollars in Munich, and Stuttgart, and Johannesburg, and he reckoned he had about as complete a dossier as you could get.

He found that Heidi Stoller was an only child, brought up by a widower-father who was born in the US. Her father had been an academic in Germany, and Heidi had taken a degree in mathematics from Cologne university, before he died.

After two years as a clerk in military intelligence in Germany, Heidi joined Zosmark in South Africa, and sharpened her skills in computer security. Two years later, she settled in New York.

She was a work-obsessed person with little time for deep relationships with men or women. She started her own business as a consultant, writing and selling software.

Her specialty was computer security. She provided an ingenious encryption system for passing information, and building firewalls which were difficult to bypass.

She gathered a specialist staff around her, as the business grew. She was one of the earliest to stumble on a market niche.

Companies were finding that people inside and outside their organisations were invading their confidential computer files. Sometimes competitors released viruses against each other, which could wipe out computer records.

Heidi's software gave companies the privacy and protection they required. She was a space-age locksmith.

Her work for Olsen started in a small way, with a genuine contract to develop security software, and their romance led him to reveal his obsession—Heidi regarded it as that—with Vance Wayman. Jed wanted his lover to know, as a matter of pride, that he could *never* accept what had happened between himself and Wayman.

In the course of her work, Heidi had already learned how insecure companies were. They locked their doors, but forgot to lock their computers; their systems were easy to penetrate—and competitors would pay for this information. Inevitably, Jed Olsen had suggested that Heidi should bring him information about Wayman's company.

The arrangement was very lucrative, although it was becoming more difficult, as computer security devices developed in sophistication.

Something in Heidi's nature was excited by this surreptitious side of the business.

Stoller Software Inc remained a reputable producer of security software but, with Olsen's influence, and a small and trusted coterie of aides of Heidi's, became at the same time a gatherer and seller of secret or highly confidential information.

Jed Olsen could afford to pay, and Heidi Stoller enjoyed the protection of her connection with him, and felt quite safe.

Olsen was so deeply involved that he could never turn against her without damaging himself irreparably. And his lineage and life were, on the face of it, immaculate.

Shortly after they met, they had sat head to head around the conference table in the office in which they were now lunching, and Olsen had said, "If you're going to rob a bank, you feel easier about it, if you believe the money belongs to you. That's how revolutionaries feel. It's how I feel about Wayman. I don't have a qualm."

Their liaison was thus perfectly suited to Heidi's talents, and Olsen's needs. The love affair lasted a few months, and faded, while a bond of common interest in the IT industry grew.

Now they could take a pleasant lunch together, and concede tacitly that what Heidi was engaged in was nothing more or less than the heist of WayCom's STELA technology—*the return to Olsen of that which was rightly his.*

The pair had fashioned the practicalities of their relationship carefully. She visited Fairford or Olsen's country estate, very rarely for important meetings. They never spoke by phone or used e-mail. They exchanged messages by a personal courier who was ignorant of the contents of the briefcase.

The paradox of the age of instantaneous communication was that only the most old-fashioned method was secure—a human messenger. And the intimate conversations they shared in Jed's bug-free office were completely deniable.

Jed Olsen returned to the worries nagging him as their lunch concluded.

"I asked you a while ago about this lawyer, Hayden, sniffing around. What do you make of it?"

Heidi already knew about Hayden, and was unconcerned. "He's there for two reasons, neither of which should trouble you, Jed. First, to protect Wayman from Cerillo. Wayman is scared that the Senate Committee will recommend termination of the contract as a result of breaches of security."

"Well he can try to protect Wayman, but he won't succeed—"

"And Hayden's other job of course is to launch a big lawsuit against whoever is buying the stolen technology—"

They both rocked back in their seats and laughed.

Olsen finished his wine, and returned to his lurking fears.

"Can we trust Charlton? She knows a lot about us, and if she were to talk—"

"Jed, she doesn't know anything about *you*. And anyway, it's a risk worth taking. Ruth's a pro. I know Ruth, and I trust her. We've worked together before. Really a small risk when you think what's at issue. Unless we hit WayCom and get ahead of them, Wayman will have you for breakfast."

No other person could speak to Jed Olsen in this way. He bunched up his long fingers angrily. "We still have contact with WayCom through Carl Leman, and others. Perhaps we shouldn't be thinking of extending the exposure."

"Leman's not performing. You need a bigger foothold in WayCom."

"First I've heard about Leman. We've had some valuable information from him. What's the problem?"

Heidi Stoller didn't share any of the details of her work with clients, and usually Olsen didn't enquire. The less he knew the better.

"I guess Leman's just tired and edgy," she said, putting Olsen off. "It's the right decision to go for Reilly, Jed."

Olsen exhaled heavily. There was a jaggedness in his normally beaming smile, more like a spasm. For a few seconds, the gentle father, the wise head of the family, the patron of a dozen charities, the church-warden, the governor of Syracuse High, the would-be Presidential candidate, faded …

His tan yellowed, his eyes sunk in bruised caverns.

"It's war," he muttered.

Chapter 10

Hayden took a commuter flight the three hundred miles to Syracuse, NY.

He wanted to get to Leman without advertising to anybody at WayCom that Leman was a suspect, at least at this stage. To call Leman on the telephone would be foolish. If Cerillo at the NSA was sifting the telephone traffic, others including Karen Bridges were too. He decided to visit at Leman's home address.

Hayden spent time in the plane thinking about Cerillo, and enjoying a gin-and-tonic. He had a small notebook with him in which he'd jotted his findings—more secure than his laptop PC.

Cerillo seemed hostile to Wayman, seemed to want to end the STELA contract. So far, neither Hayden nor the FBI had found anything which would justify this.

Sure, STELA was late and over budget, but that could be explained. No sign of fraud in WayCom's operations.

An employee had been murdered, and a woman was missing, and it was now safe to assume that valuable secret technology was being systematically looted. But so far, no sign of a lapse by Wayman. He'd apparently screened his employees properly. One of them was rotten. Not Wayman's fault.

Hayden skimmed the personal notes about Cerillo prepared by Cathy Ong: son of an Italian immigrant. A Yale graduate. Cerillo had won scholarships, but he must have been financed. By whom? Worked in Justice, Defense, and for the last decade, the National Security Agency. Always in think-tank roles. Now fifty-five, and uniquely in command of all the US's sources of intelligence. Married. One son. Reputed to work slavishly, up to sixteen hours a day.

How did colleagues feel about Cerillo? They were in awe of him. Had to admit his performance was never less than first class. But found him enigmatic.

Cerillo was a kind of spider at the centre of the web of the intelligence establishment, and as hard to read. Hayden was at one moment lulled by the benign fat man, and at another made wary by those deep, analytical eyes.

Hayden sighed, and tightened his seat belt at the request of the cabin steward. He made a note to ask Cathy Ong to find out how Cerillo's expensive education had been funded. Hayden was an old enough Washington hand to look for connections.

★ ★ ★

Hayden was installed in his room at the Bowen Hotel by late afternoon. He keyed his laptop, and read the FBI profile of Leman.

Leman had joined WayCom from Zosmark in Johannesburg four years previously. He was 38, a physicist graduate of MIT. He had been headhunted for WayCom by Digby Hudson. He was married with two children, and his endorsements from his bosses described him as clever, an effective manager of quiet disposition.

A grey man, but formidable, going places on the face of it.

Al Gerstein had also provided Hayden with the registration of Leman's car, his telephone number, a home address, and a credit search which showed Leman lived well, but did not suggest any irregularity. He was a very well paid high-flyer. Hayden timed his visit to Leman's home for about seven thirty, when Leman was likely to be home from the office. He hired a car and had it brought to the lobby of the hotel. He had a quick look at a map of the area, and drove out of the city, into a sprawling Fairmount suburb, with spacious well-treed gardens.

Hayden noted the quality of the Leman residence, a two level mock colonial construction with a pillared entrance. A house which didn't quite fit the low-key personal profile.

Hayden parked in the drive and rang the bell. Interior lights were on. A woman came to the door, about Leman's age, dressed untidily, at odds with the pretentious house.

Hayden thought she was the maid. She wore an apron, and had wispy fair hair, roughly tied back with a handkerchief, and a lined face that had suffered a lot of pain.

Hayden found she was Mrs Leman, and asked to see her husband.

"I'm sorry, my husband's still at his office. I don't expect him for ages, maybe ten or eleven."

She was edgy, cloudy eyed, anxious to close the door.

If Mrs Leman was getting the benefit of a fat bank account, she didn't appear to be enjoying it. The vacant stare looked past Hayden, at a distant flame. He guessed she was on some kind of dope.

"Will you tell Mr Leman my name, Mrs Leman? I'm a lawyer

representing WayCom. And I want to have a private word with him. I'm staying at the Bowen, on 21st Street." Hayden gave her his card on which he had written the hotel telephone number.

The woman looked distraught. Her head and arms began to quiver. "I don't understand—"

Hayden reassured her that it was just an enquiry, and let her close the door on her anxiety.

He drove the car a few hundred yards down the road. He could wait until he saw Leman's car, but that might be hours. He decided he had time to go back to the hotel.

★ ★ ★

At 8.30 pm Mike Hayden was in the Bowen Hotel gym. He clocked up the first mile on the jogging machine easily. The blond superman on the virtual reality screen in front of him flashed a message: *Nice work. You won. Try program five.*

Hayden decided to stay with program four, and pounded on, watching his progress against the superman on the screen, confident he could stay ahead.

He settled into the beat. His feet and ankles were cushioned in the Nikes. Thok-thok, thok-thok, thok-thok, the soles hit the rubber mat that reeled constantly underneath him. The golden boy was just a yard behind him, according to the screen, and sent another message: *Congratulations. Keep it up. Can you pull further ahead? I'll be kicking soon, so watch out.*

Hayden put on a little more pace and began to look around. All the machines were grouped in front of screens, so you could theoretically get the news, the stockmarket prices, and see videos of the latest pop music, as well as have your own private contest with the virtual reality athlete, all at the same time.

A bedlam of discordant noise vibrated in the gym, the gasps and groans of the unfit, the thump of the track machines, the clank of the weights, the screaming guitars of the pop group, the Barbarians ...

When Hayden had done his second mile, he resisted the golden boy's invitation to try program five, and jumped off the machine.

He decided to leave the other masochists, picked up his towel and sweater, and went outside, past the pool, to the fitness track which followed the trees around Independence Park, a two-mile circuit.

There was nobody about that he could see. The fitness freaks preferred the gym. He pulled on his sweater, tucked the towel around his neck, and set up a brisk pace on the fine gravel.

It was still chilly, with a brightness that promised a fine day tomorrow. Against the sky, he could see the plane trees' vast dark branches were beginning to stand out as the rusted leaves fell day by day.

After a complete circuit, he was pacing smoothly when a man in a long and expensive camelhair coat, incongruously wearing a Redskins' cap, stepped out of the trees.

It was only when Hayden was called a second time that he realised the man was addressing him.

Hayden reluctantly broke his stride, and stopped without replying. He didn't recognise the man, whose eyes were behind thick spectacles, and shadowed by the peak of the cap.

"Carl Leman, Mr Hayden, from WayCom," the man said in a low voice.

"Ah, Mr Leman, I was at your house tonight."

Leman came close, wanting to speak confidentially. "My wife told me. Can we talk? Maybe in my car." He looked around, worried.

Hayden gave a little laugh. "Right now, here?"

He pulled away the damp sweater that was sticking to his chest. His plan to put in another half mile, have a beer, and a hot dog—and then go out to Leman's place, was off.

"I'm sorry to interrupt your exercise, Mr Hayden, but I can't call you without somebody listening. I can't even approach you in daylight without somebody seeing."

Leman was pleading. Class performers of his kind didn't appear from behind trees, and complain that somebody was watching them—unless perhaps they were.

Hayden couldn't resist the urgency. He followed silently to the nearby car park.

There was only one car in the park, a plum coloured metalescent 4.2 Jaguar sedan with cream hide upholstery. Hayden thought it was a nice car. He had a Jag coupe himself, vintage 1985, a tuned-up V12, with a solid top. But he wasn't about to exchange chat as a Jaguar buff.

They settled themselves inside the car. A rich smell of new leather.

Leman huddled in the driver's seat, looking round the park as he did so.

"I value the opportunity to speak to you, Mr Hayden," he said, lifting one of his flabby, trembling hands from the steering wheel.

"Tell me what's going on," Hayden said.

Leman glanced at him, reluctant at the last moment to talk, unable to mouth his confused thoughts.

Hayden looked away from the man's agonised face across the parking lot. It seemed almost deserted. A park warden in a pickup truck stopped a hundred yards away to open a gate.

"The STELA 2 technology. It's being ... stolen. Sold."

"By whom?"

Leman didn't reply at first. "I need to make an arrangement with you if I talk. If I help you, some consideration ought to be given to me—"

"You've committed a crime?"

"I'm not saying more until I get immunity."

"Wait a minute, Mr Leman, no prosecutor can give you immunity until he knows an offence has been committed, and he has an idea of your part in it. And there has to be an advantage to the prosecution in giving immunity. The prosecutor needs to know what he's going to get out of it. Surely you understand that?"

Leman wasn't thinking clearly. He paused. "I'll tell you the background," he said faintly, white foam at the corners of his lips. "The STELA technology is being stolen and sold. By top executives. There was an engineer named Jack Bray who died recently. It's serious. A lot of the key information has already been passed over."

"Why have you decided to talk?"

"I'm not saying anything more now. You work something out, a deal, and I'll come back to you. But do it soon, because I can't hold out much longer"

"Do you know who killed Bray?"

Leman turned to him, the whites of his cloudy eyes showing horror. "I only heard about an accident, but I thought it might have been more than that, I thought it might have been ..."

"What happened to Mariette Stevas?"

Leman had no inkling of the tension behind the question, and shrugged non-committally.

"Do you know *anything* about Mariette Stevas?" The rasping tone alarmed Leman.

Hayden licked his lips, trying to cool his unspoken words, trying to keep his hands from reaching out to Leman's plump neck to choke some words out of him.

"If you know something, and you don't tell me, life will get very tough for you when the FBI find out," Hayden grated.

Leman nodded, yes, and looked at him fearfully.

"How many employees are involved?" Hayden persisted.

"Think about what I've said. Please, Mr Hayden. I'll have to go."

Leman fingered the ignition key, and fired the Jaguar.

"Who's the buyer?" Hayden asked.

Leman shook his head negatively.

"I can have the FBI take you in for questioning. I don't want to have to do that, but I will. I need a long session with you to work out in detail exactly what's been happening."

Leman gripped the wheel. His moist eyes, the colour of raw oysters, seemed to press against the lenses of his glasses.

"I'll have to go."

Hayden thought the likelihood of exploiting Leman's hysteria any further tonight was small. He unbent his damp body from the Jaguar.

"If the FBI take you in, Leman, it's going to be very painful. And it won't do your career any good. Think about it. Talk to me."

Chapter 11

In a booth in Dooley's bar off Bay Ridge Parkway in Brooklyn, Heidi Stoller was facing a big, muscular man around sixty, with a bullet head of cropped grey hair.

He had the rough red features of a drinker. A tuft of grey chest hair showed at the throat of his T-shirt. The expression in the deep lines around the eyes was one of amused calm. There was something controlled, even reassuring about him.

The bar wasn't Heidi's scene, but with her hair combed down, a pair of shades, a black rollneck sweater, black slacks, and no rings on her fingers, she was just another piece of pussy.

Two four-foot TV screens dominated the bar, one showing the Atlanta Braves killing the Florida Marlins, and the other a track event in Detroit. It was possible to watch both screens at once.

The commentary from each sport, mixed with the hard rock beat from half a dozen small speakers, and the talk, created an envelope of noise in the smoky space, and resonated inside their heads like a chorus of road-drills.

Heidi had to lean close to Tom Addis to make herself heard. "This is another big deal, Tom."

Addis's eyes brightened; there had to be something important behind this special invitation to New York. He didn't say anything for a moment. Then he knocked back his shotglass of bourbon.

"Sure. Count me in, Heidi."

"A neat job, Tom, an accident."

"Always—I'll have another," he said, looking round for the waiter.

"The man's name is Carl Leman. He's a very senior executive at WayCom in Syracuse. As soon as possible. Have you got that, Tom."

"Sure," Addis said, relaxed but alert. He repeated what she'd said.

"Now let's talk money," he said.

Heidi Stoller had been working with Addis since she started in business. She reckoned she knew him as well as anybody.

He was a solitary. He lived in a cabin on Lake Tacon, upstate. She got a private eye to report on him occasionally, make sure he was steady enough to do her work.

Addis boozed, hunted, fished, travelled round in his pickup to football and baseball games, and screwed a local married woman on a casual basis. That had been his life for a decade, and he showed no signs of changing.

He was an army veteran. He was fit, but he had a leg disability, and a pension, and he did odd jobs when he needed additional money, usually driving or construction work. Unless he was working for her.

He was a man who knew violence, an expert with smallarms.

Heidi had used Addis at first for small investigative jobs, inquiries, watching people or the movements of vehicles.

Addis had been a sergeant-instructor in the Marines. He was tough, used to responsibility, and street-smart.

Occasionally, Heidi had small clients—the small ones were worst—who thought they could use her services, and then say *sue me* and laugh—knowing she wouldn't sue, because she couldn't disclose how she got the information she sold.

She could have wrecked their IT systems with a virus; but that was a last resort she'd never used. Instead, she had sent Tom Addis along to see them.

He came up with the money. Mostly he just talked to the reluctant payers. One client had the throat of his dog cut, and found the carcass in his swimming pool. Another saw the top of his Aston Martin convertible burned off. They paid.

Heidi had it in the back of her mind for a long time that Addis was a resourceful man with a very cold, vicious streak.

She sipped her soda water, and ordered Addis another bourbon.

Addis half-watched the Braves, liked sitting in a booth with a classy doll, let the fuzz of the noise, and the bourbon, drench him.

Having somebody like Tom Addis in the shadows was a reserve strength, and Heidi had continued to employ him on and off, and treat him well. She believed in being prepared.

She had thought through the problem that had developed around Leman long before it happened. She wasn't like a mafia chief who could give orders and insulate himself from the cops with protective layers of accomplices. She wasn't protected by the rule of omerta.

Heidi reasoned that, for her, having accomplices only increased her exposure. The more people who knew her intention, the bigger the exposure. Heidi reduced her risk by having only one accomplice—the man who would do the job.

It was true that she might have made contact with organised

crime—she had all the information. But she was savvy enough to know she could only deal with professional criminals on a continuing business basis: it would be blackmail, in the shape of a share of the profits, until the end of her days. She ruled them out.

She therefore had to choose a gifted amateur and instruct him herself, setting up the deal to give herself as much protection as possible.

If Addis was caught, and turned her in, she would have to take her chances; it was a grave risk, and it gave her quite a high.

Addis had a tough self-sufficiency, and perhaps he wouldn't squeal, but she banked, not on that, but on the chance that he was too smart to get caught.

Heidi believed in making her own luck. Instructing Addis was like beginning a wild roller coaster ride, on rails that could split apart at any moment.

She had strong nerves. There was no point in riding the roller coaster unless you got a blast from it.

When Heidi bought Tom Addis a last bourbon, and slipped out of the booth to leave Dooley's, she had taken an irrevocable step.

Chapter 12

Hayden was awakened at the Bowen by a 6 am call from one of Gerstein's assistants. The agent said they had received a call from the Sheriff of Oswego County about a car in a stream to the north, out near Mallory—a pea green VW.

The words *pea green VW* burned in Hayden's head. He splashed some water in his face, pulled on a T-shirt, jeans and a windcheater, and met the agent in the lobby in ten minutes. They drove out along Interstate 81 past Oneida Lake. The water and the sky were shades of grey.

The agent parked in a line of county cruisers and FBI sedans on a dirt road. There was a steep ditch on one side, and a stream with deep pools on the other.

The operator of a recovery hoist had a cable around the sunken car, about to winch it out of a pool. Hayden could just make out the side of the vehicle shimmering about a foot below the surface.

Gerstein approached him. "The water's so clouded with silt we haven't been able to establish if there's a body in the car, Mike."

"Who found it?"

"Local kid cycling past. Told his mom. She rang the Sheriff's Office. One of the deputies was smart enough to remember the make we'd circulated, and checked it. Called us."

After preliminary groans from the hoist, and the straining of the engine, the VW seemed to come up quickly, like some kind of vile reptile, gushing water as it was laid on the narrow verge on its side.

In a few moments the cable was loosened, and half a dozen pairs of hands heaved the car back on four wheels.

With a cautionary word from Gerstein about damaging or marking the vehicle, two deputies strained to get the driver's side door open. Hayden stood back, sickened for a moment—there was a long pause until one of the deputies announced the vehicle was empty.

Gerstein took a look inside himself in advance of the technicians, groped around. Then he extracted himself, and straightened up, calling for evidence bags for two objects.

He walked over to Hayden, holding the bags.

In one bag, was a thin gold bangle, bent, with the safety chain broken. In the other was one of Mariette's flat-heeled slip-on shoes, oozing brackish water.

"Both under the driver's seat," Gerstein said.

"I remember the gold bracelet. I bought it," Hayden said.

Gerstein looked at him grimly, and with a nod of understanding. He had seen nearly everything in his eighteen years with the Bureau.

★ ★ ★

When Hayden climbed out of the FBI car at the Bowen Hotel, the weather had got colder. A chilly northerly wind from Lake Ontario, which smelt of pine trees, clawed at him, and cut through his thin jacket. A hint of rain clouded the air.

As Hayden collected his key, the bellhop said there was a delivery for him. He pointed to a case beside the bell captain's desk. Hayden examined the package.

It was a case of a dozen bottles of Moet et Chandon champagne, and two tickets to a performance of *Hamlet* at the Syracuse Globe on the following Saturday. The compliments card was personally signed by Vance Wayman.

Hayden would have appreciated the champagne more at another time, and he would take in the play if he had a few hours to spare. Two tickets? Every day there were reminders that Mariette wasn't there.

He had the case sent to his room. Aperitifs were secure for a number of evenings into the future.

He handwrote and addressed a thank you note to Wayman on the hotel stationery, and left it with the desk for posting.

Hayden went up to his room, and had a quick shave and shower, and changed into a suit. He climbed into a cab outside the lobby, and headed for WayCom's Strathmore Park industrial estate.

He got his pass at the front desk, and walked through the building to Karen Bridges' office. The many small communities within Le Moyne House were beginning to work, the print-room operators, the word processing pool, the travel, and planning, and payroll departments.

The high status people in departments like finance, marketing, public relations, and economic planning had slipped off their jackets, the men had loosened their ties, and just about all had fetched coffee from the dispensers in the corridors, or had it fetched for them.

The women were back from the restrooms, with their hair combed, and their eye-makeup touched up.

America was moving on in the relaxed WayCom style.

When his guide stepped into an elevator to return to the front desk, Hayden decided to see if he could speak to Carl Leman first.

His desire to corner Leman had been honed to a raw edge by the morning's events at Mallory. He suspected his approach to Leman would soon be on the grapevine at WayCom, and decided to give up trying to conceal it.

He stopped by one of the secretarial desks, and asked a girl if he could use the phone to make an internal call. She pushed the instrument toward him. She gave him Leman's extension from the screen, and he punched in the number.

"Carl Leman!" a voice said, sharply.

"Mr Leman, this is Hayden. I'm in the building right now. I'd like to see you—"

The line went dead.

He called the extension again, but a secretary answered, and said Mr Leman had left the office.

Hayden handed the phone back to the girl. She looked at him curiously.

"Could you tell me the quickest way to Mr Leman's office?"

The girl looked at the screen. "Project Coordination? Yes, sir—but that's a secure area and you'll need a pass."

She looked at the designation on his lapel tag.

"Even if I'm visiting the Head of Security?"

"Afraid so. Karen Bridges can give you a pass. Do you want me to call her?"

"No don't bother," Hayden said.

Hayden decided he would get Gerstein to go with him to Leman's home that night, and then, if necessary, they would take Leman in.

★ ★ ★

Hayden was waved in the open door of Karen Bridge's office—an illusion of accessibility—by her secretary.

Karen had her strong hands clasped before her on the desk blotter, waiting.

She wore fashionably small oval glasses with thin gold frames which gave her a studious look. Actually she was a shapely amazon, five seven or eight tall, perhaps a couple of years younger than Hayden. She had a pale, slightly freckled skin, and a mass of kinky auburn hair, shoulder length. Her pale green eyes missed nothing. She dressed down, a grey suit, and cream blouse, that suppressed the woman.

"Take a seat, Mike," she said.

Hayden slipped into an armchair. "Mariette's car's been found." He explained the journey out past Lake Oneida.

"I'm sorry."

Karen was ex-FBI. She had no illusions.

"There's a hell of a rat-stink in this place," Hayden said.

"Maybe. But we've done everything we can. Taken every precaution," she insisted.

"I hope so, or you can say goodbye to STELA 2."

Karen originated the loyalty reports on staff. Everybody in WayCom was routinely checked out—family circumstances, personal finance, activities outside WayCom, and mental and physical fitness.

Karen Bridges and her staff knew who had beaten up their brother-in-law, who was behind with the mortgage, who was drinking too much. But sometimes, perhaps, they missed the real worms.

"Do you have any surveillance on your competitors?" Hayden asked.

He didn't expect a straight answer.

Karen grinned. "We look at their websites, and read the trade mags. You know, Mike, the world is changing fast. At one time we built computers to break codes. Now the computers are *creating* almost unbreakable codes, so we can't see what our competitors are doing."

"The same applies in reverse, doesn't it? They could crack you. Now they can't."

"Sure. About even. And we have no evidence that STELA has been affected."

"If somebody's developed a computer with learning ability, maybe they've found a way to break your codes."

Karen Bridges smiled gently. "Don't even think it ..."

He told her the FBI might have to take Leman in, that Leman knew something and was holding out.

"You think you can scare him into talking before his lawyers surround him?"

"We'll try. I'm sure the fat slug knows something about Mariette."

Karen's eyes sparked. "You're personally involved. Always a bad sign."

Chapter 13

Addis was driving a grey Crown Victoria, patrolling quietly along the Fairmount avenues. He passed the Leman house twice in five minutes from opposite directions, driving easily, not pausing.

And then he parked for a few minutes on a rise a quarter mile away, from where he could see a side of the house through the trees.

The suburban road was deserted, the houses drawn back in trees, or behind walls.

The fringe of grass along the sidewalks was neatly cut, and planted every few yards with beech saplings. The sidewalks and gutters themselves were swept clean and free of any leaves or wrappers.

It was the kind of neighbourhood where many people would like to live; ordered, every home probably wired to a security alarm system, and the houses themselves, were comfortable, sprawling and withdrawn.

Another place where the residents were vulnerable. Doing a job here would be easy.

He sat in the driver's seat and rolled a cigarette and smoked.

When he had finished, he hung his arm out the window, ground the butt to a powder between a leathery finger and thumb, sprinkled it on the road, and hit the ignition.

★ ★ ★

Steve Reilly was awake at 6 am. He had a leaden feeling about the day ahead.

He slipped out of bed, and put his head through the window drapes: a sky laden with silver dust.

He could see across a vista of rolling lawn, smoothly cut, to a stream at the foot of the slope. The lawn was dotted with young larch and aspen trees, hanging forlornly in the cold air. The neighbour's chestnut pony was drinking on the other side of the stream.

Every morning lately he'd had misgivings when he saw this scene—as if it was an illusion that was going to disappear.

Laura Reilly didn't share his concerns. She lay on the bed with her back to him, her shoulder regularly rising and falling with her sleeping breath.

It had been Laura's idea when he joined WayCom and moved to Syracuse, NY, to get this big place, five acres, with a six-bedroom Spanish-style house.

They both loved the house, and at the time buying it had seemed the right thing to do, even though there were only the two of them.

At first, Reilly was persuaded by Laura that it was a good investment—but he knew now from the property pages in the local paper that prices weren't moving in any direction except down—if you could find a buyer.

Now Laura was awake.

She eased herself out of bed, long and lithe, and smooth-faced after sleep. She saw him but didn't speak. She sat on the edge of the bed, watching him choose his clothes from the wardrobe and lay them out before getting into the shower.

He was naked. He removed a pale blue shirt from the laundered stack in the drawer. He touched the silk of a blue Hermes tie, trying to decide. The feeling of dread was evaporating. He started to hum a tune.

He had a sportsman's body, tall, leanly muscled, and an enthusiasm for tennis which left Laura cold, and yet he could abandon games completely for months on end for work.

His face had a serious expression about the eyes that got to you. Plenty of thick fair hair. He wasn't going to go grey until he was much older. Women liked him.

Laura put on a wrap and went downstairs to the perfect kitchen with every known device; it was in black, with scarlet cupboard panels. She poured a glass of orange juice from the carton in the refrigerator, and sat at the breakfast bar. She held the icy glass against her temple.

She could hear her husband imitating Pavarotti as he showered. He'd want to be at the office by eight, even if he didn't officially start until later.

Today he had preliminary interviews for promotion at WayCom. So much depended on a successful result that they hardly dared to speak about it.

Laura absent-mindedly went through the ceremony of laying out a half-grapefruit, cereal, switching the coffee percolator on, and making toast.

And then she sat looking out of the window at the pond—shared with their neighbour—with its ducks and swans, and the playing fields of Stretton Hall University beyond.

As a girl from the wider spaces of Connecticut she felt more at home here than anywhere they had lived before. She didn't want to live on one of those mean little subdivisions where the developer had squeezed each family on to a postage stamp space, all overlooking each other.

Stretton Woods was a fashionable address, in a parkland of big properties, within a half-hour drive of Reilly's office at WayCom, in East Syracuse.

Over the brow of the hill at the end of the road was a new shopping mall with some snooty boutiques. Laura couldn't resist going there.

The neighbourhood had many young business and professional couples like Reilly and his wife, with their big gardens and heated pools, and their Mercs and BMWs and Alfas.

Reilly liked to go for a drink at the one of the local bars in the weekend. They were gradually getting to know their neighbours. Laura thought it could be a fun place. Reilly came briskly down the stairs, interrupting her thoughts.

He was carrying the jacket of his plain light grey suit, made from an expensive woollen worsted material. Reilly could have got by with a suit that was not quite so pricey, but Laura thought the Zegna gave him confidence.

He looked smart in the pale blue shirt with the tie he had ultimately chosen, a striking yellow and black silk.

"Making a statement, huh?" she said, putting her fingertips on his chest as he leaned over to touch her cheek with his lips.

"I'll knock 'em dead today."

He surveyed the breakfast as he spoke, not trusting his expression to back up his confident words.

"You sure will."

Laura too replied with an enthusiasm she didn't feel.

"My old pal Vance will deliver."

He winked at her, knowingly, trying to make light of it.

"Uh-huh." She buried her nose in the glass of orange juice to avoid showing her scepticism.

Old pal Vance was Vance Wayman, chief executive officer of WayCom who had persuaded Reilly to leave Mitsuko Corporation in Osaka and return to the US. Wayman wasn't a pal and scarcely an acquaintance.

Reilly had met Wayman a year and a half before at a two-day

information technology conference in Munich. Wayman was guest speaker, and he had sought Reilly out. It was an honour for Reilly to be recognised by one of the most prominent figures in the industry.

Laura knew her husband was a capable man, but it still sounded to her as though he had been stupefied by flattery.

One of the key things Wayman had told Reilly at the Munich conference was that the post of North American Sales Director was coming up in WayCom, and Reilly looked like the kind of guy to fill it. It was a job Steve Reilly coveted.

But a month after meeting Wayman, Reilly was offered a different job coordinating a computer development WayCom were doing for the National Security Agency in the US, the STELA project.

WayCom were known leaders in artificial intelligence research, and Reilly had been attracted by the offer. It was work that would revolutionise human life. But his real interest remained the big North American directorship, and he had accepted on the understanding that he could apply when the North American post came up. The Reillys had packed the few items of furniture they wanted to keep, and left Osaka for Syracuse, NY.

It hadn't quite worked out at WayCom as Reilly had thought, or as Wayman had said. The North American Sales job hadn't come up until now, but Reilly had convinced himself this was going to be the payoff.

Laura wasn't so sure. "Steve, why do you think Vance Wayman sought you out in Munich, you know, when he asked you to join WayCom?"

As soon as Laura said this, she realised she'd said the wrong thing.

Reilly couldn't maintain the veneer of good humour any longer. His mouth tightened. She was scratching at his own uncertainties.

She tried to cover up. "I didn't mean you weren't good. You were the tops, or Wayman would never have bothered. After all, he's Mr IT in the world. But how did he *know* about you—"

Reilly said tersely, "Because I guess the names of the best people in the industry get around." But he knew this could only be half the story.

"Uh-huh. Yeah, sure."

Laura wasn't going to contradict him. But she used to be in the IT world herself—she still was in a small way—and she knew there were hundreds, if not thousands, of Steve Reillys, bright guys with hot degrees who were can-do managers.

Why Wayman would single out Steve Reilly was questionable to her, much as she respected his abilities.

Reilly knew this too, only he didn't want to admit it. "You seem a bit dense today," he said, sourly.

"You don't think Wayman could have been targeting you as a key person in Mitsuko?"

"*Targeting*? What the hell do you mean? He offered me a job for Christ's sake because I'm good, not for some negative reason to screw up Mitsuko!"

"But it did screw them up, you leaving."

Laura couldn't get away from the thought that her husband's reputation hadn't travelled casually across the Pacific to the US, and come up in Wayman's hearing. To her, it looked like a planned move by Wayman, a tactic, something to handicap Mitsuko, but she didn't press it with Reilly.

Laura looked out of the window at two white swans cruising in parallel on the pond. She didn't want to catch his eye in case he could read her thoughts. Life seemed so calm and simple for the swans.

"I hope everything's going to be all right," she said softly.

Reilly choked on his coffee, and clattered the cup down on the saucer. He couldn't keep the aggression out of his voice.

"What do you mean?"

"Just, I hope you get the job."

"Oh shit, Laura! What's the point of saying that? Of course you *hope*. And I *hope*. We'll have to wait and see, won't we? I have Wayman's word."

"Cool it, Steve. I was only trying to—"

"Well, don't try!"

"Sorry," Laura said, slipping off the high stool, and going toward the door.

She knew he was touchy, but she hadn't realised he'd show it so readily. "I'm going up to get dressed."

Reilly finished his coffee, and walked through the lounge and dining room, drawing the curtains on the wide picture windows.

The Reilly's house was in an acceptable state of near-complete decoration. The walls of the rooms were papered with brilliant yellow stripes. The rooms contained a gleaming antique walnut dining table and chairs, a trio of exquisitely figured old German silver candelabra, and two comfortable dark blue sofas and chairs.

The valuable Persian rug on the floor was not meant to cover all the bare boards—they hadn't decided what to do about the floor yet. Perhaps they'd leave it the way it was. The polished cedar was inlaid with ash, and had a deep honey grain.

In the hall and on the stair landings original watercolours rested in their frames on the carpet. The Reillys were still discussing exactly where to hang them.

The dining table, the Persian rug, and the paintings and silver, had cost what Reilly thought was a fortune.

Laura viewed them as investments. Besides, she said, he had to *show* he was making it.

Every time Reilly let the morning light into these rooms, the glowing antiques and paintings emerged from the shadows like accusing strangers.

Laura was getting out of the shower when Reilly put his head into the bathroom, shamefaced. He got a full view of her, naked, lightly tanned, nicely rounded breasts and ass.

"Hey, you look good. Tell you what. When I do the final interview, how about we go out to dinner and celebrate, just the two of us?"

He was saying he was sorry in his way.

"If you aren't too busy, that would be great. Somewhere like The Green Room," she said.

"I'll call them, and get a table when we fix a date."

He kissed her cheek, and picked up his briefcase on the way out. Laura naturally chose the most expensive place in Syracuse.

Laura wrapped a towel around her, and blocked from her mind what their date would be like if Reilly missed the promotion. His career so far had been exceptional, but he never seemed satisfied.

They hardly had time to settle in London, from California, and he was thinking of the move to Japan. As soon as they were in Osaka, he was looking for something else—and this was it.

He was earning big money, and they were spending every cent of it. They seemed to need it.

She heard the crunch of his car on the drive with relief as she sat in front of the dressing table mirror in white bra and pants. She looked composed, but melancholy.

She was twenty-seven. The tension underneath didn't show all that much, she thought.

She reached into a drawer for a sweater. She didn't have to dress up. First task of the day was to drive over to Abbey Forks, to the Webster Home, where Jolie was.

As Laura looked at her own reflection in the mirror, she could see the crystal paperweight on the dresser. Pieces of paper stuck out reproachfully underneath it. They were household bills.

Reilly had brought the bills up to the bedroom to talk to her about them at bedtime. But Laura put the discussion off until after the promotion panel.

She thought they could extend their loans when Reilly had scored the job.

The house was very quiet now that Reilly had gone. Only the occasional squawk of ducks from the pond.

She could feel the solitariness. Silly fears rushed into her mind—about Jolie, about having to sell the house, or the cabin at Osceola Lake—having to admit to those around them that they couldn't afford to live like this.

She brushed her hair carefully and it fell in shiny waves on the collar of the red sweater. In the rhythm of brushing she reassured herself that Reilly would get the promotion, and everything would be fine.

Chapter 14

"There was an urgent call for you, Mr Hayden, just half an hour ago," the receptionist at the Bowen Hotel said, as Hayden picked up the key to his room.

It was 10 pm. He had spent the afternoon with Cathy Ong at WayCom's offices, reviewing the mass of information they had about the STELA team, and finished the evening with a Chinese meal in town under Cathy's discerning guidance.

They had concluded that Leman was their best hope of progress at present. It would be a matter of cracking him before he was surrounded by his lawyers. Hayden had worked out a little plan with Al Gerstein.

Leman was used to being treated with deference. Being manhandled—more psychologically than physically—into an FBI car with three or four heavy men, and riding with them, would be unsettling. It would induce an inclination to talk, to stop the unpleasantness.

The pick-up part would be stagey. Designed to intimidate.

The black car in the drive, motor running. Loud rap at the door. Loud voices of introduction. Official monotone statement of the nature of the investigation. Request for cooperation. Restraining hand gripping the arm. Then the discreet nice-guy approach. *It'll be easier if you tell us, Mr Leman.*

All this when the man was already burdened down with guilt.

Hayden had fifteen minutes before Al Gerstein's arrival, and the drive out to Leman's home with Al's team.

He took the message slip from the girl. It was a please call back from Gerstein. Hayden called the field office number from the desk.

"Developments at Le Moyne House. That's the message, sir," the duty agent said. "Al is there now, and says his previous meeting with you is cancelled."

Hayden frowned, and moved to a house phone to alert Cathy Ong, when the receptionist stopped him.

"There's another message I overlooked, Mr Hayden. It was left here personally by a caller, way earlier than the urgent one. I guess it wasn't urgent. The caller only left his name."

She pushed a slip of paper negligently across the desk toward him.

Hayden read the message: *4:0 pm. Mr Leman called at the desk.*

★ ★ ★

Mike Hayden and Cathy Ong took a taxi to Strathmore Park in thirty minutes.

When Hayden climbed out of the cab and stood on the road, icy beads of rain began to soak into his hair, and the cold attacked his face and hands.

Police vans, patrol cars and an ambulance were drawn up outside the building; there were no pedestrians, few cars.

The rain was slicing diagonally through a sodium twilight. The building was floodlit. Video cameras recorded everything happening around the perimeter twenty-four hours a day.

All windows glowed. The offices were set up for twenty-four hour working. There were relief night staff—secretaries, cleaners, telecom operators, and a canteen that served fillet steak and fries at 3 am if required.

Hayden went to the entrance with Cathy, stripped off his wet coat, and ran his hand through his dripping hair. He showed his ID to the guard, and the cop who stood beside him, and they were allowed though the barrier.

"In the shredding room, sir," the guard said, "along to the right."

The mention of the shredding room made Hayden feel queasy before he got there. Cathy Ong showed no expression, but her eyes locked with his for one second.

The shredding room was an important part of WayCom security. All the confidential wastepaper was reduced to threads. The volume of paper, including the printout from computers produced each day, was huge. Black plastic sacks were collected regularly from every office, stacked in the room, and the contents methodically fed into the machine by a member of the security staff, and then incinerated.

Hayden greeted Al Gerstein at the door of the shredding room. Gerstein was slow-moving, with patches of wetness on his suit.

"Remember Oneida Lake?" Gerstein asked. "A guy named Jackson Bray tried to circumcise himself with a chainsaw."

He jerked his head toward the shredding machine. "We got another guy playin' with unforgiving machinery."

Two medics were trying to extract the body of a man dressed in a suit, which was head and shoulders into the feed trap of the shredder.

The shredder itself was a giant version of the small portable office machine. It had a series of razor-sharp discs set in two rows, which drew the paper in, and sliced it like strands of cotton. The discs could mince a telephone directory in seconds.

A steel panelled case three feet high, three feet wide, and four feet long, bolted to the floor, housed the shredder. It had a feed tray on top.

The operator had to push a sack of paper along the slide, through the rubber lips of the feed trap about two and a half feet square. Then the razor discs took over, and drew the paper in.

There was a fraught silence in the room as the medics struggled. Just the sound of their heavy breathing, and a smell of sweat and blood. The victim's ankles stuck out from under the arm of one of the medics, aubergine socks and the clean soles of new black loafers.

Hayden could feel his half-digested supper resting uncomfortably in his stomach.

Cathy Ong was moving around expressionlessly, summing up. She had a notebook.

The medics had removed the side panels from the machine, exposing the circular saws.

The body had jammed the machine, but not before it had virtually sliced the victim's skull into pieces, and drawn in clothing from his shoulders and chest.

Blood ran down through the blades, on to the shreds in the waste pit, soaking them. Hayden could see the blood dripping.

A hand touched Hayden on the arm.

It was Karen Bridges, looking smaller and less formal in jeans and a white windcheater. "The dead man is Carl Leman. At least that's what the ID in his suit says."

"Leman? Jesus. It had to be."

He gave a desolate sigh. Hayden heard what he expected.

"I've been trying to catch the bastard since I arrived, but he's been dodging around like a damn rabbit. Scared shitless, I guess."

Hayden watched the medics lift the almost headless corpse of Carl Leman, streaming with blood, from the machine, place it on a body bag, close the bag, and move it outside to the waiting ambulance.

The ceremony quietened everybody in the room—cops, medics, and security staff.

When the door of the shredding room closed on the corpse, there was a moment of silence, while the watchers groped to get back to their tasks, and Hayden smelt the sickly smell of blood and shattered bone in the air.

Hayden and Karen Bridges waited in an adjoining office while the forensic team worked in the shredding room.

It was an awkward moment. Awkward because of the shadow of Leman's death, and awkward because of their relationship which was distant, and yet in some respects close.

Hayden groped for a subject apart from the case. "So how come you end up here as Wayman's bouncer?" he ventured tentatively.

He remembered reading in the papers some time before that in the FBI she had risked her neck in a hostage siege.

"I'm a little more than a bouncer," she said, acidly.

"I heard about the siege. Nobody does that without dedication to a cause."

He recalled the newspaper report about Karen. She had confronted a crazy holding a sawn-off shotgun on her, and two other FBI agents. There was no SWAT team to take the perp out. It had been high noon.

Karen remembered differently. "That was about psychological domination, Mike. Sometimes you can look a perp in the eye, and know he's going to crumble. It was like that with this guy Arnie Kolchek. He was an emotional sponge, clinging to a rifle butt. It wasn't as big a deal as you think. The papers write these things up."

"You disarmed him. Your buddies didn't."

"Yeah. Anyway I'm not apologising for what I do here. It's safe, which the FBI is not. And it's well paid."

Hayden had the bloodied shredder in his mind, and wondered how safe it really was, but he didn't speculate out loud.

Al Gerstein came in, the vertical channels in each cheek longer and darker. "These guys got a system. You squeak and you get iced."

He worked the coffee machine, and handed paper cups around. He went on in a low drawl that made him sound depressed. "It'd take a robust man to push Leman into that feed trap. Leman sure didn't crawl in himself."

"Let's get out of here. Can I give you a lift to the hotel?" Karen asked.

Cathy Ong came in and drew Hayden aside. "There's got to be something on the corridor videos showing how Leman got into the shredding room. No cameras in here, but plenty outside."

She was correct. Hayden mentioned the cameras to Gerstein and Karen Bridges.

"We better impound the film now. Give it a close scan," Gerstein said.

"The corridor cameras are being modified. They weren't functioning today," Karen Bridges said.

"The hell they weren't!" Hayden said.

★ ★ ★

When they were in Karen Bridges's chauffeured car, Hayden said he felt like a drink. Gerstein said he too felt thirsty. Cathy Ong knew her boss wanted this one on his own, and said she preferred to go to bed. Karen looked at her watch, and decided that duty called her to the bar.

In twenty minutes they had dropped Cathy at the Bowen, dismissed the chauffeur, and the three were side by side at Croc's on 21st and Lancaster.

Karen slipped out of her jacket as Hayden lined up three Scotch and sodas.

Hayden tried the whisky. "After tonight's events do you reckon you're under attack from a competitor?" he asked Karen.

"We don't know why Leman was killed," Karen said. "If Leman was going to squeal about espionage—"

"He was. And Leman used the plural to me. He said *senior people* were selling you out on STELA. He was looking for immunity himself, so I guess he was only one of them," Hayden said.

"If I knew there were other rats in the cellar, I'd get to them," Karen said.

"The NSA want a news blackout on this on national security grounds," Gerstein said.

Karen agreed. "Our publicity machine will ensure that all the press get will be news of a fatal accident being investigated. Industrial accidents don't make the nationals."

Hayden was thinking that if the Leman killing was as skilful as the Bray job, they would find few clues. Cerillo would be fulminating about two deaths and a disappearance, but Hayden was confident that, without further evidence, Cerillo was no nearer getting rid of Wayman.

They had a couple more drinks and talked about the goings on in the FBI mausoleum at 935 Pennsylvania Avenue, Washington, DC. Then Gerstein left.

Hayden suddenly became conscious of the warmth of Karen's upper arm against his as they leaned on the bar, and said they better go too.

When Hayden dropped Karen at her apartment in a cab, she said, "Do you want to come up for coffee?"

She said it defiantly, almost daring him to accept. As though there was something improper about it.

Hayden was taken by surprise. It was 2.30 in the morning.

She knew she was standing in Mariette's shadow, and didn't care.

All Hayden did was to move his head slightly to signal a negative.

Chapter 15

Six-thirty pm. The air had a silvery greyness; it was nearly still, but for a chill coming up from the Onondaga Lake, as the guests began to get out of their chauffeured cars and stroll through the gates, the women in cocktail dresses and the men in dark suits.

White-coated waiters were at the doors to greet them with trays of Bollinger and buck's fizz.

The party was at the Harrison Exhibition Centre on South 4th Street beside the mud coloured Oneida stream, with its fringe of young oaks fluttering just a few rags of yellow leaf. They were going to have an exclusive view of a selection of paintings from the Tate Gallery's Turner collection in London.

Steve and Laura Reilly headed for the waiters with their laden trays of champagne as soon as they were inside the door. Reilly handed Laura a glass and took one himself. The bubbles rising in the hollow stem glinted like tiny strings of pearls.

Reilly sipped the amber liquid approvingly, and was conscious of making his entrance. He wore a Hugo Boss suit of plain dark blue, with a white shirt and figured silk tie, certain that with his face and figure and undoubted skills, he outshone his peers.

And behind the relaxed smile was a sourness that these dicks hadn't recognised his true worth.

He was always proud of Laura. She was correctly uniformed for a corporation wife: the discreet platinum necklace, the diamond cluster ring, matching eternity ring, small but very good solitaire diamond earrings, and the dress Breguet watch with its diamante face. All expensive badges of status.

She wore a conservative Fendi frock, off the shoulder in midnight blue velvet which set off her golden-blond hair.

She'd got it right. She hung on to Steve's arm while he moved between groups, greeting effusively.

She was noticed but no more than that. Wayman smiled at her. She responded weakly.

She paused a little longer with Diana Wayman, a smiling centre of attention in her Guy Laroche gown.

Both Laura and Diana were a contrast to some of the wives, who looked ten years older than their husbands, dry-skinned and mummified, corporate accessories wheeled out for the occasion.

The Reillys spent a short time standing in front of Turner's radiant works, mouthing dutifully, but Steve Reilly was impatient, moving from one masterpiece to the other, turning his head to see who was close enough to speak to, or who was worth speaking to.

Eventually he deposited Laura in a corner with a tray of canapés, half a bottle of Bollinger and two other company wives, and made off for further conquests.

As Laura talked to the women, she was able to watch her husband.

Reilly was a relentless networker, seeking the players, ignoring the losers. He scored these evenings afterwards by detailing the number he'd buttonholed. Top of his list would be Wayman—whom he'd bagged for a minute or so.

Laura noticed—yes, she was sure—a woman was manoeuvring to get alongside Reilly. The woman was on the fringes. When Reilly moved, the woman followed.

She was about thirty, dark, dressed in a smart dark suit with dark hosiery and shoes. Her clothes said she was a businesswoman or a professional, maybe a lawyer, not a company wife.

Laura Reilly talked idly to her companions about houses, cars, holidays, and the children she didn't want until she'd enjoyed a few years of freedom with her husband. She never mentioned Jolie.

All the time she watched the pursuit going on. She wasn't mistaken. Pursuit it was. The woman got her chance—Reilly broke off a conversation, and she moved in on him; they began to talk.

Laura thought she saw the woman make a gesture with her head to withdraw Reilly further from the press of people so they could talk privately.

Reilly was responsive, using his eyes, his hands, looking sure of himself.

The woman was staring up at the six feet of him and cupping her champagne glass in both hands as though she was worshipping.

The two were quite separate. Nobody interrupted them.

Laura was irritated. After two or three minutes she excused herself, and pushed through to the pair.

"Hullo, I'm Steve's wife."

"Laura, this is Ruth Charlton, from Digby, Hudson."

He said it as though Laura knew who Digby, Hudson were.

Laura couldn't resist. "Digby who?"

"Digby, Hudson, the head-hunters, of course" Reilly said, impatiently.

"You don't seem to be enjoying the show," Ruth Charlton said to her, smoothly glossing over the interruption.

"Actually, I'm not one of those company wives who turn their noses up at the champagne and the works of art. But one does feel a bit of an accessory," Laura said with bite.

Ruth understood. "It's the same with me. You hardly know the people, and a lot you mightn't want to know. In a year or two it'll be a different crowd. Maybe in a different corporation."

Laura Reilly didn't think there was much she would agree with Ruth Charlton about, but this she did. Her eyes widened.

"Sure. You could be talking to anybody of almost any race or culture at these parties. The only thing the people have in common is they're pretty smart. But they don't *belong*."

"I guess they're here for the dough," Reilly said, glad his wife had decided not to maul Ruth Charlton.

"Talking about not belonging, I've been telling Steve he ought to be thinking of his next move," Ruth said.

"Oh yeah? To join whom?"

Laura was getting tired of the international junketing, but they needed the money.

"Steve could get a job very easily with any number of computer companies, I guess," Ruth said, plainly not wanting to say too much.

"It's a perennial question: whether you might do better on the other side of the world," she added.

Laura felt defensive. There was still the marketing directorship in play. She wasn't going to give a hint about that to this knowing woman. "As far as I'm concerned, Steve's doing well now. He's hardly had time to warm the seat at WayCom."

"But I can't let that inhibit me, dear," Steve said dismissively.

"It pays to think ahead. *Steve's a valuable property*," Ruth said.

"Like he's a piece of real estate!" Laura said.

The smiles on the faces of Reilly and Ruth Charlton faded.

Ruth took an address card out of her bag, handed it to Reilly.

Laura could hardly suppress her distaste. It was Ruth Charlton's wide, brash, red mouth and white teeth, and the conceit she exuded like scent.

Laura's long eyelashes flickered. She took a big gulp of champagne. Then she asked with deceptive mildness if head-hunters had any rules of engagement.

"I mean, this is a WayCom party isn't it, and you're a WayCom guest."

"A dollar has no manners," Ruth laughed.

"Head-hunter," Laura Reilly said. "You're a bloody cannibal!"

Chapter 16

Heidi Stoller sat in the driver's seat of the car at Cassidy Park. She had placed the car at the back of the viewpoint, away from the other occasional visitors.

The quarter moon was over the Onondaga Lake, and the lake burnished the thin clouds with the reflection from its mirror surface.

Delia Marris's youthful forehead and cheeks were painted in the light like an old and faded portrait.

"I had to see you because it's making me jumpy," Delia said.

She spoke into a long silence that Heidi had built.

Delia was a different beast than Leman; she was one of Heidi's own plants, found by her and introduced into WayCom by Ruth Charlton.

Delia would stay until her usefulness waned, or she was compromised, and then she would disappear.

Heidi had a real feeling for Delia, understood how far she could push her, and how necessary it was to extract her safely at the end of the operation.

It was an unfortunate fact of life that Heidi had to recruit flesh and blood agents, who could deliver secret files to her, people like Delia, Bray and Carl Leman—and Steve Reilly if he could be turned.

The amount of daily information about WayCom received by Heidi's special department in Stoller Software Inc, in New York, and processed by their computers, was voluminous—hundreds of telephone and computer communications. Most of them, unfortunately, unhelpful.

Every so often, WayCom made a slip; it might be a telephone conversation, an e-mail exchange, or an easily cracked password to a confidential file.

At rare times, Heidi Stoller was virtually inside WayCom, looking over shoulders, watching as management decisions were made.

But technical penetration alone wasn't enough. The WayCom secrets were increasingly protected by just the kind of software that Heidi Stoller sold.

The codes guarding STELA 2 were almost unbreakable. This

barrier had forced Heidi back to Sun Tzu's simple dictum formulated 2,400 years ago: *There is no place where espionage is not possible.*

Heidi's voice was affectionate. "I wouldn't worry about the Fed. Let them poke around. They won't find anything. The NSA get the FBI to carry out checks every so often. They never find anything."

"I was worried about what happened to Mr Leman. It was awful, they say. In the shredder."

"I don't know anything about that, dear. I heard he had an accident."

"Hayden, the lawyer, came prowling around the project, asking about Mariette Stevas. Mariette hasn't been at work. Do you know anything about her?"

"Not a thing, Delia. Did you know her?"

"Only by sight. Like Jack Bray."

"What was Hayden like?"

"Oh, quite OK, you know, charming, amusing. We were told about him. He's working for the company. We have to answer his questions."

"Well, WayCom are only protecting their interests. I'm not surprised."

Heidi Stoller thought about it. There was an increase of activity by Hayden and the FBI, no doubt. It meant that her intuition about Leman had probably been right—he had cracked, and talked, and the FBI were probably looking for *her*. The fortunate point was that Leman had known very little.

Heidi was not going to show any misgivings to her young accomplice. "Delia, can you get the final part of the CD scanner program we were dealing with, on a floppy? I know it isn't easy, but that's all I'll ask. Then you can leave WayCom, take a rest. Spend some of the money you've made."

The reassurance cheered Delia. She squeezed Heidi's hand. "OK. But tell me about Jack Bray. It sounds so horrible. All sorts of stories are going round the office."

"I don't know anything about Bray, dear. And he certainly wasn't a contact of mine."

"Thanks, Heidi. It ... makes me feel better."

"How are you getting along with Reilly?"

"He's nice really. I like him. He's totally pissed off with WayCom. Reckons they brought him over from Japan more or less on false pretences."

"Uh-huh. Talking about leaving is he?"

"Yes, but he's hopeful of a big new appointment in North American sales which might change that."

"Keep after him, Delia, and stay cool. I'll drop you near your place now," Heidi said, gunning the motor.

Chapter 17

At six in the morning, Hayden paused only long enough to part the curtains in his hotel room, and take in the frosty, brown patches on the park where the cold had killed the young grass.

He slipped on a pair of boxer shorts and a sweater, and did four circuits of the track, showered, and dressed.

He met Cathy Ong and Al Gerstein for breakfast in the Bowen dining room at 7.30.

Cathy had taken a table in the corner, a long way from the loaded buffet, where they could talk privately. Over scrambled eggs, toast and orange juice, they considered the case.

"From my own professional point of view as Wayman's counsel, things are just dandy. Two employees have been capped, but the Administration can't hold that against Wayman. He's followed the security rules," Hayden said.

"All right, all right," Gerstein grouched. "From my professional point of view as an FBI Agent I have two killings and a disappearance and no leads, and things are lousy. All I know is that somebody is robbin' WayCom."

"But I'm worried that we haven't had a whisper about Mariette," Hayden said.

"There's nothing from her room, or the car wreck," Cathy Ong said.

"I understand your concern about Mariette, Mike, and I'll keep you up with any developments," Gerstein said.

"Anything from the shredding room?" Cathy asked.

Gerstein lay down his knife and fork, as their memories returned to a scene which did not go well with breakfast.

"Our forensic work hasn't produced anything so far. We have a lot of prints to run through, but we expect they will be the usual operators. Leman was picked up bodily by a strong man, and shoved head first into the feedtrap. There aren't a lot of clues from an action like that, if it's done cleanly and quickly. Nothing under his fingernails to help us, no struggle wounds, nothing indicative on his clothing."

A silence, although Cathy Ong had continued her dainty eating while the other two quit.

"Look, we could approach it another way, Mike," she said.

They had been working together since the early spring, but when Cathy used Mike Hayden's first name, especially in company, she always sounded apologetic about the intimacy. The quiet Chinese woman was shy of the big, rambling Caucasian.

"I mean look at who would want STELA technology," she said.

"*Look* at them, CJ?" Gerstein smiled at his scrambled eggs, and resumed eating.

"I've been thinking about it myself," he said as he chewed.

A shortlist of corporations wasn't hard to put together. But what Cathy meant was have a look *inside* them, trawl through their computer and telecom traffic, get reports from inside agents.

If they did this, they could possibly come up with a name, a fact, some event which connected what had happened at WayCom with what was happening inside one of the major IT corporations.

Once they had that spark of connection, finding out the truth would become much simpler.

Cerillo's surveillance potential, and Stella's ability to refine and search a mass of data would make it feasible, Hayden agreed.

"A list of possibles I suggest would be Mitsuko, Fairford, KDG, and Zosmark," Gerstein said, turning to his toast, layering it with thick butter, and English marmalade.

Hayden thought about the names for a moment. "Sure. Add possibly Globe Accord. Nobody else could develop and handle the marketing of the STELA technology. One of them has to be getting the stolen information, presumably through agents who are making a pile—and killing along the line," he added, bitterly.

"Unless it's the work of a foreign government," Cathy Ong said.

"Sure, we have to put that aside, CJ. Can you persuade Cerillo to do this, Al? Look at the big players. A national security issue involving theft and murder."

Al Gerstein wasn't smug, but he swallowed his toast, and sat back, engaging both their glances, and flexed his mouth to make a heavyweight pronouncement.

"This is highly confidential. I was goin' to tell you guys since we're workin' together. Byron already did."

"I wondered why you were so quick with the possibles," Hayden said, but he wasn't too surprised.

"Yeah. Well, the NSA have been picking up a lot of stuff from those corporations through Menwith Hill and Fort Meade. Stella has been refining the trawl. Fairford is the only US company. Byron can't turn his surveillance on them without probable cause."

"And?" Cathy asked.

"Nix—so far," Gerstein said. "We can find out their chief execs' shoe sizes, but we can't find out whether they're robbing us."

Cathy sipped her tea delicately, while Hayden poured another coffee.

They were silent, thinking.

Stella, with the satellite surveillance computers, might still produce a pattern from the mass of intelligence, something strong enough to identify the perpetrator, and the scale of his operations.

Gerstein surrendered to one more slice of jam toast, and brightened. "OK. So I'll keep you in the picture on scoping the big boys. The other line is plain old unvarnished investigative work, finding Leman's killer."

"It might pay to scour the Bray file for the Nth time, too. I'll leave it to you, CJ. Could be some connection there we haven't noticed," Hayden said.

"Stella has already chewed it over," Cathy said. "I'm not going to come up with anything she missed. But our telecom and computer surveillance of the STELA team might come up with something. Anybody who's engaged in espionage will be feeling the heat now."

"Somebody else will break, eventually," Hayden said.

He was sure, but impatient.

And the coffee gave him a charge which made him reflective. "You know, when I started to come here to Syracuse to talk to WayCom, I was kinda taken in by the peaceful, laid-back lifestyle, a healthy pay check, a comfortable home with a big garden, working with bright attractive people, the chance to ski and fish a few miles up the road—"

Gerstein was listening with his cop eyes narrowed.

Cathy was following with difficulty. Her concept of lifestyle wasn't so materialistic.

Her family—her mother and young sister—lived in an apartment in a quiet suburb of San Diego. Her idea of sport, and physical freedom, was tai chi quan, and a walk in the park.

Uncertainty hovered at the corners of her lips.

"What I mean is, the shiny surface looks so good, but underneath there's greed and violence. Maybe stealing ideas beats drug dealing for profits."

"Not for Messrs Bray and Leman," Gerstein growled.

Chapter 18

Laura Reilly drove the Jeep 4WD down to Abbey Forks, where they usually did their shopping at about eleven in the morning.

Abbey Forks was an old town which used to be the centre of a farming district. Now it was a shopping and municipal centre for this part of Onondaga County.

The Abbey River and the Fabius River joined at the forks, and the town was on the high ground above the river channels. It had a town square, which was actually a big triangle of cut grass, shaded by sixty foot plane trees, where the kids could play while their parents shopped.

There was a county office, police department, courthouse and medical centre, along with three old tall white churches—Baptist, Methodist and Episcopalian, around the green.

Laura spent a little time browsing through the shirts and slacks in Dale's, the men's store, trying to think of a present for Steve's birthday but couldn't concentrate.

The row—or was it a talk?—with Steve about the new job had upset her. She hadn't realised how vulnerable he was.

Laura cleared her head in the sharp air, walking the two blocks along an oak lined street to the Webster Nursing Home where Jolie now stayed.

When they were in London and Osaka, Jolie had been at a home in Sacramento, California. Laura used to fly to Sacramento regularly to see Jolie, who was four now, but it wouldn't have made much difference, because Jolie didn't know her.

Jolie was autistic. She lived in an enclosed world of her own.

Both the Reillys believed they had to stay as close as they could to Jolie, although they had been told that there was very little chance her condition would ever change.

Laura followed her usual practice of seeing the sister on duty, and then going into Jolie's room. She usually sat with the little girl for about an hour.

Occasionally, Jolie would notice her mother, but mostly she played with the coloured blocks and soft toys around her in a way that showed she was disconnected from them. She was always silent, and sometimes very still.

The room was wide, pastel coloured, and full of gentle images on the walls. The sun poured in. Jolie was always clean and neat and calm.

The Webster Home seemed to Laura to be a good place. It radiated good karma.

The Medical Director did not pretend to be an expert in autism. He had told Laura he couldn't treat Jolie, but he said that if there were any medical developments anywhere in the world that he learned about, he would tell her.

Laura and her husband had decided that at the moment there weren't any treatments they wanted to attempt.

They had been through the long and awful trauma of discovering gradually that their tiny child, who seemed so perfect at birth, wasn't normal. And it wasn't simply abnormality. Jolie became like an alien.

Laura sat in the sun, and cuddled the child, but it was a strange experience, like cuddling an animal, because Jolie didn't react much. Sometimes it was better to sit with her on the bed, not touching, but thinking good thoughts.

At times Laura cried quietly.

When Laura had finished her visit, she said goodbye to the duty sister, and went downstairs to the entrance.

She was about to go out the front door when the Medical Director's secretary asked her if she would step into the office. Laura felt suddenly like some kind of criminal.

The secretary was a grey and shapeless elderly woman, but steady-eyed with a precise voice.

"Mrs Reilly, you haven't settled Jolie's account. I'm sorry, I know the fees are heavy. I don't know how people afford them."

Laura flushed with embarrassment. "I promise we'll do it soon."

The secretary paused, waiting for a further explanation.

Laura opened her mouth. She had to say something. "My husband is expecting—"

She was going to say a promotion, and then she had the sickening vision of the planefuls of hopefuls from Silicon Valley who would be competing with Steve.

"My husband is making arrangements …"

The secretary interrupted, "You only have—let me see—three weeks and then we will be keeping Jolie at our expense. That's not possible Mrs Reilly."

"I know."

"Jolie has to leave in three weeks, unless—"

"I understand," Laura said.

But she didn't really understand. She thought Steve had worked out the finances. She knew they were a bit pushed, but not this badly.

The secretary seemed anxious to help. She spoke very gently, picking up a copy of the account and a pencil.

"Now can I mark the account that we've met today, and you've agreed to pay in seven days, the present quarter, and the next quarter, to put you in advance in the normal way?"

Laura nodded her agreement, and the woman put a hand on her arm.

"I'm very, very sorry, Mrs Reilly."

★ ★ ★

Laura Reilly parked the Jeep 4WD in the building on West 11th Street, next to The Green Room at 7.30 and went inside the restaurant.

She had dressed carefully in a lightweight beige coat, a matching cotton dress with a brown leather belt, beige court shoes and bag. Her honey hair and light tan were shown off by the colours.

She was a little early. She sat down, satisfied with the table Steve had booked—high-backed banquette seats, and comfortably private, with a good view across the diners in the middle of the room.

She didn't feel hungry. The possibility that Steve would fail to get the job gnawed at her. Now she wished they'd decided to stay home.

The Green Room was one of the town's top eateries and already quite full. She ordered mineral water, and watched the crowd. Eight pm came and passed.

The waiter kept coming to the table and asking her if she wanted to order. By 8.30 most people in the room had moved on from cocktails, and were engrossed in their meal, and the noise level was high.

Laura was sitting in a space large enough for six, watching the big fans turning idly in the ceiling, wondering what to do. Then she saw Steve over the heads of the diners, coming in the door. He saw her, waved and began to make his way across between the tables.

She could tell even in the muted light of the restaurant that he had missed the job. His jaw was gritted as though he'd had a bad time at the dentist.

He slid into the seat opposite and looked at her squarely, the irises of his eyes like crushed ice. She put her hand over his, and waited for him to speak.

"Bastards. Fucking bastards," he said, quietly."

"Tell me what happened."

But the waiter was there. "You wanta order?"

"I've just goddamwell sat down!" Reilly snarled.

The waiter looked aggrieved. This was the sort of attitude he punished people for.

Reilly relented: "Bring me a double vodka martini, a dry white for the lady, and a bottle of mineral water. I'll order when you serve them."

Out of the corner of his mouth he said to Laura, "Christ, I don't think I could eat anything."

"Let's have the drinks and go," Laura suggested, thinking that even at a time like this, Steve wouldn't want to pay the hefty cover charge. He was like that.

But Steve Reilly wasn't thinking about cover charges. He was stunned. There was a line of sweat on his upper lip, his tie was crooked. He looked at his wife without seeing her.

"What happened?" Laura asked softly.

Reilly was silent. Laura filled in the blanks. "Drew Millar got the job?" she said.

"I've bested that guy all along the line, Laura. How the fuck could they do that?"

"You think it was stitched up in advance?"

Steve Reilly refocused on his wife. She seemed to accept what he had refused to consider. "Yeah. Yeah, I think it probably was. I didn't want to believe it. Millar could not have got that job by any rational assessment of how he has been performing, and how I have been performing. Never. Never."

"When have people ever been promoted rationally in a big corporation?"

Again, Reilly did a double-take on his wife. She understood. "You're goddam right!"

The waiter arrived with the drinks, looking mean. He banged them down on the tabletop. Neither Reilly nor Laura had mentioned food; they hadn't even opened the menus.

Now Reilly tried to be jovial with the waiter, and asked for another round of drinks, and without consulting the menu, he asked for lasagne for two, with green salads.

"How did the interviews go for you?" Laura asked, ignoring the waiter. Steve hadn't consulted her about the order, but she forgave him this once.

"Fine. Perfect. Damn well. I thought I came across with everything they wanted."

The waiter took a long time writing the small order, hovering. "Izzat all?" he asked, managing to make the words sound insulting.

Laura waved the waiter away like a fly. "Did they say anything afterwards? I mean, an explanation?"

Reilly's lips turned down at the memory. "Bridges called me up to her office. Wayman was there. Gave me a lot of crap about what a bright boy I was, and said they needed to keep me on STELA 2. I asked him if that meant the best man didn't get the job. Wayman said it was a close call."

"But you reckon it wasn't close at all."

"Not if the contenders were me and Millar. Hell, Laura I have pushed the STELA program back on schedule, while Millar has been preparing budgets. While Millar was farting digits, I've about doubled Luchinelli's progress. I've done everything except kiss Luchinelli's pecker."

"Maybe WayCom owed Millar for something."

"What? Counting beans?"

"Something we don't know about."

Laura wanted to say that Wayman was a louse to make a promise that brought them halfway around the world, and then weasel out. But she didn't. It wasn't any use stirring Steve up even more.

Reilly gulped the martini. "What's the good how much they love me if I don't get promoted and rewarded?"

Chapter 19

Cathy Ong drove Hayden out to the Leman house in Fairmont, about ten miles from the hotel.

He had a better chance to see the area than on his previous visit. It was yuppie country. The houses were big, spacious, expensive and trying to be elegant. Most looked as though they had been completed yesterday, and the turf re-laid at the same time. The roads were lined with bare saplings fighting feebly for life in the cold. The developer had left the odd fully grown beech or oak to remind that this was once an area of thick forest.

Cathy parked the rental car on the road, and they walked up the drive, past the ornamental walls and carefully tended flowerbeds. Mrs Leman opened the door.

The shock of the death had added a deep-frozen quality to the tortured expression Hayden had noticed when he first met her.

She invited them into the lounge. She sat in an armchair with her hands in her lap like a pile of small bones. She didn't question Hayden's role after their earlier meeting, and scarcely noticed Cathy.

"I can't tell you more than I already have, Mr Hayden. We settled down here three or four years ago, and then Carl joined WayCom—"

"Can you remember how he got the job, Mrs Leman?"

"No. I guess we wanted to come back to the US, and WayCom made an offer. We didn't want to have the kids in school in South Africa."

"Did Carl work in the year after he left Zosmark, Mrs Leman?"

"He was always busy doing something, but he didn't actually go out to the office."

"Did he work for WayCom?"

"He was always talking to them. And to his friends at Zosmark."

"Talking?"

"Telephone, fax, e-mail. And a lot of stuff by post. And he made a couple of visits to tidy up, he said."

"Visits?"

"To Johannesburg."

"Can you remember the names of his particular friends?"

"Oh, at Zosmark there were a lot. I can't remember now. They were a nice crowd. We had good times. I liked Johannesburg. So did Carl. He always used to say we'd be back some time when the kids were grown up."

"Did he get paid during that year?"

"I don't know. Carl always managed that side himself. Because he worked in south Africa, and before that in Japan, he used to say it was convenient to have a bank outside the US."

Hayden looked at Cathy Ong. Her face was perfectly blank.

"Do you have an old bank statement you could let me have? Can you at least remember the name of the bank?" Hayden asked.

Mrs Leman was suddenly suspicious. "I don't see how that can help solve Carl's murder."

"It might tell us who he was dealing with, who might have wanted to get rid of him."

She nodded doubtfully. "I don't have any statements. I'm sure there are none in the house. Carl's private papers are with his lawyers. I can remember the name of the bank though: Banco Nationale, Cayman Islands."

"Did it ever occur to you that Carl might have been involved in passing confidential information from WayCom to Zosmark? You know he worked on secret projects."

She frowned, surprised, and not quite comprehending at first. Then she shook her head slowly. "Not Carl, never. He was one of the most honest and open people you could meet. He went to church every week. He was more regular than I was. I'm shocked to think such an awful suspicion could come into your mind."

"It's only a thought, Mrs Leman. In my job I have to think the unthinkable. If somehow he got involved in passing information to Zosmark, that could explain what happened."

Mrs Leman was too weak not to forgive. When Hayden asked if he could see Carl Leman's study, she said feebly: "I don't know why everyone's so interested in that. There's nothing there."

"Who else has looked at the study, Mrs Leman?"

"The FBI, Mr Gerstein, and the WayCom people came. Karen Bridges. She was the one who told me what happened. They were here soon after Carl died. They took the computer. It was owned by WayCom, and they said Carl might have had some confidential office work here, and they wanted to be sure it wasn't lost."

"Carl wasn't in any fear about his life, was he?"

"You don't mean sickness—"

"I mean was he fearful that somebody was going to kill him?"

"Of course not. He was just an ordinary business executive, wasn't he? We don't have any enemies. Carl wasn't all that well, but that was just overwork."

"How do you mean, not well?"

"His nerves were troubling him. He had frightful headaches. He used to shake uncontrollably at times. He wanted desperately to get away from the secret work he'd been doing."

Mrs Leman was sitting on the couch, staring straight ahead, a trembling skeleton of a woman in her sumptuous home. Hayden was aware of how much pain he was causing her. And yet he had to go on. "Mrs Leman, did Carl have any particular interests or hobbies?"

"Why should that be of concern to you? Only the garden. And his work. And his family. And the church. That's quite enough, isn't it?"

"I'm sorry. I'm trying to understand him better, because there could be a clue there to what happened."

"Carl never neglected us, as you can see. He was ill a while back. But he got psychiatric help, and got over it."

"Was he ever in financial difficulty as a result?"

"A long time ago. Two or three years. And as I said, we were always looked after. He knew he had an illness, and got it cured."

She showed them upstairs. The rooms to the right and left were richly furnished but neglected. She pointed to the door, and left them alone.

The study, with its view of the lawns and garden to the rear of the house, had contained a powerful IBM personal computer, linked to the internet, with a laser printer, and facsimile machine. The small library of books were mostly advanced works on computer technology.

"You'll have to get Karen Bridges to tell you what she found on the PC," Cathy said.

Hayden recalled the psychological profiling work done for them by the behavioural science unit at Quantico; they had picked Bray and Leman as suspects.

"It interests me what would make an intelligent and successful person like Leman get into the dangerous business of industrial espionage," Hayden said.

Leman didn't seem to have any grudge against WayCom, or any unusual political leanings, or any special need for money. His family life with his wife was apparently workable. Even if, as Hayden thought,

Mrs Leman had a drug habit, Leman could have afforded that. He had no criminal convictions in the US. His health, apart from what was evidently a recent mental breakdown, was sound enough. He hadn't any known problem with alcohol or drugs. The security reports on him over a period confirmed all these things.

Cathy Ong was well aware of Leman's profile. "Maybe just greed."

Hayden looked around the room which was the one room in the house you would expect to have Leman's personal mark on it. He wasn't apparently a great reader, except for technical manuals. His life seemed boringly empty. He played no sport, but went occasionally to a gym. He didn't seem to have any interests—not even model trains, or collecting gum wrappers, nothing discernible. The objects on the desk were all convenience items—a mug of pens and pencils, a paperweight. The room had no personality.

Cathy Ong opened a cabinet which was filled with stationery. On the lower shelf was a pile of used envelopes, lined with plastic padding for holding manuscripts, papers and computer disks. Leman had the quirk of re-using the envelopes. She looked quickly through the postmarks—South African and local. At the bottom of the pile were several envelopes filled with papers. She emptied them on to the desk.

"Look, Mike."

Cathy Ong sprayed a half a dozen photographs over the table and turned to the window, avoiding his eyes. Hayden stepped up to the desk and looked at the spread.

He shook his head in incomprehension, picking one shot up and examining it.

They were pornographic snapshots of very young children with men and dogs; close, intimate records of sexual encounters. The faces of the children were skilfully shielded from full view, to disguise their identity, and to conceal their suffering.

Chapter 20

Steve Reilly bought two bottles of Sauterne, at the liquor store, and a French loaf, a round of Camembert cheese, and half a pound of honey-roast ham, ready sliced, at the deli in Campbell Road, and took a cab to Delia Marris's apartment in Brentwood.

With the promotion debacle still making him ache inside, he needed to get away from the office for a few hours.

She was there when he arrived, and threw her arms round him on the doorstep.

When he had rung Delia's extension at the office that morning, and suggested they leave work, and go home to her place for a quiet lunch, she had been enthusiastic. She had said she'd depart early, and be ready when he arrived. It had made him feel hot.

And now the reality. Delia looked and smelled fresh and new and different. She was naked under her bathrobe.

He hurt so much he could hardly concentrate except to recognise the throb of sexuality. It was like a wound that was bleeding, one that everybody could see, and feel faintly repulsed by.

A number of his peers had said they thought he was certain to get the post, and now they were all looking at him like he was a loser. He *was* a loser.

He put down the paper sack he was carrying, and slipped Delia's robe off when she closed the door.

Together, they pulled his clothes off, as they made slow fumbling progress to the bedroom, dropping the discarded tie, shirt, slacks and socks on the way.

Reilly pushed Delia on to the bed and made love blindly, forgetting for a moment the disappointment of the failed promotion.

When it was over, they lay quietly for a while. He stared at the ceiling, and she stared at him.

Then Delia got up, and picked his clothes up off the floor. She went to the kitchen, and brought back the food and drink on a tray, with two wine glasses and a corkscrew.

They sat up in bed and had a picnic, breaking the loaf with their hands, opening it with their fingers, and squeezing in slices of ham and the soft cheese.

Reilly uncorked the bottles and poured the wine; it was still cold from the chiller in the liquor store. But he didn't feel all that hungry. The food blocked up in his throat, and went down in half-chewed lumps.

Delia had heard he had missed the promotion. She was too new to the company to understand much about the people involved. She tried to be sympathetic.

"I'm sure something else will come up, Steve. And you have a great post already."

Reilly looked across the small bedroom toward the dresser where Delia had pinned a poster of the young, slender and darkly handsome Elvis Presley. Fuck the post he had. He was sore. He didn't reply.

His, so far, brief fling with Delia Marris had seemed to be almost unavoidable.

He wasn't the kind who was working his way through the female staff at Le Moyne House. In fact he had a definite view that it was unwise. He had seen the mayhem it could create, at its worst getting down to allegations of sexual harassment. His common sense told him that playing around with female staff wasn't worth the candle.

But Delia arrived on the scene, a new recruit for the finance department of Project Coordination. He had to show her some of the systems on STELA 2. And there *was* a spark. She was the one in a hundred person who struck a sexual spark in him. She didn't flirt. She didn't encourage. She simply had an extraordinary chemical effect on him.

And when he met her again by accident at a leaving party for one of the staff only a day or two later, it wasn't like talking coolly to another office person. She was fresh from her previous job in Mitsuko, and they had experience to share.

He had intended to go back to work that night. Instead they ended up going to a bar for a few drinks, and then to dinner at an Italian restaurant. She had asked him to go to her place. He didn't have to angle for it.

The evening was a real trip. There never was a moment when he felt awkward, when he felt he was pushing his luck, or when he felt she was pushing him.

The first time was good. Everything they expected. And the second and third and fourth weren't bad either. They followed quickly in the ensuing days.

But Reilly had already begun to think better of what he was doing, and to wonder how he could extricate himself.

He began to realise that even in this short time Delia was developing definite expectations of him, like seeing her, calling her. It was no small deal for her.

He had been trying to think what he could do to distance himself from her without making her mad—mad enough to call Laura. But this particular morning he'd felt so low, and at the same time so hot for her, and it was only a matter of picking up the phone ...

The bread was fresh, the wine heady, and the Camembert had a ripe cunty smell. He ought to have been pleased with himself, sitting in bed, eating and drinking with a naked sexy girl.

But all that came into his mind, now that the heat of his urge had gone, added to his present pain. He knew that he was an idiot to have embarked on the affair with Delia. He was storing up trouble for himself.

Delia must have sensed how far away, and how clinical he was, because as she put her arms round him, two tears escaped from under her closed eyelids.

* * *

Steve Reilly was in Block E, the windowless no-go area at Le Moyne House, where the STELA files were kept on computer.

The rooms had virtual reality panels which made it seem that they were high above a lake, with sailboats, a beach with tents and a cabin, and a thick forest of pines leading up into the mountains.

He was having a difficult top team meeting. The Italian professor, Luchinelli, leader of the project team at an astronomical salary, was performing. The other four members, which included two women, were highly qualified doctors of physics and maths were chiming in vociferously.

Reilly always found the team, if such a disparate bunch deserved the name, hard to deal with, but by a mixture of flattery, bluff and cajolery he kept them productive.

He was looking into Luchinelli's broad, olive face with its thick nose, a black walrus moustache like a yard broom, and pink lips. Luchinelli was bending around toward him, challenging.

Reilly had been told that there was a time when work had been suspended for three days by Luchinelli, while they debated what the virtual reality panels should show.

Luchinelli wanted scenes from an abattoir. He wanted war shots with helicopter gunships. They settled for a view of Arctic ice-floes in the end, but people felt cold after a few weeks, and eventually the women got their way—summer scenes from Delta Lake.

Gino Luchinelli was probably a genius, but to Steve Reilly he was as troublesome as a prima donna. He had three visiting professorships in mathematics—at Florence, Oxford and Harvard. His name was mentioned in the same breath as that of the British mathematician of the fifties, Alan Turing. He had the reputation of being the world's leading expert on semantic programming. But Luchinelli had no sense of time. He and his team might work day and night for three days, and then spend the next three debating a point of company policy.

At the top of Steve Reilly's agenda was the latest costings of new equipment, and the massive overspend on budget.

Luchinelli and Flora Stiegwitz, a black woman, were more interested in the latest memo from the Human Resources Department. The memo set out a new system of annual efficiency assessments, which managers would have to undertake with each member of their staff.

"It's another missile from the anti-personnel department." Stiegwitz said. "Everything that comes out of there screws you up. The forms get longer, and the rules more tortuous."

"It's a psychological examination in disguise," Bridget Lomas, the team's electronics expert said.

"Ignore it," Reilly said.

Luchinelli and his staff ignored anything that did not benefit them directly, particularly personnel rules. They wouldn't apply the new measure to their subordinates anyway, but they would be delighted to take half a day to talk about it.

Luchinelli wasn't going to be put off so easily. "Steve, the key word eez ere which should alert all employees to danger."

"What's that, Gino?"

"Fair." Luchinelli's walnut eyes were liquid. "Whenever you see ze word fair used in a WayCom memo, look for ze catch. Fair means you are about to be reeped off."

"Damn right. Fair ought to have a health warning on it. Something like: *If you believe this you could seriously damage your career*," Bridget Lomas said.

Stiegwitz wasn't finished yet, either. "What it boils down to is that the employee is a disposable commodity, and the purpose of this test is to improve disposability."

"Yeah, I think this is right," Reilly said, trying to think of a way of getting back to the budget.

All of the team were eccentric. Occasionally they had arguments, and behaved like selfish children. They were not above throwing a punch or smashing laboratory equipment in a temper. At times one of them would get paranoid ideas about the others, and Reilly would have to fall into the role of counsellor and therapist. They were hopeless at any form of administration. A bunch of brilliant kids.

"Why don't you draft a critique of the memo, Flora, and we'll get it away to HR. See what they say. Put them on toast about fair policies," Reilly suggested.

"Wait a minute," Bridget Lomas said. "There's a nasty angle to this efficiency assessment. We are being asked to probe and assess loyalty and dedication. Security stuff. We are being asked to brainwash our staff, or fire them."

Reilly stepped in again, to try to stop the debate which went on flaring up like a bush-fire. "OK. Nice point, Bridget. Copy the note to Karen Bridges. Give her some ginger too."

"Hey, zat's a good idea," Luchinelli said. "Toast Bridges's very fine ass too, Bridget. Flora, I vud like to see ze draft."

This seemed to appeal to them, and Steve looked at the pile of management accounts in front of him. He skimmed his cover note on the first point he wanted to make. Then one of the staff came in and handed him a telephone.

"I can't take it now," he snapped.

But the staffer pushed the phone at him, "It's urgent."

He heard a woman's voice at the other end, loud and confident. "Ruth Charlton, don't you remember, Steve?"

Of course he remembered. He had been turning over in his mind since meeting her at the company party whether he should call her, Somehow the argument with Laura about her put him off.

Laura had described Ruth Charlton afterwards as an unethical bitch, and while he didn't accept that, it stopped him reaching for the phone. Now Ruth Charlton had taken the initiative, pushed right into his meeting. She had the stones.

"You know I really meant what I said the other night, Steve. It could be a very important thing for you."

She was taking care to be vague in case anybody was listening.

"Yeah, sure. I'm busy now. I'll call you," he said, feeling awkward in front of Luchinelli.

"I know you can't talk now, but why don't we meet, and I can tell you what I have." Her voice was like warm malted milk.

"OK. I said I'll call."

"No, fix it now," she said, from milk to chilled water.

Her boldness overcame him. He tapped the diary sheet up on the screen of his laptop which was open before him, and they fixed a date.

Luchinelli raised his droopy black eyebrows and leaned close: "Women!" he sighed, with his garlic breath.

Chapter 21

Hayden walked into Karen Bridges's office. She looked away from the PC screen she was studying, waved him to a seat, and took off her glasses. She looked tense. Holding the line between Hayden, the FBI, and her employer was like walking barefoot on broken glass.

"Anything in Leman's PC?" Hayden asked.

"Nothing. A bit of downloaded porn. I'll turn the unit over to you or the FBI, if you want."

"No point."

"Tell me where you've got to, Mike."

"It looks to me as though Leman could still have been working for Zosmark. I can't understand how you could put him on STELA 2, and it's in breach of the security provisions in the contact: *No person previously employed by a competitor on a similar project shall be employed.* That's what the document says."

Karen Bridges was quite easy. "We vetted him very carefully, before and during employment. Christ, we practically knew his supermarket account by heart."

"He had a foreign bank account."

"How do you know?"

"Mrs Leman innocently told me."

"Have you ever seen it?"

"Never, and I think we'll have difficulty in examining it. Leman was obviously clever enough to cover up."

"I tell you we checked everything. Even his Revenue records."

"Hell, Leman wouldn't have told Uncle Sam! And the other point: Leman's telephone accounts—and I've seen copies—contain a number of calls to Zosmark and WayCom in the year he was off."

This was information that Stella had produced.

"We knew about that. Leman satisfied us. He had a lot of friends at Zosmark, and there was a certain amount of contact here about the formalities of his employment."

"You seem to have taken the path of least resistance. Accepting this. Disregarding that. You were taking an extreme risk with this man. You must have known it."

Karen Bridges coloured, and threw down the pencil she had been fingering violently, and it bounced on the desk, and dropped on the carpet. "We *needed* him, for fuck's sake. We're running a business. I put in my reports. Others crawl all over them, and press me about what to do!"

"It's meat and drink for Cerillo if he finds out."

"We can contest Leman ever worked on a project similar to STELA 2," Karen said scornfully.

"But he was an acknowledged AI expert before he came to you. And at some stage at least, he was probably being blackmailed for his porn interests. You wouldn't think it, to understand what the man held dear ..."

Karen Bridges protested with a deep sigh, her anger concealed. "I don't want Leman held against us, Mike."

Hayden shrugged. "I'll do my best to protect you. You're personally in the firing line?"

Karen Bridges came around her desk and stood close to him beside the door as he made to leave. She smelt faintly of flowers. She was oppressive. Her round, flecked green eyes rested on his.

She nodded sadly. "I guess."

★ ★ ★

Hayden got a call on his cellphone as he was leaving the building. It was Gerstein.

"Mike, a credit card and driver's licence were handed in to the Sheriff of Brook County this morning."

Hayden's heart thudded. "Mariette's?"

"Yeah. Seems somebody lookin' for the reward we posted on the local crimebusters channel."

Hayden had persuaded Wayman to put up the reward money. "Where were they found?"

"Dunno. Thunder Lake area, I'm goin' out there."

"I'm coming too."

Al Gerstein could have told him he'd be in the way, but he didn't. "I understand, Mike. Fine."

★ ★ ★

One of Gerstein's agents, Don Moody, blasted an FBI Chrysler to the Brook County Sheriff's office at Salim, beyond the Oneida River. It took two hours on the narrow winding blacktop.

The Senior Deputy Sheriff received them in his office with the two items on the desk before him. Gerstein examined them. Hayden stayed back.

"That's them right enough," Gerstein said.

"Tell us who found them and where," Hayden said.

"Guy name of Arkwright, lives in a hut out along Highway 37, with his wife and kids. Shoots, fishes. Grows a few vegetables. Can use the reward."

"Say where he found them?" Gerstein asked.

"By the road, he says—"

"Just the card and licence?"

"Is what he says."

Hayden stood up. "Thanks, Sheriff. Let's get out there now."

It took some map reading, and conning around the tracks of Brook County before they found Arkwright's cabin. They left the car at the roadside, and the three men walked up the slope into the pines, toward the broken-backed grey wood structure that they concluded had to be the cabin.

A skinny man in worn jeans, an old Dodgers' sweatshirt, and straw hat came out on the porch, and said "Howdy," but showed no interest.

Gerstein, standing at the foot of the steps, said, "FBI. Talk about that reward if you're Ted Arkwright."

"S'me."

"Show us where you found the card and licence," Hayden said.

"Do I get the money?" Arkwright drawled suspiciously, not moving.

"Sure do," Gerstein said.

"When?"

"As soon as the Postal Service can get a cheque to you from Syracuse—now let's get moving and look at where you found these things," Hayden said.

"OK, Mister. It's nowhere special. By the road."

He led them down the hill to the road, and walked about thirty yards along the grass verge. He stopped by a culvert.

"Hereabouts, I reckon. Just lyin' there." He pointed with tobacco stained fingers.

"Only the two items, nothing else?" Hayden asked, unhappy with Arkwright's wooden nonchalance.

"Yup. Lyin' there. I was walkin' along here."

Gerstein and Moody examined the grass. "No sign of any

disturbance. Coulda been dropped as a sign," Gerstein ventured.

Hayden winced at the man's unhelpfulness, as they made their way slowly back toward the FBI car.

"If we assume the things were dropped to attract attention, we need to look around the whole area, thoroughly," he said.

As they walked along the blacktop, they heard the thump of a motor with a broken muffler behind them, and a woman drove slowly past in an 85 Chev convertible with peeled pink paint, and the canvas hood in ribbons.

The car turned up the track toward the cabin, revving and burning oil from its exhaust. The driver was in her forties or perhaps fifties, like Arkwright, with a raddled face and wispy grey hair.

But what Hayden particularly noticed about her was her dress. He could see the dress easily as she eased past. The red and green squares of the cotton material imprinted themselves in his mind in a kind of déjà vu experience.

He left the others, and sprinted after the car. Gerstein yelled at him, but he didn't reply. Hayden caught up with the old Chevy as it grunted to a final position beside the cabin, and the motor choked into silence. He was standing over the woman as she turned to get out.

"That dress! That's Mariette Stevas's dress!" He took her by the collar and pulled her upright, the bright and stylish cloth, incongruous in these backwoods, burned in his memory.

Like the man, she too was rail-thin, and composed of some kind of hardwood, but the ferocity of Hayden made her fall back on the seat, her mouth open on her broken teeth.

Before she could speak, Hayden, eyes flaring, his cheeks livid, shouted, "Where did you get that fucking dress?"

Gerstein reached them, puffing. "Now take hold, Mike. Take hold. This is an FBI enquiry."

"That woman is wearing Mariette's dress. The one she wore the day she disappeared. For Christ's sake Al. These people are shitting us!"

"All right. Shut up. Everybody, shut up! You're not going anywheres, Mr Arkwright."

A Colt 38 appeared in Gerstein's fist, and he waved the short barrel to encourage Arkwright to come nearer. His assistant, Moody, also had a handgun and stood a little back from the group.

"Right. This is the way it is. Mr Arkwright, you will get no reward, and I am about to arrest you, and this woman, for interfering with the administration of justice. If you tell me the truth of what happened, and give me that dress and any other articles you may have relating to Mariette Stevas, I *might* reconsider. You wanta be locked up, or are you going to tell us?"

Arkwright's eyes had retreated to shrewd little pinpoints of light.

"For Christ's sake, Ted, tell 'em," the woman croaked, gathering her hair off her brow with a skeletal hand.

Arkwright put his head on one side, but his facial muscles were ossified. "Still get the reward?"

"Listen, you little cocksucker—" Hayden said, pushing Arkwright's shoulder so he stumbled.

"Leave him, Mike," Gerstein said. "You come down to the car with me, Mr Arkwright. Make a full statement. Then we talk about rewards. You don't want to go, I'm arresting you, and *taking* you, and this woman, now."

Arkwright chewed this over slowly, spat to one side, and gave a small nod of agreement. He began to move with Gerstein downhill toward the FBI car.

Gerstein looked round at Hayden.

"I'm going to get the woman to show me through the cabin," Hayden said.

Gerstein's expression said *you can't do that*, but his words didn't match: "When I've gone."

Hayden watched the trio go down the track, and then put his face close to the woman's face, smelt her decayed breath, and said, "Show me what you've got, woman!"

He pushed her up the steps, and in the front door of the cabin. The cramped living room reeked of countless stews absorbed into the damp walls. It was grimy and disordered. The woman put her hands on her skinny hips, hesitated, and then seemed to decide there was no other way.

She opened a cupboard hung with raincoats and parkas, and hanging on a peg was a shiny black leather shoulder bag. She reached it down. It was fine Spanish leather. A quality piece.

It was Mariette's.

Hayden took the bag, looked inside. Empty. "What else?"

The woman shifted a worn woollen overcoat aside. Beneath was a light grey silk anorak. Hayden folded it over his arm.

The woman moved across to a rickety dresser and pulled out a drawer. She removed a white underslip.

"That's it," she coughed.

But Hayden searched the cabin, pored over the congealed sauce and medicine bottles, pulled out suitcases full of papers, and a half-full chamber pot from under the bed, poked amongst the cardboard boxes on the top of wardrobes.

He could see nothing he could identify as Mariette's property.

The woman watched him, her mouth as tight as a drawstring, but said nothing.

"Get that dress off, because I'm coming back for it in two minutes," he said, as he went out, hit on the doorstep by the fresh chill of the pinewoods,

Gerstein, Moody and Arkwright were coming back up the track as the woman threw the dress on to the porch. Gerstein pulled a packet of plastic evidence bags from his pocket, and handed them to Hayden for his finds.

"I hope we got it now, Mike. Seems Mariette was at a cabin near here. It's deserted. Abandoned. Arkwright says he was out shootin', and wanted to shelter in a rainstorm. Saw the cabin was occupied. Stopped in the woods to look. Saw a man burying a parcel in the trees. Saw only the one man. Nobody else. No woman. Watched him. Went back a coupla days later and found the cabin unoccupied. Dug up the parcel. Found a bag with the cards and the driver's licence in it, a dress, and an undergarment. Saw the reward posted. Returned the cards and licence, and kept the rest."

Hayden listened with narrowed eyes. "Let's get to the cabin. Has Arkwright been there since? Did he get a look inside the cabin?"

"He says no."

Arkwright picked up a broken branch lying on the track and drew a rough map for them on the loose dirt at their feet. They had to go on up the hill, across another ridge and a stream. "'Bout an hour and a half."

"Let's go," Hayden said.

"Like that?" Arkwright said, pointing to their city shoes. He was wearing rubber ankle-boots.

"I got a pair of boots in the car. Part of the emergency kit," Gerstein said.

Gerstein went back to the car and put his boots on, but Moody and Hayden had to go in their shoes, following Arkwright.

They climbed a path through the pines, but as they ascended, the carpet of pine-needles thinned, and the way was scoured by watercourses. It was slippery and uneven. Soon the papery leather of Hayden's loafers was soaked and misshapen, and the stones in the stream-beds hurt almost as much as if he had bare feet.

After an hour of sweating and sliding, they came into a clearing with the cabin on the far side.

Gerstein waved Arkwright back, and he, Moody and Hayden moved gingerly forward, observing. The grass in front of the cabin was about a foot high, and untrodden.

Gerstein pushed the door open. It yielded and swung back. They stepped into the rotten-damp of the interior. There was a faint food smell. The one room had a bench in one corner, and a two-level bunk frame in the other. The walls, apart from a few yellowed newspaper clippings, were bare logs blackened with age and the smoke of fires from the open grate.

On the bench, and on the floor by the bed, there were old newspapers. Hayden saw that the dates corresponded roughly to the time of Mariette's disappearance. On the floor were empty cans, plastic wrappers, and used food cartons.

Gerstein scratched his head. "We can't do this joint, and bag all the trash. The woods need combing too. I'll leave you here, Don, to mind the shop while we go back. I'll get a squad up as soon as possible."

They left Moody and trudged back toward the road.

"What do you think, Mike?" Gerstein asked, when Arkwright was bobbing along twenty-five yards ahead.

"Two possibilities, I guess. And you'll have thought of them. Mariette could have been given another less colourful, more practical outfit of clothes for onward transmission. It makes sense. Or ... God forbid, her body could be out in those woods. The killer separates her from her ID and clothing to confuse the trail."

"Yeah," Gerstein said.

"Hey Arkwright!" Hayden shouted, and when they caught up with him, "Tell me about the guy you saw."

"I already told your pal."

"Well tell me, asshole!"

Arkwright thought about this as they walked, in no hurry, until Hayden swung on him, and shoved him back against a tree.

"Tell me before I kick your balls up into your skull."

"OK, OK," Arkwright said, fending him off. "I didn't see much. Didn't get too close. It was pissin' rain. He had a waterproof over his head and body. He was bending down, facin' away from me, diggin."

"Come on, big man, small man, old man, young man?"

"Big shoulders. Older I'd say. Moved kinda slow and hunky. Big hands on the shovel. Strong."

Chapter 22

When Ruth Charlton awoke, the sun was streaming in through the open drapes and she was stretched naked across the end of the bed. Heidi Stoller, with one arm still caught up in the folds of her oyster coloured satin bathrobe, sprawled asleep on a chaise longue a few feet away.

Ruth had a sudden frisson of anxiety in that clear moment of awakening. When she was with Heidi her life seemed to get out of control. Heidi had really ceased to be business as far as Ruth was concerned. For Ruth, Heidi had been at first like the occasional chocolate truffle or a drag on a joint—an indulgence. Now Heidi was an addiction.

Heidi wasn't as loving as Ruth would have liked, but had a restless persuasive power which overcame her. If Heidi had said black was white, Ruth would have known it wasn't true, but would have strained to convince herself it was.

They had dined the previous night at this apartment of Heidi's in New York—a beautiful dinner cooked by a French chef brought in from Lutece on East 50th Street. They had sat on a glassed terrace, overlooking Central Park, with Manhattan glowing beneath them. The claret seemed to be hypnotic and they had made crazy love after the meal ... she couldn't remember clearly, sensual images dissolved into deep sleep.

Ruth got up quietly and went into the vast white marble bathroom with its gold fittings. She turned on the shower and soaked herself—even her hair, for five minutes until she had come round properly. Her head wasn't aching; it was light.

Heidi, naked, was leaning against the bathroom doorframe as Ruth came out of the shower. She knew Heidi was going to grab her again. She let her.

Ruth was still smouldering after the night. They stood clasped together for a while before subsiding to the big woolly white bathmat. The unyielding marble slabs underneath her ass on the mat, and the lightness of Heidi's hands, made her come quickly.

Then she showered again, and began to dress in the bedroom.

This time Heidi put on a bathrobe, and sat on the end of the bed, watching.

She had ordered her housekeeper to bring apple juice, coffee and croissants with raspberry jelly.

They both ate as Ruth dressed. Ruth enjoyed having an audience. *The Wall Street Journal* was on the tray, but Heidi made no move to pick it up.

"Headhunting isn't your only accomplishment, is it?" Heidi asked.

"You mean you like my conversation?"

Heidi smiled. "I like a lot of things about you, Ruth."

"When will I see you?"

"I'll get in touch. Let's leave it that way. I'll send a messenger."

Ruth gave a little frown. "That sounds very formal. How can I get you?"

"You can't." Heidi's voice was flat and determined.

"It's awful not to be able to talk on the phone just like anybody else," Ruth said, petulantly.

"We'll talk when we meet privately."

"I can't see why you're so concerned, Heidi."

"I may want you to do some more business for me."

"So? Everybody does business. You want a top executive, I find him or her for you. Where's the big deal?"

"I don't like advertising what I do. Never call me directly, Ruth. No matter how important. Never approach me, or talk to me unless we agree first."

Ruth put her hand on her heart. "On my honour, I never shall," she said, with a tinge of scorn, thinking that all Heidi really wanted was to keep her out of sight.

"You don't accept what I've asked, do you?" Heidi was watching her closely.

Ruth stopped combing her hair, and fixed her usually dominating stare on Heidi. "Yes, I do," she said.

"All our telecom traffic is intercepted. I mean all of it. A call from a hotel lounge to a room, as much as a call from the Learjet or our offices."

"E-mail?"

"Like putting an advertisement on a website."

Ruth was nearly ready. Her near-black hair was a bit flat after the wetting, but shiny, healthy, and beginning to contract into its natural waves. She applied the red lipstick—her trademark. She had a cupid's soft lips.

"You don't think you're just a teeny bit suspicious about this?" she asked.

"Ruth, my dear, I'm doing it to people every day, so why shouldn't they do it to me?"

★ ★ ★

Steve Reilly met Ruth Charlton in her room at the Syracuse Sheraton on First Street. He was surprised that she should suggest a meeting in her room, but he hadn't commented.

"I think we should have a private talk," Ruth said in her low, mellow voice as he entered the suite, "much as I'd like to ask you to lunch with me at Billy's-by-the-Lake or some other fashionable place."

They sat at a table looking out through the birch trees to the path that wound along the bank of the Onondaga Stream.

Reilly noticed a pair of small deep water yachts moored in the stream, twenty-five footers, their sails furled, rigging tinkling against the tall metal masts. Laura thought they should buy one. Twenty-five feet was about the size he'd go for at first. A summer cruise on the Oneida sounded like fun, and later maybe Lake Ontario ...

He tried to get the measure of Ruth Charlton. He knew the reputation of her firm well. They only touched the best people. She had the flash in her eye of a person enjoying herself. Reilly warmed to her, and the confidence she radiated.

Ruth Charlton knew her brief. She had met many Steve Reillys. She knew which strings to pull, although this was, indisputably, the most difficult part of the operation. It could go quickly and well, or it could end with ruptured relationships. Ruth regarded herself as a master at this stage. It was the kind of moment she relished.

She looked at her watch. It was 1 pm. "Why don't I mix a couple of drinks for us from the cabinet, and send for a club sandwich?" she said, and he agreed.

While Ruth busied herself with two martinis and the call to room-service, they talked casually of Laura's view of Syracuse.

"I'm sorry your wife is resistant to you moving on, Steve. It's something you have to play into your career plan," Ruth said reasonably.

"You mean give in to her?"

"Sure. She has her reasons."

"She didn't like London or Osaka much either."

"What's the real problem?"

"She couldn't find a decent job. Friendships limited to my office acquaintances, you know—"

"Can't blame her for that. I'm a bit of a career person myself. But inevitably when one of the parties to the marriage is a star—and you are, Steve—the other gets towed along."

Reilly's martini tasted just right, and he stretched luxuriously in the chair. Sure, she was flattering him, but by any standards he *was* one of the best people in his field. It wasn't unreasonable for Laura to make way for him.

"I can handle Laura. Are you married?"

Ruth Charlton gave a slight negative movement of her head which answered the question, but suggested there was nothing about her personal life on her agenda today.

The martini was strong and Reilly felt the jolt on his empty stomach. He hadn't had time for breakfast. Ruth sat opposite him, and moved away the small vase with two pink miniature roses, to the side, like the first move in a chess game. Steve could feel the fixed stare.

"I hear you missed out on a promotion at WayCom, Steve. What happened?" she asked.

"How did you know?"

"I wouldn't be talking to you unless I was well informed."

She was bloody well informed. He wasn't going to tell the full story: The only person he'd ever really told was Laura. At the office, you had to pretend it all happened as you expected. You couldn't show disappointment. Although everybody knew.

But he started to talk, and in the sun, by the big window, fuelled by the vodka, it all came out.

Reilly had made a real break-through with STELA 2. You had to have a lot of qualities to coordinate that circus. He had got the various departments to work their butts off. Over five hundred people, some of them near-geniuses and hard to manage. The prototypes were on time. Testing showed they were meeting the specifications. They weren't on schedule, but since Reilly took over, they'd made up a helluva lot of leeway.

"When Drew Millar got the sales job, I couldn't believe it. Nothing wrong with him. Same level as me. But Christ, he was crunching numbers while I was managing."

"Not according to what I heard." Ruth had a sympathetic smile.

Reilly rocked back in his chair. "What I've said is true. What did you hear?"

Ruth came out with it firmly, as though it was established fact. "That Drew was responsible for keeping Luchinelli's eye on the ball. That he was the kind of hands-on manager they need in NA Sales."

Reilly threw up his arms, jolting the table and knocking over the vase of roses. "That's the most fucking ridiculous thing I've ever heard!"

"Take it easy, Steve." Ruth picked up the vase, replaced the roses, and put the vase on the window ledge.

"If that's what people think then they're looking and listening with their assholes!"

"It happens," Ruth said.

"And that isn't all. Before I joined, Wayman told me I would be in line for North American Sales when it came vacant. That was before I joined. I came here for that job. Wayman knows that."

Ruth shook her head in wonder, and patted her dark waves. "You're a smart guy, Steve, but that wasn't a smart move, not in any company. Make sure you sign the contract before you start."

"I realise that now. I guess I was impressed that Wayman noticed me. I was prepared to take him at his word."

"What did he say after the other guy got the job?"

"Shit, he patted me on the head like a good dog."

Ruth gave a steely smile. "No matter how sophisticated the management selection process, the old buddy method always comes through. Remember that, Steve."

Ruth was satisfied that she had roughed Steve Reilly up enough. He was boiling. It was at this point that she could gently introduce the possibility of working elsewhere.

"My client is a top outfit. I don't need to tell you, Steve. Your record would be regarded by them as first class."

"I have restrictions in my employment contract."

"Don't let legal formalities worry you. Let's work out a deal first, and then think about them. Thirty per cent over your present salary. That would clock up from whenever you say yes."

Reilly was astonished at the salary hike. He was already earning top dollar at his level. But the thought of being able to deal with that pile of bills, and particularly Jolie's fees, was a nice one.

"That's very generous."

"You're like I said, a very valuable property."

"Who is your client?"

"I don't want to mention any names at the moment. Let's see if we can agree the shape of a deal first. If we can, you won't have a problem with the company."

"You said or implied it was London-based at the party. Laura wouldn't be keen on going back to London, but I guess I could manage to talk her into it."

Reilly was pleased with the salary but perplexed at the way Ruth was putting it. He wasn't familiar with how head-hunters worked, and couldn't understand why Ruth wouldn't name her client.

"Look, Steve, you wouldn't even have to move house on this offer. Laura would welcome that, I'm sure."

"I don't understand. I mean, how can that be?"

"Your salary would start as soon as you accept, and we have all the formalities settled. You wouldn't actually join the company for say a year."

"Is that to cover the competitor clause in my employment contract?"

"Not exactly, Steve. One of the stipulations would be that you stay on where you are now, with WayCom."

There was a big silence. Steve Reilly confronted the laid back Ruth Charlton. The amused, dark eyes were playing on him. *Two salaries.*

"I couldn't do that."

Then Ruth Charlton got up and faced the window. She saw the small figures on the path by the stream. Who were they? To be Ruth Charlton at this moment was very exciting.

"WayCom is using you, Steve. Why don't you use them? Do you think that the board of directors are worried one iota about the career of Steve Reilly? Do you think they operate by the rules of justice and fair play? Do you seriously think so?"

"My new employer will want information from me about STELA 2?"

"Sure. Why not?" she said, casually, taking her seat as though it happened every day.

He was suddenly thinking that WayCom didn't deserve STELA 2 after the way they had treated him.

And as if she was reading his thoughts, she spoke. "Right," she said gently, "you're on then?"

"I'll consider it, I'll let you know," Reilly said, getting up to go.

The truth was that her suggestion that he should stay on with WayCom, but actually work for another company, took him completely by surprise. He didn't show surprise, but he wanted time to think.

"I could be sued by WayCom. And maybe I'd be committing

some offence against US security," he said, turning to the window, seeing those trim twenty-five footers rocking at anchor.

"Have you ever heard of anyone being prosecuted or sued, Steve? What I'm suggesting you do goes on all the time, but nobody gets sued because it's too hard to prove."

Ruth Charlton was satisfied. She finished off the rest of her vodka in one swallow. She reckoned she had landed her man. She wouldn't have expected an executive of Reilly's calibre to agree immediately. But she was sure she'd got him. He just needed time for the attractions of the proposal to sink in.

When Reilly was going out the door, a waiter brought the club sandwiches. Both Reilly and Ruth Charlton ignored the tray as though they'd never intended to eat.

Ruth Charlton shook his hand warmly. "One small point, Steve. Have the courage of your own convictions. When you accept, great, but tell nobody, not even your wife."

She closed the door, refreshed her martini, and picked up one of the sandwiches.

"Especially not your wife!" she said to herself, looking at the people on the stream path, like the little stick figures in a Lowry painting.

Chapter 23

Mike Hayden had papers and reports scattered over the desk and the floor of his operations room at the Bowen.

Al Gerstein was sipping a tonic water from the minibar, and Hayden dealt himself a Budweiser. He pulled the cap off, and drank from the bottle.

From the disposition of their two bodies you could tell it was a battle. Hayden thrown back on a chair, eyes firing shafts at Gerstein. Gerstein rocking on his heels, balancing himself on the minibar, his features shining like polished yellow pinewood.

"We raise the reward money for Mariette," Hayden said flatly. "To half a million. Wayman will back it. It's in his interest."

"Naah. It's ridiculous. Let's get our eye on the ball. Leman—"

"She's the key that could unlock this case. Nobody's going to think much about ten grand."

"Arkwright did," Gerstein insisted.

"Offer an amount that will make people take notice. Blast it through the TV crimewatch programmes. Half a mil is cheap price to pay for a solution."

Gerstein began to see the sense of it. It might work. Certainly, the cost of the case, and the value of lost technology, justified the figure Hayden had mentioned.

"OK," he said, unwillingly, after a long pause.

"Good," Hayden said, and without pausing to savour his victory, "Now let's get down to work. The little question: who killed Leman and why?"

"The obvious surmise is agents acting for Zosmark because he was wilting," Gerstein said.

Hayden took a pull of the beer. "Any connection with other helpers in the building? The WP operators, telephonists, cleaners, and so on?"

"There are about forty other people. All of them have made statements. I'll have a close look at each of them, and verify everything that's verifiable, but I don't think any could be prime suspects," Gerstein said.

"Have you looked at Karen's story about the modification of the video, Al?"

"Yes it's a very convenient excuse. It's true about modifications to the cameras. The work was under the control of Karen's department, but the actual authorisation to do the work on the day Leman died appears to have been given by somebody way down the line, without reference to Karen."

"It smells somehow. You need to have a close look at whoever authorised the work. I mean Leman didn't just happen to call in to the shredding room on the day the killer was waiting for him. It had to be an organised event."

"The work of an insider," Gerstein said speculatively.

"Or an outsider, with inside help. But how would an outsider get in?" Hayden asked.

"I've thought about it, Mike. As you know, only staff can get in through the fingerprint operated barriers, but the loading bay is entirely dependent on how good the guards are. It's a personal check," Gerstein said.

"Could be a bogus visitor calling at the front desk and being allowed through the barrier. We should verify that all visitors on the day were genuine."

"On the loading bay, we're entirely dependent on the guard's record book. That video unit was out too," Gerstein said.

"It's one hell of a coincidence," Hayden said.

★ ★ ★

Karen Bridges rang Hayden at the hotel at 11.30 pm. He was sitting propped up in bed, prowling through the mass of data on his laptop which Cerillo made available from the NSA, and sipping a nightcap of cognac.

"I'm afraid we've had another incident tonight. You better come down to Le Moyne, Mike."

"Not a death?"

Karen wouldn't discuss the facts on the phone, and Hayden dressed hastily, deciding not to disturb Cathy Ong at this hour.

He took a cab to the Strathmore Park offices. Tapes and lamps had been placed round a space outside. Light was reflecting off the wet plastic raincoats of the police.

Karen met him at the desk. When Karen had walked him to her office, he found Lieutenant Naylor, a local cop who had been on the fringes of the Leman investigation, was there, moving from foot to foot restively.

Without sitting down, or inviting Hayden to sit, she turned to him and said, "There was a security alert here tonight, Mike, and a hit and run outside. I called Lieutenant Naylor on the hit and run."

"It's a homicide?"

"Security guard. An employee was caught copying secret documents, and made a run for it, got away in her car, but hit one of the guards, and bent another car as she drove off."

Hayden got the impression that he was being called in late in events. Naylor was flicking through notes of his preliminary enquiries.

"Who discovered this? You didn't think to call me sooner?"

Karen ignored Hayden's complaint. "Luchinelli caught her in the act."

"When?"

"Around nine thirty," Naylor said.

"Nine thirty? Shit—" Hayden said, tapping his wristwatch.

"And she made a run for it," Karen said.

"And the guard?"

"Scraped him off the blacktop. Kid in his twenties," Naylor said.

"Was anybody else here?"

"Apart from usual night staff and the security men, Steven Reilly, the STELA coordinator, and Luchinelli. Nobody else in this section," Karen Bridges said.

"Who is this woman?"

"She's quite young. A junior. Been with us only a few months. Working on STELA accounts. Her name is Delia Marris."

"Access to all STELA files?" Hayden asked.

"Not all, but a lot."

"Do you know what she got away with?"

"Not yet."

"So what are you going to do about her?" Hayden asked Naylor.

"Dangerous driving causing death. We'll pick her up. We'll hand her over to the FBI on the theft."

"You might pick up her car tonight," Hayden said.

Naylor's face wrinkled with two decades of experience. "Odds against. We've got the plate number. I've put out a call. You never know. An alert cop. Or one who fancies foreign cars. White Saab convertible. We'll put someone in her apartment until we get a chance to search it."

"You're not going to send a squad to the apartment tonight?"

"I guess not. We need a handout from Federal funds if we're

going to do all these night jobs."

Naylor was tired; he had been examining scenes of violence all day. He sat down beside Karen Bridges's desk with a yawn, and began to review his notes laboriously.

"I'll get an FBI team to look over the apartment. Where are Reilly and Luchinelli?" Hayden said.

"Waiting down in the security room near the front desk."

Hayden got Delia Marris's address, and called the FBI field office. Karen told him that Luchinelli had already gone home.

"That's not very helpful."

"Luchinelli is like God. He does what he wants. I thought you knew that," Karen said.

Hayden went down, and spoke briefly to Steve Reilly, and Coughlin the control room attendant. He asked them to go to the control room with him.

"Why?" Steve Reilly asked, the exasperation showing. He was pulling up his tie, slipping into his jacket.

"I'd like to see how much of what happened we have on video."

"Screw it!" Reilly said, "I've had enough for one night."

"There'll be an FBI investigation. We do it now, it's finished. Otherwise I'm going to have to get Karen Bridges to call you in tomorrow."

Coughlin, the security controller, was cowed, ready enough, but Steve Reilly wasn't playing ball.

Hayden didn't push. There were a lot of loose ends in the story that weren't going to be tied in a hurry.

Instead, Hayden pulled out a small silver flask of cognac he sometimes carried for late nights, and offered it round.

The two men looked at him curiously.

"We'll pick it up tomorrow, guys. Let's have one for the road."

Both refused, but Hayden took a good slug. The idea of running Delia Marris to ground was something tangible.

★ ★ ★

Mike Hayden got the security desk at WayCom to call up the company car that Karen Bridges had arranged for him. He gave the Brentwood address of Delia Marris.

The car was swiftly at the entrance, and Hayden climbed in beside the driver. He was a fiftyish Czech, whose English was hard to understand, but Hayden guessed he might like to talk. And there was a hot topic.

Hayden was aware that one rule in corporate life that is undeniable is that if you want to know what's going on, ask a company driver. He is a member of an exclusive little band of brothers, who sit poker-faced behind the steering wheel, with big ears listening like the giant dishes at NASA.

Executives, when they squeeze together in the back seat of a company car, and have those few minutes of enforced intimacy as they are carried to a destination, invariably want to show their colleagues they aren't tigers. Instead of talking in technicalities which a driver wouldn't understand, they chat about what's going on which is infinitely more interesting. Who's going to get which job? How did the CEO take that setback last month? Will this deal affect the stock price? Was there a real row between those two? Who was screwing who?

The company driver overhears the exchange, and what emerges in his mind is a blurred picture of the strategies and troubles of the company. The story of Leman's death would be old gossip in the drivers' pool. And the Delia Marris hit and run was probably on the wire already.

The driver, who said his name was Kel, rolled a rubber ball in the free fingers of one hand as he drove the big black Ford. He was nervous.

Kel's nervousness was catching. The car swayed through the neon-lit streets; rain drummed on the glass and burst into rainbows.

"What do you think happened to Mr Leman, Kel?" Hayden inquired casually, taking his mind off the driving.

Kel took his time. There were some nasty intersections, and he was kneading the rubber ball dedicatedly.

Then he said, "Same as Jack Bray."

"How do you mean?"

"Yeah. Same kinda thing. Jack Bray got sliced by a chainsaw. Kinda fell on it when he was cutting lumber. Carl Leman got chewed by the shredder. See?"

Kel looked at Hayden knowingly, and Hayden wanted to say, *Eyes front*. But there was, Hayden could see, a crazy sort of lateral connection in the manner of dying.

"What about tonight's little debacle?"

Again Kel turned his head dangerously toward Hayden. "Rosie Delmer and Capel must know. Eh?"

Kel's pride in his knowledge outweighed any discretion. "They was there"

Hayden tucked the relationship away in his memory. Harvey Capel, who was leading the WayCom team on the cost overruns, seemed as dry as a dog biscuit. And of course he already knew Rosemary Delmer, Wayman's prickly secretary.

"*Where* were they, Kel?"

Kel gave a loose chesty chuckle. "On Rosie's couch, I guess. You know that big leather one in her office?"

Kel turned the car hesitantly off Broomhouse Avenue, and began to ease toward a group of parked vehicles. Through the rain-drenched windscreen flashing red-blue lights were like exploding fireworks.

"I guess this is it."

"You've been very helpful, Kel. You're off duty now. I'll get a cab back to the hotel."

★ ★ ★

The apartment was in a modern building with five levels. There was plenty of lawn space around it, with trees. The street was wide, the other blocks of apartments, spacious. Two black and whites, a laboratory van, and a couple of dark coloured sedans which Hayden guessed were FBI were parked outside.

Hayden pulled up the collar of his thin overcoat against the wet, and hurried to the entrance. He went up to the third floor. When he tried to get in, Naylor was in the doorway arguing with Al Gerstein.

Hayden was friendly. "Peace, boys. Enough for both. I didn't expect to see you, Lieutenant."

Naylor wasn't amused. "Getaway!"

With a caution from Gerstein, Naylor nodded Mike inside.

Naylor's face was set like concrete, and as pitted. Only his suspicious eyes showed any life. "You get any ideas, let me know."

A young businesswoman's apartment—a large softly carpeted lounge, with framed posters on the walls, comfortably cushioned couches and a bar, a modern pine-finish kitchen, and a bedroom with a canopied king-size bed, all of it stylish, good quality. This was a more stylish set-up, but it reminded Hayden of Mariette Stevas.

Hayden followed Gerstein into the bedroom. There was a woman there in a white anorak with the collar up, looking the other way.

"Karen, I got the impression you weren't coming over here."

"I finally decided it was wise to come. You didn't tell me you were coming," she said.

"We think alike."

He turned his attention to the room. Delia Marris had packed hurriedly, if she had packed at all, leaving a lot of her clothes. There was an open suitcase, a row of dresses in the wardrobe, other garments strewn around.

"Valuable stuff—" Hayden said, touching a brushed wool overcoat. "Shouldn't have left this behind. Useful on a chilly night."

"Maybe we shoulda got here quicker. Might have got her." Naylor stroked his chin philosophically. There were more crimes on his work sheet than he would ever solve in his career.

"We're dealing with a smart cookie, Lieutenant. Too smart to return to her apartment after being involved in a smash, don't you think?" Hayden asked.

"Yeah, maybe. Somebody else coulda come here and picked up some clothes, a friend who could play dumb," Naylor said, thinking aloud.

"Could be. Anybody else live here?" Hayden questioned.

"Seems she lived alone," Gerstein said.

Hayden began to move around. He was looking for personal papers, office memos, credit card statements, something that would give him a line on Delia Marris's personal and business affairs. But there didn't seem to be anything. Not even an old phone bill.

He wandered into the kitchen, opened the refrigerator. A carton of milk and a bottle of seafood sauce. Delia Marris dined out most of the time.

The rooms were full of crime squad technicians. Hayden was thinking of leaving, when he saw a tiny leather-bound pocket book almost out of sight on a shelf under the bedroom telephone.

One of the techs was working his way around the shelves, noting the position of objects, putting them in plastic bags—soon he would get to the notebook.

Hayden used a tissue from his pocket, and picked the book up. There were a lot of names and numbers in there. He sat on the bed and started to copy them into his notebook.

The tech didn't object. He looked bored, and said: "I'll get that later. Don't get your prints on it."

Karen Bridges was standing in front of him with her hands on her hips. "What have you found, Mike?"

"Some numbers to run through the computers."

Hayden finished copying the numbers, and got up to leave. He called a cab, told the Lieutenant and Gerstein that he had the phone numbers, and headed for the front door.

"Make sure you return the favour," Naylor grated.

Hayden noticed a business card in Gerstein's hand. "What's that"

"One of the boys pulled it out of a paperback. Been used as a bookmark." Gerstein showed him.

On the card it said *Ruth Charlton, Digby, Hudson* with an Exchange Place, NY address. The name rang a bell with Hayden. Digby, Hudson were a firm of head-hunters in New York and London who had recruited for WayCom.

"Mean anything to you?" Gerstein asked.

"Not at the moment, but it could. I'll let you know."

He walked down the path at the front of the apartments. The rain had stopped. The air was sharp. Syracuse, hidden to the north, glowed against the sky like a brazier of coals. The lights of the cab coming up the hill threw yellow globs against the hedges.

He suddenly felt thirsty. He'd stop at a bar on the way back to the Bowen, and have a couple of cold beers.

If they could find Delia Marris ...

Chapter 24

On Sunday, the only day that Reilly took off from work, he and Laura usually lay in bed, read the morning papers, made love, and went down to the local bar for a few beers and a salad.

The Harpooneer was a rather up-market bar, and they were beginning to meet neighbours, and sometimes ended up at somebody else's house, drinking and talking and listening to CDs during the afternoon.

There never seemed to be much time for household matters. A girl came in three days a week to help with the cleaning, and a man came in to do the garden, so the house didn't detain them. Sunday night was given up to getting organised for the week. But they both kept up their regular visits to Jolie, fitted in whenever they could. They usually went separately, Laura more often than Reilly.

Reilly had selected Sunday as the right day to explain his meeting with Ruth Charlton. He didn't want a row, and he knew that might happen if he tried to talk when they weren't at ease.

They had made love, had a doze for half an hour, and Reilly had just fixed two cups of coffee and brought them up to the bedroom with the papers.

Laura was lying rigid on her back on the bed, her eyes wide open. Under the silk sheet was the long neat-chested body of a model, with graceful legs.

She always looked calm, and although Reilly would never have admitted it, she occasionally made him feel a fool because she had more street savvy than he had. A kind of realism that cut through sloppy ideas.

"What have you done about Jolie, Steve?"

"I've taken out a loan on the cabin cruiser and sent a check to the home."

It was an ugly subject, their shortage of money and Jolie's expenses, but Laura was pleased that her husband had done something.

"You're not serious about leaving WayCom are you? "

"I'm thinking about it. We need more money if we're going to live this way."

He coughed. She had given him the opening he had been wanting. "I've had a further word with Ruth Charlton."

Laura turned her head swiftly to look at him: "When did you speak to her?"

"Last week," he said vaguely.

"You've taken your time telling me."

"For Christ's sake, I'm telling you *now*! I haven't had a chance, that's all. And I wanted to think about it first."

"Uh-huh," Laura said, returning to concentrate on the cut glass chandelier hanging from the ceiling. It sparkled with a prism of colours in the morning light.

"I'm doubtful about leaving WayCom."

"Not enough money offered?" Laura asked, surprised. But she'd had enough of moving around, and was glad to hear this caution.

"It's not the money—" he hesitated. "It would be a thirty per cent hike on my present salary, with bonuses. The bonus minimum is said to be $150,000."

"Well, what?" she asked, interested now. "I thought money was the important thing. God knows, we need it."

"The offer doesn't require us to move house."

"You told me Charlton was talking London. Sounds as though it could be good, Steve." Laura was up on her elbow now, enthusiastic.

"The new employer would want me to tell them about STELA 2."

"Tell them what?"

"Confidential information about the work."

"You mean, like a spy?"

"Yeah."

Laura thought about this. "Sounds exciting. I guess it happens all the time."

"Maybe, but not to me," he insisted in a reasonable tone.

"You're high-minded huh?"

"I'm doing OK where I am."

"It's the first time I've ever heard you say that. Are you running out of steam? You're not OK. We're not OK. You got rubbished by Wayman. We can't afford anything. This house. The boat. The place at Osceola Lake. Jolie's home. A holiday. Anything!"

"Wayman may be a lying shit, but don't get uptight about it. We can cut down. Sell the house. The boat. I don't want to get involved in dishonesty, Laura—that's what it is."

"Oh come on, Steve. Don't be so naive. You know guys are being bought and sold every day by these big companies like WayCom, for what they know."

"Maybe they are, but this is different. The employer—whose name Charlton wouldn't mention at this stage—wants *secret* information about STELA. It would be straight out espionage and theft—with billions of dollars at issue."

"Big deal," Laura said, "pity you can't cut yourself a slice of the action."

"I'm amazed you should say that, Laura."

"There's a lot at stake. Our home. Our kind of life." Laura saw it all vanishing.

"And you're prepared for me to betray my own company?"

She breathed deeply. "Maybe I'm wrong. I just get sick of the double standards, that's all. WayCom doesn't give a fuck about you. Twelve months from now they'll probably reorganise, and a clever dick management consultant will tell them they don't need you. Finish. Kaput. But if you sell your knowledge, that's a crime."

"You want me to take the job?" Reilly asked.

Laura was often like this after sex, very objective, cool and not cuddly. Maybe he had it all wrong.

"I want you to get your head straight. Yeah, I think you ought to seriously consider taking the job. What have you told that cow?" Laura countered.

"Ruth Charlton? Nothing yet."

Laura sat up in bed and clasped her hands around her knees. She ignored the coffee.

"One thing you might factor into your calculations, Steve, is me. Being a finance clerk is small change to you, but it's important to me. It's my job, modest as it may be. I want to work. I have the right sort of job in Syracuse. I don't want to end up serving coffee at the American Club in Tokyo or Taipeh, and I don't want to live in a compound in Jo'burg, afraid I might get raped if I go to buy a loaf of bread. I want a decent house, and cars, and a boat, and all the things we've got, without having to worry whether I can afford to go into a shop, and buy a dress or take a vacation. And I want Jolie's comfort and security beyond doubt."

Reilly put down his coffee and walked out of the room.

Laura suddenly felt very cold, although the late morning sunlight was filling the room, and falling on the bed. It wasn't over, this tug of war about their lifestyle. If they were lucky enough to avoid a head-on conflict this year, it would come up next year, or the year after that, Laura knew.

She thought of Jolie, pictured the child sitting alone and mute in that sunny room at the Webster Home. Jolie looked so much like her, and yet Jolie was a stranger ...

When Laura had asked what was going to happen about Jolie, the night they went to The Green Room, Steve said he would take care of it. And he had. But where would the next payment come from? And it wasn't only Jolie. Everything they possessed was under a shadow.

Laura hadn't told Reilly but she'd taken steps herself to pay the two quarters owing to the Webster Home. It was a piece of luck, and she had to resolve the uncertainty about Jolie. Century Bank, where she worked, had hit a whole raft of computer problems, and offered her two more days work a week. Laura had pretended to Century that she had another job offer, but settled with them for the increased hours, plus a loan sufficient to cover Jolie's account.

Laura hadn't told her husband because she wanted to see how long he would take to find the money. Now the Webster Home had two checks for the amount owing!

She could hear the splash of the shower. She examined the room again. The drapes were temporary, while she thought what she really wanted. If only events would stand still ...

Five minutes later, Reilly bounded into the bedroom as though nothing had happened.

"Come on, dreamer! A cool beer is waiting."

Chapter 25

Jed Olsen didn't like spending time alone at Springvale, his Syracuse estate, with its ten bedrooms and four reception rooms. It had been different when Diana was with him. She always had the place full of guests. He liked that. He hadn't realised how much time she must have spent inviting friends and family, and organising visits to the thousand acres of forest and farmland.

When she left, the guests stopped coming. When he tried to substitute a secretary for her, it didn't work. He had to admit, it was Diana's personal touch with people she knew and liked that made it a sociable place. And she planned the menus, and had food like fresh lobsters and clams and truffles and mushrooms specially flown in. She was always looking over the cook's shoulder.

Handing the task of organising a party to a caterer wasn't quite the same.

Now that Diana had gone, and Sherry was away at school much of the year, Olsen preferred to spend his time at his apartment in New York, or in a hotel in Washington DC, where it was so much easier to socialise.

At the moment, with Sherry home from school, he felt duty bound to spend a few days with her on the estate. They rode, and fished, and walked the hills. They talked a lot, and he tried to be as frank as he could.

Sherry was wise beyond her years; it was no use trying to kid her he was broken-hearted over her mother's departure, or that Diana had given him a hard time.

Sherry thought that her mother going off with Wayman was right and good, and he couldn't persuade her otherwise. She knew enough about his affairs with women to believe he was an incorrigible philanderer—and he probably was.

Sherry sensed very easily his dislike—too mild a word—for Wayman. She didn't like him showing it, but she seemed to accept that it was a natural enough feeling. What he had never done was to tell her how he really felt about Wayman. The fact that Wayman had also betrayed him in business—to be honest, outsmarted and humiliated him—was not a serious matter in her eyes. The Olsens had always had money, and as far as Sherry was concerned, always would have.

This afternoon, Sherry had gone with Dan and Shirley Stenhouse, the farm manager's kids, to a movie in Abbey Forks. Olsen had finished a briefcase full of work for the office, and having an hour or so before he could respectably pour himself a drink, wandered through the empty rooms of the house—empty except for the occasional stirring of a tradesman or a maid.

He went up to Sherry's bedroom. He liked to do that when she wasn't there, to get a feel about her, his child, his only child whom he didn't feel he really knew—her books, her clothes, her tennis rackets, the scent of her, the small things she valued and placed on the dressing table—a glass owl about two inches high with a chipped eye. It was of no monetary value, but she always kept it by her. She said a boy had given it to her a long time ago and it was lucky.

There were perfume bottles now, and some makeup—eyeliner and lipstick, although she never seemed to use them. And an invitation card. He picked it up.

His stomach twisted uncomfortably as he read it: an invitation to a house party from Diana and Vance Wayman. Diana had handwritten, *Darling, you must come! We're missing you so much.* The party was that evening.

Jed Olsen replaced the invitation. Sherry hadn't mentioned it, but why should she? She wouldn't have put a claim on his time if he said he had to go out for the evening, and to her, the reverse would apply.

But Olsen felt sore.

He had been looking forward to spending the evening with his daughter. And there could be little doubt she was proposing to go to Wayman's—a drive of fifty miles. It wasn't the party, it was *where* she was proposing to go that made him ache.

He went down to the study, poured himself a large bourbon, and called Art Darbey who ran a BMW concession in New York.

"Art, the red Beamer we were talking about. Can I pick it up tomorrow, around 11 pm?"

Art's reaction was a whine of inconvenience, but the words were in order. "Sunday? Shit. OK. Sure, Jed, any time you say."

Then Olsen rang Jetflights at Hancock International. With some trouble, he chartered a Learjet to fly to New York at 8 pm that evening.

He poured himself another bourbon and sat alone in the drawing room, waiting for Sherry. He hadn't noticed how dark the room was. It was bright outside, cool sun, but depressing inside. He'd get an architect to advise how to enlarge the windows, lighten it up.

By the time Sherry arrived, he'd had three big drinks. She came clattering in from the back of the house, laughing and joking with the housekeeper.

Olsen stepped out into the hall to meet her.

"Darling, I've got a surprise for you," he said.

She kissed his cheek. "Pooh, you've had a few, Pop."

"Good movie?"

"Brilliant. An oldie. *All the President's Men.* Washington isn't really like that is it, Daddy?"

Olsen's mouth twisted with words he suppressed. Sherry was an innocent. "It's a true story, Sherry."

She looked pure, and suddenly serious. "I guess I've got a lot to learn. But I love Robert Redford. He's a doll. Reminds me of you."

Olsen couldn't hide his pleasure. "I'm flattered. Do you want to hear about the surprise? You remember the red Beamer convertible?"

Her eyes opened wide. "Wowie!" she yelled. "You mean I can have it?"

"Sure can, honey. Tomorrow. We're flying down to New York tonight to pick it up."

"Oh Pop that's wonderful! You're just great. I thought you weren't going to get it after I junked the Caddy. But I have a date tonight. I'm going over to Mom and Vance to a party."

Olsen smiled charmingly. "A party's a party. There'll always be parties. There's only one red Beamer. We're flying at eight."

"No Pop, I can't do that. I promised Mom, and I kinda want to see her."

"You can see your Mom any time. Look Sherry, I've made these arrangements. The car. Flying down specially to get it. You and I together."

"Gee, I really appreciate all that, Pop. I know you don't have a lot of time to do things like that. And the car, Oklahoma! But I promised Mom. Can't we get the car in a couple of days? I mean, knowing you've got it for me is the big thing. Or maybe the dealer could deliver it up here—"

Sherry was quick to register the dark flush on her father's face. She stopped.

"If you want the goddam car, Sherry, we fly to New York tonight.

If you don't want it, if you'd rather go to a party, well go to a fucking party!"

All Sherry's glow of pleasure subsided. Suddenly she looked older and composed, pale. "It's not that I'm going to a party that's eating you, it's going to Mom and Vance, isn't it? Well, I'm sorry but I'm going, Beamer or no Beamer."

"You're not going anywhere tonight if you don't go to New York!" Olsen said, wildly.

"You're drunk. And you can't stop me."

"You're staying here, unless you want to walk fifty miles."

"What do you mean?"

"You're not taking any car from here, and the servants won't lend you one! That's final."

"I don't believe this! You're having some kind of seizure. You're sick." Sherry burst into tears and ran through to the back of the house.

Olsen felt his chest thumping. His palms were wet and he poured another drink. His head ached. Fucking little cow! Disobeying him. No way was she going to Wayman's. He'd choke her first.

He didn't know how long he'd been standing at the window—long enough to finish the bourbon and not remember he'd drunk it. Then he saw a movement outside. It was a small silver Pontiac, one of Stenhouse's cars, going down the drive at thirty or forty. He couldn't get a look at the driver, but a fury like a volcano rose inside him.

He went to the phone and called Stenhouse. Mrs Stenhouse came on the line, and he roughly asked for her husband.

"Bob, have you lent my daughter a car? Did I see her just drive out?"

"Sure Jed. She's going over to Diana's. Taking the Ponty is no sweat."

"Listen to me carefully, Stenhouse, you stupid asshole. Did it occur to you, did it come into your head, that if my daughter didn't have a car, the reason was that I didn't *want* her to have one? Did it occur to you that I didn't want her to drive anywhere tonight? Do you think we don't have cars here?" Olsen roared.

"Jesus, Jed, I didn't realise ..." The words stuck in Stenhouse's throat.

Bob Stenhouse lived a quiet life. He was a serene man and a good farmer, managing Springvale's pedigree Aberdeen Angus herds expertly. He had two children, a wife he enjoyed, a comfortable home, a satisfactory salary.

Now Olsen struck like a tornado, shattering Stenhouse's peace of mind, and scattering it like leaves in a storm. He had no words to cope with the torrent.

Olsen quivered with rage. "You're fired, Stenhouse! You hear me? Fired! Get your fucking family together, and get off this place. I'll have my lawyers on your ass tomorrow!"

★ ★ ★

Jed Olsen decided to take the Learjet to New York anyway. He couldn't stand a night in the house alone. And Sherry probably wouldn't be back until Sunday night.

He had nothing to do except work on the pile of papers he kept with him in connection with Fairford and the Olsen Trust, and he could do that anywhere. And he had an important meeting in the city on Monday.

While he finished nearly half of the bourbon, he called Alan Court at home in Abbey Forks. Court ran the firm which kept the Springvale accounts, and acted as stock agents.

He told Court he had sacked Stenhouse, and instructed him to deal with the severance, and seek a new manager. Then he asked his housekeeper to drive him to the airfield.

Any messages on his answerphone at Springvale were automatically rerouted to the cellphone he carried in his pocket. There was one. It was from Diana. He read it when he was airborne: *What's going on, Jed? Call me back, please.*

Sherry had obviously arrived at Wayman's and told her story. Jed shrivelled at the idea of Wayman's involvement in this family matter. He'd call Diana when he was good and ready.

A little while later, when his jet was preparing to land, another message came through. This was from Sherry. *Father, I just can't believe what's happened. Bob Stenhouse has been on the phone. I won't be coming home. Ring me if you want.*

She was upset. She'd think about it. Not every father was prepared to fly his daughter hundreds of miles to pick up a new red convertible. She'd wake up to realities.

Chapter 26

The phone rang in Hayden's hotel room with the urgency of a fire alarm. It seemed like the middle of the night, but the digital clock by the bed read 6.30 am.

Hayden put the receiver to his ear while he lay on the pillow. The voice at the other end was one he recognised; confident, faintly derisive, taking pleasure in disturbing him.

"Mr Hayden, this is Rosemary Delmer."

Hayden had to clear his throat before he could get a word out. "Yeah?"

"Mr Wayman would like you in his office at 8 am."

No apology. No please or thank you. Delmer loved being an iron extension of the arm of her boss.

"He's starting late this morning. What's it about?"

"He'll tell you himself."

The line clicked. Delmer had rung off. He lay in bed for another half hour, his mind flicking through the bloody images of Bray and Leman, Leman in his aubergine socks, being extracted from the shredder.

And he half imagined, Delia Marris. He had only the faintest picture of her from the file Karen Bridges had given him ... And the heavy-eyed Lieutenant Naylor, watching like a tired vulture. Hayden brought himself back to life with twenty push-ups, had a hot shower. He missed breakfast, and was in Vance Wayman's office on time.

Light flooded into the room from two walls of windows, the grey light of autumn smog over the commercial estate.

Wayman turned his back on Hayden for a moment, and walked to the window.

From this elevation, it was apparent that the building was built in a hollow, and shielded by sloping earthworks which looked like imaginative landscaping when you were at ground level. The grassed slopes which enclosed the parking lot, as well as the main building, were neatly mown and there were few trees to obstruct the no-man's land—used only by a few staff for sunbathing on fine lunch hours.

The WayCom building was in a safe space. It would be difficult to target with directional microphones or beam cameras. Hayden knew from the NSA surveillance that even a beam bent from a satellite could be intercepted by an electronic field cast over the roof.

Wayman was edgy, his face reddened, his eyes gleamed. With his salary, pension rights, share options and his slice of WayCom stock, he was a billionaire, but everything he valued depended upon him delivering STELA 2.

"What went wrong?" he asked in a deceptively mild voice, his back still towards Hayden.

Hayden knew Karen Bridges would already have told the story.

"Your vetting system. Somebody is deep into STELA 2. Not that it's a surprise. The girl got through the employment process, and possibly made a number of hits."

"Who is it, Mike, Mitsuko?"

"I don't know. We'll try to find out. She'll leave a trail."

"Find out who she's working for, and sue their ass off."

"I wouldn't be too hopeful."

"Bridges slipped up. I thought we were bombproof. God, we spend enough on vetting."

"You can never be bombproof while you employ human beings."

"So what do we do? I need human beings to perfect STELA 2. Then I'll just employ STELA 2s."

"You watch them while they work. You don't let them wander round at night copying files." Hayden spoke dryly, quietly.

The CEO looked round cautiously at Mike Hayden.

Wayman carried a burden of worries that chafed him day and night, but he was thoughtful, and always a yard or two ahead of his adversaries.

"You sayin' we're in breach of contract?" Wayman asked quietly.

"Maybe. I'll look at it," Hayden said. He wasn't going to give Wayman any comfort.

"OK. Tell me why Luchinelli or the other guy, Reilly, didn't grab this girl in the office. If Luchinelli knew enough to call Security, why didn't he stop her inside, and then call Security?"

"These are questions your people should answer. I don't know. By the time Luchinelli had got his act together, she was downstairs and out the door."

"They were probably boffing her in the restroom," Wayman said contemptuously, but he was thinking.

He was really light years away from the Marris affair. "Nobody can hit the market with a STELA 2 lookalike before we do," he said.

It was partly a declaration, partly an expression of hope.

Hayden said, "I didn't get much cooperation from Reilly on the night. A lot of rough edges. I'll put it down to the trauma. I need to see him, Luchinelli and the control room attendant."

"I'll fix it." Wayman leaned over his desk and stabbed a button. He told Rosemary Delmer to fix it.

"How does Reilly fit in? He's new isn't he?" Hayden asked.

"We call Reilly the coordinator because there are big egos out there that would be offended if we called him the director of the project. But that's what he is really, the director. He understands the technical side. He can deal with Luchinelli who's the technical head. And he understands the finances, and can handle the finance people. He's the mover on STELA 2."

"So if anyone got to him, it could damage STELA?"

"Goddammit, Mike, we've kept STELA wrapped in a blanket. One breach of security by one woman on one night doesn't mean STELA is blown. The girl could be the beginning and end of it."

"You should be so lucky," Hayden said, unwinding himself from the chair and standing up, a head taller than the CEO.

"Not just the girl. The strong odds are Leman was into you. And Bray. And I'd guess others."

Wayman wiped a hand across his forehead. He touched Hayden's arm and lowered his voice: "Mike, tell me what you find. Keep me in the picture. Everything. Every detail. I'll tell Rosemary to put you through any time you call."

"Sure." Hayden looked down on the gelled hair, met the bright, unfocused eyes, and tried to forget the crack at their previous meeting about Charlie Hayden.

Chapter 27

Heidi sat facing the silver-cropped head of Tom Addis in Dooley's Brooklyn bar. The television screens flashed on their different channels, the rock music clashed, and the customers shouted at each other to be heard.

Heidi surveyed Addis from behind her smoky glasses. He was cool. Enjoying himself. A New York bar was a treat for him. This was glamour and a good time. He was socking back the bourbons.

"You want to hear about it? Nothin' much in the papers."

She moved her head, negative.

She knew he had done the job, and the reports in the papers were innocuous. The NSA would have confirmed it was a matter of national security, and the FBI would therefore be careful what they released to the press. As an accident, what happened to Leman was hardly newsworthy.

She leaned close to Addis across the table. "Don't judge the progress the cops might be making from the papers, Tom. The FBI will be involved too. Homicide, and national security."

"I'm not worried. There's no lead."

"I hope not. I didn't expect you to do it the way you did. I thought an accident off the WayCom premises would have been better."

"Leman stuck close to home. He had his wife, kids and in-laws there. Sometimes hired a driver or his wife picked him up. The only place was at the office. I hung around a few days. You told me not to hang around too long."

"OK, well it's done now. I want you to do a big job for me. Could take a couple of weeks. There's a girl I want you to pick up. She's in the Thunder Lake area."

"I know it. I been there. Good fishin'. Who is she?"

"Her name is Delia Marris. There's a warrant out for her arrest on a hit and run charge."

Addis grinned. "You get some neat ones, don't you?"

"Tom, I want you to go up to the Lake, pick her up, drive her to

Boston, pick up a new ID for her—I'll give you the contact. Then I want you to take her over the Mexican border, and get her on a flight to Johannesburg."

"Hey, that's some tour."

Addis's eyes glinted. He liked driving, especially when he was being paid for it. And driving with a girl. He didn't think much of the risk.

"You've got to look after her and get her away. I'll get you another car. I don't want you using your truck."

"How you know I gotta truck?"

"I have to know these things, Tom. If Delia was picked up, the FBI or the cops would get to her. That's nothing against her. She's a kid. I don't want any harm to come to her, understand?"

"Sure. But say she was in danger of falling into the FBI's hands?"

"Don't let it happen, Tom."

That was all right with Addis. He thought he understood very clearly what she meant. His big head swayed on his muscular neck.

"Get a wagon with some grunt, Heidi. It's a long way."

Chapter 28

Mike Hayden went down in the elevator to the control room where Reilly and Coughlin, who had been summoned by Wayman's office, were waiting for him.

Rosemary Delmer rang him to say Luchinelli wasn't coming in to work this morning.

Reilly looked fresh in a crisply ironed white shirt with a club tie, his hair newly washed and smoothed down neatly.

Coughlin was haggard and crumpled. He'd been on all night, and hanging around after coming off duty an hour before.

Hayden slid into one of the vacant observation chairs fixed in front of the control panel. "You first, Bill. Take us back to maybe half an hour before things started happening last night."

Bill Coughlin had been in charge of the control room, and it had looked like being a long, quiet night. He had been seated in a high-backed swivel chair, in front of a semi-circle of controls. Coughlin had more dials, lights, switches and screens before him than a TV station producer.

There was a bank of video screens. Each of the screens could show one of fifty separate views, covering the lobby of the building, the underground car park, angles of the exterior walls, and the main interior corridors and offices.

Coughlin could select any miniview, and transfer the picture to one of the high-definition thirty-six inch screens in front of him by touching a button. The picture was then so detailed, you could practically smell a subject's breath.

He could floodlight the main offices of the building, and film them, by flicking another switch. And from a panel of sensor lights—as many as four hundred—he could tell whether any electrical or magnetic equipment was alive from the board room and CEO's office on the top floor, to the cleaner's locker in the basement. The equipment was capable of picking up a tiny bug in a pencil or a calculator.

Coughlin was like a man with a hundred eyes and a thousand feelers. It didn't stop with being able to *see* everything. He could speak through loudspeakers, at will, to any part of the building, and intercept telephone calls. He could open and close a series of internal steel doors to isolate areas. In some selected rooms he could release tear gas. He could switch on the sprinkler system, summon the police, fire brigade and medics, and talk to his patrolling security men—all from the big chair.

Hayden considered the human element in all this sophisticated vigilance. None of it was much good if the operator was bent, or fell asleep. He didn't doubt that Coughlin and the guards religiously kept the tapes turning, but they would also be playing cards, telling yarns, and snoozing.

Hayden guessed Coughlin himself was probably clean. The hours were long, but the money was good. Coughlin looked like an ex cop, sharpish, suspicious, and neat when he had the opportunity to clean up. He would have a spotless official record. He would have faced Karen's loyalty check: WayCom would have kept tabs on his bank account, and sent a private dick to watch him, and his friends, every eighteen months or so.

"Bill," Hayden said, "I want you to pick up the scene on the videos again, like you did for the FBI, and give us the pictures of the build-up to the girl getting out of the building."

Bill Coughlin settled down in front of the control panel, wiping his hand over his sleepy face.

"OK. This is the story. I was watching what the computer was printing out from the room sensors, around nine. Three computer modules were still working in the building. One was in an open plan office on the third floor. I had it on video." He reversed the tape fast. "There you see."

A girl was working at a screen, alone in an empty room full of dead screens. She was a long way from the camera, but they could freeze the frame and zoom in for a grainy close-up. A serious, dark-haired girl in her late twenties with a kind of ascetic charm.

"Delia Marris. I can't remember ever having seen her before, but there are so many people in the complex in normal work time," Coughlin said.

"You said three PCs were working. Where were the others?"

"In my room, on the floor above, and in Luchinelli's room next door," Steve Reilly interrupted.

"I couldn't actually see Mr Reilly or Professor Luchinelli because there're no cameras in their rooms."

"Why?"

Reilly interrupted. "Seniority. Doing very secret work. Having meetings. The corporation draws a line at a certain level."

"But whenever Mr Reilly goes to the coffee machine or the washroom in the hall, he's on camera. See."

They got a shot of Reilly coming out of the john.

"The other live part of the building was Rosemary Delmer's office. Rosemary, the chief's PA, you know?" Coughlin said.

Hayden knew. She had worked for Wayman since she was a young secretary, long before WayCom was born. She was now a shapely single woman in her forties.

"She wasn't alone in her office?"

"No, sir. Mr Capel was with her. I know that because I had them in view whenever they put their noses outside the door. No camera in Ms Delmer's office either."

From the print-out of the room censors, Couglin could also tell that Delmer and Capel were using a small TV set. "Probably looking at a film."

Hayden remembered Rosemary Delmer's office. It was spacious and softly furnished with long couches. The CEO's visitors waited there. At night the doors could be locked, and with low lighting, a liquor cabinet, stereo, TV, and a view of the illuminated lawns, it was an ideal private place for a party.

"What's the story about Delmer and Capel, Bill?" Hayden asked quietly.

"I don't know, sir," Couglin said, raising his eyebrows and rolling his eyes. "It's not the first time they've spent an evening in Ms Delmer's room."

"She isn't worried you'd know she was corralled in there with Capel?"

"Couldna been, could she? Guess they coulda been studying the company accounts—or playin' checkers," he snorted.

"Remind me about Capel," Hayden asked Reilly. Hayden had met many of the senior executives, but the view of one about another could be interesting.

There was a stony pause before Reilly replied. He wasn't interested in helping Hayden. "He rejoices in the title of Director of Corporate Planning."

"Corporation-wide responsibilities?"

"Sure."

"An important guy, huh? Friend of yours?"

"We're not here to discuss my friends."

"Does Capel have any knowledge of STELA 2. Does he understand the technicalities?"

"He coordinated STELA 1, and the STELA 2 program is a large part of WayCom's corporate plan. The answer must be yes, in a general way."

Hayden ignored Reilly's attitude, and returned to the videotape Coughlin was running. It showed that the staff in the canteen had cleaned up, and all except one cook had gone home. One telecom operator was on duty in the communications room next door, and one secretary was resting on a couch in the word-processing pool, reading a novel—Couglin had the three in view.

He went on: "OK. That's how it was before Mr Reilly and Professor Luchinelli came into the picture. Schroder and Gasparo the two guards were patrolling. Gasparo was on this level at the rear. Schroder a floor up. I have a complete print of all their movements."

Hayden wondered how much of Coughlin's story was reconstructed from the video. He didn't entirely accept the picture of an alert Coughlin watching events happening around the building. He reckoned that it was a big temptation to Bill Coughlin to push the recline lever on his chair, and lie back, and doze a little.

Hayden turned to Steve Reilly, who was half sitting on one of the swivel high-chairs in front of the control panel, swinging a leg impatiently.

"What are your qualifications for this, anyway?" Steve Reilly asked.

Reilly was a very different calibre from Coughlin. He was critical. Nothing much was going to get past him. He had been over the ground once for the FBI, and wasn't keen on going again.

His eyes searched Hayden. He would give nothing for nothing. Reilly wanted to know about Mike Hayden first—he wasn't going to tell his story to just anybody.

Hayden decided to give a little to get a little.

"I qualified in law. Thinking of a Wall Street firm. Then I liked the idea of government work, consumer and ecological representation. So I joined a Washington outfit."

Reilly digested this. "Wall Street sounds like a better deal."

"Financially, yes, Wall Street is the place."

With the intensely competitive spirit of a sharp business executive, Steve Reilly was comparing himself to Mike Hayden.

Reilly was always dissatisfied, falling short of his own aspirations. Never quite earning enough. Never quite having a big enough job. He measured himself against his contemporaries continually. And money was the index of success for Steve Reilly.

Reilly's curiosity had been appeased, and he explained he was recruited by WayCom recently for his specialty, management of computer research.

"Tell me what happened last night. Tell me in detail, beginning with why you were in the building, and how you got to find out what Delia Marris was doing."

"I didn't *know* what Delia Marris was doing. At least, not until she was out of the building. It was Gino who dropped to it."

Reilly breathed heavily, and began reluctantly, on a mocking note. "I remember I had just upset a paper cup of coffee over my desk. I was nearly finished."

"Doing what?"

"Checking some test results from the team, and trying to work out our three months' schedule. I frequently work to around 10 pm or later. I realised somebody was on line to the computer copying one of the files. I worked out who it was and went down there—to the floor below."

"How did you know?"

"You can read off the station from the screen."

"Did it concern you that somebody should be copying a file at this time of night?"

"Not really, except it wasn't necessary. The whole system is compatible. It's open to everybody who has the passwords, and they can deploy the data in any way they want."

"But you went to investigate?"

"Out of curiosity, as much as anything." Reilly said he walked down the stairs.

"Bill, can you pick up that sequence on the video?" Hayden asked.

Coughlin located the tape. The video showed that when Reilly swung open the door of the open-plan office, the fluorescents were dimmed, but there was a bright circle of light at the far end of the room, and a girl sitting before a live screen. She heard the door open, and turned in what could have been alarm. She was the only other person in the room.

"I spoke to Delia Marris. And I more or less asked her what she was doing."

The girl's reaction was on tape. She deftly removed the disk from the PC, slipped it into the small bag by her, and stood up. She had shiny, long dark hair, a pale face and a slight figure. She was wearing a tight dark dress.

"What nationality?"

"She's a Brit. From London."

Then Reilly had gone on to ask her why she was taping, and she said she was only doing what she was told to do by her boss.

"Did that make sense to you?"

"Theoretically, yes. I guess we only spoke for a few moments, and I didn't have a chance to weigh it up."

"Who is her boss?"

"Capel."

"You weren't thinking you'd found a thief at work?"

"No. She made a move to go, implying that I was keeping her unnecessarily."

The video showed him standing by the PC frowning, his hand raised in a restraining way.

"So what were you thinking?"

"Nothing. I went back upstairs."

The video showed him leaving the room, and Luchinelli, bulbous and shiny-headed in shirtsleeves, coming in.

"Did you know Delia Marris, Steve?"

"I'd met her. She was an employee."

"Not a friend?"

Reilly said no, and Hayden returned his attention to the scene on the video between Luchinelli and Marris.

This was brief. Two serious faces. Luchinelli pointing at the PC, keying up a different screen. The girl was still standing, drawing the thong on her tote-bag tighter, preparing to go. Luchinelli was remonstrating with her, waving his arms.

She moved off camera. The next shot of her was going downstairs, with Luchinelli coming into view at the top.

"It was at this time I got the call from Luchinelli," Coughlin said.

They watched the image of the girl dashing out of the open plan office, tracked from camera to camera as she ran down the stairs, and along the hall to the lobby. The camera had been focused closely on her in this part of the tape, to give them a better view. She was moving easily. But there was agitation in the attractive face. Then she disappeared from the screen.

"I alerted the guards at this point, and asked them to pick her up," Coughlin said. Then the video showed her in the lobby, using the automatic exit.

"Bill, couldn't you have barred the exit immediately you got the call from Luchinelli?"

Coughlin stopped short. At first his mouth opened on black teeth, but no sound came out. Then he said slowly: "There is a switch controls the barrier."

He looked hangdog.

"You forgot it?"

"I made a mistake. I shoulda froze the barrier. It was a panic situation."

If Bill Coughlin made a mistake he clearly had no future with WayCom. The other possibility Hayden was weighing was whether he was involved.

"All this beautiful protective equipment and she walks though it!" Hayden said, shaking his head in wonder.

Coughlin played the rest of the tape. Hayden got a picture of the outside of the building on the video monitor, and saw the girl disappear behind the parking lot hedge.

The guard who had answered Coughlin's call, was outside in the rain. Under the orange lights the area seemed deserted, empty access roads, the grassed embankments.

The video showed the guard advancing toward the road, uncertain. He evidently heard or saw a movement in a car parked near the parking lot exit, a Saab sports.

The guard was running across the intervening lawns and gardens, sinking to the ankles in the soft flowerbeds.

The car swung out on to the road. The guard raced forward, into the glare of the headlights, waving his arms to stop the girl.

"Foolhardy guy," Hayden said.

Hayden was suddenly aware from the video that the car wasn't going to stop.

They saw how the Saab swerved, and slid on the wet road, revving in low gear. They had a snapshot vision of the girl, her mouth open, her face terrified in the frame of dark hair, fighting the steering, virtually standing on the accelerator as the rear wheels spun.

The front right of the grille of the Saab smashed the front fender of a parked Buick, swung toward the guard, and although there was no sound on the system, the impact with the guard's bent body seemed audible, a sensation of crushing of flesh and tissue.

The white car snaked away into the darkness. The guard's body lay crumpled like a wet sack of trash.

Chapter 29

On a Monday morning, Jed Olsen, looking clear-skinned and alert sat languidly in a chair in the office of Jeff Salmon of Kingsdorf & Co. Kingsdorf were the investment bankers who led the consortium which had financed Fairford for the last fifteen years. Salmon, plump and creaselessly blue suited, was the senior director responsible for the most important accounts. Jed Olsen had known him for years.

The room was perfectly quiet. Jed Olsen faced Salmon across a coffee table, savouring the silence. No sound of traffic from Wall Street. No hush of air-conditioning.

"I can't remember how long it is since you were in this room, Jed."

"About ten years, I think." Olsen remained unhurried.

He knew that Salmon would be racing to try to find reasons for the visit, and he wanted Salmon to worry a little at first.

Although the two men had met regularly over the years, it was always for lunch at the Oak Room of the Algonquin or the Racquets Club, or for drinks in the evening at the Princeton Club. Fairford were good clients, and there was no business that couldn't be disposed of over the second martini. So there had to be a special reason for this visit.

Salmon radiated the ease and assurance of an unctuous priest, but his first thought was that Fairford was in trouble.

He had checked the account—the overdraft was slightly higher than at this time last year, but well under the lending limit. He got an update from Moodies on the credit rating. No change. He spoke to a financial analyst at Goldman Sachs who specialised in computer companies. The stock had been drifting down for a long time because WayCom had taken over as market leader, but Fairford was rated a sound blue chip. Salmon spoke guardedly to a friend on *The Wall Street Journal*. Nothing.

Then Salmon had begun to get really worried. Olsen must be looking for a better deal from him, or he might be thinking of moving his account. But at the moment, Jed Olsen wasn't disposed to talk—

not about finance.

"Yes, you've changed the room a little since I was here", he said, standing up, putting his hands in his pockets and walking around proprietorially.

Personally, he thought the room was a botch, bookshelves and panels in black Japanese lacquer and a white oriental rug.

"This is a lovely piece. I remember it."

He put his hand on a refectory table, polished walnut which shone like amber. He wasn't trying to flatter. The table was a beautiful piece of furniture, and he did remember it.

"Oh yes. We've had that for years. Supposed to have been looted from a Cistercian abbey originally, Rievaulx I think."

Jed Olsen took his time with the Miro, and the Gauguin, hanging on the wall. They weren't in the same league as the set of French 19th and 20th Century masterpieces owned by the Olsen Trust—most were on loan to the Guggenheim, but a select few graced Olsen's homes, and those of his brothers and sisters.

All Salmon would know about Gauguin was the price they bid at Sotheby's. The paintings here were part of the Kingsdorf investments, and could vanish overnight, along with the George III antique merchant's desk, and the refectory table, if the balance sheet of Kingsdorf required it.

Jed Olsen resumed his seat and slowly came to the point of his visit. He had learned, he said, without saying how, that WayCom were deeply in debt over STELA 2, and were planning to refinance with the Kingsdorf consortium of banks.

"Jeff, I think the question I want to ask you is whether you're going to play on my side or not?"

"What kind of question is that, Jed? We've worked together for years, smooth as butter." Fairford were just the kind of client bankers love, a secure business, and a high level of borrowing.

"You're planning to refinance WayCom."

Salmon understood immediately. Everybody knew WayCom had bested Fairford. "I can't talk about other clients. You know that."

Jed Olsen coloured a little, and the frank blue eyes burned brighter. "Don't fuck with me, Jeff, if you want me as a client. We'll talk frankly. We'll *assume* you are going to refinance WayCom. If you do, you won't have the Fairford account. Is that clear?"

Jeff Salmon was not a man of discretion and judgement. His mind worked more like an electric circuit. It rang up numbers. If he could have Fairford or WayCom, which one was best? Which would earn the most for Kingsdorf?

"I hear you," was all he could manage. "Nothing has been finalised, Jed."

Olsen was satisfied that Salmon was wilting. "You'll look back and value this day, Jeff. WayCom are not only heavily in debt, they face a Senate Committee hearing and are likely to lose their big defence contract through fraud and corruption."

Salmon's fleshy countenance stirred. "That's hard to believe. I mean, I'm not doubting you, Jed—"

"I'll give you a couple of people to call. Important people. You don't have to take my word for it. Byron Cerillo, intelligence chief at the NSA, and Senator Sam Jankovic. Wayman paid off to get the contract, and the cost overruns are fraudulent. He'll be indicted."

Salmon was uncomfortable. "I don't know what to say, Jed. I need to look at this."

"There's another angle you might like to consider, Jeff. We can do a lot of business in future if you're on my side. In a year I expect to stand down from Fairford. You know where I am in the nominations. I think I'm going to make it, and if I do, I can be a good friend to Kingsdorf. I'm offering you a win-win ticket. You'll have Fairford which will take the lead again when WayCom falls, *and* you could have a line into the Administration."

"I realise that very well, Jed."

Salmon's mind had already covered this possibility. Olsen was right. Worse still was the prospect of rejecting Olsen, losing Fairford, and finding Olsen was then President. Kingsdorf could be shuffled to the back of the queue in some big financings if the President took a dislike to them.

Olsen stood up, and extended a hand to the banker, who proffered three plump fingers, too torpid with worry to rise.

"Let me know in thirty days whether you're with me or not, Jeff."

* * *

Jed Olsen felt sure of his success with Salmon. Bankers were congenitally risk averse. WayCom was a bigger client for them, but far more risky. They wouldn't refinance WayCom.

He treated himself to a glass of champagne and a platter of raw oysters at the Cafe Pierre on 61st, and felt ready to speak to Diana. He called her on his cellphone from a quiet booth in the restaurant.

Diana's voice changed as soon as she recognised him. The light flutter deepened. It was her serious-issue voice, a steady low note which signalled she was trying to be reasonable and was very much under control.

"Sherry arrived here Saturday evening Jed, very upset about you trying to stop her coming to us. And then half an hour later Bob Stenhouse called from Springvale and told us you'd fired him for lending her a car. I can't believe this—"

Olsen moved the phone slightly away from his ear and bared his teeth at it, but said nothing. He'd let Diana run out of steam.

"Don't you understand Sherry is a woman now? A person in her own right. You can't forbid her to do things any more. When you can't get your own way Jed, you start behaving like Genghis Khan. You may be a big shot, but you can't *force* Sherry to do things. You may get away with this behaviour at Fairford, and with your political pals, but it won't work with family. It won't work Jed." She paused.

Jed Olsen, fulminating, unable to stop himself, leaped in. "Don't tell me how to manage my daughter, you bitch. Sherry would know how to behave better if she had a mother who wasn't so busy consorting with a rag salesman!"

Diana was still in the cool and reasonable mode. She ignored the crack.

"Vance and I were shocked to hear how you've treated Bob Stenhouse. He's a decent man, and you've always said he's a fine farmer. I don't believe that even you would go so far—"

The mention of Wayman making moral judgements on him made Olsen's temples throb. "Stenhouse is a bone-headed asshole. He's made a lot of mistakes, and this was his last one. He's fired and he'll stay fired."

Diana's voice trembled, but was low. "You're a treble A shit, Jed. Absolute. Vance says if Stenhouse is fired he'll give him a job on our place. He reckons a guy wounded in somebody else's family argument deserves a bit of consideration—"

Olsen wrenched his collar open, and loosened his tie. The veins in his neck were swollen, his voice full and thick. "Don't quote that hustler to me. I'll see him down the drain he crawled out of!"

Diana's measured reasonableness was now as thin as a thread. "And another thing. Sherry doesn't care about the car. But she does care about what happened to Bob. She won't be coming back to you, Jed, not now or on any other vacation."

"You—" He felt like saying "you rat-fucking whore!" but he took control of himself, and the line was dead anyway.

Olsen gripped the cellphone in his fist, like a live rat that he was about to crush.

A cough intruded. A young waiter smoothed his hand nervously down the silk lapels of his jacket.

Jed Olsen blinked at him, hardly seeing. "Excuse me, Mr Olsen. Did you call?"

Chapter 30

Gerstein called at the case-room Hayden and Cathy Ong had set up in a room at the Bowen interconnecting with Hayden's.

He stood in the doorway approvingly.

The room had a work table, a laser printer and their laptops, and several cabinets full of hard copy. From here, Hayden sent regular updates to Gerstein on his progress, and received the result of the FBI crime-tech work online in code. It had been a fair exchange of information to date.

"I got the reports on the Brook County cabin," Gerstein said.

Hayden had waited anxiously for the FBI report on the cabin. Al Gerstein's decision to call with the news, instead of sending an e-mail, gave Hayden a sense of foreboding.

He was a little relieved when he saw that Gerstein's usually sombre manner was replaced by a breeziness.

"Some little progress folks. First, an extensive search of the area with heat-seeking detectors hasn't revealed anything. We're just about certain there's no body buried there. Second, Marietta *was* there. We have her DNA from her family, and we have matched some DNA prints in the garbage—drinking straws, bottles, juice cans."

"There's still some hope, then," Cathy Ong said.

"I guess there is," Gerstein said, carefully.

Hayden was flooded with relief, but he tried to take an objective line. "We have to pick up Marietta's trail soon. According to you, Al, the Bray file is dead. Leman's looks like going the same way. There isn't the slightest hint of who the paymaster is in all the detail we have about Leman's life and family. Yes, he was on the take. That's all we know."

"Like most hits, there's no personal relationship involved, nothing to trace unless there's a clue at the scene," Gerstein said.

"Do we have any idea yet how the killer got inside—if he was an outsider—and how he got Leman to go to the shredding room?" Hayden asked.

Gerstein pulled a piece of paper from the breast pocket of his suit, and studied it.

"I think I might have found something. I've covered the guards on the loading bay, and the desk clerks. Their records are in order. Neither the guards or the clerks recall anything useful to us."

"Are they kosher themselves?"

"I've seen their bios, and they appear to be. I think the answer is much simpler. Leman left the STELA unit around thirty minutes before he was found dead. That's recorded. One of the STELA girls says he had a call from the desk. He also had a recorded visitor, Mr Willets. No company ID. The visitor could have used one of the lobby phones to call Leman, feed him a story, lure him down to the desk. Mr Willets—nobody remembers him—was in the building, personally admitted by Leman, for fifteen minutes. His pass was handed in at the desk, and clocked when he left. The clerks tell me it's quite common for staff and visitors to use the downstairs meeting rooms, which are in the same corridor as the security room."

"Time enough to push him into the security room, and into the shredder," Hayden reflected. "It's feasible, and it demolishes the idea of inside help."

"Seems audacious," Gerstein said, critical of his own reasoning. "And we should be able to pick up this guy from the lobby video."

"I think I'd buy your theory, Al. It just doesn't take us anywhere. As for the video, the killer will have been aware of it, and wearing some kind of disguise. What about Delia Marris? She's our real hope."

Hayden had a biography of Delia. She had a degree in computer studies from Leicester University in England. She was a chartered accountant (English qualification). She had worked for IBM previously. She was twenty-five and unmarried. A South London address was given as her home, as well as the local address in Brentwood. She had been considered too junior to be profiled by the FBI.

Gerstein consulted his notes. "Coughlin, the security man. Coulda been implicated in her getaway. I don't think so. He's an ex-cop whose record is clean. Married with three young children. He's been suspended for negligent misconduct—for not closing the barrier and stopping Delia. He swears he knows nothing. We can tap his phone, keep an eye on him, but I don't think he's our man."

"Nothing on the car? It's fairly conspicuous," Cathy asked.

"She'll have dumped it," Gerstein said.

"OK. You have the list of phone numbers I got from Marris's apartment. Anything on them?"

"Nothing. A few work contacts that seem appropriate. Convenience numbers like a hairdresser, supermarket delivery, you know. And the Digby, Hudson number—"

"Ruth Charlton. I remember. I wonder if she's legit? Not much point in approaching her without something to shake her with," Hayden said.

"What about Capel and Delmer? Both in the building on the night," Gerstein said.

"I'll have a word with them, if you like," Hayden offered, and Gerstein agreed.

Cathy Ong had sat by silently, listening. "I've run both Capel and Delmer through the NSA computers, and Stella," she said. "Outwardly clean potatoes. They haven't tangled with authority."

"I wouldn't have expected it. We'll have to go softly with these two, they're plugged in at top level. And presumably they'll be edgy about their affair. That's why I'm leaving it to you at this stage," Gerstein said.

★ ★ ★

Mike Hayden called Rosemary Delmer from the meeting room he had organised on the second floor at WayCom. "You know what I'm here for, Rosemary. I'd like to see you some time."

"I do know what you're doing Mr Hayden. I'm no part of it. There's no need for us to meet. We'd be wasting time."

"I have to be the judge of that, Rosemary, so let's make a time—"

Rosemary Delmer was very good at conveying her feelings through her voice. She was an artist on the telephone. It was her chosen instrument. She took a long pause.

"Rosemary?"

"Yes, Mr Hayden?" Her tone was bored but tolerant.

"I insist."

She was clipped, efficient and too smart to go on resisting. She just wanted to register resistance.

"Very well then. Suppose you come up here between 11.00 and 11.30. That would be the best time to fit in with Mr Wayman's work."

"Uh-huh—no. That won't be satisfactory. I'd like to see you here, in meeting room number 3."

Another pause, with the sound of her slowly indrawn breath. "No, Mr Hayden. I need to be here. Affairs of state. Sorry. You come to me. I'll be pleased, even though I can't help you."

Hayden knew it was essential to get Rosemary Delmer off the

throne she occupied, to get her sitting in front of him, giving him her full attention. Otherwise she'd destroy their meeting by answering calls, and interrupting to give instructions to others. Her office was like Grand Central Station.

"No, I want to see you in meeting room 3. I don't want a trial of strength on this, Rosemary. I've been promised cooperation. Do you want me to speak to Mr Wayman?"

Rosemary Delmer paused, knew from Hayden's stony tone that he would go to Wayman, and Wayman would back him up. She had at least two assistants in the adjoining room who were capable of handling her desk. There was no reason not to go. She could look a damn fool being *told* to go trailing down to number 3.

"I don't think we need bother Mr Wayman with such a piddling point," she said in her best utterly bored voice.

★ ★ ★

As Rosemary Delmer went to the washroom before going down to meet Hayden, she tried to work out how far her presence in her office, with Harvey Capel, on the night of Delia Marris's flight, was likely to come out, and what it would mean.

She was sure it wouldn't matter to her boss. He was a tough brute who took his pleasures where he found them, and wasn't critical of other lifestyles. As long as she did her job with super-efficiency, she was safe from him.

Rosemary had come to relish the evenings she spent with Harvey Capel at the office. As the CEO's secretary she often helped to entertain his guests, and her room had been furnished with that in mind. And it had a nice outlook over Strathmore Park.

Using her office at night was comfortable, convenient and private, assuming Vance Wayman wasn't around. She and Harvey usually had quite a party—champagne from the bar, snacks, music. Rosemary had fixed it with Security to ring her should anything happen outside the room that might disturb them.

She had known Harvey Capel since he joined WayCom fifteen years before as a junior executive. But it was only in the last five years, when she had become the CEO's secretary and personal assistant, to give her the full title, that she and Harvey had become close.

In her time at WayCom she had experienced a number of unsatisfactory affairs with colleagues. She felt that in most of them she had been undiscriminating, and had been exploited. But with Harvey, it was different. He was older, and he was very senior. It was a serious relationship.

For quite a long time, Rosemary had made no claims on Capel at all. She was simply an enthusiastic lover. He didn't interest himself much in her life outside the office, although he occasionally visited at her apartment. Since she lived with her mother until recently, it wasn't ideal. Nor was going to a hotel; it was too coldly premeditated. Rosemary understood and accepted all this, although their evenings at the office must have been widely known.

And then there was Harvey's wife, Gloria. Rosemary knew Gloria from company parties, and felt very confident alongside her. Gloria was not only a drinker, but she'd let herself go to seed. She had a sagging belly and cellulite thighs, and the skin on her cheeks was like crumpled paper. She made Rosemary feel youthful and sexy.

The only concern Rosemary had was the slow progress toward living with Harvey. Now that her mother had died, there was no need for them to meet in the office, and she had asked Harvey to move in with her. But Harvey *still* liked to meet in the office. He said it gave him a lift. It was tied up with Harvey's dislike of Vance Wayman. Harvey used to say it gave him satisfaction to see Wayman's guests sitting on the couch where they had been screwing the night before.

Sometimes Rosemary wondered about the extent of Harvey's interest in Wayman. He was always asking questions. And Rosemary, to show her confidence in Harvey, had got used to answering them. To her, it was not a breach of confidence, but never-to-be-repeated talk between lovers. It happened every time they were in her office.

On the night Marris was caught, she remembered Harvey flicking through Wayman's diary; Rosemary always kept a hard copy on her desk.

"Hayden?" he had asked.

"The lawyer. Vance wants to sue the NSA for payment on STELA, and he wants to sue the guys selling his technology, if he can identify them."

"What's this meeting with Kingsdorf?"

"The bankers. He's trying to arrange a refinancing. You know, you do this every time. Ask questions."

"I've told you Rosemary, pure curiosity. I'm interested to see how the guy does it."

"Sometimes you seem more interested in that stuff than you are in me."

"Darling, making love to you happens to be a unique opportunity to do two things. Have the best sex in the world, and satisfy my curiosity about the great man you work for," he had said. Harvey was a nice phrase-maker.

"When are we going to be able to get together permanently, Harvey?" she had replied.

It was the first time she had ever been so blunt about it.

"Give it time. I have to arrange things with Gloria. I know the children are older now, but I have to run it past them. I don't want a battle, lawyers, lawsuits. It would upset you too."

And then he had embraced her, and she had felt horny in spite of herself, and coming awake with his hands crawling all over her, and he unclipped her bra, and she slipped her skirt and pants off, and they had done it again on the same old spacious soft red leather couch.

She had listened to the endearments he whispered to her as he pressed down upon her. Her half-open eyes could see only the whiteness of the ceiling. She had told herself his words were true.

Before the washroom mirror, Rosemary dismissed the memory. She smoothed her brow with her fingers, and tucked away an unruly curl. She was ready.

★ ★ ★

The meeting room was windowless, an air-conditioned and brightly lit box, with a long artificial wood-finish table and a dozen padded chairs with chromium legs. The walls were bare.

Hayden had a lined notepad before him, and Rosemary's personal file. She sat facing him on the opposite side of the table. She sat demurely straight with her ankles crossed.

She wore a dark green dress which had a hint of formality about it, but showed plenty of chest. Her invitingly rounded figure had heavy breasts. Her dark hair with straw coloured lights was neatly moulded, powder and pale lipstick perfectly in place.

Hayden could feel the pulse of being in a small, quiet room alone with a sensual woman.

When Rosemary Delmer looked at him with her flecked brown eyes, she created an intimacy.

"All right, Mike, ask away."

She switched to his first name without a qualm after their previous bitchy exchange.

"I believe you were here the night Leman was murdered "

"Murdered? I thought he had an accident, as far as we know. I wasn't here in the office. And I can't tell you any more than I've already told the police. You've seen my statement I assume."

"Agent Gerstein showed me. OK, the night Delia Marris was caught by Luchinelli. You and Mr Capel were working on a presentation for Mr Wayman, which needed to be ready by nine in the morning. You were in your office with Mr Capel until the police arrived. You have a set of TV monitors in your room—"

"They were off. I never saw anything."

"We can confirm that from the control room," Hayden said.

"Well they might have been turned down rather than off. I told you we weren't watching them. What do you mean confirm? I'm telling you the truth."

"You knew Leman?"

"He was a name on paper, a face. A senior executive. I spoke to him on business."

"No contact outside the office?"

"He was at company receptions and parties I was at."

"Mrs Leman?"

"The same. The Lemans weren't friends, and barely acquaintances."

"Did Leman usually work late?"

"I think all the top executives do, but I don't know specifically about him."

"Steve Reilly and his wife?"

"I've met them the same as the Lemans. But they're fairly new."

"Did you know Marietta Stevas?"

"The missing clerk from STELA? No. I can't recall I ever heard of her—until I read her name on reports going to Mr Wayman after she disappeared."

"Your work for Capel was personal? I mean, the CEO's secretary doesn't usually get tied up in preparing presentations for other execs."

"Yes. It was personal. Harvey's a friend."

"You've both been with WayCom for quite a while. You must know each other—"

"About that. Don't ass about, Mike. Harvey and I care for each other."

The flecked eyes were dancing.

Rosemary Delmer wasn't as stuffy as he'd imagined, but she wasn't telling him anything that would surprise any of the WayCom staff who knew her.

"I see, just a casual thing—" he said, airily.

Rosemary's reaction was instinctive. Her mouth tightened, her shoulders squared. "I said Harvey was a friend. A sincere friend."

Hayden thought she had invested heavily. It wasn't a casual affair.

Diplomatically, he changed the subject. "Do you know anything that might suggest that Carl Leman or Delia Marris were stealing confidential material from WayCom and passing it to another company?"

"Nothing. I thought Leman was regarded as one of our best people. As I said, I don't know Marris."

"Do you know anything about espionage here at WayCom? I mean staff stealing secret material and selling it to competitors."

"Nothing. I never knew it happened. But then I'm only a secretary."

Hayden felt the wall. He was up against it. There was probably a goldmine of gossip and rumour which she could give him, some of which might be useful. But she wasn't playing.

"I told you I couldn't help you, Mike."

When she had gone, leaving her fragrance on the air, Hayden banged his fist on the table in frustration.

She was hiding behind all the myriad things a secretary doesn't know officially—but knows perfectly well. She had shut the official door in his face. That might be because she was implicated.

He reserved his decision on the voluptuous Rosemary Delmer.

Chapter 31

The house lights went up in the theatre at the Syracuse Hyatt on 12th Street as Steve Reilly concluded his presentation on "The Civilian Uses of Artificial Intelligence".

Looking and sounding very assured with his strong jaw line and penetrating but warm voice, he took a round of applause.

His audience was a select band of executives from McKinsey & Co, the management consultants, from all over the US.

It was WayCom policy to develop the spin-offs from the STELA contracts as fast as possible. Huge markets were expected to open up as intelligent robots undertook the more mundane tasks of mankind, controlling household work, automatically ordering provisions from supermarkets, regulating and operating public transport, and providing their operators with personalised information about their needs. People like McKinsey had to understand what was going on.

The presentation was visionary. It looked forward to a robotic world with greater leisure and freedom for individuals. It sent the message that WayCom were on top of the technology, and expected to be world leaders in a vast new splurge of manufacturing and marketing. The McKinsey consultants were goggle-eyed as Reilly painted a picture of the future like a latter day H.G. Wells.

Reilly took half an hour of enthusiastic questions, and he hardly had time to step down from the podium to the floor, before he saw Ruth Charlton standing at the back of the theatre, demure but somehow threatening with her pale face, dark hair and red lips. Reilly had thought Ruth's proposition over carefully. He didn't, couldn't, agree with Laura. Laura's good opinion was important to him, but at last he had decided to oppose her on this. That was why he had stalled Ruth. It seemed the easiest way.

Reilly had dealt with Ruth Charlton by not going back to see her. She would have had to be stupidly thick-skinned not to understand his failure to respond, yet here she was.

Three or four days after their meeting, she had started to call his office. Reilly instructed his secretary to say he was in a meeting.

The Predators

Ruth had called at least three times, with messages to say it was urgent. All this must have made Reilly's failure to respond clearer.

Ruth Charlton was at his elbow by the time he had taken a bacon pastry and a glass of orange juice from the buffet.

The men who were questioning, and congratulating him, moved out of the way in a gentlemanly reflex as the determined woman pressed forward.

"Hullo Steve," she said, taking his arm. "I thought your presentation was wonderful. You're a gifted speaker, you know. You almost made me believe that we'll have robots doing heart bypasses."

She drew him away from the crowd so they could talk, just like she had at the company party.

"How did you get here?" he said, suspiciously.

"I told you before, I'm extremely well connected. I have a valid invitation, I can assure you."

The cool way she said it made Reilly realise she wasn't trying to look big. She had sources inside WayCom.

"But you're here to see me?"

"Exactly. It's no good getting your secretary to put me off. We have to talk Steve. If we don't, things won't go well for you."

She was looking up at him, clear-eyed, calm, and perfectly sure of herself.

Reilly was amazed at her words, spoken as though she was his boss.

"What do you mean? Are you threatening me or something?"

Ruth Charlton bit daintily into a fried prawn. She smiled. "Yes. You're on the ball today."

Reilly waved away a plate of canapés and concentrated on the impudent eyes. "Well, you can—" the obscenity rose in his throat, but never came out. "You can forget it!"

Ruth Charlton watched him closely, a slight smile on her lips. "Tough guy, huh?"

"You can stick your offer."

"I don't like people talking to me like that," Ruth said, selecting another prawn, but maintaining the charm.

"I can recommend these." Her white teeth bit into the succulent flesh.

Her enjoyment annoyed him. Her nerve—coming to his presentation and holding a gun to his head.

"You've had my answer," he said, turning to go, brushing her off.

She clung on to his arm still. He could feel her fingers tightening.

"All I'm asking, Steve is for us to talk. Nothing more. If you feel the same afterwards, I'll do what you suggest with the offer."

His temper was rising. "There's nothing to talk about. It wouldn't matter how much you were offering. I'm not your man. Now, if you'll excuse me, I have to get back to my colleagues—"

"Wait a minute." She leaned toward him almost affectionately.

He was starting to pull himself away by force, to withdraw physically from her clutches.

"I know about you and Delia Marris, Steve."

She paused to watch the effect of this shot. Reilly, to give him credit, didn't react much. A little tighter mouth. A couple of lines on the forehead.

She went on, "And if I act, and I will, in twenty-four hours you won't have a job with WayCom or a reputation. You won't work in any major IT corporation again."

"If you *act*?" he said, his face creased with a frown.

"Try and be a wise guy, rather than a tough guy."

The words stopped Reilly. He groped for what she could know. But he couldn't ignore the knowing glance, the gleaming lips. He couldn't afford to walk away. He had to get to the bottom of her meaning.

"OK. Let's talk. Where?" His tone was snappy.

"That's my boy. Actually, when I say talk, I should have said that a friend of mine will deal with it. You'll be talking about things I don't understand. You need to have two people talking the same language—"

"You mean information technology? Who is this person? What's his name? How many people are involved?"

Steve Reilly's skin had lost its sheen, and his usually smooth and cheerful expression had been destroyed by hollows of concern.

"Never mind. No names now. My friend will find you. You'll like her. She's quite personable, and attractive too."

They arranged the meeting in one of the bars after the presentation had concluded.

Ruth would have liked to say that Reilly should have woken up earlier instead of trying to be holy, but she liked to keep business on a polite level.

"And be there, Steve. Or Vance Wayman will get a brown envelope in the post."

★ ★ ★

Perhaps Delia Marris had been sent to WayCom to trap him. Reilly wondered about that as he waited for Ruth Charlton's friend at Luigi's Wine Bar in the Hyatt, after the reception.

She was half an hour late. He had consumed three screwdrivers. He hoped she would never come, but he couldn't leave.

Then a tall blonde woman slipped agilely into the seat before him in the booth.

Where Ruth was dark, she was fair. Her dress was azure blue cashmere wool, and left much of her honey coloured chest and shoulders naked. She was long-necked, and this was accentuated by her drawn-back hair. Her smile was fixed. Her pale eyes suggested an intelligent and calculating mind.

"I didn't think you'd be in too much of a hurry to decide I'd stood you up," she said, and Reilly noticed the slight German accent. He gestured toward his near-empty glass.

"Spritzer for me please."

He ordered the drinks and they settled down facing each other in the booth. It was private.

Heidi sampled her drink with enjoyment. "You're not saying much, Mr Reilly."

"I don't even know your name."

"Don't look so miserable. Everything's going to be all right. My name doesn't matter for the moment. All you need to know is that I know everything."

He sniffed. "What are you talking about, everything! There's nothing to know. I've done nothing wrong."

"Delia Marris." The blonde's eyes glowed.

He had decided there was no point in denying what he had been doing with Delia. It was a matter of finding out how much this woman really knew.

"I don't think what happened with Delia was very important, and wouldn't be seen as important by management. People are screwing around all the time," he said, showing irritation.

Having conceded the point he was sure he was in the clear.

"Quite right. Oh this really is refreshing," the woman said, sipping.

Reilly waited. He'd misread her. His admission didn't seem to mean anything to her.

The blonde stirred the cocktail stick caressingly. "But it's not sex that management would be interested in. Sure, you're a big healthy boy getting your share. No problem. It's whether you were working with Delia, trying to get secret files—"

"Shit! I'm not. I wasn't. There isn't a scrap of evidence." Reilly's contemptuous voice went up a few tones.

"No? Really?" she said, opening her shoulder bag, and taking out an envelope.

In the envelope were photographs. Her hands moved gracefully over the prints, spreading them over the table. The diamond on her finger caught a fragment of light in the shadowed bar.

The prints were 35 mm enlargements, taken with a telephoto lens, showing Reilly with Delia in her car, in a restaurant, going into her apartment.

Reilly assessed the collection quickly, painfully.

The shots didn't necessarily imply they were lovers, or even great friends. They were fixes of serious, tense moments between two young people. The black and white prints magnified the feeling. They recorded the moments that might occur between two people who were lovers—or who were working together on a difficult task.

Somebody had watched very carefully to get the photographs. They showed intimacy.

The blonde was very casual. "Of course this is just background. It doesn't prove anything. But it covers a period when certain computer files were copied, and stolen by Delia Marris. It shows association."

Reilly was still trying to weigh up how damning this was. "So I knew Delia Marris, so what?"

"And you lied to the FBI about it. In the statement you gave Agent Gerstein, you said you didn't know Delia Marris except as a fellow staffer. You didn't say you were friendly with this girl and used to go to her apartment."

Reilly felt desperate. A castle of suspicion was being erected out of nothing.

"For Christ's sake, it was too embarrassing to admit, and it wouldn't have contributed to the inquiry!"

But the blonde woman had all the answers. "Maybe you had a reason for not telling, a good or bad one—who cares?—but the point is you lied to a Federal agency in an espionage investigation about your association with a spy. It's undeniable. You lied."

"Look, I never *knew* she was a thief or a spy or whatever she was!"

"Really?" the woman said carelessly.

She paused to let her words cut deep into Reilly.

He closed his eyes wearily.

She withdrew more prints from a second envelope. "When we

put the first lot of shots, and your lie, with these, the plot thickens —recognise them?"

Reilly felt the shock of seeing frames that he had already seen—on the Le Moyne House video.

There were several frames of him with Delia at her desk. They both looked strained. There was again a suggestion of intimacy, but it depended upon what you wanted to write in for dialogue. Again, they could have been lovers or co-workers.

"How did you get these?" Reilly asked.

The blonde ignored the question, and collected the photographs like a dealer with a pack of cards. She tapped them with a fingernail and made an audible sound.

"Taken together the whole lot makes you look suspect, Mr Reilly."

"If you want to think the worst, maybe, but I don't see they're in any way conclusive," Reilly said evenly.

He was an experienced debater. It was part of his job. He was used to being confronted with surprise facts that weakened his case. And he was used to thinking of instant replies, and fighting back. He tried to sound assured, to write off the collection.

The woman laughed. It was a low and ladylike sound. "Oh you're right there. They wouldn't prove anything in a court of law. But you're not going to be tried in a court of law—"

"Exactly!" Reilly interrupted. "And anybody with any common sense isn't going to believe a bunch of flimsy suppositions."

The blonde wasn't fazed. "Oh no? Be real Mr Reilly. What would *you* do if you had doubts about the loyalty of one of your staff, and billions of dollars in issue, possibly even the survival of the company? Do you expect Wayman to give a wise middle-of-the road ruling? Would you? Do you expect him to say to himself that he has to be careful to be fair to Steve Reilly? He'll be careful to be fair all right—to the company!"

Steve Reilly was corroding inside with anger and self-loathing, as he looked at the chillingly beautiful woman.

He could have reached across the booth and clawed away the composed mask which confronted him. The bitch was absolutely right. He would be gone. Finished.

Chapter 32

Mike Hayden had a heavy file in his hand as he sat in his office at the Bowen, reading.

Cathy Ong was sitting at the desk, with big black-rimmed spectacles on, peering at the screen of her laptop.

"We need to give some thought to questioning Harvey Capel, CJ," Hayden said as he flicked through the pages.

Capel's personal file carried an interesting but unwritten message. He was the top graduate of London Business School in his MBA intake. His performance on other courses was brilliant. He had served WayCom almost all his career. His marks for loyalty and dedication were impeccable, but he had missed a series of critical promotions which would have taken him up to main board level—although he had still achieved a very important position.

Capel hadn't bonded with his peers, and the result was shown in the guarded comments on his assessments: *An intellectual approach rather than practical. Inclined to be cynical. Attitude sometimes superior.*

"There's the epitaph on a man's whole career here," Hayden said, closing the folder. "Once you get a tag on you like being a superior kind of bastard in a corporate hierarchy, you can never shake it off. Capel's been damned for a long time."

They talked about how to approach Capel. While it had been important to get Rosemary Delmer out of her native habitat, it was equally important to catch Harvey Capel out of his. Capel was officially in touch with people at high level on an almost daily basis. He wouldn't be able to be so distant as Delmer. But it was a matter of getting him in the right environment. It was no good interrogating Capel in meeting room number 3; that could lead to stiffness and non-cooperation.

"Better to have a beer with him at the country club, approach obliquely," Cathy Ong said.

She had found that Capel was a member of the Jamesville Country Club, and that he generally had dinner there, and stopped for a drink on Wednesday or Thursday nights. Capel didn't seem to spend a lot of time at home with his wife.

"I can get you a corporate guest card from WayCom. They're one of the sponsors. And you can go out there," Cathy said.

★ ★ ★

The club was an important amenity for the top people at WayCom as well as those from the other big employers in the neighbourhood. The Jamesville had a fine golf course, huge indoor and outdoor pools, a sailing lake and dozens of tennis, basketball and squash courts.

The clubhouse was based on the old family house of the James's where they had farmed thousands of acres a century ago. And it still preserved some of the grandeur—the high columned entrance, and marble hall, the elaborate plaster sconces and architraves, and in the foyer, a collection of large oils of long forgotten Georgian gentlemen.

Hayden made his way to the bar, furnished with gaudy tartan drapes, and matching chairs. It faced across the lake which glistened like black marble. A mist was gathering above the water.

The room was nearly empty. He searched for Capel whom he knew only as a sharp negotiator heading the WayCom claims team.

Hayden found his quarry imbibing his first whisky-and-soda, alone.

Capel recognised him immediately. "Ah, Mr Michael Hayden. You've run me down finally, have you?"

Capel leaned back on the bar. He looked deliberately casual in a well-cut tweed suit, and a brocade waistcoat. The waistcoat was a florid touch in keeping with a man who knew there was no gain in conforming. His face had the puffiness of a regular, heavy drinker. His eyes were red, but the glance was sharp.

"As a matter of fact I have come out here to talk to you."

"I thought you might. Business and pleasure. I'll buy you a drink."

Hayden accepted a malt Scotch and the two took seats at a convenient distance from the bar. The room would fill up in the next hour when members called in for their nightcap or a game of cards, after having had dinner at one of the club's dining rooms.

"You've got a difficult task in front of you, Mr Hayden."

There was no point in trying a "call me Mike" routine. Capel was congenitally a stand-off person.

"Perhaps you can tell me what's happening, around here and then I can see for myself," Hayden said.

"You know as well as I do. There's always an Iscariot."

"Did you know that Carl Leman was employed by WayCom in breach of the contract—you arranged it, I think?"

"No. You think young Carl was a spy? Who for? No, let me guess. His last employer. Zosmark. South Africa?"

"Looks like it to me. You don't seem surprised."

"Why should I be? If I were ten years younger I might do it myself."

"You don't have any sense of loyalty to WayCom?"

Capel laughed and finished his drink. "Loyalty to what? A board of fat directors. Loyalty to the sleek and shifty Vance Wayman, who loves me as much as his mother-in-law? Loyalty to my snakepit of colleagues? How can you be so naive?"

"What about loyalty to the US Government? This is a US contract."

"Oh God, patriotism. I hadn't really thought of George Washington and the Stars and Stripes. Anyhow, the point doesn't arise. Nobody made me the offer, Mr Hayden. Too much of an old has been. And I haven't got the nerves for it. I like a quiet life."

"You don't like the WayCom management, do you?"

"I think they're swine, but that's being too hard on swine. These are incompetent swine."

"A man of your ability could be CEO," Hayden said agreeably.

He wondered how such a conceited man would handle the comment. There was an element of truth in it. Capel was the *nearly* man, the one everybody had expected to succeed, who didn't.

Capel's flippant façade dropped, and he looked at Hayden seriously for the first time. "Actually, I'd make a damn good CEO. Better by a mile than that asswipe Wayman. But these things are not to be. My ambitions were put away long ago."

Hayden was amazed by the brazen arrogance. "You never had any suspicions of Leman?"

"Never."

"There was nothing personal between you? No antagonism. No dispute?"

Hayden could see the deliberately languid Capel coming awake under these questions.

"Nothing. What's your standing to ask these sort of questions, Mr Hayden?"

"My client's being robbed, Mr Capel. Systematically robbed by employees. I'd like to know who they are. So, what's your theory about what happened to Leman?"

Capel could have shut up, but he liked to parry words. "Oh, dear me. Is this a question in a management psychology test? Give two alternative explanations of what might have caused executive X to end his life in the shredder. Well, I don't have a theory, and I certainly don't *know* what happened."

Capel had decided not to cooperate. Hayden could feel the breeze, and he tried another avenue. "Reilly? Anything you can help me with on him?"

"I'm expected to grass on him, am I? Well, I haven't any scruples. I would if there was something to say. All I can add is he's a young man of little experience, and immense over-confidence."

"You have a close relationship with the CEO's secretary?"

Hayden had Capel on full alert now, but Capel was taking trouble to preserve his urbanity.

"Why not? She's a rather attractive woman for her age, wouldn't you say?"

"And it's just a romantic interest, is it?"

"Get screwed, Mr Hayden."

Hayden paused, but Capel had slammed the door on the subject of Delmer. "And Marris, one of your employees: was she doing any work allocated by you the night she fled?"

"She certainly wasn't. She was one person in a big team. I hardly knew her. Look, Mr Hayden you're flannelling around, getting nowhere. Why don't we have another drink, and talk about the championship golf?"

"Am I getting nowhere? I have losses of secret technology. I have a top executive who hates his company, his CEO, and his colleagues; who is having an affair with the CEO's secretary, the person who knows the CEO's private business; who has employed one thief; who has no moral scruples about espionage; and who, according to his lifestyle, appears to be independently wealthy of his salary."

Capel paused to take this in, particularly the implication that his background had been under scrutiny. But why not? The FBI and the NSA had the resources and he was necessarily one of the bugs under the microscope. Then the corners of his mouth twisted sarcastically.

"Bravo, Mr Hayden. All sound and fury signifying nothing!"

Chapter 33

Jed Olsen sat at the boardroom table at Fairford, drumming his fingers on the polished oak, waiting for Heidi Stoller. She was due to present her security report on Olsen's artificial intelligence team.

Heidi made a report every two or three months, because Olsen had come to fear that all their work, and their investment, would be destroyed by loss of key people to a competitor, particularly WayCom.

He watched the AI team like the commandant of a gulag.

He drew on a small Dutch cigar, one of the three or four per day that he allowed himself, but the fragrance left a peppery irritation in his nose and mouth.

Heidi appeared, ten minutes late, and with no apology. But Olsen was pleased that she looked so assured, in control, and took her lapse of manners without comment.

After Jed's secretary had shut the door and left them alone, Heidi took her time arranging her papers, sipping her coffee, adding more sugar to taste, sipping again, lighting a cigarette and blowing a satisfied plume of smoke at the ceiling.

Her white cotton skirt and jacket with gold threads clung to her lithe figure, and the line of her court shoes emphasised her graceful ankles, but Jed felt no stirring in himself. He might as well have been looking at a shiny illustration in *Vogue*.

"Good news?" Jed asked.

"Not entirely. On the face of it, all the Number 1 team appear reliable. We've looked them over carefully. Examined their private affairs and their assets. Nothing untoward. I suppose that's good news."

Olsen paled visibly. "It's Haffner. Don't tell me it's Haffner."

"It is."

"What have you got?"

Peter Haffner was leader of the Number 1 team. He had a first in the mathematics tripos at Cambridge, and was one of perhaps fifty people in the world who understood a level of mathematics which was beyond others. He was the key person whom Wayman had not enticed away. Jed Olsen had nurtured and rewarded Haffner ever since.

"Haffner spent more time with Luchinelli and Stiegwitz than one would have thought appropriate for rivals at a recent conference."

"Deep professional interests," Olsen said plaintively, anxious to justify.

"You may be perfectly right, Jed. On the other hand he could have been discussing the possibility of joining them."

"Is that all?"

"No. I'm told he's becoming increasingly restive about the flow of material. At first he was grateful for a kick-start, it boosted his ego, but now it's become painfully clear to him that he's receiving stolen property."

"The pathetic maggot. What do you suggest?"

"We could throw a scare into Haffner. Remind him how deeply committed he is already. Point out that he isn't a vestal virgin any more, and could wind up in prison."

Jed Olsen was instinctively sceptical. He had made it a policy to court Haffner. He entertained Haffner on occasions, acted like a friend. He knew the man.

"You think so? Haffner is a very strange and clever animal. He could react in a way we don't expect."

"By talking? He doesn't know where the stolen material comes from. He can only assume it's WayCom," Heidi said.

"No. Haffner isn't the kind to go to the FBI. He'd think he was putting his head in a noose, and he would be. He's deeply complicit. What he might do is just go right on doing what he wants to do, join Wayman, and to hell with us."

Heidi agreed slowly. It was a serious and almost insoluble problem. To lose Haffner would be unthinkable.

"We're playing for big stakes, but we mustn't act hastily." Jed Olsen said vehemently, soothing his fingers over his temples, trying to ease his tumultuous thoughts.

"You don't have long to consider this one, Jed."

Olsen sank back in his chair, his forehead a net of wrinkles.

Heidi tried to imagine him as President, coping with a sudden war emergency.

Olsen leaned forward suddenly, brightening. "We're close to the Senate hearing. Don't forget, the hearing could accomplish everything we want. We can't risk prejudicing it. I talk to Haffner first. But I'll tell you one thing certain. *Haffner will never join WayCom.* It will never happen, whatever the inducements. We've come too far to go back. If Haffner goes, he'll go in a box."

A silence fell in the room, Jed's slightly bloodshot blue eyes were fixed on Heidi's.

"I understand. That's the spirit, Jed," she said with an iron smile.

★ ★ ★

Reilly settled into the same booth at Luigi's Bar in the Hyatt where he had first met the Ice Maiden. He ordered a martini, and she arrived a minute later, precisely on time.

She looked different this time, wearing big shades, her centre-parted hair falling straight to her shoulders obscuring part of her cheeks and jaw line. Very little of her face was visible, and the swan-like throat was covered by the rollneck of her grey brushed wool sweater. She was expensive but anonymous.

She ordered iced Perrier. This would be her last meeting with Reilly in a place where she might be identified by a stooge set up by Reilly. She knew from her detector that he wasn't wired, and judged the meeting safe.

She began without preliminaries. "I'm awfully glad you're agreeing, Steve. You're a mature guy doing the sensible thing. I believed you would."

Reilly had desperately tried to think of a way out. But his nerve-splitting conclusion was that his position was impossible. He *had* to agree to Ruth Charlton's proposal. If he didn't, he was finished anyway. Wayman would fire him instantly over Delia Marris.

The mere possibility that he and Delia were working together was too strong to be overlooked. And if he was fired, he'd never get a decent job in IT again. He wouldn't have a reference, or be able to get one. And the word would spread that he wasn't trustworthy. None of the major corporations would touch him. He'd have to start over in a completely new field. It was a risk he couldn't take. He had a career—and he was going to the top.

If he picked up Charlton's offer, he had a better than even chance of getting away with it at least until he could find a way—perhaps by changing his employer—to extricate himself. He would have to be very careful. He would have the money. He wouldn't have to make the embarrassing economies he'd been planning, like selling the boat, and the place at the lake.

And the other advantage was Laura wouldn't find out anything about Delia Marris. If he told Laura about Delia, asked her forgiveness, he knew what her response would be. Assuming she forgave him, she would probably hold the affair over him forever. She was like that. She'd never forget.

Heidi preserved a businesslike calm but couldn't quite resist the sense of triumph. How easy these venal little men were to manipulate when they let their peckers work the keyboard instead of their fingers.

"What about the job Ruth Charlton is supposed to have organised. Who's it with, and where?" he responded shrilly.

"One thing at a time, Steve. Let's get a good flow of information going first, and then we'll get to talking about that."

Reilly's face reddened with anger and frustration. "Horseshit. There's no job, is there? There never was. It's straight blackmail."

Heidi's cruel amusement was noticeable, despite the shades.

"It's no use getting annoyed," she said, as though talking to a child. "We're going to do this my way. You got yourself into this."

"What do you want me to do, anyway?" He was surly.

"You should be telling me what you can do. I want the specifications, complete, for the prototypes you're building. And I want a copy of the programme log. I want Luchinelli's latest papers on semantic programming."

"Now wait a minute, that's a mountain of information—"

"Copy it and get it to me. $100,000 bonus every time you make a delivery. It'll help with the payments on the cabin cruiser."

The bitch *knew* about the boat.

"It's dangerous—"

"There's nobody better placed than you. You coordinate. You have access to everything. You understand enough about the technology to know what we want. Go to it."

Reilly was sickened at what he was undertaking, the impudence of her request. His bowels felt weak, painful, but he didn't show it.

Heidi Stoller smiled her electric smile, teeth and lips gleaming. She reached into her handbag and slipped out a bulky brown envelope.

"This is on account. We pay in advance."

As she walked out of the bar, Reilly's fingers closed around the envelope, and he could feel the thick packets of banknotes inside. In spite of his reluctance, despising himself for being a fool, he had a pulse of excitement about the money.

★ ★ ★

The room at the Hilton on 23rd Street in Rochester, NY, overlooked the Gracewell Gardens. The wych elms were whipping in the wind, and the few people who chose to walk on this afternoon, bent over against the biting northerly.

But Jed Olsen was comfortable. The lime and soda was soothing.

He never indulged in alchohol on occasions like this. He could relax. There were no bugs, cameras or recording devices in the room. He had to protect himself if he was going to talk frankly with the man on the couch opposite.

Olsen liked to renew his feel for this man by meeting him personally every few months. And the meetings had to be on territory where nobody would connect that they were talking about the business of WayCom.

Olsen had been working with Capel for a long time. They were in a sense friends, or at least that was what Olsen pretended and Capel believed. And in many repects there was no reason why they shouldn't be seen—very occasionally—in public together. Both were high in the IT industry, and their connection had started many years before at IT conferences.

Olsen usually met Harvey Capel in Rochester, sometimes in New York. These meetings in a private room at a good hotel had become a regular event. Capel would take a room, and Olsen would drive or fly in for an hour with him.

Olsen, always holding out the ultimate prize of a major post in his own company, was wary of the man beneath the surface charm.

Capel was a guileful operator who had provided Olsen with a mine of information about WayCom—not espionage in the true sense of the word, not handing over plans and drawings and confidential files, but vital tactical information about WayCom's corporate plans, often accompanied by detailed figures from Capel's almost photographic memory.

Capel had never handed over a document, a tape or a disk. He simply talked. And as the talk was all deniable, Capel could never be convicted of an offence, or found to have breached confidence in a civil suit. He was a fatal leak in the hull of Wayman's great flagship.

He had earned his corn from Olsen, a huge sum, which made his official salary look meagre, paid from an anonymous source into a Swiss company account which Capel maintained. That of course was a weakness, but Capel counted on the fact that Jed Olsen could never let it be known that he was implicated in the slightest way in bribery. And they had concocted a fictitious arrangement for the payment of consulting fees.

"The US Government are stepping up the pressure. The FBI are all over the STELA contract, to see if we're living up to our promises to keep it secret," Capel said.

"I know. You're not worried personally?"

"I can run rings around them. It makes life more interesting."

"Good. But don't be too confident. STELA 2 will enable WayCom to build an unbreachable wall around itself. That's why I need more help from you, Harvey. How is Wayman taking it?"

"He's shitting bricks. Meetings with bankers. Reassurances to stockholders. Getting his lawyers to harry the Government for payment. He's at the end of the road financially. STELA's bigger than him and she's throttling the life out of him."

"Good. But it doesn't mean we can let up. This is as much a *kill Wayman* exercise for me, Harvey, as it is for you," Olsen said quietly, his palm supporting his handsome head. Harvey Capel sipped his Campari soda and thought about this. He knew the Olsen-Wayman history well, and had no doubt of Jed Olsen's vitriolic hatred of Wayman.

And it was, as Olsen suggested, a kill Wayman exercise for him too—not killing literally, because Capel was not a physically violent person. Destroy was a better word. He fervently hoped to see Wayman downed. To have a hand in bringing him down would be a supreme satisfaction, and then to move to a top job at Fairfield, and a place on the board …

Their mutual malice against Wayman was what held the two men together. Capel never thought of himself as a mere money grubber.

He tried to remember when it had all begun—years ago, before Wayman appeared on the scene. He was the coming man in Daltech, as the company was called in those days, plainly superior to his colleagues in every way, and devoted to his work.

He had been especially strong in finance, but had a marketing and sales flair too. And he had the brain to understand the technical people, to interpret their ideas in a way that was marketable.

As a manager of men his style was perhaps old-fashioned. He didn't waste words, or suffer fools. He said it the way it was. He was a damn good manager. Everybody had agreed that he would head the company one day.

Then Wayman appeared, a New York rag merchant who had hardly read a book in his life, and took over Daltech.

Capel hadn't been slow to understand Wayman's qualities—which were so unlike his own. Wayman was instinctive. He didn't think, he felt. Wayman couldn't be bothered with plans and processes. His decisions weren't arrived at by fine reasoning. They were based on simple pragmatism and, Capel had to admit, were so often right.

But it wasn't Wayman's natural talent that worried Capel. Capel's own ability was strong. It was the fact that Wayman had used him as a gopher over the years, worked his butt off, flattered him, promised the moon, and—it finally became evident—never intended to deliver.

Wayman was a liar who used him, and despised him.

Capel's perception of this didn't appear overnight. It took years and years of irritating grains of grit silting up in his mind. Disappointments.

Harvey Capel was very successful by most men's standards. But he'd given in return, brilliance, and supreme effort, and received only empty promises.

He should have been on the WayCom board by now. He should have been lifted to a new dimension of power. But it hadn't happened, and after a while he could see that it wasn't going to happen. That was why he had responded eventually to Jed Olsen's approaches.

It was some consolation to feel you had your knife into Wayman's enterprise, and that it was bleeding.

And so the meeting with Jed Olsen. A couple of days in Rochester, good restaurants, the theatre, a nightclub, girls, the casino. Money no problem.

He had the urge to spend. The fact that he'd made the money secretly gave him a special high when he spent it.

The problems of Fairford seemed remote to Capel. Seven or eight years earlier he might have been trembling with anxiety to please Olsen, but now he had become so used to his role he could lie back and contemplate it more objectively.

Capel projected a contrasting aura to a person as perceptive as Olsen. On the surface Capel was witty and lighthearted, but underneath, Olsen sensed a deep, nihilistic cynicism like a cold metal plate in Capel's chest.

"I was going to ask you about Carl Leman," Capel began slowly. "Horrible death."

Olsen looked at him vaguely. "I don't know anything about it other than I read in the papers. We're not *that* anxious to put the skids under Wayman that we'd kill off his executives."

Capel pushed his glass away, and turned unseeing toward the window.

"I suppose it's all a coincidence. Jackson Bray's accident. Then Leman. And the missing staffer, a girl, Mariette Stevas."

"I really don't know anything about it, Harvey, and I'm rather surprised to think you thought I might," Olsen said sharply.

There was a quiet in the room. The wind was lashing the trees outside, exposing the black fingers of the branches underneath the thin leaves.

"I didn't mean to imply that you would be involved. There was this girl Delia Marris who was caught stealing a tape and got away—"

"God, Harvey, I don't want to listen to this. You know the industry. Everybody is hungry to advance the technology. Everybody is watching everybody."

Capel felt a little easier. He hadn't seriously believed that Olsen or his company had anything to do with Delia Marris, or the deaths, and he knew how predatory the industry was. The proximity of physical violence unnerved him, and it was good to be reassured.

Olsen smiled thinly. "Anyway, I wanted to say how important your loyalty to me and your discretion are in our business. I want to talk about the Senate Committee hearing. My lawyers will be getting in touch with you to prepare affidavits detailing Wayman's payments to the generals and the President."

Capel would be taking a decisive step when he swore an affidavit traducing Wayman. His years of work with WayCom would end overnight. It was a big step.

Olsen followed the unspoken train of thought. "There's no way back, Harvey."

Capel understood. He felt a coldness, an uncertainty he'd never felt before. *No way back.* He looked at Olsen, at the almost maniacal light in his eyes, and wondered how balanced Olsen was.

He, Capel, was bitter, but Olsen was corroded, eaten away by his passion to get Wayman.

Olsen made an excuse, and instead of staying to dinner, left. When he had gone, Capel felt like stone.

He sat down, picked up his glass and saw the few last dregs of blood-red Campari at the bottom.

His mind dwelt on the angle which even a man of his intelligence had pushed into the background: Olsen was spending millions of dollars in the assault on WayCom. He believed that Olsen wasn't implicated in the deaths, but even so he sensed that there were no limits for Olsen.

He himself was now going to be drawn into the heat of the battle. *No way back.* The implied threat. A sudden sweat prickled on his forehead and a moment ago he had been casually sipping his drink as though it was a game!

He suddenly didn't feel so keen about his tickets for the Moonlight Club.

The attractions of the girl from the agency, whom he'd dated for the night, paled—even though her charms were so graphic on the photographs the agency had supplied.

Chapter 34

Hayden and Cathy Ong were in the suite at the Bowen.

Cathy Ong had been working every night and her glazed skin was dark around the eyes. She was making one of her reports.

Hayden himself was no longer as laid back as he had been a month before. He had started with an objective interest in peeling away the layers which obscured WayCom, and finally come to a tense-jawed impatience, watching, listening above all else for a clue to Marietta's whereabouts.

"What I have done," Cathy said quietly, "is to have a look at the main AI scientists over the past ten years. They move around. They meet at conferences. They belong to national committees. It's interesting."

"Makes sense to have a look at the whole bunch," Hayden conceded.

"Well, Luchinelli and Stiegwitz, the two WayCom geniuses, used to work for Fairford, in the days when Fairford were doing the most advanced work on artificial intelligence. Left after an argument."

"So no love lost there. They're not likely to be sending their research results back to the old firm. Would there be any exchange of ideas at a super-scientific level, conferences, over the heads of their employers?"

"I doubt it. All sides are under confidentiality undertakings," Cathy said.

"They don't always mean a lot in practice."

"Maybe not, but it's a hotly competitive area. Every company hoping to take a lead. Big reputations. Big money. Lots of adulation. I gather that there are definite bounds to these conferences. The nerds only explain what's already either patented, or on the market, or they speculate about the future. Of course, what happens on the side is something else."

Hayden followed her. "I guess it's fair enough to assume the conferences are a highly competitive area academically. So there's no leakage. Only espionage."

"Exactly, Mike. I've also been looking at the top people in the research teams of each of the AI research corporations. I was looking for common links with their opposites at WayCom. I've matched their educational backgrounds and employment histories. And as much as we can find on their activities outside the company they're working for. Stella has analysed all the data, and effectively she's saying there are no useful connections, other than the one I've mentioned: Luchinelli and Stiegwitz formerly working together at Fairford."

"Who is the leader at Fairford, since they're within physical reach?"

"A guy named Haffner."

"So what do we know about Haffner?"

"He's a lot younger than Luchinelli, and some say brighter ... he's gay. Very single-minded. Hoping to make an even bigger name for himself than he already has. A visiting professor at UCLA. Has worked for Olsen for many years. Apparently very loyal."

It occurred to Hayden, that if Fairford were quietly boosting their progress with espionage against WayCom, some member, probably the boss of the research team, would have to be complicit.

Every piece of stolen information would have to be fed to the research team, who would want to know where it came from. Every valuable piece of information would amount to a clever, perhaps a brilliant technical insight, for which somebody would want to claim the credit. Who better than the leader of the team, dazzling his people with his inventive mind?

He rehearsed the idea with Cathy.

"Yeah, now you mention it, I guess it's a bit much to think of the researchers sitting in their lab while stolen secrets flutter down anonymously from above," she said.

"Sure, and let's be practical. You couldn't trust a whole team to handle material they knew or guessed was stolen. Somebody would sing. But suppose the stolen technology came secretly to the team leader, and he filtered it through to his team as his own. Only he would know."

"Right, Mike. But let me be practical now. Suppose we put every head of every AI research team outside WayCom under suspicion. How are we going to investigate them?"

"Yeah, yeah, I know we can't approach research bosses in South Africa or Japan or Britain—unless we go through their justice system, and that would take an age. But we might remember that there is one AI boss in the USA, other than Luchinelli: Professor Peter Haffner."

"You're going to look at Haffner then?" Cathy asked.

"I'm thinking about it. You've talked me into it."

★ ★ ★

Mike Hayden spent the afternoon in the WayCom offices with the team of lawyers and accountants looking at the cost overruns.

He had only half his mind on the negotiations. The room was full, the tables stacked with files, and computer screens flickered at every elbow. Hayden let his colleague, John Bloomstein, lead on financial matters, and on this particular afternoon he kept quiet and watched.

It was like a poker game, between WayCom and the NSA, each lawyer and executive playing his cards quietly to win a surprise point: millions of dollars were changing hands.

Cathy Ong could see Hayden wasn't all that interested, and whispered that she had something to show him.

They left the room, and went for a walk in the chill afternoon sun outside the building. Cathy Ong showed him a print-out.

"These are the prime corporate suspects, Mike."

There were three names on the list: Zosmark (South Africa), Mitsuko (Japan), and Fairford (US).

"These are the companies with the most significant AI experience, actively pursuing research. They would have a deep interest in getting hold of STELA technology," Cathy said.

"And the NSA have had Zosmark and Mitsuko under satellite surveillance?" Hayden asked.

"With Stella doing a data analysis. Right, because there are no prima facie grounds for getting a warrant from a judge against Fairford."

"Fairford is the Olsen family company. They wanted the defence contract, and didn't get it. And presumably they're hoping to get it if WayCom falls over. OK, so what about the other two, CJ?"

"We've trawled through a mass of their computer communications, and been inside some of their systems for almost a month, but nothing. We have a picture of what they're doing, but there's nothing to show any kind of connection with WayCom."

"Maybe Stella is telling us we don't have to worry about Zosmark and Mitsuko," Hayden said.

"I'm not so sure."

Cathy Ong was thinking that left only Fairford amongst the big players, and she found it difficult to believe they would infiltrate WayCom.

"Jed Olsen has too much to lose. The STELA development may come to him anyway."

"Nothing like making it more certain," Hayden said.

"Think the unthinkable, huh?"

"It isn't so unthinkable, CJ. And Olsen is known to dislike Wayman."

"Come on, Mike. Including a couple of murders? I can't imaging Olsen besmirching his family name. He's angling for a political appointment too. I don't think he'd let his company get engaged in espionage."

"Sometimes powerful men overreach themselves," Hayden said. But he was inclined to agree with Cathy Ong.

Olsen was unlikely to be a candidate for their investigation.

★ ★ ★

"Another call about Mariette, Mike," Gerstein's phlegmy voice said over the telephone in Hayden's room at seven in the morning.

Hayden's head was suddenly as clear as a mountain stream. "Where this time?"

"Thunder Lake area. Place called Dry Creek, maybe fifteen miles from the lake."

The FBI had received a lot of calls as a result of the posting of the reward. Hayden had been right. They had sent a couple of agents to interview each caller, and carefully mapped the areas in question. To date, the callers seemed to have been mistaken.

"What do you make of it, Al?"

"Mariette was sighted, if it was her, being pushed into a battered Dodge utility truck by a man described as of strong build with short silver hair."

"Ties in with what Arkwright said."

"Yeah. And it's not too far from where Mariette's car was found. It's the most hopeful call yet."

On a sudden impulse, Hayden said, "Do you have any objection if I go up there?"

Gerstein's chest wheezed with discomfort. "I do, Mike. Stay out of it. Do your lawyering. Protect your client."

★ ★ ★

Mike Hayden spent some time each day at the WayCom offices, according to a schedule he had worked out with Karen Bridges. He had the use of a company meeting room.

Hayden and Karen finished late at the office reviewing the security clauses in the NSA defence contract, and Hayden drove her to her apartment. As they drove he told her about the information on Mariette.

"Do you feel responsible for her, because you're the guy that saw her last" Karen asked.

"Hell, no. She was working her shift. I agree with Al that she was a greenhorn, but that's down to the NSA. No, I just care for her, Karen, that's all. Look, do you fancy going up there again, around Thunder Lake?"

Karen gave a small smile. "We'll get into trouble with Al."

He glanced at her as he drove. The FBI training was all there.

"Yes, Mike. I'd like to."

It was something maybe he shouldn't have offered to do, drive her home. But Karen had a fascinating attraction and repulsion about her, and he was feeling low after Marietta's disappearance. It was a momentary feeling which lowered his resistance on formal rules like not messing with people you work with.

When they reached Karen's apartment, she invited him in, and he accepted as he knew he would. She poured him a scotch and they sat in her lounge, far apart on different sofas.

"Well, are you going to tell me what your report to Vance will say?" she asked.

Maybe she had lured him into this privacy so she could ask, and get a good chance of an answer, to a question that worried her above all others.

"I guess there's no reason to keep it a secret. I think you're in line with the contract, not perfect, but enough to satisfy the Defense Committee."

She smiled broadly, put down her drink, and came over to sit beside him. Not touching, but so close, so he could feel her warmth.

"Well then, Mike, my job is done. I don't have any axe to grind."

He was a little taken aback at her candour. She was assuming a hurdle to what they both wanted had been removed.

"Let's have dinner, anyway," he said.

He chose Oswego's on 2nd Street, which specialised in French cuisine, with a nice line in Creole and French-Canadian food. It was tasty and informal. He had thought about the atmosphere. He didn't want white cloths, candles and hushed voices.

They had a small table against the wall on one side—not the best in the room, but one of the most private. Oswego's had dark green carved panelling, and brass fittings which shone in the shadows—kitschy perhaps but comfortable.

In the few minutes that Karen had excused herself to change, she had wrought quite a transformation from the businesslike security chief: she wore a white jacket with gold brocade stitching over her dark tube skirt, gold pendant earrings and a matching chain necklace. Her crinkly auburn hair had been allowed to escape from a band.

When they had settled themselves in the seats, and he had ordered drinks—sparkling water for her, gin and tonic for him—she sighed, put her elbows on the table and looked straight at him. Questioning green eyes.

Hayden liked her. Like Rosemary Delmer, although at quite a different level, work was the centre of her life. Over the weeks he had found out more about her, and perhaps remembered things from the past that he'd forgotten. They had a way of talking frankly.

She had no brothers or sisters. Her father disappeared when she was a little girl, and her mother was dead. She had friends but, in super-mobile America, they were scattered around the continent, people she went to high school and university with, or people she had met on summer work schemes. She rarely saw them except for a vacation weekend.

She went to the gym, took small parts in amateur productions of the WayCom theatre, attended an adult education class in Impressionism, had parties with her acquaintances—but the centre of it all was her job. And Hayden fitted in at the edge of this pattern, because he was, in a sense, work.

And it was the same with him. He worked ten or twelve hours a day, less for the money than because he thought he was doing a useful job and he got a kick out of it. It was a big slab of his life. If he was going to change that for a relationship—as he had learned from his first marriage—it would have to be a very weighty one.

He had found out that hot sex plus an easy relationship didn't add up to a sum as big as the pull of his work—not yet anyway.

She covered his hands on the table with hers. She smiled. "Come on, Mike. Let's order something nice."

★ ★ ★

When Mike Hayden parked his car in the Bowen Hotel lot it was nearly 1 am.

He had driven back from Karen's apartment in Hart Forest very slowly. He felt buoyant, and in a sense guilty at having enjoyed himself while Mariette was in limbo.

Neither Karen nor he could face the meal at Oswego's, seafood, in a hot red sauce over rice. At any other time, with a bottle of cold chardonnay, it would have been delicious.

They had picked at the food in silence. It congealed on the plates before them.

The noise from the other diners in the restaurant became too intense to bear. Finally, with hardly a signal between them, they knew they had to go, not even hearing the troubled queries of the waiter about whether anything was wrong with the food.

They didn't switch on the lights at Karen's apartment. The moonlight coming through the windows was enough.

Making love had been a silent, self-contained passion for each of them. A hopeless attempt, in one intense spasm, to share all the pleasures they feared they were never going to share.

He lay beside her for a while afterwards, wide awake.

Then he got up, dressed in the dark, and the last thing he heard before the front door clicked behind him, was a sob from the bedroom.

★ ★ ★

Hayden preferred to maintain a presence at Le Moyne House while he was trying to put the claim together, because he was able to speak to staff casually, and little by little he built up a feeling for the company, learned things he would never have heard outside.

One morning as he passed Rosemary Delmer in the corridor she greeted him, then hesitated, and seemed to decide that there was something she wanted to say to him. She stopped and turned, on impulse.

"Mike, can I come and see you?"

He said sure, anytime, and by noon she was seated across the desk from him in the meeting room.

He could see her eyes were red and swollen, the only change in her otherwise immaculate presentation.

He guessed that it was the Capel affair that was driving her. It had been going on for a long time without resolution. The gossip was that Capel was playing her for a sucker, and never intended to leave his wife.

"I think there are a few things you should know, Mike. They might make a difference to your investigation. They're about Harvey."

She reddened. It was anger rather than embarrassment.

The night before she had finally pinned Harvey Capel down. Perhaps she had a drink too many. But after dinner in her room at the office—she took infinite pains to ensure that every meal they had there was a picnic delight—she had given him the ultimatum: stop stalling, and tell me when you're going to move in with me.

Harvey had flannelled. Rosemary had lost her temper. She knew, had suspected almost for two years, that he wasn't going to take their relationship further. At last she'd run out of patience, and trust.

"I'll be glad of the help, Rosemary," Hayden said.

Rosemary looked around. "Is this room secure?"

"I wouldn't bank on it."

"You don't worry?"

"I work for WayCom. I tell them my conclusions. So they listen in. So what?"

Rosemary sat silently for a moment, summoning up the will to talk. She pressed her palms flat on the table. She had small, soft hands like a young girl's.

"Harvey's going to give evidence to a Senate Defense Committee inquiry on the STELA contract. He's going to say Vance Wayman gave gifts to get the contract."

Hayden couldn't help showing surprise. It was a heavy allegation.

"Who got the money, and how much?"

"Two generals and the President. It was a campaign donation for the President, but Harvey says there was an understanding about Wayman getting STELA 2. I don't know the names of the generals. The campaign donation was $350,000 and the generals got $200,000 each."

"How does Capel know this?"

"Harvey used to be boss of the STELA programme. He's the one who put the STELA 2 bid together. He says Wayman told him he was sweetening a couple of generals. And that the President was a friend who would support Wayman in return for campaign support."

"Explosive stuff. Is there anybody who confirms what Harvey says?"

"Yeah. A Senator. An old guy. A Polack. From the Midwest."

"Who approached Harvey to give evidence?"

"Jed Olsen."

"Fairford. The guy who wants to get the contract. It figures."

"The guy who hates Wayman's guts like no other—except of course Harvey," Rosemary chimed.

"Why?"

Rosemary Delmer explained what Hayden in part had already learned. The new pieces for him were the capture of Mrs Olsen, and Olsen's personal affront in what Hayden had assumed to be merely a business move by Wayman.

"Did Capel ever try to get confidential information out of you about WayCom?"

She bridled. "Mike, I'm a very good PA even if I say so myself. And I know my duties. Harvey was sure curious about my work, but I gave nothing away. I think Harvey was interested in me because of my position. I think he wanted to find out what Wayman was doing."

"You think he might have sold info?"

"He hated Wayman enough to do it, but I don't know if he did."

Rosemary had said enough to prejudice Capel without getting herself into trouble. She was burning. And there was the Olsen connection again.

But Hayden reflected that Olsen, shrewdly political, couldn't be faulted for collecting affidavits that might upset the Defense Committee and win him the contract. Why not, if Wayman's actions were so improper?

★ ★ ★

Hayden heard the motor change down as the Buick he was driving pulled up the steep rise into the pines at forty five. He had the side screen down, and cold fresh air whipped around the interior.

He had covered about twenty miles of the run to Dry Creek, in the Thunder Lake area, where he had an appointment to see Mr and Mrs Sorrel.

Hayden had pored over the FBI agents' report of their interview with the Sorrels, and their subsequent follow-up report of inquiries in the towns and homesteads nearby. The reports were thorough but added nothing to the Sorrels' story.

He was giving in to that urgent feeling that he could have done better himself. In a less emotional mind, he would have admitted he didn't have the skills of a trained FBI operative.

It was the same kind of impatience that left the passenger seat in the car empty. Karen could be helpful. She had a lot of skills he didn't have. But this was uniquely to do with Mariette, and he decided to leave Karen out. Karen and Mariette were oil and water.

He was soon deep into the hills where the road was a single ribbon of blacktop occasionally monopolised by timber trucks, their gears screaming on the slopes.

Dry Creek, population 210, was announced by a skewed and peeling sign, and beyond it, there was little evidence of Dry Creek the town.

Hayden drove on several miles, and apart from a few houses and an auto-wrecking yard, assumed the town was scattered in forest on either side of the road.

He found the Sorrel residence, a cabin with lean-to additions, down a long dirt road. The cabin sat in a quarter acre of mown grass surrounded by a chicken wire fence.

Hayden stopped behind a muddy Japanese SUV. When he got

out of the car he could hear the rush of water in a nearby stream.

Jay Sorrel came out to meet him, a young timber worker with a thick neck and bulging forearms. His jeans were as tight as some women like to wear them.

They shook hands and Jay Sorrel showed Hayden into the parlour, a neat room with old couches and a worn carpet square, dominated by a huge black TV set.

Mrs Sorrel came in, a slight woman, pale with her dull hair drawn back to a knot at the back of her neck, and rimless glasses. She looked delicate alongside her muscular husband.

She offered a drink and Hayden declined. Both the Sorrels were attentive. Plainly the prospect of the reward had its effect.

"I wondered if you had any information to add. You're around the county day by day. I thought you might have seen something more," Hayden said.

"I'd have come forward with it smartly if I had," Jay Sorrel said.

Hayden questioned them in detail about the man, the woman, and the truck.

Sorrel was clear about the pickup being an 89 or 90 Dodge because he used to drive one himself.

Hayden slipped a photograph, which he had taken from Mariette's photo album, out of his pocket.

"That's her," Mrs Sorrel said. "My, she's beautiful. Course, when we saw her, she was—well at the time I thought she was—drunk, and her head was hanging all over the place, and the man was holdin' her up. But that's her."

"Sure is," Sorrel added.

Hayden felt hollow, and stood up. If the Sorrels were right, Mariette could be close.

"Can we go and have a look at the site now?" he asked.

Sorrel drove Hayden a few miles down the road in his big Jap 4x4 to the place where the couple had seen Marietta. It was a crossroads where there was an old general store, a bar, and a filling station.

Nobody was in sight. The damp buildings seemed to be sinking into the forest. There was a fleck of cold rain.

"Just here," Sorrel said, pointing to an area in front of the bar. "I figured they'd come out of the bar, but hell they coulda come from anywheres. There's more places than you think in the trees around here."

Chapter 35

Steve Reilly quit the office at 5 pm for once, and drove home to Stretton Woods. When he arrived, Laura, a bandanna round her head, and a half-empty sack of groceries in her hand, had heard the scrunch of the car on the gravel, and opened the door.

"Hey, you're early! Has WayCom self-destructed or something?"

Reilly tried to look pleasant. He gave her a peck on the cheek, and walked past into the kitchen, where Laura had been stacking the refrigerator.

He threw the brown envelope on the table. "A present for you."

Laura, immediately curious, and an enjoyer of surprises, picked up the envelope and split it open with her fingernails. The banded bundles of $100 bills tumbled out.

"Wowie!"

But her initial pleasure froze quickly as she fingered the notes, puzzled. "Where did you get this?"

"I guess you'd say from my new employer," he said, cynically.

"In cash?"

"Yeah. A down payment. $100,000."

Laura looked at him hard, trying to catch up.

"Uh-huh. You never told me you were going to do this. You seemed against it. What made you change your mind?"

Reilly was hesitant. Laura got inside his head easily, and there were things there he wanted to keep hidden. He broke away from her eyes, and looked out the window at the pond, rippling in an afternoon breeze.

"You know—Jolie was on my mind—and the Osceola place—I want to keep it as much as you do—and all the shit we've had from Wayman, and everything …"

"Quite a conversion." Laura weighed it up. "I guess I don't know you sometimes, Steve. You do this. The opposite of what you say—"

"I thought it over, dammit! It's what you wanted!"

"It's your decision. Don't try and hang it on me. And you don't seem very happy. You have just brought home a hundred grand, and you are unhappy. What's with you, man? We should be going out to a champagne dinner."

"You don't understand. Laura."

"What's to understand? You've just taken a new job."

"I don't think there is a job. It's just money for information."

"You haven't signed an employment contract?"

"No. I don't even know where the information is going. I don't know who my employer is."

Laura frowned, but not for long because it was bad for the skin on the forehead.

"Shit, you amaze me. You're supposed to be the hotshot businessman, and you get into a back-alley deal."

"I did it for us, for Jolie."

His voice was thick with emotion, and his mind swayed like an uncertain tightrope walker when he thought of telling *why* he really did it, of telling about Delia.

Laura thought Steve behaved like a kid at times. However good he was as an executive, he was piss-poor at handling his own affairs. He needed a keeper.

But the mother in her warmed to him. "OK, Steve, you've done it for us. So what the hell. We'll pay off everything we owe. Let's enjoy."

He agreed with difficulty. He couldn't share her easy optimism.

"It's dangerous. I could get caught. I could go to prison."

"What *is* the matter with you, Steve? You didn't have to get into this at all. You've always known how dangerous it is. You *must* have calculated you could pull it off. Why, when you've hardly started, are you bitching about getting caught?"

"Chicken, I guess."

It was all Reilly could think of, and he felt small.

She went up to him and slid her arms around his neck.

"Well, be a man, my man. You got yourself in. Now do a good job, get the money, get everything paid off. Let's have some fun holidays abroad. And when we've got a decent bankroll, get yourself out. You're a clever guy. You can do it. And take me tonight for cocktails at Leo's and dinner afterwards."

Reilly went upstairs to change while Laura mixed the drinks. She was going to bring them upstairs on a tray, and they'd have them as they showered, really king size whiskies and dry, with lots of ice in mega glasses.

Upstairs, Reilly doused his head under the cold tap first. Hell,

Laura made it sound so easy, and so right.

He was on his own. He could look after himself. He'd bale out in plenty of time. He *was* a clever guy, and he could turn these events to a considerable profit.

Chapter 36

Jed Olsen met Senator Sam Jankovic outside the east wing of the National Gallery, and they walked together down Madison Drive, away from the Capitol. The tall and graceful Olsen, with the portly Jankovic hardly up to his shoulder.

Olsen recalled that the pair had walked in Central Park about a year before, in just such weather, coldish, sunny, with a few dusty and moulting chrysanthemums in bloom, but he didn't mention it.

"What can I do for you, Mr President-in-waiting?" Jankovic asked, when the small-talk subsided.

Jankovic had lots of silver curls, a pink complexion—babylike, not a drinker's—and a set of lines round the eyes and mouth which produced an image of good nature. Only the eyes moved uncertainly at times.

Jankovic was a fighter for the underprivileged, born in Bethlehem, Pennsylvania, son of a Polish immigrant furnace worker.

"That may be jumping the gun a little, but it's nice to know I have your support, Sam."

"Until I die," Sam Jankovic said.

He was an emotional man, a ham actor, and his voice broke. "I owe my life to you, Jed. I acknowledge it. I'm not understating. You're a merciful man."

Jed Olsen moved his lips a little to show he was repelled, but never commented, and Jankovic would not have seen the reaction.

"Sam, I need your help."

"My Lord Jesus, if I can help you Jed. I ask nothing more than the chance."

★ ★ ★

A year ago it was Sam Jankovic who needed help. Jankovic, the trustee of a home for children with learning difficulties, St Catherine's in Allentown, Penn, approached Olsen as a trustee of the Olsen Trust. The Olsen Trust was one of the main donors to St Catherine's.

At first, Olsen thought Jankovic's wish to see him, and talk about

St Catherine's, was the usual begging bowl approach. There would be a new wing to be built, or a new gymnasium. Jed Olsen would hear Sam Jankovic out, and probably persuade the board of the Olsen Trust to make a grant.

But it was nothing like that.

Jankovic insisted on coming to New York, declined lunch, saying he was too sick at heart to eat it, and told Olsen the story.

The two men had walked in Central Park. Despite a chill in the air, there was enough sun. Soon, they ceased to notice the joggers, and buskers, and bums on benches.

Sam Jankovic was caught up in an investigation by the St Catherine's trustees. A complaint had been made by two parents about sexual abuse of their children.

Two members of staff had been investigated, and found to have falsified their employment applications, by failing to disclose previous convictions for offences involving children. They were summarily fired, but that still left wild allegations by the parents, about abuse of the children by unnamed *others*—not staff members, but so-called important people.

"It's spreading like gangrene, Jed—"

Olsen and Jankovic had been on speaking terms for years. They were members of the same party, but not friends. Why Jankovic should reveal this to him wasn't immediately clear. But he knew Jankovic's fuzzy, nice-old-man manner, concealed a cunning, life-time politician.

"You're involved personally, Sam?"

"I'm involved, Jed. I can't deny it."

"You mean you've been touching the children?"

"God help me, I have. I don't know what to do. I think my life is over."

"What do you want me to do? I mean, your trustees will investigate. Maybe they'll call in the police or the DA's office. I can't stop them."

"I don't know what you can do. I came to you because the Olsen Trust is a big supporter of the St Catherine's Home. I don't know whether you know my fellow trustees, but you're kinda towering above them. They depend on the Olsen Trust. Maybe you could talk to them, get some sense into this thing—"

"Isn't the investigation justified?"

"Sure it is. I deserve the gas chamber."

"What did you do?"

Jed Olsen didn't entirely believe in Jankovic the penitent. He waited while Jankovic with many holy incantations worked himself up to tell.

"I did bad things with two of the girls. About fourteen years old. Beautiful kids. Beautiful and affectionate. No moral sense or understanding at all. Just wanting to be cuddled."

"You fucked them? Raped is the correct legal word I suppose."

Olsen looked down on the bobbing silver head beside him, determined to have it out clearly.

"Yes, God help me. One of them is pregnant."

"Yours?"

"Not necessarily. Other people were involved too."

Jed Olsen was no stranger to depravity. He'd seen or heard most of it, although he was a straight up hetero himself, with no inclination toward young girls.

But he could understand Jankovic. Religious. With a sex life at home that had dried up. Attracted by the innocent and pure sexuality of a fourteen year old, who wasn't going to be judgemental about anything, who liked a nice, kind man who bought candies, and made nice feelings come in her.

It was hard to accept the utter fraudulence of this genial old man.

"Rape of a mentally retarded minor. You're in deep trouble, Sam. You could go away forever for this. At your age, you'd never come out."

"I'm dead. God forgive me!" Tears came to Jankovic's eyes.

They came out of Central Park opposite the Plaza Hotel.

"Let me buy you a drink, Sam. You look as though you need it."

When Jankovic refused, the two parted, but not before Jed Olsen patting Jankovic's arm in a brotherly way, said, "Leave the problem with me for a couple of days. I'll give it some thought, and call you."

Olsen felt no pity for Sam Jankovic. One part of him would have been pleased to see Jankovic fry in hell, but Jankovic could be useful. A trusty ally in the Senate was always worth having.

Jankovic served on a number of key committees. He was well regarded by the party, close to the President—whom Jed loathed—and had been an important fundraiser. Jankovic could be a mine of useful information, and perhaps a day would come when he could help Olsen.

Jed Olsen decided.

It took twenty or so telephone calls—about two or three hours of his time in all, and several hundred thousand dollars of Olsen Trust money.

The Olsen Trust paid for the services of a lawyer, to advise the trustees of St Catherine's. The lawyer pointed out to them that the evidence of identification of the perpetrators was weak, contradictory, and inconclusive.

He also advised that the courts would be reluctant to convict on the evidence of a mentally retarded child, without additional supporting evidence—and the supporting evidence was dubious—or the lawyer said it was.

The trustees of St Catherine's decided that the prejudicial effect of the inquiry on people of otherwise good reputation, outweighed any obligation to take the case further, but to avoid any lingering suspicion about practices, St Catherine's would be closed.

The children involved in the abuse complaints were sent to different homes, including the new Dorneyville House in Allentown, established by the Olsen Trust.

The trustees and most of the staff of St Catherine's, except Jankovic, and another as involved as he was, either joined the board of Dorneyville, or the staff.

Dorneyville House was superbly equipped in comparison to St Catherine's.

The parents felt justified that their complaints had closed the home, and it was some satisfaction that their daughters were now in new, secure and more comfortable surroundings.

Jed Olsen eventually came into possession of statements by the children, and other witnesses, copies of which he handed to Jankovic. Olsen had read them and they were nauseating.

"I'm afraid there's always the possibility that this could come back to haunt you Sam, but I don't think you ought to worry too much about it," Olsen had said.

He deliberately left the shadow of the sword of Damocles suspended over Jankovic's guilty, sin-racked head.

★ ★ ★

Sam Jankovic, seasoned operator that he was, knew that payback time would come round, and he was ready, even anxious, for it.

"Anything, Jed."

"I've talked to you before about Wayman, and I want to be sure the Committee nails him for corruption. You'll be there Sam, that's where you can help. One of my lawyers will get in touch with you, and take you through a line of questioning. A crucial part will be your own conversations with Wayman, about his donations to the

President's re-election fund."

"You want me to say he asked for assurances that he would get STELA 2?"

"Yeah. And that he had two generals in his pocket—Rollins and Skidelski."

"It could ruin them, Jed."

"Sam, understand me. I don't give a fuck about two, two-bit generals. I want Wayman skewered. Are you with me?"

"Sure, Jed, sure." Jankovic moved his curly head as though it was a lead weight.

"And the President's involvement. I want your help there."

"You want me to say the President knew what Wayman's price was?"

"Yeah. That's what you told me."

"It was kinda an implication, Jed—"

Jankovic halted and turned, looking up to the proud, burnished face of Jed Olsen. His voice was weak. "I have to say that, don't I?"

"Yes, Sam, you do."

Chapter 37

Hayden faced Wayman with Rosemary Delmer's story. He had a duty to tell his client. Wayman took the news with surprising calm, not attempting by gesture or interruption to show a reaction.

Hayden felt the irony of Wayman's remarks about Charlie Hayden, the unlucky man who got caught stealing. Perhaps Wayman himself was going to get caught doing something worse than stealing.

"Looks like we've got action on two fronts," Hayden said. "Olsen is planning to take you down at the Senate Committee, and perhaps score the STELA 2 contract himself, and somebody, I guess a foreign government, is buying your technology from your employees."

"As far as Olsen goes, these are lies, Mike," Wayman said calmly. "I made a campaign donation to the President, but there were no strings attached, and if Capel says there were it'll be on his word alone. There can't be any supporting papers."

"What about the Polack Senator. Can you identify him?"

"That can only be Sam Jankovic. I don't know why Sam would want to lie about me. I can understand Capel. He feels he's been screwed. Actually he's been highly promoted, too high. But he feels screwed. Jankovic I can't figure."

"And the generals?"

"OK, I entertained them. No money ever changed hands."

"The entertainment won't look good."

"I have to do business. I didn't do anything wrong. I think the generals attended a couple of company receptions. Nothing special, nothing personal ... I'm trying to think of the tie-up between Jankovic and Olsen. There has to be one—"

"Capel's perfidy doesn't surprise you?"

Wayman had an intense look, as though he was a doctor or a psychiatrist studying a patient.

"I shoulda taken more interest in the guy. Then maybe I woulda dropped to him. Capel's been pushed gently away from the big-time, because he ain't big-time, but he's able. Very smart. He's been useful. I guess he hurts. So he wants to get back at me. He thinks he's good, but he ain't as good as he thinks he is."

Hayden asked whether the disloyalty bothered him.

Wayman laughed. "Disloyalty? You think I expect the Capels to thank me? To salute me? Naah. There's money, power and pride. I gotta dish it outa the pot in the right proportions to every man jack in this outfit. I get the mix wrong for just one of them, I get a kick in the balls."

Chapter 38

Steve Reilly sat in his office area in the suite next to the laboratory occupied by Luchinelli and the STELA team. The secretaries and assistants who had work stations close by had gone home.

His palms were damp with sweat, and he had a cramped feeling in his chest. The task he was about to perform always brought out the symptoms of a physical illness.

He was waiting until he was sure Luchinelli, who had left a few minutes ago, was clear of the building. He told himself it was only necessary to keep clear-headed and calm. It was just after seven, and the lab was empty.

Reilly had been amazed at Laura's cool acceptance of what he was doing, and her uncomplicated enjoyment of the money. It cleared his mind, strengthened him. Her support made it a game he had to play, no mistakes allowed.

Reilly thought through what he had to do carefully.

The most secret development files on STELA were in a self-contained intranet computer system, in the secure laboratory. The laboratory was under surveillance by video cameras twenty-four hours a day.

The small intranet had PC monitors for Luchinelli, and each member of his top team. There was one spare PC, usually used by Reilly. He accessed the system to collate reports, assess costs, and monitor the progress of the components of the STELA master plan.

There was no way to hack into the system from outside, because there were no links to other systems, even if somebody knew the entry codes. The only way in, was to use one of the PCs in the lab. When Reilly occasionally did this, the entry was recorded. WayCom security required certification that all recorded entries were legitimate.

Reilly's first idea was to go into the laboratory at a time that wouldn't cause any concern, when Luchinelli and his closest associates weren't there, and there were few of the other seven or eight people present. A lunch break seemed the most obvious time. Luchinelli and his team were given to long wine-fuelled lunches at times, perhaps for three or four days in a row, when they weren't working sixteen hours a day and subsisting on carry-outs. But the room, Reilly noticed, was never entirely deserted at lunchtime, because some worked through at their desks, and others took flexible times.

He would have to use the unoccupied PC, copy a file, and erase his entry—the work of ten minutes, at the outside, on these powerful machines.

After that, all the evidence that would remain would be the videotape held by Security—if ever anybody got suspicious and looked at it. Reilly's presence at a PC in the lab was not open to question. The only concern he had was that somebody might suspect he was doing something beyond his normal duties.

Reilly was helped by one further event which arose from the eccentricities of the research team. For a long time there had been complaints at team meetings about the surveillance cameras. Up to now, Reilly had very reasonably pleaded the management view. But that had not stopped Luchinelli covering the cameras from time to time.

"I canna scratcha my balls in the offiz vizzout a security guard vatching," he complained.

The team all seemed to share this paranoia, and covering the cameras became a regular practice. Although Security complained, Luchinelli was unrepentant, and he was so important that Karen Bridges did not dare to disturb him.

After a while, Security stopped sending a guard up to the lab to ask why a particular camera had been covered.

For his first few forays into the secret files, Reilly took advantage of the covered cameras in the middle of the day. He was able to complete the operation successfully each time, although on the last occasion, Lucy Sherriff, one of the linguistic experts wandered back into the lab, sat down beside him, and asked him what he was doing.

She was entirely unsuspicious, and trying to be friendly. She thought Reilly was a doll.

He managed a smooth lie about monitoring progress. It was a dangerous moment. Lucy Sherriff was a clever woman, and she would remember their conversation in any subsequent investigation.

He then decided to try to work after normal work hours, with covered cameras. He could now cover them himself without Security getting alarmed or anybody in the team noticing.

Reilly keyed the code into the door pad, went through the security door to the main laboratory and seated himself before the spare PC.

The covers on the cameras which had been in place during the day were undisturbed. The virtual reality screens were dead. The lights were dimmed.

A succession of PCs on desks shaded off into greater shadow, some of the screens still live, showing the mobile introductory display, letters of the alphabet tumbling through space.

He knew the filing system well, and the daily and weekly passwords. He ran faultlessly through the sequence. Then he punched one of the key files in the program log, slipped a blank disk into the computer, and started to copy.

At the end he would have to go through an elaborate procedure with the machine to wipe out its record of the transaction.

The taping was completed in a few minutes. Then Reilly began the sequence to erase the entry. It was one of the special functions he had been at pains to learn.

He heard someone coming along the corridor. In the still building, footsteps clicked on the rubber floor tiles. He had to hurry.

His attention was diverted slightly, and he didn't notice that the cursor had stopped a line above his entry. He hit the delete button, and instead of wiping off his entry, wiped another.

There was a way of getting it back, but he stiffened in panic. He didn't have time to go through the retrieval procedure.

He switched the machine off, and retreated with the disk in his pocket, wondering how the mess would be interpreted tomorrow.

He waited behind one of the privacy screens which Luchinelli's team had arranged around their monitors, hoping the person would go to the other end of the L-shaped room and give him a chance to slip through the door.

From behind the screen, he watched the figure, trying to see who it was. There were only two or three spotlights on in the room, throwing direct light down on the desk beneath, leaving the rest of the room in shadow.

He made out a stately form, costumed in black, bending over the desk. And then the smell of hamburger and fries, and the crackle of the paper sack they were in.

It was Flora Stiegwitz. She was a short distance away, with her back to him.

He could reach her in a second, stun her from behind, and get out the door before she saw him. Inside his throbbing head it suddenly seemed the only possibility.

It *was* possible—and if he didn't act—the consequences were a pit of uncertainties, crawling like maggots. One sudden blow, hard enough to put her down.

He had almost started forward, when Flora straightened up, and turned towards him. She showed no sign of alarm.

"Hi, Steve, I didn't know you were around."

She popped a french-fry between her prominent teeth.

He hardly had the breath to reply. "You know, just checking—"

He suddenly had uncontrollable hands, and pulpy legs.

Flora snapped a main light switch on. "Gee, man. You don't look well. Got a chill or something?"

"No, I'm fine. Got to get away now. Don't work too late."

He fled through the security door.

★ ★ ★

Reilly couldn't sleep. It was the thought that he might have killed Flora Stiegwitz, the sheer madness of the idea.

He was no killer, and yet he had been ready to strike her down, would have struck her if she hadn't turned round. He sweated, agonised.

And something else had happened when he got home that he wanted to forget.

He and Laura had a drink and a light supper before they went to bed. It was about 11 o'clock, and Reilly liked to get to bed early, and get an early start in the morning. But before bed, he always checked though the mail—usually bills—and telephone messages on the answerphone.

On this night there were some routine calls about personal business, then a tear-croaky voice, and his finger recoiled from the play button.

A woman. *Please Steve call me at this number as soon as possible. I'll be waiting. It's 7 pm.*

The woman gave the number. It was Delia Marris. The desperate voice at the end of the line didn't move him at all. She was wanted for criminal offences. He cursed her, and felt a start of fear for his own safety.

While he was wiping the message tape, Laura had come into the study. She paused at the door. He felt uncomfortable, waiting for her to speak.

"Steve, I played the messages. Who was the girl wanting you to call her?"

"Somebody I've been dealing with in New York getting a quote on a finance package for supplies."

The half thought-out explanation came out glibly.

"Why call you at home in the evening?" Laura said, edgily.

"Because I *asked* her to call me here or at the office," Reilly snapped. "I want the goddam information in a hurry."

"Sounded kinda emotional, you know, personal," Laura persisted.

"Well it wasn't fucking personal!" Reilly shouted. "Do I have to submit to cross-examination about my calls? What in hell is needling you?"

The incident had passed uneasily between them. And if, as Reilly guessed, his line was bugged, Karen Bridges, or the FBI, would be on to him.

He didn't call Delia. He went to bed and struggled half the night with how he was going to explain the call to Karen Bridges or the FBI. He slept fitfully, and when in his dreams, he thought he had the answer, it dissolved.

Laura, disturbed by his restlessness, asked him at about 3 am if being a spy was getting to him. He was too proud to admit it was, and blamed the food in the company restaurant.

It was all right for Laura. For her, it was spend, spend, spend. The first payment had been enough to take care of their immediate debts. Reilly had warned her that the company checked up on free spending staffers, but Laura was having a ball.

★ ★ ★

At the office the next morning, although he felt his life was coming apart, all Reilly's defence systems were working clearly.

He hovered in the laboratory, waiting until Jimi Rudik, the most junior member of the team, was collating the computer access entries for the security report.

When he was sure Jimi had seen the problem, he interrupted, let Jimi explain it to him—a disappeared entry, and a new one last night. Reilly insisted on taking the problem over.

"I'll have a look at it, and complete the report to Security, Jimi. Leave it to me."

Jimi, a nerd who was sensitive about being allocated a junior administrative task, and bored with it, agreed readily.

Chapter 39

Hayden met Cathy Ong for breakfast at the Bowen. They had a quiet table overlooking the park, where they could plan their day.

Cathy was sipping tea and flicking through a pile of print-out, when Hayden arrived at seven. When she looked up at him, he thought her glance was particularly animated.

She pushed across a Stella report. "One of Stella's intercepts on the Reilly's home phone."

Hadyen read the paper. *Please Steve call me at this number as soon as possible. I'll be waiting. It's 7 pm.*

"Reilly? Shit! Where's the number? Do we know?"

"A bar at a place called Thunder River in the Adirondacks. I also have a tape of the voice," Cathy said.

"Thunder River. Thunder Lake. It's where we got a sighting of Mariette," Hayden said, feeling a sudden and painful stirring.

Cathy slipped the tape into a small portable player, and a plaintive, trembling, female voice emerged from the static.

"It's Delia. Stella identified the voiceprint. The location makes sense. Hiding out for a while. Maybe waiting for somebody to get her out of the country. Feels distressed. Calls a friend," Cathy said.

"What sort of a friend?" Hayden asked.

"Well, it doesn't sound like a business call, so—"

Hayden gave a cynical smile. "Lovers or fellow spies, or both."

A check on Reilly's background had already revealed his financial problems. He was behind in the mortgage payments on his house, his lakeside cabin, and his boat. Both Gerstein and Hayden thought this might make Reilly vulnerable to approaches, but they considered he was too new a recruit to have got into espionage—although they didn't rule out entirely the fact that he might be a plant.

Hayden thought the odds were against Reilly being a plant. His meeting with Reilly had suggested he was dealing with a dedicated, and rather selfish man whose career was his main interest in life.

"I don't see Reilly doing anything to besmirch his shining curriculum vitae," Hayden said.

"But there's just one thing," Cathy argued. "We have the accounts for Delia's cellphone, and her home phone. And of all the numbers she ever rang, Reilly's is the most frequent."

"She had legitimate business reasons to talk to him at one time," Hayden said.

"Sure. That might account for the office line. But why so many calls from her cellphone and her personal phone? I'm talking about maybe ten calls in the two weeks before her break. And I've checked on their official business. Actually very little. Some, yes. But Delia was a number cruncher in Finance, and he is coordinator of the whole project."

"They were probably lovers, but the theory could be they were working together? Uh-huh." Hayden dwelt on it.

"I guess we should turn this over to the FBI and the police immediately—and Karen Bridges," Cathy Ong said.

"Al Gerstein will have the Stella report. Karen will already know," Hayden said. "She's bound to be monitoring the line too. I'd like to go to Thunder River and try to locate Delia, before she gets buried in law enforcement procedures. I need to see her on her own, try to get a line on who's behind her."

Hayden was also thinking that it would be a step nearer Mariette.

"You'll have to take Karen. She's effectively your client," Cathy said. "Will Al agree to you going ahead?"

"I shouldn't think so."

"You could just go. I could ring Al after you've got a start."

"I value Al's help more than that, and I sure as hell won't get it if I bolt after Delia."

★ ★ ★

As Hayden predicted, Al Gerstein warned Hayden about obstructing access to a wanted felon, but grudgingly agreed that Hayden and Karen could leave for Thunder River first, provided they took no initiatives, and handed over to him when he arrived.

While Hayden was waiting in Karen Bridges' office for her to clear her desk for the journey, he took a call from Wayman. The mogul was buoyant: "I got some friends of mine to have a look at Jankovic. About a year ago. Sex inquiry at a kids' home. Very bad. Allentown. Interstate issues. FBI were involved. Get Gerstein to show you the file. And call Barney Sefton in Allentown. Rosemary has the number. Olsen baled Jankovic out."

Hayden chewed on this while he waited. It was almost unthinkable that Olsen was setting up the evidence for the Senate Committee hearing. But Wayman seemed to assume this as a matter of course. If Olsen was pressuring Jankovic to give false evidence, things were dangerously haywire, and Hayden thought he'd talk it over with a pal in the Justice Department and get some ideas on how to handle it.

Hayden and Karen Bridges left Syracuse within a half hour. Karen Bridges supplied the wheels, a Caddy Fleetwood from the car pool.

As soon as they were on the road, and Karen was manoeuvring through the city traffic, she said: "You don't have to do this, Mike. You're doing it for Mariette, aren't you?"

He looked at her after a moment, and moved his head slightly to agree.

She drove expertly. Mike Hayden lounged beside her, and when they cleared the city and suburbs, watched the dark area of pine forests and lakes unreel before them.

Instead of stopping for lunch they had a coffee and donut carryout from a diner. They didn't talk about *the* case. They talked about other cases—Karen's with the FBI. Some of Hayden's. In the intimacy of the car, their exchange of experiences warmed up their emotions almost to the point they were at when they had dinner at Oswego's.

The drive took four hours east up Interstate 90, then through to Boonville on 46, and climbing up 28 and 30 past Tupper Lake.

Karen stopped at the Four Seasons motel five miles outside Thunder River. They decided to check in. There wasn't much accommodation in Thunder River, and it was less conspicuous to stay out of town. They would need the evening, and at least the next morning to locate Delia. The motel stood alone on high ground above the road, surrounded by trees. It was spacious and newly decorated, catering for the hunting crowd.

Hayden looked at his watch. It was 3 pm. "I reckon Gerstein will be a couple of hours behind, so we better use our time well."

Karen came by Hayden's room to collect him for their visit to the town. He was getting his gear out of his weekend bag. She came into the room through the open door without knocking.

"Hey, this is better than I imagined. I was expecting the Bates Motel Mark 2," she said, approaching behind him, and slipping her arms around his waist.

To Hayden, it was the most natural move in the world, what their closeness in the car had inspired. He put his hands on hers, and then turned to face her, and press his mouth against hers. She melted.

"We better get to business," he said, pulling away regretfully.

She was disappointed, but sensible. "Sure."

The wild flutter of her eyes, and her quickness of breath told him that he wouldn't be able to resist her tonight, didn't want to.

★ ★ ★

Thunder River, they found, wasn't so much a town as a logging centre. It was at the crossroads of three deep slashes in the forest, along which the cut logs were drawn by tractor, to a lumberyard, and loaded on to trailer trucks. Where the main road passed the lumberyard, it was stained for hundreds of yards with nicotine coloured dirt, ground into the blacktop by the rigs.

Alongside the yard, was a windowless shed with a neon sign saying *Bar*. Beside the bar, was a restaurant with broken slat-blinds, advertising pizzas. There was a scatter of other anonymous sheds, and a few cabins set back in the trees. The pine hills around threw the area into blue-black shadow on this afternoon. The place was deserted.

Karen took the Caddy slowly through the metropolis and parked down and off the road at Hayden's suggestion.

"You mean we're going to walk back through all that shit to the bar? What about my shoes?"

Hayden looked down at her virgin white Reebocks. Karen was also wearing jeans, and a blue anorak over a plaid shirt. A dark velvet band held her auburn hair down.

"What do you want to use those shoes for, shopping at Bloomingdale's? Karen, this is how I think we should play it unless you have a better idea. We're married, and we're looking for your sister, who's had a breakdown, and run away."

Karen was amused. "Married, huh? Where's my diamond engagement ring, my eternity ring, my wedding band?"

"Take the ring you've got on your right hand, put it on your left, and turn it round."

"Enterprising and economical. All right, husband, come on."

She arranged the ring, linked her arm in his when they were out of the car, and they walked up the road to the bar. Before they went in, she stopped him. "Hey, wait a minute—our marriage hasn't been consummated."

Hayden said, "It can be done later. Consummation is retrospective."

"I'll hold you to that," she said.

Inside, it took a few moments to discern anything in the gloom. And there was a smell of sawdust, and beer, and dank tobacco, and woodsmoke.

"Jesus," Karen breathed, "it's just like the Ritz."

A few brooding faces were eventually lit up, like Halloween pumpkins with near burnt-out candles. Three men swayed over the pyramid of light on a distant pool table.

The bulky bartender steered toward their end of the bar table. Hayden ordered a couple of Pabst Blue Ribbons, told their story when the bartender served them, and flashed a photo of Delia.

The bartender showed more interest in them than the photo. Who was this city suit, and the doll in tight-assed jeans? His small eyes weighed their story up, and found it wanting. No, he couldn't assist.

"Too bad," Hayden said. "I have a hundred bucks for anybody who can give my wife and I any genuine help."

An electrode behind the barman's eyes energised. "Your wife's sister, you said? Tough when it's family."

He was watching Hayden slip out a leather notecase, and extract a hundred dollar bill. Hayden flattened the bill on the counter, and began to slide it toward the barman without taking his fingers off.

The barman's eyes followed the movement. "Why don't you try Ryker's cabin, past Logan's Yard. There's a young kid stayin' there some days now, lookin' a bitty like the shot you showed me. Lookin' mighty lost too. I seen her in the pizza parlour—the wife works there. That's where the kid eats."

The barman didn't usually make a hundred that easily, and he disappeared the note instantly when Hayden's fingers released it.

When Hayden and Karen were outside the bar, Karen said: "You make it seem easy Detective Hayden. How long have you had your gold star?"

"It wasn't a long shot. If you're not a hunter or a shooter or a logger you stick out in a place like this. I bet a number of people around here have noticed Delia."

"What's the next move, Captain? Will we take Ryker's cabin by storm, or shall I call up a police chopper, and a SWAT unit?"

"Very funny. Let's find the cabin now. In half an hour we could be talking to Delia," Hayden said.

"While poor Al is mobilising the mighty FBI."

"I'm a bit worried how he's going to take this," Hayden said.

"Think about it tomorrow. If we can talk to Delia, it'll be our first real lead."

They walked past Logan's Yard, inactive, with its rusty dozers and cranes reigning over a graveyard of torn logs. Beyond the yard, half a dozen damp cabins crouched in the pines.

Hayden and Karen were approaching the cabins when a mud spattered black sedan drew up behind them, a door opened, and Gerstein appeared in a dark blue windcheater.

"Thought I better see how you guys were progressing. Any news?" he said.

Hayden looked at the car, laden with men, and told Gerstein about Ryker's cabin.

Gerstein ordered his men to stay put in the car, and walked with Hayden and Karen to examine the exterior of the cabins. No names on the doors. The mailboxes on the road had numbers. The cabins looked deserted, although probably earlier in the year there were plenty of vacationers to fill them. One had the rusty, wheelless shell of a seventies Chevvy in front.

"We better knock on a few doors," Karen said, and they moved past the car hulk toward the door of the cabin.

The dog came from behind the cabin with a deep throaty yelp that make Hayden realise it was big before he saw it.

Very big. A German shepherd, crossbred with a species with high shoulders, possibly a Doberman. The dog lunged at them, barking hysterically, its nose drawn back over open rows of teeth.

Hayden snatched up one of the small planks of timber rotting on the ground, and attempted to hold the animal off. Its jaws were flecked with foam. The three of them had no option in the onslaught but to back up on the porch of the cabin.

Hayden kept Karen and Gerstein behind him. But he soon realised that the fury and energy of the dog was going to beat him. The dog danced from side to side, always moving in, its mouth like a bear trap. Blows from the plank of wood missed or had no effect.

Then he heard Gerstein say *Screw this*, and there were two quick explosions in his right ear, blasting him sideways. The dog let out a shrill sound, and nose-dived into the dirt, twitching, blood pouring from a huge hole beneath one of the wild eyes.

"For fuck's sake!" Hayden shouted.

"That feller was asking for a couple of Hydra-Shok hollow points," Gerstein said.

In the instant of silence, he patted the blue Smith & Wesson 38 in his hand. "Never go anywhere without it."

Hayden sat on the porch and looked at the dog, venom still pulsing in death.

"We're really up the creek now. People will be around in a minute.

Chances are that Delia will get a whiff that something is going on, and bolt—"

"Somethin' I kin do for y'?"

A wide shouldered man came swaying across the grass, close cropped silver hair, mirror shades over a red swollen face, oilskin jacket and logger's boots.

Hayden said they were attacked. "Whose dog is it? "

The man didn't seem concerned about the dog. Touched it with the toe of his boot.

"Kept tellin' him to tie the bastard up. Yeah, I know the guy. He ain't about now. Back maybe seven tonight. Name of Powers. Lives right here." He pointed at the cabin.

"OK, we'll come back later and make our peace," Gerstein said. "We're in a hurry, and we're looking for Ryker's cabin. You know it? It's one of these."

"Ryker? Sure. Come here."

He walked to the side of Power's cabin and pointed down a path through the trees. "Right along there to the end, and maybe a further hundred yards on the left. Can't miss it. Got this old tractor in front."

Gerstein called up his men on the hand-radio, telling Hayden and Karen he was going to stake out the cabin, and they better stay out of it.

Hayden and Karen walked back to the main road.

"Al's doing this the wrong way. He's scaring the girl and her minder off," Hayden said.

"Patience, Mike. The FBI have their ways."

They kicked the mud off their shoes on the blacktop, and Karen complained about the brown stains on her trainers. They huddled for a while in the damp cold air with the pines bending around them.

A fusillade of shots cracked in the silence.

"Let's go see," Hayden said.

The FBI men had entered the cabin with the rusted tractor in front.

"Goddam place is empty" Gerstein announced from the porch, as Hayden and Karen approached. "Doesn't look as though it's been used."

"You got the wrong place, Al. Delia & Co will have bolted," Hayden said.

"Another day, another dollar" Gerstein said carelessly. "I'll go back and talk to the guy at the bar myself."

He led his men back to the car.

Hayden and Karen started back along the path toward the cabin where they had encountered the dog.

"Ryker's cabin wasn't where the bartender said, was it?" Hayden said.

"Let's make sure," Karen said. "After all, you paid a c note."

They walked about a hundred yards, and saw an old woman coming cautiously down the steps of one of the cabins that were linked to the path. She was swaddled up in a long brown coat and headscarf, only her dry-walnut face visible. Hayden asked her where Ryker's cabin was.

She took a long look at them. "You're goin' the right way. Ryker's is back there on the rise."

"Can you tell us which? There are half a dozen places up there, no names, only numbers," Hayden said.

The old woman thought about this. "Ryker's a junkman, see? Boilers, refrigerators, mowers—junk. All around. Y' can't miss."

"You're sure? Because a guy said Ryker's was down here." He pointed toward the cabin the FBI had forced.

The old lady's chin went up with annoyance. "Cain't be too sure. I only lived here sixty years."

"Is there an old car out front?" Karen asked.

"I remember rightly, there is."

"And he has a dog, very fierce?" Karen added.

"No dawg." She rasped a small laugh. "Too goddam mean t' feed a dawg."

"Let's get back there," Hayden said.

They thanked the woman and jogged back up the path. "What do you think?" he asked.

Karen was running easily alongside him. "The guy gave us a bum steer because he was Delia's minder, and the dog was probably his. He was buying himself a bit of time to get Delia away. Probably thought we were Feds."

"Yeah. That's about how I read it. A real cool man to pull that one," Hayden said.

When they reached the back of Ryker's cabin, they noticed, as the old lady had said, it was a litter of rusting scrap metal parts. The cabin looked as closed and deserted as it had when they first approached. They went on to the back porch and listened.

"Can't hear anything," Karen whispered.

It was no use trying to look through the windows; they were covered with filthy muslin.

"Do we call Al?" Karen asked.

"We didn't come here to wank around," Hayden said. "You go round the front. I'm going to knock first, and if there's no response, break the door open."

Hayden reckoned the dry, warped frame would yield to a kick.

"OK. Be careful. That guy is probably one smart operator," Karen said, and went around to the front.

Hayden hit the door, which was locked, hard with his fist, and shouted. Then he listened for a moment. Complete silence, other than the soughing of the pines.

He stepped back and launched a flat-footed kick against the door which had almost his whole weight behind it.

The door burst open, and he was propelled into the kitchen space by the force of his own charge. He had to take a few seconds to accustom himself to the shadow. Nothing stirred, except Karen, who had left the front of the shack, entering behind him, a gleaming Sig-Sauer.30 glinting in her fist.

Hayden worked out the plan of the cabin quickly. A kitchen opening to a living space with a table and chairs, and three rooms to the side with closed doors—the bunkrooms and bathroom. He could see into the living space from where he stood. It was deserted. The rooms were sparsely furnished but tidy. The kitchen smelt of soap.

"They've gone," Karen whispered.

"Could have disappeared into the pines for a while."

"There's nothing personal around," Karen said, and Hayden picked up that the place had been swept and tidied.

Hayden walked on the creaking boards and cautiously opened the bathroom door, then the first bunkroom. Four bunks, one with a riffled bed cover, but no personal possessions.

Karen went for the other bunkroom, gun first. Hayden heard her cry, and rushed in after her. The blinds were drawn, but there was enough light to see a large open suitcase on the floor, folded clothes on a dresser, and a double bed. On the bed, a woman's figure, in slacks and sweater, face-down.

Karen pulled back the curtains, and Hayden raised the woman's shoulder.

The way she was collapsed into the mattress with her face buried made her seem lifeless.

Hayden had the sudden fear that this was Mariette. He had a glimpse of the white cheeks and staring dark eyes as he lifted. Her skin was warm on his hand.

"Look," Karen said, pointing to the back of the woman's neck.

The hair was sticky with glistening blood, not immediately noticeable against the darkness of her hair.

"Better leave her for the techs. There's nothing we can do," Karen said, as Hayden relaxed his grip and the lifeless form slumped into the bedclothes.

"It's Delia all right. She must have been killed while Al was messing around trying to imitate Waco," Hayden said.

"Executed is the word. One neat shot to the back of the neck," Karen said.

★ ★ ★

Hayden called Gerstein on his cellphone, and he and Karen searched the cabin. The rooms had been cleaned, and Delia was packing to leave. From soft cigar butts in the trashcan, and an empty bourbon bottle in the other bunkroom, they concluded that there had been a man there, probably overnight. There were no fresh car tracks in the mud outside. Empty Fido cans in the trash suggested the dog had been with the man.

Gerstein arrived with the local sheriff's deputies, and Hayden and Karen made their statements. The sheriff's officers seemed relieved the death concerned a girl from outside the county, and involved the FBI. Hayden and Karen went back to the motel.

The discovery of Delia's body had cooled the ardour that had been building between them. They ordered steak and fries in the dining room, but left their plates largely untouched, and sat in the bar afterwards in front of two whiskey and sodas.

"I think Al's hamfisted approach, gunning down the dog, and then taking a half-hour out for a set piece siege triggered Delia's death," Hayden said.

Karen was inclined to agree. "She was warm. She'd just been shot. Maybe the guy figured the chances of getting her away were limited, and he decided to shut her up. Or maybe he went there to kill her, we interrupted, and he bought the time to finish the job."

It was nearly 9 pm when Al Gerstein walked in. He did not look happy. "You guys shoulda called me before you hit that cabin."

"Yeah? Well you fucked up, Al. She was one exposed female, and she won't be having words with anybody."

"Hey, it's an even chance that by the time we arrived, nobody could have saved her," Gerstein insisted.

"That's an even chance we might have saved her if we'd moved quietly and more quickly!" Hayden said, showing his distaste.

Gerstein was angry at having his methods questioned, and he took the offensive, pointing a blunt, tobacco-stained forefinger at them.

"Don't get in the way, however important you think WayCom is. The court will come down on you like a hammer."

Chapter 40

The High Trees Golf Club near Syracuse, NY was one of the finest championship courses in the country, designed by Arnold Palmer. It was also a very exclusive establishment, open only to those approved by the ten person members' committee.

High Trees had much the same nomination procedure as other clubs, but final approval rested with the committee in a secret vote, in which one black ball would end the applicant's chances forever.

The members tended to be senior business and professional people, because the annual fees were high, but there were no religious or racial barriers to entry, and both men and women were admitted as full members. High Trees regarded itself as a liberal establishment.

Jed Olsen liked the club. It was a place where he could reckon on meeting influential local people. An afternoon there was never spent merely on sport; there was always the satisfaction that he had either learned something useful, or moved his own interests forward. You couldn't go there without meeting a sprinkling of the most prominent politicians and business people in the area.

Byron Cerillo accepted Jed Olsen's invitation to join him at High Trees for the day with satisfaction. Although it was not part of his world, on the pay of a government servant, Cerillo loved the sense of richness that enclosed him from the moment he drove through the gates and up the drive to the clubhouse.

It was a vast and beautifully manicured estate, blooming in season with honeysuckle, camellias and rhododendrons of all colours. There were artificial lakes reflecting the artful bridges that crossed them, stands of oak and larch and maple and ash that seemed to have been arranged to complement the variety of the species, like mixed flowers in a vase. The effect, on a huge scale, was like a Chinese pleasure garden.

Although Byron Cerillo had a penetrating mind, and understood the theory of golf—the movements of the swing, the various positions of the hands and feet, the functions of all the clubs, better than most, he was not a steady player, barely able to keep to his official handicap of eighteen. He had come to golf late in life.

Jed Olsen was just the reverse. He had played as a boy. He had his own style. The skill had never left him. He could go out one day a month and play his grooved game to plus four.

He played half a dozen holes with Cerillo, gave Cerillo a stroke a hole, sometimes two, and thrashed him soundly. Cerillo usually didn't bother to putt out. At last, Jed, bored, suggested they should go and watch the demonstration game, and Cerillo, crimson with embarrassment under his olive skin, hastily agreed.

The exhibition match between two pairs, Tiger Woods and Mark O'Meara, and Fred Couples and David Duval, was an exclusive private showing for a gallery of the great and the good of about two hundred. Olsen and Cerillo followed the players in the chilly sun for half a dozen holes, watching some of the finest golf in the world, and then retired to the glassed in club terrace to drink long gin and limes under the yellow awning, free from the bite of the weather.

"How is the WayCom case, Byron?"

"The reports I have from our investigating team indicate gross overcharging, probably amounting to fraud."

"Do you have evidence of dishonesty?"

"Not specifically, only gross behaviour."

"And the security breaches?"

"They're very serious of course. I don't have a final report on them, but what I do have indicates that WayCom haven't followed the procedures—"

"Good. And I have two people who will testify to Wayman soliciting the contract for payment."

"That should about clinch it as far as the Committee is concerned. The NSA position will be that we propose to terminate dealings with WayCom."

"And Fairford will I think be the only possible contender who can take over. Very satisfactory. You've done well, Byron."

"I think I've only acted in the national interest, Jed," Cerillo said, righteously.

Jed Olsen shot him a critical glance, and covered the derisive curl of his mouth with his hand.

He changed the subject. "High Trees is looking wonderful, isn't it, even at the fag end of the season?"

"It's a fairyland. Jed, I was thinking how good one feels here, how far away from the cares of the world—"

"Yeah. It's not a place I'd want to share with everybody. I hold no bar to persons of any race and creed belonging here—provided he or she can pay the dues, but there are some specific people I don't want to see on the tee, or have to stand next to in the club bar. The nice thing about High Trees is that one can decide. It was one of the pleasantest days of my life, Byron, when I rolled that little black ball into the slot on Vance Wayman's application. Look around here, Byron. Beautiful. You won't ever see that shitbird Wayman."

Chapter 41

On Saturday morning, when Steve Reilly was getting ready to go to the office at about ten, he heard a scrunch on the gravel outside. He looked out the upstairs window to see a white Olds with Hayden at the wheel. Hayden sprang out and ran up the front steps.

Reilly calmed himself, looked in the mirror and put on a resolute face, and then went downstairs. He was in a light coloured sports jacket, open shirt and jeans—uniform for Saturday at work.

Hayden, admitted by Laura, was perched on a bar stool, sipping a tall glass of orange juice. Laura was arranging the toast and coffee on the kitchen table.

"Mr Hayden says he wants to ask you about that call on the ansafone, Steve." Laura looked taut.

Reilly frowned. "Which call?"

Both Hayden and Laura had been expecting a smarter response, and their faces showed it.

"You know which call," Laura said in a low, trembling voice.

"The one from Delia Marris, Steve, at 7 pm two days ago. We've identified the voice. We know where the call originated." Hayden too was very quiet.

The pony in the field next door nickered.

Reilly tried a different tack. "Look, we can talk in the car. Or maybe after work. Right now I have a meeting at the office, and I'm late." He made a move to go.

"That's bullshit, Steve," Laura said.

"I would have thought you'd support me, Laura," Reilly said peevishly.

"I think it would be better if you stayed, and answered a few questions. It's easier with your wife here. If I have to talk to her on her own, I may only get half the story."

Steve Reilly checked himself at the door, came back and sat down at the table, pushing his untouched breakfast plate away. In just the time it had taken him to cross the floor he realised how unwise it would be to walk out. He was going to have to field some very hard balls, but he could do it.

"OK, so it was a call from Delia Marris. So what? She's gone on the run. She calls a colleague at the office. I guess she wanted help. I don't know. I never tried to call her back."

"You lied to me," Laura said flatly. "What was it you said? A business call from New York about software?"

"I didn't want to worry you with the thought that Delia Marris might be asking me for help," Reilly said smoothly.

Laura sniffed, and turned her attention to Hayden.

He appeared to accept. "Sure," he said. "I can understand Delia might want to call a colleague. But you told me she wasn't any sort of special friend of yours. She wasn't a working colleague. You were very senior to her, and in another department."

Reilly shrugged, trying to think of a way he could insist that Laura shouldn't be a party to this conversation.

"I knew her. So what? I think we talked about common experiences at Mitsuko. I can't control who she rings. Look, this is an office matter. I resent you coming here and bringing things into my home."

Laura looked suspicious, watching the ball batted between the two men. She said it was better they all talked together. Her face was pale, still. "I want you to talk here."

"And you don't have any right to talk to me, Hayden. I don't *have* to answer your questions," Reilly persisted.

"It's true, you don't have to answer me. But I'm working for your employer. I have your employer's permission to speak to you, and if you refuse, I'll let WayCom know, and refer it to the FBI. You'll have to talk to them."

"Steve, don't be so pig-headed. I want us to talk together, *now, here*," Laura insisted shrilly.

Reilly was at war in his chest, but unable to give a sign. He thought that Laura, spurred by petty jealousy, was disregarding the risk she must know *he* himself was taking in selling information. She wasn't covering for him like a good wife.

"OK," Hayden said after a silence, judging that Laura had prevailed. "Perhaps, Steve, you can explain to me all the calls to you from Delia's apartment and her cellphone before she ran away. Calls to the office, and here."

"Oh, Steve—" Laura's reaction was instinctive, her voice burred by the weight of infidelity uncovered.

"Yes, she called me about business," Reilly said, toughing it out, but feeling his defences crumbling.

"Steve," Hayden said gently, "this is a woman you've denied knowing. We're talking about maybe ten or fifteen calls in her last two weeks. You never had any business with her that would justify that many calls from her apartment."

"Oh, for Christ's sake own up to it, Steve. You were screwing her, you bastard!" Laura unleashed her fury.

There was another long moment of silence in the room. Reilly looked from Hayden's slightly impatient interrogation to his wife's almost uncontainable rage and pain. His lips twitched. He was cornered.

His eyes became damp, not with remorse, but with bitter disappointment at having been caught out. He hated himself for an instant. But he thought quickly. A passing sexual involvement was a minor offence, and nothing to do with his employment.

"Yes. I admit it. It was nothing. She meant nothing to me. I met her on only a couple of occasions, and she got a fix on me. Called me all the time. It was awful. She was lonely and unsure of herself after Mitsuko. And I was a kind of link with Mitsuko. I was doing what I could to put her off. I was worried and overworking. I made a hell of a mistake. It was all over before she ran out."

Hayden swallowed as though the explanation was indigestible. "Steve, it looks as though you were helping her with her espionage activities—"

Reilly cut Hayden off sharply. "No, I wasn't! I categorically deny it. I never had the slightest idea what she was up to. I was just afraid that the FBI would connect me because of the affair. That's why I tried to conceal it."

Laura Reilly sobbed, and then got up, and went silently upstairs.

Hayden assessed his target. He wondered whether at last he'd got the truth from Steve Reilly.

Reilly watched the lawyer, wondering whether he had said enough. The thought that his own activities might be fully uncovered sent chills through him. He had too much to lose to tell Hayden the whole truth. If he was going to go down, Hayden and the FBI would have to drag him down inch by inch.

"Look, Hayden, I'll probably lose my job if WayCom find out about this. They'll *assume* I could have been involved in espionage, and they'll drop me. Guilt by association. Unless you say that you believe me," Reilly pleaded.

"I don't want to make your life any more unpleasant than it

already is, Steve. I'll make my report of your explanation. It's up to WayCom to believe you. By the way, Delia is dead. She was murdered yesterday. She kept tough company."

★ ★ ★

Steve Reilly worked at his desk until he heard Luchinelli leave the laboratory at half past nine, the last to go. He was hungry, but on these nights, his stomach was in a knot, and he suffered the pangs rather than eat.

The call from Delia had put him in peril. He was suspected, and in danger of being discovered, but if he didn't go on divulging information to that icy bitch, she would rat on him to WayCom and he would be finished anyway. He *had* to devise a way to finish with her.

Luchinelli shambled past his door.

"Donna overdo it, Steve."

Luchinelli had a file of papers under his arm. He took secret documents in and out of the office without question. "I tink we haff nearly arrived. Soon. Three months maybe."

"Great, Gino. I have all the staff in place waiting for your test runs. Better early than late."

"Very efficient, Steve. Since you come, we go faster. Now I go for a leetle Barolo and pasta. You want to join me?"

"I have a schedule to finish, Gino."

"What about the Marris woman, Steve? I hear she's dead. The papers donna say much. Death in suspeecious circumstances."

"It's a national security blackout, Gino. There won't be much in the press."

"What do you teenk happened?"

"I don't know. Maybe she was killed to shut her up."

Luchinelli's bulging eyes shone. "Eet's a dangerous world out there."

"You should have more personal protection, Gino. Like Karen offered."

"Perhaps, perhaps. Already I have Karen Bridges' dogs sniffing my ass day and night. I can't go anywhere weethout being watched."

"Just so long as they are Karen's dogs."

Luchinelli was suddenly cast down, and he grunted, and moved away down the hall. Both he and Flora Stiegwitz had repeatedly refused to have a personal bodyguard.

Reilly waited for another fifteen minutes, and then pulled on a pair of latex gloves, dimmed the light in his office, and punched his way into the lab.

He had carefully checked a few hours before that the covers were over the two video cameras which would record him in this section of the room, a McDonald's sack over one, and an old sweater of Luchinelli's over the other. Luchinelli had not disturbed them.

He quickly slid into a seat in front of the spare PC, switched on, and booted up the main STELA programme. He ran his eye down the file menu, and selected the third in a long list of programming files. The other two files he had already copied and delivered to the Ice Maiden.

He had only a hazy idea of what he was stealing, although he knew it to be of great value. These files contained the data from which the main software for STELA would be written. They were like background papers—the "how" of it.

It was Reilly's intention to work through the entire menu. Already, the Ice Maiden had shown the urgency of her need, and pressed him to proceed quickly.

He had toyed with the idea of passing material that was useless, but it had quickly become apparent to him that the woman, or her bosses, appreciated very quickly whether any material was valueless. He couldn't afford to frustrate or anger her. Bray. Leman. Delia. His mind could hardly grasp the significance of this chain of death, and its links to him.

He taped two files in the stillness of the lab, and quickly went through the procedure of eliminating the record of his entry. As he switched off, and slipped the disks in his breast pocket, he became aware of a sound, close, that had been masked by the low hum of the computer. It was a person, he was sure of it. He cut the lights and waited in the dark.

The noise had come from outside the door. Somebody was coming in. It was a rerun of the scene with Stiegwitz. It could probably be her again. Or Luchinelli. He had to silence whoever it was, and get out unseen. Or he might bluff his way out.

He had a number of reasons for accessing the computer. No, he couldn't bluff. He was sitting in the dark. An innocent man wouldn't be sitting in the dark in a top-secret lab late at night! And it was too late to change now—the door was opening.

Reilly felt physically ill, and the sweat poured off his forehead. His hands were wet inside the latex. His career reeled before him in a minisecond—the striving for top marks at UCLA, the slaving to produce his doctorate, the swift corporate moves that took him near to the top of the executive tree, the pride in his own intelligence and brilliance: all that splintered and smashed.

Reilly moved quickly in the dark to the most distant part of the L-shaped room. He had to hope that the person wouldn't explore the far end. He scuttled like a rat, cringed down behind a desk. His confidence, ever since he was a kid, in his ability to be a move ahead of anybody pitted against him, was gone. It had been an illusion.

The razor sharp Steve Reilly was grovelling on the floor, with his career and his freedom in issue. Despair rose up in him like sewer water in a gutter.

The intruder had switched a small spotlight on near the door, and now moved down the room in the shadows. He or she didn't seem to be bent on business, only on watching and listening. The person moved slowly. Suspiciously. Reilly could see the figure. Too big for a woman. It was Security.

He nerved himself for what he had to do—get to the man unseen, knock him cold, and get out. His fingers closed on the weapon he had brought just in case this happened—a paperweight in Danish glass enclosing a tiny rose, and shaped like a ball, half the size of his fist, and heavy.

The figure came closer, and then turned slightly. Now would be the moment, but Reilly was crushed behind the desk. Reilly eased himself to a position where he could spring up. He tightened on the paperweight in his hand. He had to hit hard, but not too hard. Images came up in his mind with horrifying speed. A smashed skull. A murder trial.

The man turned away, still listening. Steve Reilly unleashed himself, and sprang forward, powerful thigh and calf muscles driving him. He swung the paperweight.

But in the instant, the intruder sensed a presence and swung back. Reilly's blow with the paperweight crashed on the man's shoulder, and there was a gasp of pain.

Before Reilly could strike again, the man had his wrist. They stumbled together in the darkness. Reilly struck a series of chops with the back of his free hand to the throat and neck.

The man's fingers clasped Reilly's throat, and Reilly broke them away with the strength of desperation. He could win and he would.

The man stumbled back, Reilly on top of him, pinning the man's arms with his knees, and raising the paperweight blindly to hammer it down on the upturned face.

Fear and blood-rage coursed through Reilly, the desire to pound the man into insensibility.

But he stopped. An anticipation, as vivid as reality, of the smell of blood and death stopped him, a stench too evil to bear. He leaped away and made for the open door.

The man, very fast, was on him. From behind. Tripping him in a football tackle. Bringing him crashing to the floor.

The paperweight rolled out of Reilly's hand. The man's knees jabbed into his spine. The man's shoulder weight bore down on Reilly's neck, pinioned him to the floor, crushing his lips into the rubber flooring.

"Reilly, you motherfucker!"

Reilly's worst fear started at the voice, and the aura of tobacco. Gerstein.

★ ★ ★

It was 9 am. The three men and Cathy Ong sat around the table in the sharp artificial light of one of WayCom's anonymous meeting rooms. Hayden, Gerstein, who was rubbing his shoulder reflectively and had an abrasion on one cheekbone covered with a plaster, and Reilly. Reilly had a crisp white shirt on, his bright tie well knotted, and his hair immaculately combed.

Gerstein played with the two disks he had taken from Reilly the night before. Reilly had chickened out of killing him. Gerstein had no doubt that Reilly *could* have killed him. He fingered the paperweight in his free hand. It was lethal.

"You've got some explaining to do," Gerstein said in a deep tarry tone.

Reilly's quick brain had already scrambled through the possibilities of saving himself, of glossing the story in some way that would put him in the clear. He could say he was coming out of the lab, and thought Gerstein was the spy, so he tackled.

But if Gerstein checked on the disks, and he would, he would find they were unauthorised copies, and unregistered on the access list. Reilly could say he found the disks—the spy had made copies, and put them aside to be collected later. But then there were the latex gloves. An honest observer wouldn't be worried about fingerprints.

Reilly wasn't going to give in easily. He started haltingly to explain he had been on watch in the lab, trying to catch the spy. But Hayden interrupted.

"Steve, if you give us another fairy story, I'll tell you what we'll do. We'll simply put the facts before Karen Bridges. You. Al. In the lab after hours. You with two discs. Unauthorised copies. You know what she will do. She'll remember you were with Delia Marris on the night she fled. She'll have you suspended, *whatever* your story. You'll never get back again."

Reilly nodded. He knew that was true. Fancy stories didn't matter. Finding the correct answer didn't matter. All that mattered was that WayCom had a senior executive who *might* be putting them at risk. Enough to finish Steve Reilly. Reilly watched Hayden sullenly, feeling for a way out.

"You lied to me when I was questioning you about Delia, the night she ran. Then, after your phone call from her, you admitted your love affair, but denied espionage. Now we have the whole truth," Hayden said.

"No," Reilly protested, still battling to save himself. "I wasn't working with Delia. I was trying to catch the thief, because I thought I might get blamed for losses." Reilly's voice was hoarse with desperation.

"Why wear gloves?" Hayden asked.

"To avoid getting implicated myself as the thief."

"I'll make a deal with you," Gerstein said, cynicism in every note. "You help me, and I'll take no action against you. If you don't, I'll probably charge you with theft or an attempt."

Reilly realised he was right on the edge. At least he would stay afloat a little longer. "I'll help all I can. It's what I want to do. But I've told you the truth."

"You're going to be in serious trouble if this isn't true," Hayden said.

Steve Reilly wasn't going to give the game away. His face tightened. Everything he had ever worked for was at issue now.

"Look I realise that if you put in a report on this I'll be suspended, and shit tends to stick. I hope you two guys realise you've got my career in your hands, and you could ruin it, just on suspicion—"

Reilly watched the two men as he spoke. Gerstein, glowering, suspicious, but following every word. And Hayden, applying a lawyerly balance of the scales. Christ, he could just about see the scales of justice, weighing up in Hayden's head.

Reilly knew then that both the men were aware that they had no more than suspicions to go on. He continued his pleading—but calmly, maturely. It wouldn't be effective to snivel in front of this pair.

"I want to ask you to be fair to me. Leave me out of any report to WayCom until you get further. Then you'll get the real culprits, and I'll be in the clear. I swear what I've told you is true. I'll take a lie detector test if you want. And I'll help you in every way I can. You can't lose on this—"

Hayden looked at Gerstein and saw agreement there. For himself, Hayden thought Reilly could be the smoothest liar he had ever met.

"OK. Let's get it on the record," Gerstein said, flipping on the tape recorder on the desk.

★ ★ ★

Reilly had already carefully vetted and re-edited his story in his own mind, before he ever began to speak. What he had decided to do was to tell almost the whole truth, but to give affairs such a twist that he would rid himself of the Ice Maiden. It would be an elegant solution, solving a number of problems neatly.

Reilly frankly admitted his short affair with Delia Marris. He strongly denied he was in complicity with her in stealing STELA technology. He told why he was disenchanted with WayCom, and was thinking of leaving.

It was pure coincidence, he said, that he had been approached by Ruth Charlton of Digby, Hudson at a party about a new job, and she had fixed a meeting with a woman whose name he didn't know, and never found out. As soon as the woman suggested theft, he said, he walked out.

He didn't go so far as to implicate Ruth Charlton in espionage, because he would have been unable to explain why, instead of walking out at *that* stage, he went on to see the unknown woman.

He said he had been given a date and place by the woman, to meet her, if he wanted to take up what he thought would emerge as a genuine job offer. He did not mention the meeting was only brought about by blackmail, because that would have led to the realisation that he had already sold out.

When he finished, Gerstein clicked off the recorder. It was a reasonable story. And more than that, for Hayden and Gerstein, the unknown woman, and the prospect of a rendezvous with her, was a line to the paymaster.

"Do you think Charlton is genuine?" Gerstein asked.

Reilly knew she was deeply implicated, and he would have relished pushing her into the mire, but he couldn't afford to.

"I don't know. Quite possibly. She never gave any sign to me."

Hayden was puzzled. "Why did you see a person who was unnamed before the meeting, about a job with an employer who was also unnamed? It doesn't sound like the move of a high-flyer who is used to being courted with job offers."

Reilly had already thought of an eminently suitable lie to cover this. "My talk with Ruth was more about the market. About different countries. About where my wife might like to be. Ruth said there was a lot going, but we never mentioned an actual job. That was why she passed me on to the other woman. This woman was going to be specific—"

"Why wasn't the woman's name mentioned?" Hayden pressed.

"The arrangement was to meet in a bar, and it was more important that I recognise the person by sight. A name wasn't much use to me. As I say, when we did meet, she refused to give her name."

"Well, who was she supposed to be—?"

"Another head-hunter, I guess. I considered I was following through on an opportunity—"

Reilly gave Gerstein and Hayden the time and meeting place with the Ice Maiden. They would never know it was one of a series of meets at which Reilly handed over secret information.

His plan was the Ice Maiden would be arrested at the meeting place. She would gain nothing from implicating him, but in any event, it would be her word against his, and hers would be completely devalued.

He left the meeting room with both Gerstein and Hayden looking satisfied. He had given them the Ice Maiden, and in one neat move, cut the cord with her, and left himself with—what was it now?—$250,000.

It was an incredible world: a few hours ago he'd been caught with stolen goods, and tried to fight his way past an FBI agent. Now the FBI thicko, and WayCom's dumb lawyer had swallowed his tale.

He felt really strong and invulnerable as he returned to the STELA unit. There was the problem with Laura, about Delia, but Delia was dead, and he'd apply his persuasive powers to Laura. She'd come round eventually.

Chapter 42

Mike Hayden and Al Gerstein walked together in Independence Park, alongside the unoccupied jogging track. It was a cold day. The trees were now bare and the wind whistled shrilly in their branches. Hayden outlined his plan.

"You can pull Reilly in any time, but he does more good for us, the way I see it, by stringing along. We get him to set up this woman. We grab her—"

"Not a bad first idea, Mike," Gerstein said, the ravines in his face softening to something like a smile. He pulled his jacket more tightly around him.

"You don't like it?" Hayden asked.

"Suppose we get the woman. She says nothing. Clams up. What do we have? Can we indict her for receiving stolen secret technical information? No. It's Reilly's word against hers. Reilly a tainted witness. She comes up with an explanation. It's a mistake. She makes smoke. We get nowhere near the people really responsible."

Hayden could see the sense of it. "Uh-huh, so we have to get her to lead us to them. We wire Reilly. We follow her."

"That's more like it, Mike. And we take a lot of photos. Try to match her physiog with our database. We trace her car. Possibly pick up her prints. Get a credit card line on her. When we know who she is, and what she does, we watch her, see who her friends are. Get it? Somebody out there has a lot of sophisticated equipment and money. Surely not this doll, but somebody. Whoever's behind this."

They agreed to set it up.

"Let's get back to the hotel, and I'll buy you a drink," Gerstein said.

In the warmth of the bar, over two straight JDs, Gerstein moved to Ruth Charlton.

"We need to talk to her," he said. "She's implicated. And she's a real lead. Reilly may be a lying slimeball, but he has no reason to involve Charlton, unless she really is involved."

Hayden thought they wouldn't get anywhere with her. She would be far too smart. Gerstein said it was a step they had to take.

"People get nervy" he said. "Even mafioso. When you start asking them questions. Even their denials worry them."

He was experienced at shaking people up. "I work on the old cop principle, Mike, that most convictions are based on perps spilling their guts. First you throwing a scare into a guy, razz up his nerves a little, get him looking over his shoulder, get him looking over your shoulder at a ten-year stretch. Then you get a little cooperation."

Hayden tossed off the whiskey and clapped his arm around Gerstein's collar. "Al, I don't doubt your method is effective. But it won't work here. You or I go to New York. We have to press her to see us, point out the gravity of events on the phone. She agrees to see, say me. She's all prepared. I go to her Exchange Place office. Low-key super luxury. She's sitting on her throne in total command. And Al, she's a diamond-cutter. I'm not dealing with a nervous preppy—"

"You can still rattle her," Gerstein said.

"Yeah. I can give her a sleepless night, make her look into the abyss. But the point I'm making to you Al is that she's not going to show the slightest sign to me. Now I'll buy you one."

Gerstein took his time about agreeing, and only when he'd tasted the second drink.

"We watch her then?" he said.

"I reckon. You see, Al, if I was to take her through everything Reilly has said, including Reilly's description of the other woman, she'd obviously tip the other woman off. This blonde doll would drop Reilly. We'd get nowhere."

"OK, OK, we watch Charlton. Do nothin' meantime with her," Gerstein said.

★ ★ ★

Hayden went over the plan carefully with Steve Reilly and Al Gerstein at the FBI field office on 20th Street.

Reilly was alarmed that Hayden and Gerstein wanted him to act as a decoy. He had given them the time and place the Ice Maiden would pick him up: 3.30 in the afternoon, outside the diner on 23rd and Elm.

He had expected that the FBI would simply stop her as she cruised past. Now he was finding that their plans were quite different. He protested at first, but had to give in. He was slightly apprehensive about dealing with the woman again. It wasn't that he was scared of her, but she had a ruthless quality about her that made him uneasy.

Reilly had to pretend to Hayden and Gerstein that he had never been in touch with the woman previously, except in the bar. But he already knew the routine. She would roll past, and if she was satisfied he was alone, pick him up.

She wouldn't stop the car. He'd have to get out in the street, and jump in while the car was moving. If she followed her usual routine, she would drive around, rarely stopping while they talked, and drop him when she was ready. He had never been in the car for more than five minutes. She always had a different car.

The plan was that Reilly would wear a wire, and the FBI would be in position around 23rd and Elm to take photos of the car and driver. No attempt would be made to interfere.

The FBI would rely on tracing the car, getting ID from the photos, and the record on Reilly's wire. There would be two FBI cars, anonymous, on the street, to watch and follow, but not to apprehend.

Hayden listened as Gerstein constructed the plan.

★ ★ ★

At 3.25 on the day, Reilly stood on the sidewalk outside the diner. Hayden watched the scene from a room above the sidewalk.

This was a sleazy part of town, a street of bars, clubs, and wire-covered second-hand and auto-parts shops. Reilly, in a windcheater, open shirt and jeans, rocked on his heels over the gutter looking into the traffic haze. He had a bag with some impressive but useless floppies in it.

Hayden was virtually above Reilly's head, the second floor above a laundromat. Al Gerstein had secured the empty room, and one across the road, and set up observation and cameras.

Hayden had a nagging thought that the woman would be too smart to be taken in by the set-up, but it wasn't his scene. Al Gerstein was an old hand at this. Hayden sweated and waited.

At 3.35 a black Mercedes 350 which looked as though it was going swing past the observation post, smoked rubber and nearly halted. The passenger door swung open, and Reilly moved quickly inside.

"Son of a bitch!" Gerstein muttered.

Hayden saw a dark figure in the driver's seat for a fraction of a second before the door closed, and the car rocketed away.

"She's got dark glass!" Gerstein spat. Their hopes of getting a snap of her through the car windows were zilch, but they photographed the car and plates.

Gerstein called the FBI cars on the street on his two-way radio. "Try and get a snap of her without being seen, willya, Lance? I'm askin' for the moon. The Merc has sunglass."

Agent Lance Devitt's car was nearest. There was a heavy sigh on the airwaves. "No way, Al. We're a hundred yards behind. She's goin for it!—well, Jesus, lookit what happened! Your guy Reilly is out of the car. She's pushed him out in front of us!"

Hayden had field glasses trained on the two cars which were now at least two hundred yards away down the road, wet but shimmering with light. He saw the Merc brake, and the door fly open. Reilly's body was ejected into the street, and his bag.

The car behind the Mercedes, not an FBI car, an old eighties Ford, huge and sluggish, lurched toward the kerb to avoid ramming the Mercedes, slid on the damp surface. The Ford ran over Reilly's body.

The Mercedes accelerated, slewed right with a muffled scream of tyres at the first intersection, and vanished.

The driver of the Ford was out of his cruiser, looking down at what he'd done.

Devitt's voice grated on the radio. He'd lost the Mercedes. The other FBI wagon never got a look in.

Gerstein called an ambulance, and he and Hayden ran down the road. They hunched down beside the peeling panels of the old cruiser to peer underneath.

One glance was enough to tell Reilly was dead. One of the Ford's wheels had gone over his throat. His head had just about been squeezed off.

The driver moved his vehicle a few feet, and Gerstein dropped a blanket which the distraught driver gave him, over the body.

"He was a screwed-up guy but he didn't deserve this," Hayden said.

Gerstein turned toward him pale and hoarse. "Maybe she knew Reilly was wired. She didn't know until he stepped into the car. She could have had a detector. It was always a risk that she'd have a detector. We had to have a wire, and we had to take the chance."

To Hayden, it sounded as though Gerstein was dictating his report. "I guess so. Do we have enough to trace her—the car? If it's a rental there'll be papers, credit cards," Hayden said.

"We'll try. Now we've lost the car I doubt it. Car will be from out of state. With false plates. Possibly even resprayed. Using a dummy but valid credit card. If she's as well prepared as she seems to be, this could be what we'll find. Nothing. But we'll try."

Gerstein showed a ray of optimism: "At least we know one of the people we're looking for. We'll get to her."

Hayden was thinking they should have grabbed the Ice Maiden as he'd suggested at first. At least they'd have had a chance of getting her to reveal her masters. And they'd have got her name. Found out where she worked. The trail might have been there.

He pushed a hand through his hair in perplexity. 20/20 hindsight was never a comfort.

"I don't know how you put this in your report, Al."

"Another fuck-up, and don't you say I told you so," Gerstein said, rubbing his still sore ribs, while they both watched Steve Reilly's body being stretchered to the ambulance.

Chapter 43

Hayden was sitting on a hard, creaking chair in Gerstein's office at the FBI field office.

Gerstein had put Capel through exhaustive surveillance, and traced money in a number of his bank accounts. Although Capel was clever enough to use offshore accounts, the NSA search and the Stella assessment of the data had revealed the banks, and the names of the dummy corporations which Capel used. Capel was worth at least twice what his annual salary would have produced over the years, and had no other known source of income.

"Looks very suspicious," Gerstein said.

"And this is a guy who hates Wayman's guts," Hayden said.

Hayden suggested that they should see Capel again, this time the interview would be at the FBI field office, a seedy and stark business-like setting.

"I'll get nowhere with Capel if we are leaning over the bar of the Jamesville club. That's home territory for him, and it was fine to open the dialogue there, but we have moved to a new picture."

When Hayden called Capel and tried to set up the meeting, Capel was elusive. He claimed he was too busy. Hayden said the interview would be in the presence of an FBI agent, and if he wouldn't agree, then Hayden would get Wayman to instruct him to cooperate.

Capel sounded jaunty, and he knew his rights, but he was jolted. "This is a free country. I don't have to talk to you, whatever Wayman says."

"Do you want to be taken in for questioning officially by the FBI, in connection with an enquiry into the theft of secret technology and murder, or do you want to help?" Hayden asked him to think about it, and rang off.

Gerstein listened and smiled. He was sure.

"I know the type," he said. "Thinks he's as clever as shit, and he is, but he doesn't appreciate *yet* how scary it is to get close to the grinding wheel of the law. When you start talking indictments, these smart guys' blood turns to water."

An hour later Capel called Hayden and agreed to meet. Capel jibbed at visiting the FBI office, but Hayden thought the atmosphere for the meeting would be about right. Capel was a cocky son of a bitch, and it would be necessary to cut him down to size.

Within two hours of Capel's agreement, he arrived at the field office, and sat down at a gleaming white plastic table before Gerstein and Hayden. He was affable, but chastened.

Gerstein switched on the recorder, and made an introductory statement identifying the date, time and parties. This was disturbing for Capel. The slightly airless, windowless room, the procedures.

"OK, Harvey," Hayden said, "let's have a general chat before we put together a detailed statement with names, addresses and dates. We've done quite a study on you. We know all about your foreign bank accounts and phoney corporations. Who has been paying you off?"

"Do you mind telling me how you know about my private affairs?"

"Certainly. You've been under surveillance as a matter of national security. We have a version of STELA that sifts and tracks information through international banks. We know what you're worth."

Capel was disconcerted, thinking himself above the scrutiny which he knew was almost a routine part of operations in the industry. "I don't believe you know anything."

Hayden pushed across a page of computer print-out. "Doesn't that summarise your overseas holdings?"

It was a list of banks and corporations operating accounts from the Caribbean to Switzerland.

"Our search system is very effective," Gerstein said.

Capel couldn't conceal the dismay on his face as he considered the list. "The fact I've made a little money doesn't make me a crook."

"In your case it does. You've defrauded the IRS. You should have declared all this to them. If we don't get help from you, we'll be handing the information to the IRS. You know you can do a long stretch for this."

Capel looked from one to the other, pale, his thin fingers twitching nervously. From the detached and flamboyant executive, with his brocade waistcoat, bow tie and tweed suit, he seemed to shrink suddenly to being a wrinkled and emaciated man in overly ostentatious and ill-fitting clothes.

"If I help, what then?"

"We can't make any promises," Gerstein said, "but the more helpful you are, the more easily it will go with you."

"I've never given away or sold any WayCom secrets, and I have never been approached with any proposition."

"So where did all the money come from?" Gerstein rasped.

"From successful investments. I can prove it."

"That's your story. But remember, if we find you haven't come clean with us, we'll hit you with everything."

Hayden shook his head in disbelief. "Mr Capel, this doesn't look good."

"I swear I have nothing more," Capel smiled thinly, now feeling that Hayden was groping in the dark.

"You're going to be called to give evidence at the Senate Defense Committee enquiry against Wayman? Whose initiative was that?"

"I was asked to testify by Jed Olsen and a couple of NSA officers."

"Which officers?"

"Chiefly Mr Cerillo."

Capel explained the evidence of bribery by Wayman. Capel said that Senator Jankovic could give similar evidence.

"How come you're so friendly with Olsen?" Hayden asked.

"I am a rather senior person in the industry. So is Olsen. Naturally we've met."

"How did Olsen know you could swear an affidavit about bribery by Wayman?"

Capel hesitated, then decided the truth would do him no harm. "Because one day, over a drink, I told him."

When Capel had gone, Al Gerstein said, "Prize louse, isn't he?"

Chapter 44

Ruth Charlton drew her pashmina wrap to her throat and huddled near the entrance to an apartment block on 83rd Street, near Central Park, New York. It was a chilly night, but the cold was peripheral to her. She watched the entrance and windows of a sixth floor apartment across the other side of the street.

There were people, brightly dressed, coming close to the big windows on the sixth floor occasionally. It looked as though there was a party going on up there, as more youngish, stylish people, mostly women, arrived, and passed glitteringly and noisily into the ground floor entrance to the building.

Ruth herself looked as though she was dressed for a party. She wore silver shoes and her black dress sparkled with silver threads.

"Hi, doll!" A big shadow of a man lunged at her out of the darkness.

"Fuck off or I'll blow your head off!" Ruth snarled, moving the arm which held her evening bag to reveal a snub nosed Colt 38 five shot.

The man veered off, stumbling. "Jeez, lady!"

Ruth returned her attention to the bright windows. The feelings that ran in her were confused. Her veins were coursing with a kind of molten pain. Her head pounded. Heidi was up there, with another woman. She was sure about the other woman, young and pale and buxom and schoolgirlish. And she was out here on the street. Ignored.

She thought she might try to go in, but in the end she lacked the brass neck to face the officious porter without an invitation. She pulled the cellphone from her bag, and her finger hovered over the button for Heidi's pre-set number. She had never used it before.

Ruth bent away from a cloud of dust and fumes stirred up by the traffic. She pressed the pre-set and send. The phone buzzed four times, and then, in a sudden panic, Ruth cut off the call before connection.

If Heidi had lifted the receiver, it would be like injecting a slow-acting but fatal poison which would claim them both. She imagined the chocolaty burr of Heidi's voice, full of gentle invitation.

"Heidi—it's Ruth!" But the dial tone was buzzing in her ear. Ruth stumbled away into the darkness.

Chapter 45

Mike Hayden had an early morning call at the Bowen hotel from Al Gerstein. "Do you know WayCom's back-up arrangements for their files?"

"I know they have a store near Rochester. Guarded like Fort Knox. I checked it out with Karen. Don't tell me somebody has been into that," Hayden said.

"Tried, I'd say. There was a fire, and an attempted robbery there last night. A lot of the contents destroyed. Nothing missing as far as we can tell."

"Hey, this is turning into a military action."

Hayden drove over to the Rochester address. It was part of an industrial estate of small factories on two- or three-acre sites. From the outside the security unit looked much like any other on the lot. It was one level, painted cream, windowless, topped by an air-conditioning plant. The identity of the occupier was confused by a small nameplate bearing the title of a subsidiary company of WayCom.

Inside, a separate ferro-concrete bunker, two levels deep, had been constructed, with a ramp leading down past a steel grille. The interior of the main storage area, formerly filled with filing racks containing tapes, disks, and hard copy files in boxes was full of scattered mounds of charred rubbish which still smouldered.

Hayden and Gerstein wore oxygen masks for the inspection.

When they came out, Gerstein said, "The fire started in the compartment where the artificial intelligence material was stored."

"Somebody trying to put WayCom's AI unit out of business?"

"Robbery that went wrong, I'd say," Gerstein said.

"Hell. Very determined people."

"I guess lifting the back-up files is a fairly logical way to get yourself into the AI know-how," Gerstein said.

"Can you reconstruct what actually happened here?" Hayden asked.

"With a little imagination. There's a shift change at ten o'clock pm. Goes through until six. Shortly after the change, the three security guards were overpowered by masked attackers, knocked out with ether, blindfolded, tied and locked in a storeroom.

"The guards got no opportunity to hit the emergency button connected to the local police depot. We find one person on the guard list missing, and think he was the inside man, looked after the timings, let his pals in, stopped anyone getting to the emergency. We'll check this guy out carefully because he was employed through an agency, had references etc. But I guess we will find everything was false and he fooled the agency.

"The thieves were interrupted on the job by the arrival of a roving WayCom security patrol. The thieves detonated a charge as a diversion, or had an accident with it, or set a fire, and fled. They obviously didn't want hand-to-hand violence, and maybe were worried the WayCom boys would get backup quickly.

"The vehicles the thieves were using, a couple of grey Isuzu 4x4s, had the plates covered, so we have no lead there."

Hayden was thinking it was quite an assault. He saw Karen Bridges coming up the ramp with a pair of her security men.

"It's a mess isn't it?" she said as she extricated herself from the oxygen mask.

"But you've lost nothing?" Hayden asked.

"Nothing has been taken, as far as we can see, but we've lost back-up material—hard copy, disks and tapes, damaged in the fire, that we'll have to replace."

"Is that going to worry you?"

"No, provided we replace promptly."

"If the thieves had got the STELA material, how much of your work does it cover?"

"All of it. The practice is to move back-up material here from Le Moyne on a weekly basis. Every department at Le Moyne has a back-up register, and they have to keep it up to date, moving product into the store, and out of the store when it's outdated."

"How can you be sure you've lost nothing?"

"There's sufficient evidence amongst the damaged material, but I'll have a team go over it again."

"Are you going to be under fire for a security failure?" Hayden asked.

Karen bridled. "I think our system worked reasonably well. I mean an armed intervention is something you can't protect yourself from entirely. Don't forget it was our security patrol which stopped the theft."

Hayden was left wondering whether there would be some kind of assault against the lab at Le Moyne House, or perhaps against Luchinelli personally.

★ ★ ★

Hayden was reviewing their progress with Cathy Ong. Or rather, the truth was, Cathy was working, and he was sitting looking out of the window at the approach of winter in Independence Park.

Just when a possibility of tracing Mariette came up, it seemed to disappear—and leave no trail. With Delia Marris's death, that line closed. With Steve Reilly's death, the line to the blonde woman closed.

Cathy said: "I have been reading the e-mail from the chief exec's office, Mike. You ought to know Wayman is in trouble with his bankers. He has tried to renew a loan with them, and failed. He's not getting a good response from other bankers. I've checked with contacts on Wall Street and there's an issue about WayCom's credit rating. Mike? Are you reading me?"

"Sure, sure."

Hayden had been intercepting telecoms from the chief exec's office. The system was easy to get into. Stella hoovered up the data and scanned it.

"If WayCom is in financial difficulty, it could be an additional reason why they might lose the STELA contract. I'll ask around Wall Street myself and see what the word is," Hayden said.

Hayden made calls to a few friends in the big banking houses. The answers he got confirmed that WayCom had problems, and the stock had started to slide on the NY Stock Exchange.

Hayden rang a friend who worked in the office of Kingsdorf, the lead bank in the syndicate financing WayCom.

"All I can tell you, Mike, is that Jeff Salmon didn't regard WayCom's credit rating as good enough for a renewal. I'm not giving away any confidences. The Street knows that. And the other thing is, we act for the opposition. The Street knows that too. We have too big an exposure."

"You mean IBM?"

"No, Fairford."

"But you've financed both WayCom and Fairford up to now?"

"Yeah but the exposure is too big. We have to go with the winner."

"Fairford?"

"Right."

Hayden could feel the strength of the tide that was turning

against WayCom. Financing problems, falling stock, it had probably been robbed of invaluable technology, there were cost overruns on STELA 2, the project was behind schedule, and forces in the Senate were lining up to take away their prize contract.

Hayden went down to Washington to see Cerillo. He thought he'd make an attempt to head off the slide on behalf of his client.

Cerillo settled him in his office and asked for the reason for the visit.

"I thought I'd tell you I've checked out WayCom security very carefully. They're abiding by the contract strictly."

"But that's ridiculous. We know of at least four serious leaks. Bray, Leman, Marris and Reilly."

"Well there's a small issue around whether Leman ought to have been employed, in view of his history, but the others are just thieves, crooks, who got into a position to steal."

"Because WayCom didn't check them out correctly."

"No. I've been through that. WayCom did everything they were bound to do. They weren't lax. WayCom isn't responsible for the criminal acts of others."

Cerillo's complexion darkened. "Four leaks in the barrel seems to suggest the barrel is wanting—"

"Not necessarily. WayCom has been, maybe still is, under siege from employees who have been bought by somebody—"

"What about the cost overruns?"

Hayden's firm had completed a detailed analysis of the overruns which Hayden had studied carefully.

"The way I read it, the charges by WayCom are heavy and unauthorised in some cases but they fall far short of fraud. This is a contractor trying to claim every cent he possibly can, but it's not dishonest."

"Not dishonest to be a couple of hundred million dollars over the correct figure?" Cerillo asked.

"Right. Wayman will insist to his dying day that his figures are right, and yours wrong. The answer, as always, lies somewhere in the middle. We'll compromise. It's not fraud."

"We'll see what the Senate Committee thinks," Cerillo said.

"We'll fight every centimetre of the way."

Cerillo was weighing the fight he had on his hands, his eyes hooded under heavy lids.

"Another thing, Mr Cerillo: I'm beginning to see Fairford coming into the frame very boldly. First, they seemed to have blocked

WayCom's refinancing with the bank. Second, it is Jed Olsen who is behind some of the evidence for the Senate Committee. It's him or his lawyers gathering it. Third I know there's a lot of bad blood between Wayman and Olsen, a kind of vendetta. I had ruled Fairford out of our list of corporate suspects as far as the theft of technology is concerned, but now I'm thinking they should be back on the list."

Cerillo's eyebrows flickered with disdain. "Don't let your imagination run away with you. Olsen is a powerful competitor sure. And, I believe, right up with his research on AI. A natural successor to Wayman. But that's free enterprise. You can't blame him for playing hardball. And as far as the espionage goes, now I'm asking, where's the evidence?"

Hayden had to concede there was no evidence to link Fairford to the thefts.

"Wayman only has the STELA contract by his fingernails, Mr Hayden."

He sat hard-faced, and silent. Hayden said nothing. Then Cerillo said coldly, "Thanks for coming in."

Hayden walked out. He had never realised how much Cerillo had invested in getting rid of WayCom. He had no idea that Cerillo could be so emotional. His first thought as he passed down the long polished corridors was that he should have been more agreeable with Cerillo.

He met Cathy Ong at the Washington Monument and they went for a pizza, and then sat on a seat by the Reflecting Pool in the thin sunlight. Hayden felt depressed, but Cathy was quite cheerful.

"You told him how it is, Mike. That's all you can do."

While they were sitting Hayden saw Cerillo again. Cerillo, a small plump man in a light beige suit. He was with a taller man who had a flock of greying hair that glinted golden in the sun, slim, ruddy-faced and fit looking.

"There's Cerillo, CJ, the little guy with the waddle. Having a stroll and a confidential talk with the big man in the shapely suit—he's familiar—"

"Isn't it Jed Olsen? I've seen his picture a few times. And seen him on TV. He's quite a star."

★ ★ ★

At 6.30 in the morning, two dark, battered Ford sedans, loaded with men, hardly visible behind smoked glass, eased up Fairway Drive, Montrose near Syracuse. They entered a spaciously lawned estate of condominiums.

The architect had managed to convey layers of interesting shapes, with three separate blocks of ten levels, no one apartment looking into another, and each with long open terraces. A ground-mist about a yard in depth lay on the grass. The occasional, newly planted birch tree, stark without leaves, reached out of the cloud.

The drivers selected a block and drew up outside the entrance. Hayden eased out of the back of one of the cars, while Gerstein and his team assembled quietly for the word go.

Hayden followed Gerstein and the others as they confronted the two security guards in the lobby. The guards were speechless at the unyielding FBI faces. ID folders passed under their noses.

Gerstein and his men headed for the tenth floor, some in the elevator, some by the stairs. On the tenth, there was only one penthouse. Gerstein rapped on the door, and when he heard a scuffle on the other side, identified himself, and held up his ID to be seen from the peephole. His men were ready to force the door with a crowbar at a sign from him.

It was not necessary. Peter Haffner opened the door, hastily drawing a black silk dressing gown around his tall, thin figure in agitation. He fell back feebly as the FBI men crowded in, slicking his long hair back and whinnying in agitation like a nervous horse. Hayden followed.

Gerstein, heavy and menacing in visage, but meticulously polite, persuaded Haffner to sit down in his daringly odd black and white lounge.

Gerstein explained that they were investigating the theft and receiving of secret government IT technology, and that the FBI would be talking to all the scientists working in the major AI companies. "In the US, that's Fairford. You."

Gerstein questioned Haffner gently about whether he or his team had ever received secret IT information from an outside source.

Haffner had a nervous, girlish chuckle. "Of course. From all over the world. Meetings, conferences, published papers in scientific journals. Not really secret, but hinting at secrets, you know. We watch like magpies."

Gerstein lit a cigarette, disregarding Haffner's request not to smoke.

"Do you have a warrant for this?" Haffner asked, his superior mind beginning to pace ahead of Gerstein's.

Gerstein showed him the document. Haffner looked at it briefly, agitated by the banging of doors and cupboards made by the agents who were searching the premises.

He became more serious: "Look, we're advancing pretty well by our own efforts, and I can't help you. There doesn't seem to be much sense in approaching me this way, a dawn raid, as though I'm a common criminal—"

There was a ropy laugh at the door, and one of the agents appeared with a youth of about eighteen, naked. "Will ya lookit I found. In the bedroom wardrobe!"

The youth fled from the room in a tide of heavy laughter, and jeers.

Chapter 46

Jed Olsen had heard of the fire at a WayCom facility in Rochester, but he knew no more. This was brought to him as routine industry news. But the item was short on detail. He asked Heidi Stoller because he knew she would be regularly screening all WayCom telecom traffic.

They were meeting, as they occasionally did, on a back road on Olsen's Springvale estate, where there was a deserted farm worker's cabin. Today the weather was too cold to occupy the cabin without taking the trouble to heat it, and they sat outside in Olsen's Lincoln, with the heater on.

"I didn't even know WayCom had a facility in Rochester. What do they use it for?" he asked.

"It's a back-up store. A self-contained vault. They had a fire."

"Nothing to do with our ... operations, Heidi?" Olsen asked cautiously.

"Not at all," Heidi said dismissively.

Olsen's brow creased. "I was going to say that I don't want anything to rock the boat this close to the Senate hearing. Things are coming together. WayCom has financial problems as well."

"Maybe *we* should have thought of this, Jed—grabbing the back-up files." Heidi smiled.

Olsen laughed. "I can see that. Robbing their back-up material is a neat and simple solution. I like it. But it's too ... violent, and obvious. Like a bank hold-up at lunchtime. The FBI would never let up. Instead, we've managed a stream of information which keeps us nearly abreast of WayCom, and the FBI will never crack our sources."

For a second Heidi's stare cooled. She was inclined to agree that the FBI would be unlikely to get them, but Jed Olsen was the man who was curiously persuading himself that he had adopted a non-violent option. He knew of the deaths of his informants, and yet by a mental somersault, imagined he was unconnected to them. Heidi wondered what the US would be like with Jed Olsen as President. For her, the strong, square-jawed, alpha-male look that Olsen projected was an illusion.

Olsen had brought a silver flask filled with fine cognac, and they shared a drink. Olsen was confident that Wayman would fall at the Senate Committee, and they drank a toast.

Heidi had saved one piece of information until they had talked for a while. It was bad news, although she could cope with it. She had no qualms about lying to Olsen, or giving him slanted versions of events, but this subject was one which could cause Olsen to erupt. And she couldn't keep it to herself.

"Jed, I don't want you to worry about this, but you need to know. It's about Haffner—"

Olsen's warm contemplative mood changed to one of threatening storm. He started: "Don't tell me—"

"Haffner's OK," Heidi interrupted sharply, "and I believe as loyal as ever. But you know he's had cold feet about the material we've been feeding him."

"What do you mean? Haffner wants to get ahead, to claim the credit, to win the laurels—"

"Sure he does. But he's had such a rich diet, he's worried he'll be implicated in the theft. Originally he was greedy, and happy with the slow trickle. He could feed his team nicely, and claim to be a genius. But recently he's had a torrent, and he's been wetting himself. Not conscience. Just a worry that he's now in very deep."

"I'll get him in to the office, I'll reassure him. Leave it to me," Olsen said, waving his arms, brushing it off.

"It's not as simple as that. The geniuses at the FBI have apparently at last realised that one way to find out who's behind the thefts might be to approach the top research men in the industry."

"The FBI have actually *seen* Haffner?"

"Yeah."

Olsen momentarily looked drawn. The jaw and square forehead had a skull-like quality. "Jesus! What happened?"

"Gerstein and his goombahs visited Haffner early one morning at home. Had him scrambling out of his silk sheets. But I think Haffner acquitted himself well—after all, he's rather bright—but he was shaken. I saw him afterwards, and he was shaken."

Heidi didn't mention that Haffner had been questioned about whether he could identify *her*. And the Feds had described her to him. There was no point in worrying Olsen, and she was sure that Haffner wouldn't talk, at least at this point.

"What should we do?" Olsen asked, at a loss.

"Don't worry, Jed. My people will get to Haffner, and we'll keep him out of play until the Committee has decided. Let's say officially that he will be going on a holiday abroad for three months."

Olsen accepted weakly. He was seeing the obstacles begin to stack up against him. He had a sudden perception of the enormous risks he was running.

Chapter 47

Hayden ran up the stairs to the FBI field office on 21st. It was raining outside, and the stairs smelt of damp raincoats, and were dark like the day outside which didn't seem to have fully dawned yet.

The desk woman nodded him through to the inner sanctum, untidy rooms strewn with boxes, PCs and outdoor equipment packs which made it look as though the FBI had just arrived, or was about to go.

The big man was in his shirtsleeves, with his tie pulled loose, hunched in his chair over his paunch, frowning. He was studying dozens of detailed sheets of the surveillance on Ruth Charlton. He grunted, "Get yourself a coffee." Pointed to a duplicate set of the documents for Hayden.

Hayden sat down and started to read. Every move outside Charlton's apartment, every phone call private and business, had been logged since they had decided to watch her. He flicked to the summary sheet.

Stella's analysis had produced a reference to afternoon tea at the Algonquin, and a shopping expedition at Christian Dior, both in the company of a woman with long straight fair hair aged about thirty-five. The elusive woman that the late Steve Reilly had identified—perhaps.

"I *told* you it was worthwhile," Hayden said.

"Could be the dame. I'll get our operatives to switch on to her, if Ruth meets her again. We'll get her address, photos, identify her before we step in," Gerstein said.

Hayden fetched a paper cup of coffee from the dispenser in the hall, and settled down again. "Al, we've been seeing this as the tip of a big international conspiracy, but maybe it isn't. Maybe this is a local job. Olsen could be more in the frame than we think. Olsen and Cerillo."

He could see immediately that Gerstein didn't like this idea.

"You're getting it out of proportion, Mike. Olsen is a go-getting businessman who happens to hate the guts of his adversary, and Byron

Cerillo simply wants to get the best deal for the NSA. There's no conspiracy there."

"Suppose Olsen has been paying Capel, and Capel is perjuring himself."

"Interesting speculation," Gerstein said lightly.

"Capel's got a lot of money, and he'll be going some to show he got it by shrewd investments—"

"Leave it to the IRS," Gerstein muttered.

"And Jankovic. Wayman gave me the word on him. There's an FBI file. Very interesting. I pulled the file as part of our investigation, and I was going to talk to you about it."

Gerstein was taking an interest now. His small brown eyes had a nasty glint. "Yeah, I know, but you didn't tell me Mike."

"I'm telling you now. I put in the file request myself because you weren't around."

"You're not runnin' the FBI, Mike."

Gerstein's bureaucratic training was coming through. Hayden had submitted one of the FBI request forms they used jointly without mentioning it.

"We're cooperating. Working together. I'm levelling with you, Al. Jankowitz was the subject of a sex inquiry relating to a children's home. There was an investigation. A decision not to prosecute. The home itself was disbanded, and the children transferred, which was what the parents wanted. Who was behind the charity that resettled the children? Jed Olsen."

"You're suggesting Olsen got the dogs called off Jankovic, and in return, Jankovic is paying back with perjured testimony?" Gerstein said.

"Could be. We might find Olsen has a hold over Cerillo, as well as Jankowitz, and he has an unhealthily close relation with Capel. His three stars."

Gerstein thumbed his nose wearily. "Mike, my brother held up a gas station. What does that make me? Let's get back to three murders, a missing person, and the theft of secret technology."

★ ★ ★

Hayden faced the brilliant glass wall of the extraordinary machine that was so creepily like an attractive and solicitous woman. He thought Stella might be capable of the kind of lateral thought which doesn't come easy to humans.

When Gerstein and Hayden used Stella, they usually interrogated her by encoded e-mail, and her replies were immediate. But it was a stilted way of communicating.

Occasionally, if they were visiting Cerillo, they took their files to the Defense Department building and had a "personal" meeting. They both preferred to be face to face with Stella, because it was faster and more subtle than e-mail. You could follow small trains of thought as they came to you.

One of the things that puzzled Hayden was how much Stella knew about *them*, Gerstein, Cerillo, Olsen, Wayman, the Senate Committee hearing, and himself. Hayden looked for an opportunity to be alone with Stella to satisfy his curiosity.

The opportunity came when he returned to Washington after his meeting with Gerstein at the field office. Gerstein was with him at the Defense Department, and he left when he had dealt with his own queries.

"I have a few more questions, Stella."

"You're positively identified Mr Hayden, please proceed."

"Can you give me an outline of the testimony proposed at the Senate hearing?"

"Mr Cerillo will say the NSA no longer have confidence in Mr Wayman or his corporation on this contract, because of cost overruns and breaches of security procedures. Senator Jankovic will say Mr Wayman bribed two generals, and paid money to the President's re-election campaign after receiving promises from the two generals of the award of the contract. Mr Harvey Capel will confirm conversations with Mr Wayman that requests were made for a deal, and it was done. Let me give you the precise detail, or you can download copies of the affidavits if you wish—"

"That won't be necessary, Stella. Thanks. What is the connection between Mr Cerillo and Mr Jedadiah Adams Olsen?"

"I can give you the common points in the history of Mr Cerillo and Mr Olsen. You'll have to deduce whether any of these are the connections you seek."

Hayden felt a sense of awkwardness or embarrassment, asking a machine to give him information he would have hesitated to request from an employee of Cerillo's. He seemed to be behaving in an underhand way.

"Fine, go ahead—"

Stella swayed a little, and consulted the PC screen before her: "Mr Cerillo's scholarship to Yale was funded by the Fairford Corporation, and the Milstein Trust. Mr Olsen is an officer of Fairford, and related to the Milstein family. Mr Cerillo is a member of the High Trees Golf Club, and the Liberal Club. Mr Olsen is also a founder member of the High Trees, and a member of the Liberal. Mr Cerillo's half brother James received a similar scholarship, and after employment here at the NSA, joined the Fairford Corporation."

"Where did you get this information, Stella?"

"From staff records, *Who's Who*, political and commercial directories, the company registers, and FBI and NSA files. You can download a detailed list of sources—"

"Not necessary, thanks Stella. What are you going to say if Mr Cerillo asks you what questions I've asked?"

"I'll tell him your questions, and my answers." The bland smile.

Hayden wondered if either Gerstein or Cerillo would check up on him. He doubted it. He was a kind of passenger in their enterprise.

★ ★ ★

Nathan Flint, Chairman of the National Security Agency, sat opposite Hayden over a coffee table in his office. He had protruding pale jaws and a white fluff of hair. His cheeks were limp with non-expression, but his eyes darted uncertainly round the room as Hayden told his story.

Flint saw the shadows of official inquiries, and questions in the House, and special prosecutors, as Hayden spoke. He wished Hayden a million miles away.

"Aren't you getting unnecessarily alarmed, counsellor?" he said when Hayden had concluded. "I recognise of course that you have suspicions, but no more than that."

"There's a point where you have to act on suspicions. You should have surveillance on Fairford, and the FBI should search their offices, and see if there's any evidence of stolen tapes and files—" Hayden said insistently.

"Try to get sense out of research material?" Flint asked, the corners of his mouth turning down emphatically.

"You should be *trying*—"

"I hear you counsellor. I'll certainly talk to Byron, but he has my confidence, and the confidence of everybody on the Hill. Equally, the FBI team. Gerstein's an old stager. We all have to go along with their findings."

Hayden had wound himself up for this difficult meeting, and now he felt exhausted, depressed.

When Flint walked Hayden to the door, he added: "I'll give all you've said further consideration, Mr Hayden, but I think events should be allowed to take their course—"

* * *

The small office at the Justice Department was as untidy as its occupant. Books were stuffed into shelves at all angles, files stacked on the floor. The PC rose out of a mound of papers, the only sign that somewhere down there was a desktop.

Jeremy Segal had been a friend of Hayden's at NYU. He was the law review type, probably the best legal brain in Hayden's final year. Jeremy was plump and untidy in appearance, with thick spectacles he was constantly adjusting with a forefinger on the nose-bridge.

The common interest between Hayden and Segal had been fiction and booze and bridge. Both had been voracious readers and drinkers, and hooked on bridge to the detriment of their studies. And both were outsiders. Hayden carried Charlie like an albatross, and Segal, quietly clever and fat, had been the butt of classmates since junior school.

The two men were standing in Segal's office. They high-fived, and promised to make a date for a drink before Hayden sat down to tell the story. Segal seemed to be soft and sloppy, but his eyes were steady on Hayden like a couple of steel ball-bearings.

"Shit, it sounds bad, but bad, Mike," he said when Hayden had finished. "But there's nothing there, is there? I mean a businessman can help a Senator in trouble. He can be friendly with an executive in a competitor company. He can be friendly with the head of an intelligence agency. He can be a member of the family that paid for the education of the intelligence man. He can want to get hold of a contract held by his competitor. He can hate his competitor's guts, for good reason, or no reason. But it doesn't mean he's improperly screwing his competitor out of the contract, and it certainly doesn't point to espionage against his competitor."

Hayden had to agree. It was a sobering vision he needed. "But the way I see it, Wayman is going to lose the contract on perjured evidence."

"You believe that, Mike. Maybe you're right. But that's what the process is designed to test. The evidence. You'll have to let the hearing happen, and see how it goes. I'd guess, in the end, you'll find some foreign outfit is sending its agents in, with loads of bucks."

Hayden chewed on this, gave sigh of resignation, and thanked Segal. They switched to pleasant memories over two cups of coffee which tasted like engine oil.

Hayden hesitated for a moment as he came down the steps of the Justice Department Building. There was a beam of sunlight. Before heading down Constitution Avenue, he sat on the plinth of a sculpture in bronze, a jagged piece like a broken gate.

A couple of bums also shared the plinth. The one nearest gave him a leery grin and offered his can. Hayden politely declined. The bum shoved out a dirty, mitted hand.

Hayden flipped the bum five bucks. He always felt better when he did that.

He figured he was in a minority of one in his views.

* * *

The next day Mike Hayden was with Gerstein at the FBI building on Pennsylvania Avenue when he got a call from his office in Washington. It was his secretary Dora Leonard.

She said Ralph Gurney the senior partner wanted to see him immediately. Dora didn't know what it was about.

Hayden tried to call Gurney back several times, but got the run-around. Gurney wasn't in or he'd just left for a meeting. Always the calls ended with Gurney's secretary saying they were expecting Hayden back as soon as possible.

He tried to work out what could be eating Gurney. He had a premonition of bad news, something unexpected rising out of the Washington mire.

The next morning, with his head still thumping from a nightcap too many, he took a cab to the offices of Stuart & Durwood in Bay Street. It was 10 am. No time for a workout at the Bayview Sports Club. He was very late.

His colleagues, he could see through the glass panels when he was on the fourteenth floor, were hunched over their books, or making calls, or punching their PCs.

He felt a stab of guilt; they would have been there since seven. One or two looked up as he passed along the passage, but none gave a sign of seeing him.

There was a pile of mail on his desk, a list of calls, and a note for him to see Mr Gurney urgently.

Dora Leonard came in: "You OK, Mike? Anything I can do? Hey, you don't look exactly great."

She put a hand on his arm, and then neatened his shirt collar inside the lapel of his suit. Dora was motherly.

"I'll be fine. I've got a few problems, that's all. Like this." He pointed to the pile of work.

Dora moved awkwardly. "Mike, I've had Gurney's secretary on. She keeps calling every half hour to see if you're in."

"What's with him for chrissake?—I've been at the FBI and in Syracuse on business."

Ralph Gurney was the oldest of the partners by nearly twenty years, a sort of father figure amongst them.

"I still don't know. I was asked to get you to go upstairs as soon as you arrive."

He crumpled up the summons to see Gurney, and dropped it on the floor. Ralph Gurney was nice on the outside, bathed, clipped and perfumed to perfection, laid-back, liberal in his views, charming, but Hayden wasn't sure whether there was any real flesh and blood underneath the Savile Row suit. However, Hayden trusted Gurney who had been behind the move to get him to join the firm.

He straightened his tie. Gurney always made him feel untidy.

★ ★ ★

Ralph Gurney had been in his office for three hours when his secretary told him Mike Hayden had arrived.

Hayden came into the room looking flushed. He knew what Gurney's opinion of him was, his hair an inch too long, his tie unnecessarily bright, his suit too light in colour for the Stuart & Durwood style—late getting in to the office, imprecise in the time he took for visits to clients. There was a casualness about Mike Hayden that Gurney couldn't accept.

"Sit down, Mike. I'm glad you finally got back—"

Hayden took it as a rebuke. "I've been at WayCom, Ralph. Working for our client."

"Sure you have. I don't have any problem with that. I know that you're doing an important job."

"Thanks, Ralph." Hayden was looking at him unblinking. Gurney was a law-machine, the subject of legend in the office.

Gurney smoothed his hand over the breast of his monogrammed, hand-made shirt betraying a slight pain. "An overstretched pectoral. I'll have to take the bathroom exercises more easily," he smiled.

And perhaps lengthen his walk to the office, Hayden thought. Ralph Gurney had ploughed the same old furrow between his penthouse apartment in Hudson Towers, and his office in the Citibank building for ten years, ever since his marriage had broken down. He had chosen one of the firm's young lawyers—twenty years his junior—and the liaison had only lasted a couple of months.

Gurney didn't do anything but work; he told everybody that he enjoyed it. While he put in twelve or fifteen hour days at the office, six, sometimes seven, days a week, money piled up in the bank. It was shovelled into his share portfolio, and investment trusts, by his broker. He never took a holiday. What was the point of going to a hotel in the Caribbean, or on the Riviera, on your own? He made occasional visits to his club, the Princeton, and his sister in Newport, Rhode Island.

Gurney tried to feel his way gently into what he had to say.

"Byron Cerillo from the NSA called me. He told me in confidence what the implications of your present work are."

"So?"

Gurney was massaging his chest, uncertain how to continue. "It sounds as though you're rubbing the NSA up the wrong way—"

"Cerillo's trying to screw Wayman. He doesn't have a case. I told him. It's that simple."

"He doesn't see it that way—and you know, the NSA have been good clients in the past. We could get a lot of work from them in future. Government work is our specialty."

"You want me to short-change Wayman?"

Gurney had elegant pale hands, with manicured and buffed fingernails. He eased the double cuffs at his wrists. His hands played over the papers like an ageing concert pianist. After a hesitant start, he was moving more confidently now to a finale.

"Maybe you should quit, Mike."

"I'm not going to do that. I don't know what's going down here. I want to find out. We have a duty to Wayman. I feel I should stay with it."

Gurney put his fingertips together calmly this time. The truth was, he didn't feel much, didn't feel pleased or regretful. As he got older his emotions were drying up. The chest pain had gone. He touched his wrist. His heartbeat was normal. He'd done what the senior partner had to do.

"I thought you'd say that, Mike. I just had to raise it with you, that's all."

Ralph Gurney looked fussily at his platinum Cartier wristwatch. With all the warmth he could muster, he said, "Take care, Mike. I don't like this case all that much. Cerillo wanted to rattle me. Put pressure on you. He's a strange man."

"Thanks for the support, Ralph."

Hayden left the office with Gurney's unspoken fears in his mind: Cerillo was also a powerful, and possibly a vindictive man who could do their firm a lot of harm.

Chapter 48

"This guy may not have very big muscles, but he's smart. Very, very smart." That was what Heidi Stoller had told Tom Addis about Peter Haffner.

Using a couple of investigators he had recruited himself, Tom Addis had watched Haffner's movements for two days. The objective was to pick a moment to snatch Haffner without causing any alarm.

Addis had been able to locate an empty apartment which had one small frosted bathroom window looking directly toward Haffner's apartment. A grossly inflated short-term rental for the apartment, and a glazier, provided Addis with the viewpoint he needed.

The investigators Addis hired were routine leg men from an agency, used to sitting around for hours on end, noting the movements of adulterous husbands, and wayward daughters. They logged the most tedious comings and goings of their target—when he went into a room of his condo and switched on a light, when he walked on his terrace and tended the flower baskets, when he walked through the grounds to the corner store.

From these boring reports, and Heidi Stoller's surveillance of the telephone line, Tom Addis had a sufficient picture of Peter Haffner's daily life. Haffner was followed from his home to his office each day. Every stop he made was monitored.

Peter Haffner lived a solitary and simple life. He cooked and cared for himself in the Montrose condo, and spent long hours at the Fairford laboratory. All his contacts seemed to be the mundane ones that kept life going—visits to the supermarket, the post office and the laundry.

Addis decided to take Haffner inside, or just outside the grounds of the condos when he was on his morning walk at around seven thirty. Addis reasoned that was the time when there were few people about, and Haffner would be least on guard. Addis knew he had to protect against the possibility of an emergency call from a cellphone in Haffner's pocket. He would have to move quickly.

Addis paid off the investigators, and on the night before the snatch, stayed at the viewpoint, hoping to get a few hours sleep on the mattresses they had laid on the floor of the bare lounge room. Haffner had arrived home at 11 pm from work, and appeared to have gone straight to bed.

At 6.30 the next morning, Addis was alone in a navy blue van, cruising the roads that intersected the lawns of the estate. He kept Haffner's block in view, and would not miss his quarry's slender, active figure in a tracksuit when he emerged for his walk.

★ ★ ★

Hayden stood on the terrace of the Montrose condo for the second time in a fortnight. Haffner had a display of late chrysanthemums in purple, red and pink, in pots along the edge. The evening was cool, but not cold, and the sky a mauve that matched the flowers.

At the dawn raid on Haffner, a few days before, Hayden had sat on the sidelines and watched. Haffner had been plainly disturbed, but Hayden thought only by surprise, embarrassment, and a natural neuroticism at having his space violated by muscular men in dark suits. The search yielded nothing, and there was no computer on the premises.

When they had returned to Syracuse in the car after that raid, Hayden and Gerstein had agreed they were still steering blind on the rattle-them-if-you-can theory.

But Hayden insisted that they should watch Haffner, twenty-four hour surveillance, and intercept his telephone traffic. Reluctantly, Gerstein agreed. Gerstein said he had started proceedings to question other research heads through the Japanese and South African agencies, but it would take a time to set up, and God knows when they would get any results.

Hayden had the feeling that the watch Gerstein had set up after the first raid was tardy and half-baked. Gerstein complained they couldn't get a satisfactory observation point. It was the way the apartments were built. The transcripts of the reports were sketchy and useless.

Eventually, when it became screamingly apparent to Gerstein's operatives that the apartment was deserted, they swooped again. The condo was cold. Haffner had disappeared. And he and the FBI had the leisure to examine the rooms again.

Hayden could see from the patio how carefully sheltered the other condos were from his direct sight. And being on the tenth floor hadn't helped.

"He's skipped," Gerstein said, coming out on the terrace and lighting a cigarette. "This place hasn't been occupied for two or three days. Hasn't taken much by the look of things. There's a wardrobe full of suits and sportsclothes."

"And the latest information we have from his brother in Rochester is that he's abroad on holiday. If we had been watching Fairford—"

"Mike, don't go down that road again. Cerillo won't wear it. And I won't either. We have to have probable cause. We have to believe an offence may be being committed."

Hayden left it. Fairford kept cropping up in their findings, and every time he raised a point about them it was squashed. It was a sore spot. Now Haffner had disappeared. The odds were that he would be abroad when the Senate hearing took place.

Hayden looked into the darkening sky and thought it through. Suppose, just suppose, Haffner had been using stolen technology, and suppose he was feeling weak and exposed, beyond his depth in very dangerous water. After all, he had been raided.

Suppose Haffner might think of confessing, or that those close to him thought he was weakening ... The natural step to take would not be to kill Haffner, because he was too valuable, and his death might send the message that he was somehow involved in receiving stolen technology. The natural step would be to make him disappear for a while, particularly during the Senate hearing.

"I think we need to keep a lookout for our friend Haffner. His absence may be quite innocent. But it may not," Hayden said.

"Sure," Al Gerstein yawned.

★ ★ ★

As a matter of form rather than enthusiasm, Gerstein detailed a couple of agents to make inquiries in the surrounding condos. Find out whether any resident knew Haffner, or had some information about him.

The agents came up with two facts. A for-sale apartment overlooking Haffner's had been occupied by men for several days at the crucial time. The tenant next door was curious, and troubled about who his new neighbours were going to be. He could only identify the men very vaguely as three tough looking guys, like plumbers in suits. The tenant said they had camera equipment with them.

Gerstein's boys picked up a load of fresh prints in the empty apartment, and a bill from a tradesman for the clear glazing of the bathroom window. A run of the prints through the FBI computers identified an ex con man Bill Gundy who had done time for bank fraud, now traced to an investigation agency in Rochester where he did repo work.

"Looks like a break for us," Gerstein said, grudgingly.

"Yeah," Hayden said. "I guess what the tenant thought was camera stuff could have been surveillance scopes."

"I'd reckon."

Hayden thought about it. Haffner under surveillance by somebody other than law enforcement officers. "What does it mean?" he asked Gerstein.

"Could mean a whole lotta nothin' as far as we're concerned. Maybe Haffner's wife is after him."

"He isn't married, you know that."

"Well, somebody setting up a palimony suit. Chasing him for debt. Lookin' to persuade him to share his research. I dunno. The guy's an asset. Bound to have people sniffin' round. But I can't see how it necessarily connects with us, Gerstein said."

"Unless somebody wants to stop him talking, particularly during the Senate Committee hearing."

"One among a number of possibilities," Gerstein said, as he made plans to interview the firm of inquiry agents. "But don't forget, his office and his family simply say he's on vacation somewhere they don't know where."

"Next item," Hayden said, confronted by the immovable Gerstein.

Gerstein held a paper up in front of Hayden as though it was noxious. It was a facsimile from the Sheriff of Brook County. The half million reward was still posted for Mariette, and Sorrel could still smell the money.

"Guy is ever hopeful," Gerstein said derisively.

"I think Sorrel is genuine," Hayden said.

Hayden read the document. Sorrel had been carefully looking around the area to see if he could see any trace of the Dodge pickup, or the man. According to the Sheriff, Sorrel said he had seen the man in a place called Dry Creek, about twenty miles from the first sighting. He was now driving a different vehicle, a GM van coloured dark blue. Sorrel reckoned he had information about where the man might be staying.

"This could be the lead we need," Hayden said.

Gerstein agreed without enthusiasm. Hayden thought Gerstein had given up Mariette for dead. And maybe he had too.

"I'll get Don Moody to go up there right away," Gerstein said, putting the fax beside him, like the condo report, as though it was one of a dozen things to do.

"But surely—" Hayden was expecting Gerstein to say he'd send half a dozen agents.

Gerstein caught his feeling. "Don'll call us if there's any action."

"I'd like to go up and see Sorrel. I could—"

"You keep the fuck out of it, Mike. You blind-sided me once before up there. Cooperation only goes so far. This is a law enforcement operation."

As soon as he left the field office Hayden got Cathy Ong on his cellphone and asked her to call him back with the Sorrel home number.

It was 9 pm and Sorrel had just got in. He was delighted to talk. He'd scoured the district like a detective. Hayden had assumed that Delia Marris had chosen Thunder River on the run, and that the oldish man with short silver hair came from afar. It looked now as though he could have some kind of set-up in Brook County, wherever he lived.

"You come up, Mr Hayden, and I'll show you where I think his cabin might be."

"Any sign of the girl?"

"He was alone, both times I saw him. I followed but he kinda got away."

Sorrel had already been warned by the FBI that the man was dangerous, and Hayden thought that even half a million dollars wasn't going to be an incentive to get all that close.

"Can you pinpoint the actual cabin?"

"Not the actual, but I think it's one of maybe four five out of Dry Creek ten miles north."

Sorrel seemed basically honest. Hayden decided on the spot. "I'll be up there at say 4 pm. Meet you at your place."

"Ok fine. Guess it's worth calling in sick. I'll take a look around in the morning."

"Take care," Hayden said, and rang off. Sorrel wanted to earn his money.

★ ★ ★

Hayden sweet-talked Gerstein into letting him go with Don Moody to Dry Creek. Gerstein extracted a promise that Hayden would act only under Moody's instructions.

It was a bright blustery day with little traffic, and Moody wasted no time. He drove with his bladed nose pressed forward like a prow, and his lips compressed into a tight line. They rolled up to Sorrel's cabin in a cloud of dust, the FBI Ford reeking of hot vinyl and oil and carbon fumes. It was ten minutes short of 4 pm.

The studious looking Mrs Sorrel came out to them. She looked calm enough, but her fingers worked anxiously, rucking the front of her apron.

"Jeff ain't back. Went out around nine this morning. I expected him back before this, long before."

Moody and Hayden sat in the car without saying anything immediately. And then Mrs Sorrel's natural hospitality asserted itself. "Y'all had a long drive. Come in for a drink, stretch y' legs."

When they were inside the parlour with their hands around a glass of Mrs Sorrel's homemade lemonade, Hayden said, "We ought to head up the road, Don, to where Mr Sorrel said he had made the sighting."

Mrs Sorrel stood by the door, watching them with one eye, and her two young children in the next room with the other. Don Moody pulled out a map. He had pinpointed the place. He showed Mrs Sorrel.

"How is the road from here?" he asked.

"It's rough. But its been worked over for the winter coming. should be safe enough. You can't miss. Just keep straight ahead. Only timber tracks to the side. Y' can't get lost."

There was an awkwardness in the small room. Mrs Sorrel's unexpressed worry darkened the air. Moody was taciturn. Hayden didn't want to offer her reassurance, because he thought that might worry her more.

The two men came away when they had drained their glasses, saying they'd keep an eye out for her husband, and promising to call in before they left the district.

Moody stomped the car up the track to the road, wheels spinning, and dust, blown by the wind, smoked past them.

After they passed through the Thunder Lake township, the blacktop gave way to gravel which had been regraded in recent days. The surface was loose, and untracked yet by traffic, and rocks from the coarse mix were flung up by the wheels, drumming on the under-chassis. The banks at the side of the road had been cleared and shored up, and on the drop side, parts of the Armco barrier had been replaced by new grey strips.

They hammered on, the car sliding on the loose surface as Moody extracted all the speed he could, past high embankments, and steep falls.

Over the top of a rise, where the road narrowed, they ran down alongside a small lake which lapped close to edge. They were still about ten miles from their destination. There was a collection of cars in a viewing bay—two were County Sheriff's cruisers with lightbars on top.

Moody pulled in, showed his ID to a deputy, and explained their presence. The deputy knew about the FBI contact.

"Right, man. We think the body we're tryin' to recover from the lake—" he pointed a finger at three open boats clustered together on the smooth surface, with men working from them, about two hundred yards away—"could be Sorrel, the guy who gave the info for our report."

"Why Sorrel if you haven't got the body yet?" Hayden asked.

"His truck down there, under that tree."

The deputy said his name was Darren Shervey, and he was in charge. They had been called out by a motorist who noticed the empty truck, and an overturned dinghy in the water.

"We've got an ambulance, but it's no good. The guy's dead," Shervey said.

Hayden walked down the road to the small bay beside the lake, with room enough for just one vehicle under an oak tree.

He hauled himself up inside the cab, more to say he'd been there than in the hope of finding anything. The instrument panel compartment had the usual collection of auto manuals, and a pair of canvas work gloves. There was a heavy plastic rain slicker behind the seat.

Fastened to the dash was a tear-off notepad, and a ball-point on a cord. Something was written unsteadily on the pad. Hayden tore off the paper, and held it closer. It looked like a registration number.

"Looks like Sorrel might have written down the number of the vehicle of his aggressor, Don." Hayden handed him the slip.

Moody and Hayden went back to the rescue team, and scrambled into a boat, with another deputy. This time they were dressed for the task. They both wore jeans, trainers, and warm sweaters. Hayden drew the centre seat and had to row them out to the recovery scene.

The body had been freed from a tangle of fishing line, surfaced and lifted clear of the water, and was being laced on a light stretcher by a paramedic.

A County frogman was still in the water, his hands clasped over the gunwale of one of the boats.

"Guy had the line wrapped all round his arms and throat. Ain't no way that coulda happened by natural action of capsizing, and going down," he said.

The boats returned to the shore, one of them towing the capsized fishing dinghy.

Moody showed Shervey what Hayden had found in the cab of the truck. Shervey copied the number into his notebook, and said he'd run a check.

"You going to look at the body?" Hayden asked Moody.

The stretcher, still covered, had been lifted clear of the boat and rested on the roadside, waiting to go in the back of the ambulance. It was a couple of feet away from them.

Moody was about thirty, and not all that experienced. He didn't like looking at stiffs any more than anybody else, but he suddenly realised he couldn't represent the FBI at a crime scene without at least glancing at the victim, fruitless as that might be.

"Sure," he said as though he'd planned it all along, and he leaned over and pulled back the sheet.

It was Sorrel, grey faced. The dull, open eyes, had shining whites. Sorrel's sweater and hair were coated with mud. One or two small cuts on his cheeks bled feebly. His throat was red-lined. His arms were at his side, the big, scarred hands set like claws. The paramedics had not disturbed the corpse more than necessary for transportation, to give the forensic pathologist as much scope as possible.

"Seen enough?" Moody said to Hayden, and flipped the sheet back to cover the body. Sorrel had tried too hard for the half million.

★ ★ ★

They continued their drive to the north.

"This guy must have snagged Sorrel, and eliminated him without hesitation," Moody said.

"Sorrel was an amateur. The person we're dealing with is a pro and an expert," Hayden said.

"What hope is there for the girl, with a guy like that?"

It was a thought that had plagued Hayden. The man was a killer, and he removed obstacles by killing. What could Mariette be but an obstacle, a serious threat to his safety? When you thought about it, there was no logical reason why Mariette should be alive.

"I don't want to think about it. I just want to get the bastard," Hayden said.

Moody reported to Gerstein on the phone, and passed on the number Hayden had taken.

Hayden counted off the miles from Dry Creek to the place where

Sorrel had said there were several possible cabins for their quarry.

Moody stopped the car in the nearest passing bay. The sun had gone in, and the clouds were banking up, white slashed with grey and yellow. The wind scythed through the pines. It was 6.30 pm and the light was failing.

"I guess it's on foot from here," Moody said.

"I think we find a motel and hit this place early tomorrow morning," Hayden said.

"Or we go home, and call in the big boys," Moody said hesitantly.

"Do that and we might as well not have come up here. With Sorrel dead, we're not taking back anything new."

Hayden wanted to go on. His mere illogical hope that Mariette was alive had revived. And therefore every day counted.

Moody thought about it. He wanted good marks. "Yup. We'll be falling over ourselves in the dark, soon."

He swung the wheel, burning the car round in a full circle, and drove south. They had to coast down to Thunder Lake for the nearest motel, the JB SupaMotel—with an agonising stop, to keep their promise, at Sorrel's home.

Shervey's cruiser was outside the gate. Mrs Sorrel was strangely composed, with the children keening slightly on her skirts. Both Moody and Hayden made a stumbling attempt at condolences, and came away quickly, leaving Shervey weighing down the couch.

"I know it's no consolation to you, Mrs Sorrel," Hayden said at the door, "but if we're on the right track, I'll see you get the reward."

Hayden had a shower at the motel, and sat with Moody over a glass of draught beer in the bar.

Moody talked about his climb from a trailer in Oklahoma where his mom had a brood of four kids, and no pa, through Oklahoma University law school on scholarships, and charity, and night work on auto repairs. The FBI was all he ever wanted. He loved the Bureau and was proud of it.

"I heard about you," he said.

Hayden felt this was coming. This was the offset for telling about life in a trailer park. Moody had been at the bottom of the barrel, so there was no inhibition in talking about someone else who'd been there too.

"Your old man. Charlie Hayden. Some guy."

"I'm not him," Hayden said.

Moody laughed. "Might as well be. You're famous for it."

★ ★ ★

Moody and Hayden planned to be on the job at 6.30 am in the morning. Hayden found he didn't relish Moody's conversation all that much, and went to bed early, after a surprisingly tasty baked local trout.

Hayden lay awake for a while. Sorrel's death pointed to a local presence, and there was every chance that he had enough information from Sorrel to run this big old man to ground.

Then Hayden slept well, stirring occasionally to the sound of the wind in the pines. It reminded him of the summer house the family used to have beside the sea in Maine—in their better days.

In the morning, he had breakfast—coffee, orange juice and toast—in his room, checked out, and met Moody in the car park.

They were at their destination near to the planned time. They couldn't find a better place to leave the car than a passing bay. Getting concealment off the road was impossible. The only laterals were private tracks to cabins, the rest led to either steep banks or steep drops.

Hayden got out and stretched. It had rained heavily overnight. The woods would be slippery and damp. But the cloudy sky was already glaring with jagged slices of sunlight. And there was warmth.

Hayden noticed that Moody had a gun in a belt holster, covered by his sweater.

"You're at risk here, counsellor," Moody grinned.

"I can handle it."

"That keen on the girl, huh?"

"Let's stop jerking off, and get on with it," Hayden said.

Hayden was waiting for Moody to give some kind of summary about how they might move, together or separately, whether they were going to circle the area and watch from a distance, or pinpoint individual cabins and try to get close, how long they were going to give themselves for this part of the exercise—or at least discuss these possibilities. He said nothing.

About a hundred yards from their position there was an entrance, with a mailbox. Moody headed for it, presumably expecting Hayden to follow.

"Look, in case we get separated, we'll meet at the car at say ten. OK?" Hayden said.

Moody looked at him as though he had never thought of it. "Sure, man."

"And do you have a spare car key on the ring?"

Moody nodded slowly affirmative, curious. "You going to boost the wheels?"

"I don't know what's going to happen. Suppose I have to bring the car half a mile down the road to pick you up. Say."

"That's not goin' to happen, pal. But I don't mind you have a key. Saves friggin' around if you're driving." He slipped a key off the ring and handed it to Hayden.

Hayden would have preferred to get into the pines and recce the road for half a mile to identify the cabins, but he didn't say anything. The track twisted into the darkness of the tree trunks, and Moody began to walk along it. He never looked back at Hayden.

Hayden moved off the road, into the pines and stood still, listening. He figured the cabin on this lot would have several acres all round it. He could move quietly toward it with good cover, avoiding the road. He didn't particularly want to follow Moody. He felt unsure of him.

Fortunately the trees were closely planted, straight and well grown, with trunks about a foot in diameter. The branches, to a height of perhaps ten or fifteen feet, had withered in the lightless zone, and it was possible, by bending a little, to walk easily on a carpet of pine needles.

Hayden had a small compass on a penknife that he had never needed to use seriously for direction-finding. Now it told him that if he wanted to keep his back to the road, he should move due east.

He heard a dog start barking, and some noise from Moody's direction. After a few minutes, he could see ahead the outline of a tin sided cabin, that looked as though it had once been a trailer.

He watched through the trees to pick up some movement inside. He sidled along to get a view of the lean-to which covered a practically prehistoric ex-army jeep, encrusted with rust. Squatting in the middle of the track was a peeling red Toyota. He could hear a young kid's voice from inside the shack. And the cry of a baby. An old man with rubber boots and rope suspenders on his trousers came out the door, scooped up a pile of cut firewood from the stack by the door, and went inside.

Hayden was looking at an old scene of rural poverty, and there wasn't anything here for him.

He made sure the track ended at the cabin, and made his way back through the pines to the road. There were no cabins to the south, because the roadside fell sharply away, a hundred feet, to a riverbed. On the west side there was a steep bank, so the property there was inaccessible, at least from where Hayden was.

He decided he would enter the forest near each entrance on the right-hand side of the road, and recce, until the time for his rendezvous with Moody.

The next property was deeper in the woods, built of milled timber, with dogs, fortunately locked in a shed. There was a small road grader in the driveway, and the place looked to Hayden like the home of a county employee.

Hayden used the same method on the third property which was falling apart, and deserted.

It was now 8 am and he was saturated with sweat, and dripping water from the trees. His clothes felt heavy on him with a chill against the skin from the wet. He had seen or heard nothing of Moody.

When Hayden started to think whether it was remotely possible that Mariette could have been brought here, and kept in confinement, he pushed the thought from his mind. If the killer had killed one of his own, Delia Marris, why should Mariette survive?

Hayden entered the fourth lot, and this one was different. His view from the pines showed that the track forked at least twice, shortly after the entrance. All the tracks were deeply pitted by rain and heavy vehicles, but all looked drivable.

He trekked parallel to the nearest branch of the track, until he came to a clearing. All the timber had been cut for a hundred yards, in a swathe about three times the width of the track. It was inviting to walk on the soft wet grass, but he kept pushing through the pines, fending off the twigs that seemed to want to find his eyes.

At the end of the clearing there was a thin stand of trees. Now he could make out a cabin, a substantial construction of logs, stained grey by weather, with a roof of faded, red painted corrugated iron.

Shielded from the cabin by the trees, Hayden stepped out into the clearing. A weakness suddenly went through his bones, and his vision became unsteady—in that millisecond, he thought he was going to pass out.

He moved his legs again slightly, before he realised the ground beneath him was giving way. Instinctively, he flung himself back toward the trees.

Hayden grabbed the nearest trunk and held on, dropping to his knees, while behind him he heard the crackle of thin wood collapsing, and the thud of falling earth, and the tearing of grass, and the metallic clunk of metal on metal. Then silence.

He turned to the hole that had opened behind him: poking through straw and grass and dirt, at the bottom of a four foot deep trench, were the wide, clamped jaws of a bear trap. The closed teeth, oiled blue steel, flecked with dirt, caught the light.

Hayden put his forehead against the sappy trunk, and let a surge of body heat scorch across his wet skin.

When he could stand steadily, he picked up a dead branch about four feet long and stripped it. He would have to probe every foot of the way—or go back.

Then he heard a rustle of movement in the clearing and saw Moody, fifty yards away, striding toward the cabin, his sweater knotted around his neck. Impatient, and perhaps tired, he was taking the easy way, shielded by the trees.

Hayden let out a strangled, dry-throated cry.

At that same moment, Moody hesitated, appeared to hear, looking across toward Hayden with a red, glistening face—but his next stride brought a sickening crack.

The long grass around Moody collapsed. He threw up his arms as his legs plunged into the trench. Above the sound of falling debris was the sickening clash of the teeth, and Moody's animal howl of agony.

Poking the stick into the ground ahead of him, Hayden worked his way along the line of the trench. He calculated that there was a whole ring of bear traps around the cabin. There seemed to be no movement from inside the cabin. No smoke from the chimney. No apparent sign that they had disturbed anybody.

As he moved, he heard a low moaning sound. The sound seeped into a long cry, like somebody who had cried so much, they had nothing left. It could easily have been a dog. A dog or a child. Moody had slumped into the trench almost beyond view.

Hayden reached him, and pulled the grass cover away from the trench. The trap had taken Moody across both legs just below the knees. He was semi-conscious. The hole was drenched with blood. The razor sharp incisors had bitten in to the bone.

Hayden reached down beside Moody, and slipped the 38 from Moody's holster and, only looking to feel the safety, slipped it under his belt.

He slid down into the trench beside Moody. He looked at the mechanism, which on one side of the jaw contained a hub with a metal tap, levers and screw holes.

He tried to figure out the way to release the jaws. He tried to force the jaws open, but with all his strength, and the lack of leverage, he could only manage an inch. Moody screamed as Hayden had to let the jaws close again on the flesh and bone.

Hayden realised Moody could die of shock if he left him to get help. He had to solve the mechanism of the hub. He calmed his mind to finger the various taps and levers, trying one after another, sweat running into his eyes and blinding him.

He was desperate with anxiety for Moody, and impatient with the mechanism. Then, by pure luck, in response to his frantic movements, there was a metallic snick, and the jaws were loose.

Hayden opened the jaws out, releasing Moody's legs, and then lifted him out on to the grass. He lay Moody on his back. He slipped off his sweater and T-shirt, and tore the T-shirt into strips. He made two rough bandages, and tied one on each leg.

"I can't do any more for you, Don. I'm going to call in help," Hayden said, pulling on his soaking sweater.

Hayden didn't know whether Moody heard him or not. He went through Moody's pockets, and found his phone in a belt pouch. He had dialled Gerstein, when there was a roar from behind the treeline. He flattened on the grass.

A dark coloured van was heading out from the vehicle port by the cabin, behind the trees, wheels spinning and throwing up mud and stones, to the road. Whether the driver saw Moody and Hayden or not, he kept going.

Hayden listened as the high revving died away on the highway, and became conscious Gerstein was on the line. Gerstein would already have known from the display on his unit, that this was a call on Moody's phone. Hayden could hear his gruff call to Moody.

"Al. Mike. Moody got caught in a bear trap. He's in a bad way. Needs medical help. The jaws have taken him just below both knees."

"Where in hell are you? Canada?"

"Our car is fifteen miles north of Dry Creek, in a passing bay. Take the fourth driveway on the right past the car, you'll find us three hundred yards from the highway. A dark coloured van just left here. Seems to line up with Sorrel's description. Turned south if I heard right, towards Thunder Lake."

"OK, Mike. You guys supposed to be reconnaissance, not a goddam assault force—" He rang off.

Moody seemed to be more awake now. He appeared to have understood Hayden's conversation with Gerstein. "I'll be OK till Al gets help. You can't sit here like a duck on a pond. Better take a look round."

Hayden was anxious to find out whether anybody was left in the cabin. It was a thought that Mariette might be left behind. He moved slowly beyond the trench, working the probing stick anywhere there might be a trap, and in twenty minutes had made a circuit of the cabin. It occurred to him that the cabin itself might be booby-trapped, but he dismissed it. Whoever was in there had set up a warning system with the traps. The cabin seemed deserted.

Hayden approached a blind wall, and eased along to look in a grimy window. A bunkroom. Empty. He got bolder and tried the warped back door. It was unlatched, and swung open.

A smell of sludgy drains and stale milk greeted him. He stepped into a filthy kitchen. In a few moments he found each of the rooms empty, but plenty of signs of life: food scraps, empty liquor bottles, disturbed bedding, ashtrays crammed with buts, a television guide and a TV set, old clothes draped over a chair, and a noisy refrigerator containing ham, eggs, tomatoes, and milk.

He stood in the middle of the parlour and looked about, careful not to disturb anything. A forensic examination would show how many people had recently occupied the place, and possibly whether there was a woman amongst them.

Hayden's eye strayed to the floor of shrunken and twisted timbers, worn smooth, and rippling like a lake. A stained Native American mat was placed on one corner of the floor, and topped by a couch with springs that showed through the seat. It was the positioning of the couch and rug, in relation to the rest of the room that he noticed— oddly off centre.

He pushed the settee along, and pulled away the rug. There was a trapdoor underneath. He was not exactly surprised, because he had been half-looking for a cellar, or some form of underground storage. There was no space in the roof—the rooms rose open into the eaves.

Hayden lifted the cellar door, and saw a ladder disappearing down into blackness. He couldn't locate the light. As he looked for a candle or a match, he heard the distant pock-pock of a chopper. Al Gerstein was putting Moody's health above any question of stealth.

He found a flashlight. He wrapped toilet paper around the handle gently, and knelt over the hole, spying what he could with the beam. There was a smell in the cellar like an old persons' home—loose bowels, and disinfectant. It was a big space, perhaps fifteen feet square, shored up with thick beams, and damp. No human presence.

He saw a bunk, a cupboard stuffed with clothes, the door leaning open. And another curious wooden construction in the middle of the floor. The light touched a length of steel chain on the bed. Hayden felt nauseated.

The helicopter was louder now. Gerstein would have no trouble locating the clearing, and putting down out of range of the traps. Hayden decided he had time to go down into the cellar. He climbed down the ladder and confronted the article he could not at first identify, which in the dark, looked like an old fashioned wine or fruit press.

At first Hayden's mind was reluctant to identify it for what he knew it must be: a set of stocks, which would clamp the wrists and ankles of a human being, only a little more sophisticated than those used for village punishments in past centuries.

Whoever had slept in the bed—Mariette—had been chained. The stocks by day, and a chained bunk at night. The clothes in the cupboard were worn women's garments. What Mariette must have been through sent waves of pain and fury through Hayden.

He could hear voices outside. The chopper was down. He made to leave, splashing the beam of the torch around the cellar one more time to make sure he would never forget.

He saw a bottle on a tray in the corner. He looked more closely. It was a jar of powder with two hypodermic syringes. There were several loose packets with the brand Supernova. He'd seen them before. Cocaine. He guessed the jar contained heroin. It certainly wasn't icing sugar.

He pushed up the ladder, out of the cabin, to the light and the breathable air. He didn't really hear Gerstein's angry questions about what he had been doing.

★ ★ ★

Hayden didn't feel like waiting around for Gerstein's forensic team to finish their work. He would read their report in the quiet of his office. He wanted above all to leave this place behind.

The chopper which had taken Don Moody to hospital would be returning for the FBI men, and Hayden suggested to Gerstein that he could pick up Don Moody's car and drive back. Gerstein agreed at first, and then, ever a bureaucrat, pointed out Hayden wasn't insured to drive that car. Hayden told him to fuck the insurance.

"Gimme the gun first, then," Gerstein said, holding out his hand for Moody's gun.

Hayden turned the Ford and headed south down the gravel highway. It passed through miles of undeveloped wood and wasteland with only the occasional abandoned cabin. He was cruising, tired, his one positive thought that they could find Mariette. He tried to see how they might get a line on the blue van, but his mind was too exhausted to concentrate.

Hayden saw the Mack semi-trailer, a shiny black rig, high and sassy, with Virginia plates, and chrome on the smoke stack and wheel-discs, come churning down the hill behind him, columns of dust flaring up from its wheels.

The Mack had a four-axle trailer, and a heavy load under canvas the way it handled. It hesitated very close to Hayden, a few feet away, long enough for Hayden to clock the number. The rig came up close behind with its evil looking black and chrome snout filling the rear vision mirrors. Hayden thought it was tailgating him, deliberately getting up his ass. He hit the gas and left the rig behind.

After a few miles Hayden forgot about the incident, but in a couple of minutes the Mack was coming up behind him again.

He decided not to let it bug him, and settled down, with the cruise control on the Ford at fifty-five. The weather too was unfriendly. The sky had greyed over in the afternoon, and now showers of rain darkened the whiteness of the granite chips on the road and the embankments. There was no other traffic on the winding ribbon of highway.

South of Dry Creek, the side of the road was heavily forested with beech and oak and ash, and the branches were practically bare of leaves. The black arms of winter waved threateningly. The highway fell away sharply on each side, leaving a steep twenty foot bank down to the trees.

Suddenly, the black Mack appeared beside him, a high-pitched scream coming from its axles, throwing clouds of spray. The sensation of horror hardly had time to gather in Hayden's chest before the rig moved quickly across from the crown of the road to jolt the Ford.

The sound was no more than a leaden thunk of denting metal, and the impact a neck-bending jolt, but the dark shadow of the truck filled the driver's side windows as though a black blanket had been thrown over the car.

Hayden lost control, and the Ford snaked. He lifted his foot first, uncertain, and then stamped on the pedal, but neither move rid him of the monster shrieking alongside.

The first movement of the Mack had merely been a feint, and it was followed by a solid blow that smashed the car sideways. The invisible driver, high in his cab behind smoked glass, positioned the rig precisely, and struck with a grooved swing like a pro golfer striking a ball.

The Mack disappeared in a fountain of rain, dematerialised,

howling. The gleaming gravel, slippery as an ice-rink seemed to rear up underneath the Ford, and then drop away, tossing the car off.

Hayden was flying into a grey void. The scarred and broken tree trunks rushed forward, bars set to break him. Then a paralysing shock, which sparked a network of searing pains through him. And darkness.

★ ★ ★

Hayden's head cleared in a few seconds. The crumpled nose of the car was jammed between tree-trunks. Smoke and oily steam seeped into the car. He was almost choked by the airbag inflated around him. The broken trunk of a young beech had come through the windscreen on the passenger side.

Hayden forced the door open, driving his shoulder against the resistance with all his strength. He was able to open it just enough to slip through. As he did so there was a low boom, like a bass drum being struck softly, and the car was enveloped in flame.

He crept deeper into the woods, and eventually hid, crouched in a pile of wet underbrush a hundred yards away.

★ ★ ★

Hayden and Gerstein walked through the light drizzle with their heads down, across the parking deck, pushing between cars, toward the lighted entrance of the Bowen hotel.

"Am I being irrational?" Hayden asked.

"Better question, Mike: are you paranoid?"

"It was about as deliberate a move to run me off the road as you could imagine."

Gerstein breathed heavily. He allowed only a possibility. "Coulda been a nut"

"The fake plate, the timing—lonely road—two vehicles—"

"A nut might choose that scene, and he would fake his plates—"

Hayden felt tired and bruised. He believed the shunt was connected to the case, and if it was, it meant he was getting hot.

What he wanted to do was to pour himself a very big Scotch, and crawl into bed. He wanted to put a pillow over his head, and consign himself to oblivion for six or seven hours.

"Thanks for bringing me back, Al."

Hayden went up to his room sat on the bed, and poured a Scotch. He drank the Scotch with water from the bathroom tap, rather than go up the hall to the ice-machine. He eventually fell into a disturbed sleep, fully clothed on the bed, vipers crawling around inside his head.

Chapter 49

There was a big party at the Karamanlis in New York, and Sherry was there with her mother, and Vance Wayman.

Jed Olsen was holding court in the centre of one of the reception lounges, shaking hands, talking as people seemed to almost line up to greet him, when Diana, Sherry and Vance Wayman moved past.

Wayman swerved off in the other direction, touching Diana's arm gently as he did so, to signal he was better out of it. Diana and Sherry turned to Jed. There were greetings.

Sherry came reluctantly forward and let her cheek touch her father's quickly, and then stepped away. The onlookers' attention was soon attracted elsewhere, leaving the ex-family trio alone in the centre of the floor.

"Oh come on, Sherry, you don't bear a grudge against your dad do you?" Jed Olsen said, annoyed by his daughter's coolness.

"I can't forget what you did to Bob in a hurry. Messed up a good man, who did nothing wrong."

"Well we have different points of view about that. I—"

"Jed," Diana said, "what's the point in pursuing this?"

"You might at least talk to your daughter, act like a mother—" his voice dropped.

What he was going to add was, "instead of a whore". But he could stop the words coming out. And he did. His chest pulsed, his heart seemed to ball into a fist, and drum against his ribs.

Sherry stepped between them. "We're not going to have a family difference at the party of the year. I need a bit of space, Dad, to think things over. And if you want me back, please lay off Vance. He's a nice guy. I don't know what you're planning at this Senate Committee, but I know it's bad for Vance. You're going to hurt Mom, and you're going to hurt me—"

Jed Olsen had difficulty in getting his breath as his eighteen-year-old daughter laid down stipulations for their friendship, stipulations relating to *his* business, *his* career.

"Your mother and you have chosen to get involved with Wayman.

That's your problem. He's a sleazeball, and he'll get what he deserves—" Olsen said, forcing a kind of mildness, despite the vitriol of his words.

Diana for once lost her famous cool. "You oaf!" she hissed, almost loudly enough for other guests to hear, and she raised her arm and flicked her fingers in his face.

Jed Olsen caught Diana's wrist, and dug his fingertips in deep. She grimaced with pain. "You hurt my arm, Jed. I ought to let the people here know it."

"You wouldn't do that, would you?" He spat out the words confidently.

Just then, Sherry stepped between them. "But I would," she said.

She glared at her father, and he was momentarily taken aback by her determination.

He looked around the room, and through to the adjoining rooms. The guests were taking their pleasure with only an occasional glance at the celebrity pair, and their daughter.

Diana Wayman hustled Sherry away into the crowd.

Olsen stood for a moment, alone in the centre of the carpet, the gladiator feeling more like a deer in a clearing in the forest, nervously waiting for the attack. He fancied the people had become as still as alabaster busts, watching him. Olsen put his head up, and stalked away.

Chapter 50

"You persuaded Moody to go in there?"

"I didn't persuade him, Al. We both agreed that to make a decent report, we needed to get a closer look."

Gerstein was displeased with Hayden again. He was slumped over his paunch at the field office. "You guys went too far."

Hayden wanted to say Gerstein should have sent in a hit squad, but he didn't argue. He was too anxious to find out the result of the examination of the cabin. He looked away out of the window, and eventually Gerstein went on.

"Well the good news is, Mariette may be alive. She was definitely in the cabin. Slept in the bed in the cellar," Gerstein pronounced.

Hayden looked at him. "Chained up, and shot up," he said, with a mixture of relief, and pain.

"Oh you saw that, did you, on your private inspection? I guess, yes. DNA on the hypodermic. Hers. Drug of choice, heroin. Coke too."

"Not her choice. What a scumbag this man is."

"Another piece of news."

Gerstein soothed his stained fingers over the tongue of short black hair on his forehead. Hayden got a sense that this was a more important announcement in his mind.

"Two men in the cabin. The perp—we have his DNA from the Ryker cabin, and the Arkwright cabin. And *another*. We have his DNA."

Gerstein's little eye-slits were crimped in anticipation.

"Don't tell me. Haffner."

Gerstein exploded in a laugh which collapsed into a phlegmy cough. "You get the prize!"

"Now we only have to find where this screwball has taken them. Great. Really, really great," Hayden said.

Gerstein affected not to notice the sarcasm, because he was impressed with their progress.

"So Haffner wasn't on vacation. He was and is being held by a perp who is working for those who are behind the espionage," he said.

"It means my theory was right, Al. Haffner is seen as a weak link. He knows too much to be allowed his freedom at this time. He's in protective custody. That means our target company is Fairford. Olsen."

Gerstein's head swayed around uncertainly. "Maybe. A big hypothesis. And Mariette?"

Hayden couldn't think straight about Mariette. "Hostage, maybe. Or sexual plaything of a psychopath. Perhaps both."

★ ★ ★

Hayden was in the goldfish-bowl of darkened glass, looking out at late autumn's yellow and black remnants of forest.

Wayman had his stockinged feet on the desk.

It was two days before the Senate hearing. Hayden had told Wayman he was in big trouble. On the edge of losing STELA 2, and facing a corruption inquiry, Wayman had vowed he would take Jankovic down with him, and publicise Olsen's personal prejudice.

"You'll just have to face the legal process. It's like a grinder. If you're hard enough material, you'll come through."

Jeremy Segal's advice was echoing in Hayden's head.

Wayman sneered. He had no confidence in judicial processes. "You haven't helped me much, Mike."

"There's one card we can play. The FBI have evidence that Haffner is being held illegally. Haffner is Olsen's key man. If the FBI are prepared to say that there is reason to believe that Haffner is being silenced because of his involvement in espionage, that could halt any immediate moves."

Wayman's eyes glowed for a second, then died. "Yeah. I see it. But the FBI won't play ball. Gerstein is in this with Cerillo. Let Stella have a look up his ass. She'll find a briefcase full of dollar bills"

"I don't believe that."

Hayden's words were flat and cold and what he believed. He needed to add something soft to avoid rudeness. *Vance* would have been enough. But he had never been able to bring himself to call Wayman by his first name.

"Your Daddy would believe it!" Wayman said savagely.

★ ★ ★

Cathy Ong met Hayden at breakfast in the hotel looking hopeful.

Talking over their table was more important than the enticing smells of the buffet.

A check on the vehicle registration which Sorrel had provided before his death led eventually to a second-hand car dealer in Rochester, who sold the navy blue Renault van to a buyer named Steven Craig. Craig, who paid cash and left no true address, appeared, according to the FBI, to fit the description of the killer.

An urgent request for information on the van to all the city and county law enforcement officers in the Rochester-Syracuse area had produced no result.

Hayden wasn't too surprised.

"But the TV crimewatch reward has produced several sightings," Cathy said.

"The problem with those is where do we go from there?" Hayden asked. "And how many are chancers or nuts who want publicity?"

"There's been another development," Cathy said, passing a paper across to him. "An e-mail server has passed a message received by them to the FBI."

Hayden read the message: *inform fbi hafnr bway 9*.

"Al says they can't trace the sender, but maybe we can work out the message," Cathy said.

"It looks like a distress signal from Haffner. Tell the FBI I'm at B'way—what is that?—Broadway?—number 9. Perhaps the guy was able to lay his hands surreptitiously on a PC or a cellphone for a few seconds."

"Broadway sounds mostly like a road, or perhaps a geographical area, a suburb," Cathy added.

They passed on the toast and juice, and decided to have coffee in the office to save time. They went upstairs. Cathy spread an enlarged Rand-McNally map of Syracuse and the surrounding counties on the work-table.

"I've marked the blue van sightings in blue just to be complete. The only point to notice is that two sightings, from different informants, happen to be in this area." She indicated an area west of the city.

"What are the red marks?" Hayden asked.

"All the official references to *Broadway*. You can see there are three. All of them are roads."

Hayden could see the point. "And a couple of sightings are close to a particular Broadway. Nice work, CJ."

This was in the Westvale area of Syracuse.

"Are we going out there to look around?" Cathy asked.

"I'll have to call Gerstein. And you don't want to get involved. This guy's a killer. Hell, you know that."

"Isn't it premature to tell Al?" Cathy asked with an impish smile.

Hayden would like to have gone out there immediately, but he owed Gerstein. He called and told him.

Gerstein listened to Hayden quietly, only the scratching of his breath coming across the wire. Then he said, "Brain of America. Thanks for the info. And let me add: Fairford have a disused factory premises at Westvale, known as Broadway 9. Take a nap now while I deal with this, willya?"

"Right, Al, right, you already got it. You guys are wide awake today!"

"Gedout! And Mike, stay away from Broadway 9. I'll keep you informed."

★ ★ ★

Hayden drove to Le Moyne House to report to his client. He could see Wayman when he wanted, but otherwise he kept Karen Bridges in the picture. He outlined events at Dry Creek to her in her office. She took off the oval gold spectacles and fixed her big green eyes on him, her attractive but strong white hands clasped calmly before her. He regretted now that they had made love together, not because it wasn't good, but because it left a question mark hanging over every meeting. Hayden didn't quite know how to take her, and he was far too preoccupied with the case to think much of his own personal life.

He had a slow burn about the killer. He felt he had to find the man. One part of him wanted to kill the man for what he'd done to Mariette. At the same time, he felt Karen was expecting a statement from him about their relationship. Was it a one night stand, or the beginning of something more?

"So Mariette's still alive? I'm glad to hear that, Mike. Really. What she has been through, Jesus! This guy is something else."

"He's a fucking psychopathic monster. In one sense, she's no safer today—perhaps less so—that the day she was taken. I don't know whether we can save her."

"Leave it to the Bureau. You can't do it. You look a helluva worried man, Mike. I told you you'd lose objectivity—"

"The latest is that the crazy, and Haffner, and Mariette are probably holed up in an old Fairford works at Westvale. The FBI have traced them there."

"Nice work," Karen said, and she was ahead of him. "You want to go out there?"

Hayden let the question rest for a moment. "Yeah, I want to, but I don't know whether I should. Gerstein wants me to stay out of it, and I guess I've signalled I would."

There was a slight shine in her eyes. Perhaps she was thinking back to her days at the Bureau when a stakeout or a raid was in a day's work. "Want me to come?"

She put the question lightly, but she meant it.

He nodded yes. "But is it any of your official business?"

She turned sideways, opened the draw of her desk, and removed the shiny Sig Sauer. She placed it carefully on the desktop, holstered, with a packet of shells neatly alongside. She touched the cream gentian flowers in the vase at her elbow absently, still without looking at him.

"It depends how you interpret my job description. Looks like the people holed up at Westvale are behind the thefts from my employer. I'm in charge of security."

Hayden took another tack. "We could lose Gerstein's help. I've got two strikes against me already: Thunder River, and Dry Creek. I don't know what Al reports to his superiors, but I can guess he's saying that but for my interference, he could have wound the case up long ago."

Karen wasn't impressed. "If he's saying that, it's shit. We've helped him a lot. I don't think he has a beef. But I can tell you, imaginative reports can explain why you haven't solved a case, and assist your promotion. You want to go?"

Hayden did. He was thinking he *had* to go. And in many ways he couldn't have anybody better than Karen with him. She knew all the stealth assault caper. She was doing it for him, not for WayCom, but he didn't care.

★ ★ ★

Karen and Hayden cruised Westvale in one of the WayCom fleet of Chevrolets. They went along Third Street, and turned into Broadway. Hayden knew roughly from a map where the old Fairford works were.

This was an area that had been hit by the recession, broken advertising hoardings, empty factories, and abandoned shops, covered with posters and graffiti.

Hayden looked around as they slowed to a crawl.

Many properties lay back from the highway behind barricades of junk. Broadway was certainly broad. It had a wide centre strip that sprouted grass and weeds a yard high. The tarmac surface was wavy, and littered with wide and deep potholes that drivers had to skirt or suffer the shock of driving through.

He found the old Fairford lot, and Karen Bridges pulled over.

Pressing into his side was a Colt 38 seven shot, and bulging in his trouser pocket, a packet of shells—presents from Karen. He didn't tell her how little experience he had with firearms. When she handed him the smoothly blue Colt to him, she clicked the safety, and spun the chamber expertly.

"I expect you know how to use this," she had said, not as a question, more a statement.

Hayden guessed that in her estimation, every man worthy of the title knew how to use a handgun.

It was a clear day, and the brightness seemed to draw the colour from this trashed part of America. Everything Hayden could see through the windscreen, the signs, the old buildings, looked faded. A column of dust was whipped along the tarmac by the wind.

"What do you think the FBI are doing, Karen?"

"Thinking about it."

"How should we move? You know a lot more about this than I do."

"With only two of us? Common sense. We have a few acres of old buildings there. I figure our friends are deep in the heart of the place. They wouldn't be sitting at the front windows, would they? We slip down the track at the side of the property next door, get deep in, and find a place to get through to the Fairford site. I'd guess the fence is down in places, the way it looks from here. We can probably walk on to the site. How we get into the buildings, we'll have to wait and see."

Karen pulled a key ring from her pocket and jiggled it in front of him. It had a number of picks on it, as well as keys.

"And when we get in?" Hayden asked.

"Stay a few yards apart. One person moves at a time. The stationary person covers the mover. Then the stationary person comes up, covered by the mover. Step by step, like that. I lead."

"I'll be joining a SWAT team before long."

"And Mike. When we've sussed the joint out, we decide *together* what to do. One likely option being to retire and get help. OK? Understood?"

Hayden agreed.

Karen parked the car on a disused lot a couple of hundred yards down the road, and they made their way along the track of the disused property at the side of the Fairford site. They were both in jeans and dark sweaters, and Karen had provided two plain baseball caps from her office wardrobe.

The sign on the Fairford site, which had been painted out when the factory closed in a recession a decade earlier, was peeling to reveal the Fairford name. They were on course.

Hayden was calm. Somewhere inside himself, he could feel a flame that would come on like an oxyacetylene torch when his mind dwelled on the man.

It was as Karen had predicted. They eased through a rotten hole in the fence, and stepped on to the Fairford land, thick with wild grass and weeds. They examined some of the outbuildings for signs of life, before choosing an empty wing which was part of the main complex. The site had been vandalised, and many of the windows were broken. One broken window had wooden boxes stacked under it to enable entry from ground level.

"If they're here, they're in some part of the main building. We get in here, we move the same as I said," Karen whispered.

She picked the padlocks on the door, and they eased away the chains. They slid inside and listened. Hayden could hear the wind, a door creaking. Nothing to alarm him.

Karen moved in the lead, through the wing, deeper into the centre of the complex. The rooms were littered with old tables, shelving, filing cabinets, old PCs, and daubed with paint by intruders. The artists' attempts at the erotic were merely laughable. In one corner was a pile of excreta, and there was a stink like a urinal.

Karen kept ahead of Hayden in staged runs, the handgun gleaming in her fist. He hadn't removed the Colt from his belt yet. He didn't want to get into a shooting war. He wanted to feel his hands on the man.

Hayden did his best in true cop style to cover Karen's runs, and make his own. Whenever he felt awkward or exposed, the gas torch in his chest would spurt. It was worth the exposure.

They came to a glass ceilinged, open area which had served as an atrium. The glass cover was shattered. Rainwater had poured through and rotted the floor fifty feet below. Around the walls were four levels of offices joined by a gallery at each level, and at the far end, a wide flight of stairs, and the lift shafts for the now defunct elevators.

Hayden crouched out of sight. "We can't go in there," he said.

"We need to find a place where we can get a view, remain out of sight, and listen. A quarter hour of listening might be instructive,"

Karen said.

In fifteen minutes Hayden had located a small office with a window opening on the atrium, and they installed themselves inside. The window was broken in its lower corner, a hole six inches around which gave a clear view, and hearing, if they wanted it, or they could be obscured behind the glass, still with a view.

They sat on two empty boxes, huddled together, looking out, and waited. Hayden was turning in his mind the difficulty of searching the complex without being seen or heard.

In some way, they were going to have to circumnavigate the space facing them, because it was under view from a hundred angles and places. Their idea of finding the perp was becoming difficult, and dangerous, and foolhardy.

As they crouched together, Hayden could smell Karen. The vague waft of musky perfume the only clue to her femininity. She moved her leg against his, and slid toward the window.

Hayden followed her eyeline, and saw a man had appeared on the third gallery, virtually facing them. He was wearing a maroon tracksuit top, and had long lank hair and a frail face.

It looked like Haffner. Behind him and to the side, perhaps holding him, was another man, hardly distinguishable in the light at this distance.

Karen had crouched down over the back of a broken chair, resting her elbows. From under her bulky sweater she had drawn not the shiny gun, but a different weapon, which Hayden had never seen. It had a thin six-inch barrel, a mini-telescopic sight, and a longish handle that made her two-handed grip comfortable. She was sighting on the man.

"What in hell're you doing?" Hayden whispered, knocking the weapon as she squeezed the trigger.

The bullet tore out the rest of the pane of glass, and sent a crack echoing through the atrium. The men were gone.

"You stupid dick!" Karen snarled.

"We've got to take Haffner alive. He's the only link to the whole shitball. And we want the other guy too!" Hayden said.

Karen holstered the gun, waving her head around as though Hayden was a nutcase.

"You probably just passed the death sentence on Mariette and Haffner," he said.

"Crap," she said.

"What are you trying to do? You didn't even have a clear shot at the killer."

"Since when did you become an expert in armed assault? Stick to your torts, baby!"

Hayden made a gesture of hopelessness. "You've blown it now. Why don't you keep your head tucked right up your ass, and we'll go home. Tell Uncle Al. He'll fucking well fry you. Let's go."

He gave a sharp movement of his head in the direction of the door.

★ ★ ★

They spent a few minutes working their way back gingerly toward the wing they had entered. Hayden was in turmoil. He was thinking that the killer would be alarmed by the shot, and make a break for it—he surely wasn't going to hole up, and risk a firefight.

There was still a chance of getting to the killer Hayden calculated, and he had almost decided that he alone might return to the atrium, when Karen mouthed silently, "We got company."

Hayden looked outside to see two or three men in grey overalls with rifles, bullet-proof vests and metal head protectors. It was Gerstein's force, and Karen and Hayden were between them and the killer.

They sat with their backs to the wall, and heads down, like troops in the trenches, while Hayden figured what to do. He was still scorchingly angry about her gun-happy tactics.

"Sooner or later they'll get up to the outside wall. I'll call to them then, tell them who we are. Hope they don't start shooting," he said.

"A woman's voice, and I guess they'll respond—"

"OK" Hayden said.

"But it was a woman's fucking gun that we needed earlier!" Karen said, grating the words out between her teeth.

"Wrap it up, will you?"

They sat quietly, listening to the grunting and stamping as the FBI men positioned themselves outside.

When Karen judged the Bureau men were in position, and about to enter, she called out to them. Her low voice would have been easily audible through the row of broken windows above them. She stated who they were. Silence.

A few minutes passed before a voice told them to move out of the wing doors.

At the same moment, gunfire broke out in the atrium. A blistering crackle of automatic weapons that came resonating down the wing.

On impulse, instead of following Karen, Hayden started to make his way back to the atrium.

Karen was nearly at the door before she looked around, and realised he wasn't following. He had only a glimpse of her face, rippled with exasperation, before he went on.

When he got back to the atrium, the space was full of gunsmoke, thick enough to prickle the eyes. FBI men, sited in half a dozen different places, who had approached from other wings, were pouring fire into the third level—where the men had appeared.

On the way out with Karen, Hayden had seen a passage behind the atrium which would enable him to get to a secondary set of stairs. He went along the passage, and up the stairs to the third level without exposing himself. He pulled out the 38.

He guessed there would be more than one entrance to the rooms likely to be occupied by the killer and his prisoners. He was hoping like hell now, that Karen had told the FBI, loud and clear, that he was still in here.

But in the mayhem of gunfire, his head throbbed, and he was no longer reasoning clearly. He had an urge to get to the man which he knew was slightly manic, and overcame his fears. It had some of the demented unstoppability of a cavalry charge.

He stepped into the first room, and Gerstein was there. He jerked his head around to Hayden. Gerstein looked red-eyed and crazed. He had two men with him. They all had Ruger Mini 14 semi-automatics.

The FBI men began firing, tearing the thin wood of the movable partition which enclosed the adjoining room to shreds, wood chips and dust clouding the air.

Hayden shouldered Gerstein so hard, Gerstein stumbled sideways on one knee, and Hayden thought for a moment that in surprise and rage Gerstein would turn the gun on him.

"You want to kill everybody?" Hayden shouted.

The FBI men stopped firing, and there was a moment of incredible silence in the haze of gunsmoke.

The powder pinched Hayden's nostrils. He could see through the holes punched in the screen. The next room was empty.

Gerstein gave him a fierce look, and led his men past the partition. Hayden followed.

From the empty cans of beer and cola and a half eaten packet of donuts, it looked as though the room had been used as a refuge. It contained only a trestle table, and a few hard chairs. Along the walls, crates of abandoned office equipment, vandalised lamps, printers, fax machines.

The FBI men filtered slowly down through the building, Gerstein muttering on the radio to his section commanders. Hayden followed, learning that the whole force had lost sight of the killer, and his captives.

The assault team gathered silently at a side exit from the building. Gerstein's commanders were assuring him by radio that they had covered every inch of the premises.

They stood in damp, knee-high grass and weeds, confused. Hayden was waiting for a sign of Mariette's presence, but there was none.

"Shut up!" Gerstein said, as the muttering broke out.

Then they all heard a vehicle engine starting, a couple of quick growls, and the whine of low gear.

"It's over the fucking fence," Hayden said.

Gerstein swore, and began to lead his men up, and then down the fence-line to find a way through. In twenty yards he found a hole, and squeezed through. Two of his men followed, and Hayden pushed in next.

Gerstein ordered them to spread out. They scattered amongst the cluster of small red-brick buildings on the site.

Hayden was on his own, with a gun in his hand, creeping along the blind wall of a building without a clue what he might find at the corner. He listened at the corner and, hearing nothing, came gingerly round. He was faced with an empty alley. He ran quietly down the alley. At the end, there was movement. He could hear a motor revving slowly, and somebody moving around. He took a careful look.

Ten yards away was the dark blue van, its exhaust popping as it idled, with the grey haired man hefting the tall skinny figure Hayden recognised as Haffner, into the back.

The man looked up from his task and saw Hayden. He pulled Haffner in front of him as a shield, slammed the rear doors closed, and dragged a terrified Haffner, his arms and legs stiff like a scarecrow, towards the cab.

Gerstein came round the corner of the building a hundred yards away, the Ruger in firing position at his hip. He loosed off a magazine as soon as he saw the van, punching out its windows.

Haffner broke free, and hit the ground.

The killer gave up Haffner, and concentrated on getting the van away. He revved the motor, hit first gear, and spun the wheels on the grass as he snaked past Hayden, and Gerstein, down the track toward the rear of the lot.

A punishing burst of gunfire from Gerstein at the rear of the retreating van seemed to have no effect.

Hayden ran to Haffner who squirmed in agony. He had taken a slug in the arm.

Gerstein called an ambulance, while his on-site paramedics stopped the bleeding, and gave Haffner tetanus, and morphine.

Hayden assumed Gerstein had no unit watching the road which served the rear of the lots. His men hung around awkwardly although it was clear they were relieved the stakeout was over. They waited for Haffner to be moved.

When Hayden could get Gerstein alone, he said, "You damn nearly killed Haffner. That's your lead in him!"

"The perp could have slugged me."

"He had his hands full of Haffner, and trying to drive."

"Yeah, well, I wasn't goin' to debate it with him. He's a nut."

"How many rounds did the FBI fire back in the building, Al? A thousand? How many did the man fire? One, two, three?"

Gerstein's lips lifted off his stained teeth like a dog getting ready to snarl. "Listen counsellor. I got men with families here. Doin' their job. We don't take chances."

"Or prisoners," Hayden said.

★ ★ ★

When Hayden called Wayman and told him they had a wounded Haffner, who probably wouldn't take much persuading to talk, he wasn't as optimistic as Hayden expected.

"Ya sure you're goin' to get an opportunity to talk to him, Mike?"

Hayden was assuming Gerstein and he would talk to Haffner together. "I think so."

"My bet is, you'll find Dr Haffner is incommunicado. Doctors, family, his employer, the FBI—but not you."

After his report to Wayman, Hayden took a taxi to the Bush Memorial Hospital. He was disappointed at Wayman's negative reaction to his good news. But when Hayden got to the hospital he began to think Wayman was right.

Haffner's ward had a permanent duty sister at the desk, and she wouldn't let him enter, even though the word was that Haffner was fit enough to see visitors. Also, she had an FBI agent standing guard about a yard away. She said Dr Haffner had a very limited number of people who could see him at present.

As luck would have it, Gerstein and an assistant came out when he was talking to the sister. Hayden hailed him.

Gerstein didn't give Hayden a chance to speak: "No, Mike, you can't see him. One, he's too sick. Two, this is an FBI investigation. Send some candies, and make an appointment for a month from now."

Gerstein marched off, leaving Hayden gasping. Then Hayden saw a man he recognised coming down the hall, tall, well-suited, with longish, wavy, silver-gold hair which caught the light and shone. A young woman walked at his side with flowers.

Hayden stood back for Jed Olsen. Olsen stared at him curiously, as though he had met Hayden, but didn't quite remember who he was. Olsen and the girl were admitted by the sister immediately.

Hayden drove away from the hospital reflecting on Karen and the FBI's killing assault on Broadway 9. And the way that ranks had closed around Haffner since, cutting him out. And maybe leaving Mariette even further out.

Chapter 51

The next morning Hayden called in at the field office for his routine briefing with Gerstein. When he went in, Gerstein had cleared his desk, and was sipping a carton of coffee. He waved Hayden to a seat, and Hayden had a feeling that the atmosphere had changed. They weren't going to have the usual working session.

"What do you have for me, Mike?" Gerstein said brusquely, hardly looking up.

Hayden was surprised. "Nothing. You're the one with all the news. Forensics on the hideout at Broadway 9, the Haffner story."

"Uh-huh. Tests show the same three people as at Dry Creek."

"So Mariette is still alive!"

"I'd say."

"Do you have any plan to apprehend this lunatic?"

Gerstein made a helpless gesture. "He's disappeared."

"And Haffner. Is Haffner going to admit he has been in receipt of stolen technology?"

"I don't think he has. I think we can bin this hypothesis. Haffner thinks he was abducted to give info to the people who have been stealing your client's work, but the plan went awry."

"What does he say about the guy holding him?"

"That he's only a stooge. A heavy. And a nut. Probably knows nothing about the espionage operation."

Then the question about which Hayden was deeply apprehensive: "Mariette. What does he say about her?"

"She's there. We know she's there. Zonked out on drugs most of the time."

"Could Haffner talk to her?"

"He only knew of her presence just before they moved to Broadway 9—though he knew there was somebody else at Dry Creek. Haffner says she was too spaced out to talk sense."

"Why is the man keeping her?"

"Haffner doesn't know. Like a pet. The creep seems soft on her."

Gerstein sat back, and then reached his in-tray from the shelf behind him, as though the meeting was over, and he was going to start work.

"Al, can I see Haffner?"

"No, you can't Mike. That's final. Oh and one other thing. Sorrel. Had a long needle inserted in his brain from the back of his neck, and removed, before he was tipped out of the fishing boat."

★ ★ ★

The brother of one of Hayden's partners in DC was director of orthopaedics at the Bush Memorial Hospital. Hayden asked his partner to call his brother, and persuade him to see Hayden. "What's the favour you want, Mr Hayden?" Dr Flexner asked Hayden in his consulting room at the hospital, screwing up his eyes as though lawyers were a rare genus.

Hayden explained.

Flexner was still mystified. "You people sure get into convoluted situations. But OK, if this patient is being held incommunicado as you say—sounds screwy to me—I mean the FBI, you have to trust them—I guess I should do what I can—which is not much—and you'll have to leave if there's any adverse reaction from the patient—and I don't want to be any part of this anyone asks you, you took the passcard yourself."

He reluctantly reached a pass from a holder on the wall.

"Look, Mr Hayden, I'm trusting you with this. And you'll have to be discreet about how you use it."

He handed Hayden the card which explained that the bearer was engaged in checking computer systems. "This will get you into the ward."

★ ★ ★

Both the duty sister and the Federal agent were different people to those on duty when Hayden first called, and he passed into the ward after normal visiting time in the evening without a query.

Haffner was in a private room. He was sitting on a couch beside the bed in a dressing gown, reading a magazine, when Hayden let himself in. Hayden could see from the parting in Haffner's robe that his chest was strapped up, but he looked well, and moved without pain. He seemed glad of the interruption.

Hayden guessed Haffner didn't know of the walls that had been constructed around him. Hayden reminded him who he was.

"Come and sit down," Haffner said. "I remember you in the FBI group that came to my apartment."

Hayden asked him how he got his message out on e-mail.

"My jailer was using e-mail. He left the machine to go to the john. My hands were free enough."

Hayden said he knew the young woman who had been at Dry Creek, and in the factory, and was anxious about her.

"Yes, the girl. I suppose I was suffering from shock myself, and didn't take things in as sharply as I should have, but I didn't know she was at the cabin until the day we left, when Mac—that's what he told me to call him—brought her up from the cellar, all dirty and stinking and only half conscious."

"She was drugged."

"I realised that. Mac seemed quite, I don't know, anxious to see she was comfortable. Kinda soft on her. I didn't understand how she fitted in."

Hayden told Haffner the complete story as he understood it. He explained who Mariette was. Haffner already knew a little about Bray and Leman—certainly knew they were dead, and had suspected that their deaths had something to do with espionage. Of which he was a beneficiary. Hayden recounted the murder of Delia Marris, clearly down to Haffner's captor, and that of Sorrel.

Haffner listened with riveted concentration. Hayden felt the sensitive wheels inside that highly intelligent head were sifting and weighing the story.

"What have you told Mr Gerstein about your part in this?"

"I guess I've kind of stalled him. I have to think of my own interests."

"What I'm saying to you Dr Haffner is that this is big and won't go away. You may think Olsen is your benefactor, but he's the person bankrolling the goon who held you. You came within a few inches of being killed. When it suits him, Olsen will have you killed to save himself. He doesn't want you dead yet, because that might cause questions at the Senate Committee. But later, if he fears you will weaken, he'll wipe you out like Bray and Leman and Marris and Sorrel."

Haffner paused, folded the magazine absently and pushed it away on the couch. "It's hard to believe. Jed Olsen. I mean, goddam …"

"He doesn't do these things himself, he just gives the orders."

"But still—"

"The technology is worth billions, and Olsen hates Wayman," Hayden said quietly.

Haffner was unconvinced. "There's always a little leakage about secret projects. Somebody disloyal. It's endemic in the industry. It's about human beings, and the way they are. That's why, when I started to get secret material, I thought, lucky me."

"But it's gone on and on, a concerted program of espionage involving murder."

"Mr Hayden, I can tell you, I didn't have a single qualm at first."

Hayden could see Haffner was an unworldly man. Life in the laboratory had its passions, but they were sheltered.

"I believe you. Perhaps even Olsen felt the same way at first. But once on the path, you go on."

Haffner frowned, and wrenched his mouth bitterly. "But if I talk, my reputation will be ruined, and I'll probably go to prison."

"You'll get off a lot easier if *you* are the one to bring it out in the open."

"I accept that, but—"

"Do you seriously think these thefts, and deaths, are going to shrivel up and dematerialise?"

"No, the pressure will get worse, I agree, but—"

Hayden could see Haffner was following him. A drop of sweat ran from Hayden's hairline down his temple, wriggling like a transparent worm in the overheated room. Then another, as he strained to persuade.

"And can you in your conscience withstand the pressure?" Hayden asked in a low voice.

For the first time he noticed the flexing of the muscles in Haffner's jaw. "Maybe not."

"And can you trust Olsen not to kill you?"

"He nearly did ... OK, Mr Hayden. What do I have to do?"

★ ★ ★

Haffner and Hayden walked brazenly out of the ward without challenge or recognition. The nurse on duty, and the FBI guard, were only interested in people going in.

Hayden drove Haffner to the Bowen Hotel. When he had checked in, Hayden handed Haffner the phone and suggested he call the hospital, explain he was discharging himself.

Hayden called Wayman, told him he was right about Haffner being gagged, and explained that they were together now at the Bowen.

"Nice work, Mike. I take back what I said about your help. Shit,

I know you've been on the case. What does Haffner say?"

"That he's prepared to admit that a woman colleague of Olsen's fed him with info. He knew that he had access to somebody else's research. Didn't think too much about it at first, since he says it goes on in the industry all the time. After a time, he became alarmed at the flow of secret material, and has now decided to tell all."

"Now, all you have to do is keep Haffner alive for the hearing," Wayman laughed harshly.

★ ★ ★

Gerstein roared at Hayden over the telephone, "I'm going to indict you, you fucking asshole, interfering with justice, abducting an FBI witness!"

"Hey, wait a minute, Al," Hayden said in his friendliest tone. "We had a briefing. You told me Haffner was off the hook. He wasn't a witness to anything according to you—"

"I'll indict, I said! You'll end in the pen, like your old man."

"I advise against it, Al. I have a tape that just happened to be running when we talked about Haffner. Every word you said. I'll let you have a copy."

Gerstein cut the call.

★ ★ ★

Hayden sat at his desk in the ops room at the Bowen, head in hands, thinking about Gerstein and his attitude. Cathy Ong looked on, trying to contribute to this new line of concern.

At the time, Hayden hadn't given much credence to Wayman's remark that Gerstein was crooked. Wayman was a man who thought low, made cruel remarks. But Hayden asked himself now whether Wayman might be right.

Gerstein hadn't exactly thrown himself into the inquiry. He was late in getting to Thunder Lake, he sent Don Moody to Dry Creek instead of a squad, he came in to Dry Creek by chopper scaring every crow within miles, he and his team used excessive fire-power at Broadway 9, and didn't seem to care if they gunned Haffner, and Gerstein had declared Haffner hadn't any useful evidence. All these events might be capable of innocent explanations, but they stacked up.

"Do you think Stella would have anything?" Cathy asked.

It was an idea. Turn the machine on its master, as he had done with Stella and Cerillo.

Hayden expected his access to Stella might have been cancelled.

But it hadn't. He punched her up on e-mail, and then decided to go personally to the Defense Department building when he was in Washington.

★ ★ ★

When Hayden had retired to his hotel room, and was having a shower and a large nightcap of Scotch, there was a knock at the door.

He was wary. Somebody who didn't want to report to the desk. He looked out of the peephole.

A woman. Karen Bridges.

He opened the door. She put her head on one side demurely and asked if she could come in.

Her hair had been washed and combed out so it glinted. She wore a short skirt and jacket, high heels. Not the tough broad in jeans and sweater whose face was creased in antipathy last time Hayden had seen her.

"Vance told me. You've been moving," she said, impressed, entering.

Hayden didn't know whether to believe Wayman had told her. She was probably taping everything on the line.

"I'm getting there, slowly."

"Can I talk to Haffner?" she asked.

"If you want. If he's not asleep. Don't take long. The guy's a bit weakened. I didn't think you'd want to speak to me again."

He cracked a smile with difficulty.

She sighed seriously. "I guess we have different ways of doing things, that's all."

He phoned Haffner, and took her to Haffner's room briefly. When they came away he said, "He'll stitch up Olsen."

"Yeah, I guess. That's it then?"

"Not exactly. There's Mariette, that psychopath, and the fair woman, or had you forgotten?"

They were standing outside Hayden's room, looking, for the want of anything else, at the trays of half-eaten food that guests had left outside their doors for room service to collect.

"I didn't mean it that way," she said. "Mike, let's have a drink and make up." She pressed against him, firm but yielding.

"I've got to work tonight, sorry. Another time."

★ ★ ★

Hayden was awakened in the morning at six by a noise in the hallway outside his bedroom, high frantic tones. He threw on a dressing gown, and went out.

He recognised the night manager frantically giving orders to his staff, people with startled looks on the faces. Hayden asked him what was wrong.

"Somebody forced their way into the room you reserved last night for Dr Haffner, and he isn't there—"

"See anybody?"

"None of the staff saw the intruder. He appears to have searched the room, and left."

Hayden walked down to Haffner's room. The frame of the door was split where it had been forced with a crowbar, the empty room trashed, drawers pulled out of the dressing table, bed upended.

"You don't need to worry. Dr Haffner hasn't been abducted. He left last night," Hayden said. "The intruder was too late. I'll take care of his account."

Fortunately, Hayden had arranged with a local private investigator for Haffner to be taken away to a safe place. Haffner had been collected last night, and would be kept safe and delivered to Washington, to the Senate, for the hearing.

Hayden had come to the point of suspecting everybody. The only people who knew Haffner was at the Bowen, apart from Wayman and himself, were Karen, Gerstein, and Haffner's family—unless Hayden was being watched, or the phone lines he had used with security devices weren't so secure.

Hayden's suspicions turned to Karen, and her oafish performance at Broadway 9.

★ ★ ★

Hayden got an early plane to Washington, and went straight to the Defense Department building. He produced his pass, and was admitted to Stella's presence.

He interrogated her about Gerstein. All he got, apart from Gerstein's CV, was that he had been transferred from bank fraud investigations after an internal bribery inquiry in which he was acquitted. That didn't necessarily mean that Gerstein was a dirty potato, but it could be an indication.

Stella had nothing on Gerstein's personal finances except that he lived in a condo in the Meridian Hill area of Washington. Cathy had already run a credit inquiry on him which simply showed he was solvent.

Then Hayden tried Stella on something she was good at: "What running strands of coated wire across the floor. The lawyers were coming in with armfuls of books and manuals, and the clerks were fussing over the microphones and place-names.

Wayman settled down inconspicuously at the back of the room, and before Hayden left him, Karen Bridges appeared, her usual ginger halo neatly coiffured. She asked Hayden what was happening, and he gave a confidently vague answer.

Hayden prowled the corridors outside the committee room, waiting for Cerillo, Olsen, Jankovic, and Capel to arrive. He anticipated they would be surrounded by a flock of lawyers, and so access would be difficult.

He already knew James Orbach, the principal lawyer behind the affidavits of Jankovic and Capel, and Orbach would behave like a fullback. Letting Hayden through to his clients would be like conceding a score.

Hayden accosted the bunch of them when they filed into the waiting room a half-hour later. But as he thought, Orbach insisted that Hayden talk only to him. Hayden knew he'd get nowhere. But Cerillo wasn't Orbach's client, and Cerillo, ever cautious, was prepared to talk.

The pair walked down a passage away from the waiting rooms.

"I'm not sure whether I'm wasting my time, Mr Hayden."

"On the contrary, Mr Cerillo, you're saving yourself the embarrassment of a lifetime."

Hayden could only see the whites of Cerillo's eyes as the large head was turned toward him in the dark passage.

"That will take some justifying."

They went down the corridor and stood by a small window looking out to Union Square. It was shadowed and cramped where they stood, and Hayden was looking down on Cerillo's shiny skull, with the great brown orbs beneath, like a strange sea creature.

Hayden told Cerillo he should withdraw the testimony from Jankovic and Capel.

"Jankovic is trying to cover up sexual offences against a minor, and Capel is going to be indicted for tax fraud. On allegations as serious as bribery of high officials of government, they have no credibility."

Cerillo was startled and quiet. The luminous eyes, reflecting the light from the window, settled on Hayden.

"That's for the Committee to say, Mr Hayden. The allegations of Jankovic and Capel are going to take some while to resolve, even if you attack their credit. Wayman is in financial trouble. He's had breaches of security. The Committee will be very unhappy."

"I think we should have a private and confidential meeting with Mr Olsen. I believe he's here, in the building. You see, the security breaches result from espionage, and there is evidence of a link to Mr Olsen."

"Preposterous, Mr Hayden."

"Preposterous or not, you should hear me out in Mr Olsen's presence, and then we might agree what evidence can be put to the Committee."

Cerillo thought quickly, and glanced at his watch. A smile hovered at the corners of his urbane mouth.

"I'll see if we can indulge you."

★ ★ ★

From the small window, Hayden could see clear to the Lincoln Memorial, flaring in the winter sun. He waited, hands in pockets. He reckoned he had about thirty minutes to make a deal before the hearing got underway, and perhaps crashed out of control.

Wayman's shining face loomed at him. "I asked you to take a seat in the committee room, Mr Wayman, and let me do my work for you." Hayden had no time left for friendly civilities.

"Jesus, Mike, it's my fuckin' company. My business. Any dealin' I wanna know."

Both men became aware of a movement along the passage, and looked in that direction. Cerillo and Olsen had been approaching, but now, on seeing Hayden and Wayman, had stopped. A light from a window near them illuminated them faintly, the fat frog Cerillo, and the tall, noble Olsen.

"Listen good, Wayman," Hayden mouthed between tight lips. "I am going to talk to these two men for you. You stay, and there'll be no talk. If you want to screw up, stick around."

The street kid in Wayman flamed for only a silent instant. Then he was still. Then he stuck out his chin and marched away in the opposite direction along the passage.

As Wayman retreated, Cerillo and Olsen advanced.

"Difficult client, Mr Hayden?" Cerillo asked with a flutter of amusement.

Hayden moved his jaw non-committally. "Let's talk."

"I'm not sure I should be here" Olsen said. "I have an extremely expensive lawyer only a few rooms away. But the view is splendid, even if these windows are rather mean."

"Time's running short, Mr Hayden," Cerillo said.

Hayden began in low key. "I'm asking you not to present the Jankovic-Capel evidence. I'm not going to attempt to persuade you it's perjured. All I will say is that if you go ahead, Professor Peter Haffner will give evidence linking Mr Olsen to espionage at WayCom. And I remind you, that the espionage is linked to a number of killings."

Cerillo and Olsen were expressionless in the silence that followed. Two men suddenly cast in stone.

"I'll leave you for a moment. I'll walk to the end of the passage and back. Then you can tell me how you want to play it," Hayden added, and he moved slowly away.

When he returned, Cerillo was alone.

"You mean this man—what's his name?—Haffner, is prepared to stick his neck in a noose?" Cerillo said incredulously.

"Somebody has to level, eventually."

Cerillo was still again. Hayden could see the small tracery of blood vessels at his temples.

"Look," Cerillo said, "I'll make a deal with you, Mr Hayden. Keep Haffner out, and I'll withdraw Jankovic and Capel."

"So you'll be talking about cost overruns, nothing about security?"

"We won't blame Wayman, put it that way, for the breaches of security. It'll be espionage by persons unknown."

They parted. Hayden thought Cerillo had been quick on his feet, anticipating the danger. He wanted to protect Olsen.

The PI Hayden had hired was now in one of the witness rooms with Haffner. Cathy Ong was with them. Hayden greeted them abruptly, and asked them to wait.

Hayden now had some sense of control. He spent fifteen minutes on the phone to Jeremy Segal at Justice, getting his view of the rights and wrongs, and then went back to report to Wayman.

It was two or three minutes before the hearing was due to start. Senator Latham, the Committee chairman, and all his members were already in place. The room was packed.

Wayman gave Hayden a scowl, anticipating a failure. Hayden fished him out of the back seat, leaving Karen, and escorted him down the aisle to the two vacant seats available to them in the front row.

"What happened?" Wayman whispered.

"Better wait and see," Hayden said.

Senator Latham banged his gavel, and called the room to order as Wayman and Hayden took their seats, a half a minute ahead of time.

The Senator announced the review of several defence contracts in a low voice, gabbled the serial numbers. The first was ITC 4042, known as STELA 2.

The Senator was brisk, almost impatient. He asked for an opening statement from the Director of Intelligence at the National Security Agency.

Byron Cerillo, ignoring the pile of notes before him, blandly explained that apart from problems on cost overruns, and a lapse in the schedule, the contract was proceeding satisfactorily.

Wayman was astounded. "Shee-it!" he whispered.

There was a murmur of approval from the room. Hayden looked across at Wayman. Wayman nodded and smiled enthusiastically.

Senator Latham asked for details on the costs and delays. Cerillo responded with a summary, and the Senator said they didn't sound too bad. He joked that they would hear a lot worse today.

Senator Harden said he was surprised there were no issues, and that the NSA were satisfied with performance. He raised his thick grey eyebrows questioningly. What he could not say was that the scuttlebutt that he had heard in the corridors outside said exactly the reverse.

Cerillo smiled indulgently, and repeated that the NSA were broadly satisfied, but that was subject to continued progress being made to resolve costs, and speed up the schedule.

"What about the question of espionage?" Senator Harden asked.

The audience was suddenly at attention. Nothing had ever been said publicly about espionage against STELA 2, but the gossip in the passages and waiting rooms outside the committee room was thick with it. Senator Harden was on touchy ground.

"It's under investigation by the FBI. I can't say more."

"Have there been serious losses?"

"I don't think any losses can be assessed. I have to leave it to the FBI to complete their investigation."

Harden accepted with a curt nod. His experience on the Hill told him things had happened which he, as a mere representative of the people, would never learn.

Wayman leaned over feeling he had missed a move in the game. "What did you do, Mike? It was a breeze."

"I made a deal with Cerillo: bless STELA 2, and we don't call Haffner."

Chapter 53

The Senate chambers were deep in shadow. The light glowed dully on the wooden panels. The portraits of the politicians in the corridor had heard many whispered secrets. The two men walked slowly, one very tall, and the other short and rotund, moving quietly. The tall man radiated silent ferocity. The small man spoke gently, surely.

"There will be another time Jed. The Committee will reconvene to hear new evidence, perhaps as little as six months from now, and then you can bring forward Jankovic and Capel. But now, while Haffner is loose, you're in danger, Jed, and we would only be compounding that danger by trying to press ahead now."

★ ★ ★

After the hearing, Hayden had a brief view of Jed Olsen in the crowd. Olsen wasn't surrounded by his usual retinue. He was alone, his head cast down, his usually glowing expression gaunt.

Wayman wanted Hayden to dine with him and his wife at the Four Seasons, but he refused. When Wayman's limousine had swept him away, Hayden was left with Karen Bridges on the sidewalk. They headed down the Hill, toward the Monument silhouetted against a sky that was now darkening and angry.

"You've got one happy client," Karen Bridges said.

"At a price. We should have had a full and open hearing."

"Don't be a purist, Mike. Vance has got what he wanted. You delivered for him. With the testimony of Jankovic, Capel and Haffner, the hearing would have snowballed into a major inquiry, probably with a special prosecutor. And taken months or even years. Vance may even have lost the contract."

"We still have to nail Olsen."

"The FBI will do that if he's guilty. You're getting it out of proportion, like I've said before. It's the Mariette factor."

Hayden looked at her coldly. She smiled and took his arm but it didn't warm the chill he felt at the mention of Mariette's name.

"Why don't you take me to your place, and give me a stiff whisky to warm me up?" Karen said.

* * *

Hayden called a cab, and took Karen to his apartment. She pulled her coat and scarf off and dropped them on a chair. She slipped her jacket off too, and flexed her shoulders in the cashmere sweater she wore underneath, which showed every curve as though it was glued to her.

She wandered around the rooms, stopping at times to look more closely at the titles of some of the books lying around.

When Hayden had poured a double malt on the rocks for her, she sat down, taking the glass. "Hey this place is nice, Mike. Very you."

"What does that mean?"

"Oh, kinda ... untidy, comfortable, no bullshit, a certain pizzaz—like that."

He couldn't work out whether Karen thought this a good combination of qualities or not.

Karen was in a seductive frame of mind, her green eyes caught the light, and her ginger hair, which she shook out of the hairdresser's mould, seemed to be aflame. But Hayden found it difficult to follow her on-off passions. One moment squirming with desire, another, cool and verbally abusive.

But he was warming to her as always, and wanting to put out of his mind the tangle of the case. His mind moved several frames forward to persuading her to lie back on his duvet, and ...

"Look," he said when they had finished their drinks, "I've got work to do tonight, Karen. I'll call you a cab to your hotel."

When Karen had gone, he rang Al Gerstein, told him about the hearing.

"I already heard," Gerstein said.

"Any progress on the perp?"

"None. He disappeared again. We have some sightings of a blue van. We're pushing the reward on TV."

Another quite different thought had been troubling Hayden. "Al, Haffner is a material witness. I have an affidavit from him. I reckon he's at risk. He's a link to Olsen, and the blonde woman. He needs protection while you sort out his evidence."

"Hey, who's running the FBI? I'll deal with the case, Mike."

"Don't think too long. The guy's in danger!"

***

The next morning Hayden fetched four newly baked donuts filled with jam and cream from the bakery on the corner of M Street, and took them up to the apartment.

He and Cathy Ong sat at the table getting some early sun through the glass, and having breakfast. Cathy made the thick Costa Rican filter coffee he liked. It had a kick like a saddle bronc.

They talked over what they had learned from Haffner. Haffner's immediate contact had been the ubiquitous blonde woman, but Haffner had added one important fact that took them beyond mere physical description. She was an IT expert.

She understood the nature of the material she was providing, and what part it could play in developing STELA 2. Haffner had met her on four or five occasions. The conversations had been brief, but Haffner was sure he hadn't been talking with a mere messenger.

"We have this description. I can almost see her," Cathy Ong said. "Although the woman is a fairly common type."

"And she's in the industry. And from what Haffner says, no ordinary nerd. She's a mover. Is she in a big corporation? Could be, but I don't think so. She's an independent, a small company person."

"Search all the small IT companies for a tall blonde in her thirties?" Cathy smiled. "That's a tall order."

"No, we can't do that."

"Maybe she's been brought in from abroad—the foreign accent," Cathy said. "A loner, working for a foreign government."

Hayden sighed. "Not a loner. Too much org behind everything she does. But still, it's a whole lot of maybes. Nothing we can home in on, and search or analyse … Haffner couldn't be holding out on us, could he? Just trying to think the unthinkable."

"I believe we've pumped him dry," Cathy said.

Hayden wasn't sure, and despite Cathy's insistence that there was a whole lot more information about the case to review, he pushed the pile of files she laid in front of him aside, and pulled on a leather jacket.

The truth was he wasn't very interested in part two of his legal brief—find out who had benefited from WayCom technology, and sue the ass off them. He was interested in finding Mariette. The lawsuit was secondary.

He went downstairs and made a short call to Haffner to ascertain he was in the Syracuse apartment Hayden's PI had arranged for him, waiting for the FBI.

"Let's get back to Syracuse. I want to talk to Haffner some more before Al takes him in", Hayden said to Cathy.

Chapter 54

Heidi Stoller could enter the Springvale property by a side road which led directly to the cabin. Olsen deliberately kept the cabin empty for this purpose.

Heidi and Olsen were sitting on folding chairs on the porch, looking over several hundred acres of lush, well-fenced pastureland to a distant pine plantation. Olsen had brought vodka and orange, and asked the housekeeper to let him have a bag of cookies. It was noon on a cool sunny day as they sipped their drinks from the Waterford crystal glasses that Olsen also provided.

"You didn't want to come?" he asked.

"I'd have preferred not to, Jed. Only your insistence has brought me. I've sold the business. I'm about ready to leave, but—"

"Where are you going?"

"Oh, Europe for a while. I don't know long term."

She seemed to measure her destination against this place. "You have a wonderful home here, Jed."

"I always think of it that way. Even if I don't have a wife."

"At the moment! You'll marry again. Maybe two or three times. Why did you insist on me coming up, Jed? Our business is finished. We both agree it's too hot to handle any more."

"Heidi, we have to talk about Haffner. He's in Wayman's hands. And he's going to do me in. Tie me to the stolen technology. And possibly to other things," Olsen said, with a sick look.

He couldn't bear to think of the killings, let alone mention them.

Heidi thought for a while. If Haffner talked to the FBI he'd implicate her too, even if he couldn't identify her precisely. And it was a fair bet that eventually the FBI would find out who she was. She'd never be able to return to the 'States. If Haffner didn't exist, the trail would go completely cold.

"OK, Jed. I'll get somebody to deal with Haffner. You'll need to let me have a large sum in cash."

★ ★ ★

Addis was a man of the mountains, and he'd chosen to return, and make his hide, in another part of the Adirondacks. In the cities he felt constrained and wary, always looking over his shoulder at somebody looking at him. In the hills and mountains he felt free, with a dozen directions to run, and the comfort of thick almost impenetrable forest around him, cut by rivers and lakes, each one a road to freedom.

Addis wasn't for running. He didn't think he'd have to run. All he needed to do was snug down awhile, and let the FBI get bored. After a few months he'd think about buying some classy wheels, and maybe hitting Vegas with that pile of bucks he'd earned.

Heidi Stoller knew exactly where Addis was. She had helped him set up his hides. She had never actually been to Newcomb Lake between Mount Marcy and Kempshall Mountain, and she drove up Interstate 87 past Lake George and Pottersville, turning off at Blue Ridge.

In a couple of hours she was standing outside a cabin tucked away at the end of a long, rough path, with a sheltered view of part of the lake. The tall grey-black walls that formed a basin for the water rose sheer into the mist.

Heidi was wearing light walking boots, lined waterproof trousers, a fur trimmed black leather coat, leather gloves, and a voluminous white woollen hat which covered all but the area from her eyes to her chin. She had a capacious leather bag slung over her shoulder.

She stamped her feet with annoyance, and to assist her circulation. Addis wasn't home. The cabin was locked. Her breath spouted in a feather of steam as she breathed. The cold ached at her neck, and crept down the skin of her back.

Then she heard a noise inside. She moved along the porch trying to look in the windows, but each had a net curtain. The noise was like a child crying. Had she come to the wrong cabin? She recalled the reference points: this was certainly Addis's cabin. Was he inside, perhaps ill?

She saw a movement in the curtain. She moved nearer to the dirty windowpane: a white face looked out at her with big, shadowed, unseeing eyes.

Heidi was at first alarmed, then reassured. It was the face of a child, Downs Syndrome perhaps, mentally deficient. What she couldn't get was the connection with the Addis she knew, the tough ex-marine. The curtain dropped back into place.

A dog snarled behind her. Addis was walking toward her along the path, a bull terrier on a leash towing him, with a sack of groceries under one arm. He recognised her, gave his easy smile.

"I didn't expect to see you."

He reined in the growling, salivating dog, and stopped short of the porch, making no attempt to go inside. Wanting an explanation.

"It was safer to see you personally, Tom. I want you to do another job."

"I don't know about that, Heidi. I about done enough."

It went through Heidi Stoller's mind, that if she were to kill Tom Addis now, she would then be quite safe. That of course would leave Haffner. Haffner was more of a risk for Olsen. Haffner might not even be able to identify her conclusively.

In the pocket of her coat was a flat Walther PK 22. The small lead bullets had shock-points which spread on impact. Her gloved fingertips rested on the edge of the handle, inside her pocket.

But then there was the person inside the cabin who had looked out at her.

"Tom, I'm bloody well freezing out here. Please be kind enough to invite me inside, give me a drink, and let's talk."

Addis had grey bristles on his cheeks, and a look around his wrinkled eye sockets that still suggested calm shrewdness to Heidi. He showed little concern, and spoke in a low positive voice.

"We can do our talkin' out here."

"I saw the girl you've got inside," Heidi said. "What's the point of trying to conceal her?"

Addis looked round at the lake behind him. The wind whipped a pattern on the surface of the water. The light was fading as the clouds massed. There were flecks of rain in the air.

He flipped away the cigarette butt he had been chewing, reluctantly drew a key from his pocket, and stepped up to open the door.

Addis had lost the easy smiling eyes now. He looked as hard as granite with his silver head and cheeks, but Heidi felt she was boss.

The living room of the cabin was dark. Heidi walked into a wall of smells, stale body smells, damp clothing, rancid frying fat.

Addis lit a lamp. The girl was half lying on a couch. Her white face shone in contrast to her drab clothes. She moved, whimpered. Her hair was unwashed, and hung in sticky strings. Her legs and feet were bare in the cold. The dressing gown wrapped around her was half open on her bare breasts.

Heidi looked down at her, but the girl made no sign.

"She'll get cold even if she is stoned," Heidi said.

Addis didn't appear to listen. "I don't want any more work, Heidi.

Can we agree on that?"

"Give me a whiskey, please Tom. Who is she?"

But Heidi Stoller knew almost for sure who the girl was, although she'd never seen her. Addis busied himself at the sinkbench in the corner, reaching a bottle of Jack Daniels from the shelf, and filling two shot glasses.

He came swaying back toward her, offering a glass. "Straight up. You don't need to trouble yourself about her."

"It's Mariette Stevas," Heidi said, tipping the glass in her gloved fingers, taking a dignified but large swallow.

The girl heard her name, and looked round stupidly. She never spoke.

"Don't trouble yourself," Addis repeated heavily.

"Instead of doing what I paid you to do, you've messed around with her," Heidi said frigidly.

If the girl survived this she would be a menace to Heidi ... Heidi was thinking how the situation could be recouped.

She could kill Addis now, one shot a few inches from his face. Then the girl. Then leave the gun with Addis's prints on the handle. The gun was not traceable to her—second or third-hand, $500 from a junk shop in Harlem. It would look like murder, followed by suicide ...

She wanted to ask Addis what he did to Delia Marris before he killed *her*. After all her care to try to get Delia out of the country, Addis had betrayed her, Heidi, in that case as well. He must have delayed taking Delia to Mexico, and then killed her, giving Heidi the excuse that the FBI would have taken her if he hadn't acted.

She was seeing Addis in a new light. The stolid, unfeeling backwoodsman who could bring death as readily to a man as a bear—ideal for her purposes—was actually a sexual psychopath. His level, experienced stare had become a concussed look under Heidi's probing.

Heidi wasn't alarmed for herself, merely doubtful about what to do. What had begun as a simple mission to tidy up her activities by arranging to deal with Haffner, had become a complicated puzzle with dangerous implications.

She remained standing in the centre of the room, facing Addis, and looking from him to the girl. She finished the drink in a single hit.

"Whaddya want, Heidi, a refund?" Addis grinned.

The minutes were moving by relentlessly, and Heidi was conscious that the time of decision was with her. Her memory of Delia, and her understanding of what Delia, whom she really cared for, must have suffered, gave her pain.

She should simply kill Mariette now as a menace to her own freedom, but she couldn't. Delia and Mariette had both been abused beyond belief.

Heidi had never killed before, but it was a firm principle of hers that if she could give the orders, she must be capable of carrying out the deed personally. And she felt calmly able.

She had liked Tom Addis in a distant kind of way, admired the rock-like amorality of the man she thought he was, but now it would be a pleasure, a vindication of her feelings for Delia, to kill him.

But putting the Walther to Mariette's white forehead. No. She couldn't do that. It would be like killing Delia.

Heidi squared herself. Life was full of risks, and she'd have to take the risk of letting Mariette be. She would be out of the country before Mariette recovered enough to tell her story. She felt she still had a grip on Addis, and he would do her bidding.

"The business isn't finished, Tom. Finish it. It's as much in your interest as mine. You've let me down once. I want you to make sure you don't with Haffner. He's the last canary. Then we can all live quietly."

★ ★ ★

When Heidi let herself in to her New York apartment she experienced a sudden jolt—the break with the past. She faced a bare foyer of dusty marble, littered with packing cases.

It was what she had ordered: all her valuable rugs, antiques, paintings, furniture, crystal and silverware to be packed and stored. And now the sight of the shell, with only the drapes hanging in forlorn splendour, shocked her. The end of an era. A highly successful era.

She walked about on an inspection tour, her heels clicking unnaturally on the bare marble and polished wood floors.

When she went into the study, a woman in a white belted raincoat with long black wavy hair was sitting, legs crossed, on a box, sipping from a champagne glass. An opened bottle of Krug stood beside the woman. The woman wasn't looking at Heidi, but must have been aware of her approach.

Then Heidi saw the small, circular, gilt mirror on the wall beside an empty bookcase that the packers had forgotten. The woman was watching her in the mirror.

"Hullo, Ruth," Heidi said.

Ruth swung round toward her, and she could see the dark circles round Ruth's eyes.

"I thought I'd come and share a drink with you. I didn't realise you were leaving."

"I'm staying at a hotel right now. I got a good offer for the place, and thought I'd let it go. Get somewhere else—"

"Liar!" Ruth said, lighting a long gold cigarette. "You're running. Where to? Paris? Vienna?"

Heidi didn't attempt a denial. She had deliberately not been in touch with Ruth Charlton in recent weeks. She was beginning to find Ruth's devotion rather trying. But Ruth, to give her her due, had observed Heidi's rule not to make contact unless Heidi initiated it—until now.

"You shouldn't have come here. I was about to arrange a meeting for us. I haven't been able to do anything lately, because I've been out of town," Heidi said.

Ruth looked at her hollowly, without trust. "What's such a big deal about coming round for a drink? I thought you'd be pleased to see me."

Heidi could feel the hysteria building in Ruth, and had no wish to foster it. "Ruth, I am glad to see you. But I'm worried about the casual, unplanned contact, that's all."

She stepped forward and put an arm around Ruth's shoulders, smelling the lustrous hair that had once charmed her so much. Heidi kissed her cheek.

"I want you to go now."

"Are we going to meet?" Ruth asked in a plaintive, croaky voice.

"Sure," Heidi said, struggling to think of a secure place.

Chapter 55

Hayden had a meeting with Gerstein at his office in the FBI building later that day. Gerstein had a cagey look about him as Hayden entered. The anger had gone. He didn't get up.

"Siddown." He waved Hayden to a seat.

"I oughta arrest you," he said, "but I'll hear what you've got to say first."

Hayden decided to mount his own offensive instead. "I didn't know you were a friend of Jed Olsen's, Al. You should have told me. It would have explained a few things."

"Like what?"

"Like a certain reluctance to see Fairford in the frame for espionage."

"OK, so I got in to the High Trees Club through Olsen. That what you're on about? So did one of our directors. No secret about it in the FBI. A genuine gesture of thanks for our help in other matters. And I'll tell you, and don't you ever doubt me, if I've got evidence against Fairford or Olsen, I'll indict. Clear?"

Hayden nodded. He wanted to accept the assurance. He wanted, above all, to continue to work with Gerstein.

"Mike. You get in my gunsights with frolics of your own, and I'll blow your ass off."

Gerstein held out his hand.

"Peace, Al," Hayden said, touching the hand with his own.

Gerstein frowned. "Right, then. We got a line on the blonde. Surveillance of Charlton shows she visited a Central Park penthouse apartment recently. The place is owned by a sham company, but the occupant is Heidi Stoller, an IT consultant who runs a small company in New York producing tailor-made security software. Stoller fits the Reilly description."

It sounded like the woman they were chasing, right down to the connection with IT security.

"So the old gumshoe method pays off in the age of supertechnology. How are you going to handle it, Al?"

"Take her in. No frills. Reilly's testimony is no use, but it's a guide. Haffner should be able to identify. We'll get a photo to him as soon as we locate one. Bound to be something in the trade press."

"You'll get her for receiving and handling stolen property, but not murder. There's a circumstantial link with the killings, but no evidence," Hayden said, dissatisfied.

"Correct," Gerstein agreed. "But it's progress."

"You need the man."

"We do."

"You need to get Mariette back. She must have a story."

Chapter 56

Ruth Charlton turned slowly in front of the mirror, admiring the line of her peach silk gown, worked with silver motifs. It was a trifle too glitzy perhaps, but clinging, and luxurious.

And then she glanced at her diamond wristwatch for the third or fourth time in ten minutes. Heidi was late.

She looked around the spacious room without seeing it, the minimalist white of the ceiling and walls, the feeble watercolour paintings, the pale bedcover with gold threads. She pulled back the sheets and smoothed her hand along a pillow. Here, she would dream tonight with Heidi.

A doorbell rang in the next room. She touched her breast, and glanced one last time in the tall mirror. She forced a smile. Her face was so pale, her lips ruby red. She skipped through the connecting doors into the reception room, and opened the door to the passage.

The smile fell away frostily from her cheeks as two waiters in white jackets wheeled in a laden trolley, with champagne in an ice-bucket, and dishes under bulbous silver dish-covers. She fell back as the waiters began to lay the walnut dining table, bent to their task, affecting not to notice her.

Ruth retreated to the bedroom, closing the connecting doors until the waiters had gone. She checked her watch again. She returned to the reception room.

The silver and crystal had been set out on a white cloth, with table napkins, and plates for appetisers. The repast remained hidden by a variety of gleaming dish-covers. There was a faint smell of roast chicken and an indefinable sauce in the air. The lights had been switched off, and three candles had been lit.

The white-draped oval table looked like an elaborate coffin lying in state.

Ruth put her hand round the cold neck of the champagne bottle, ignoring the napkin, and poured herself a glassful. Cold water from the outside of the bottle ran down her wrist, and dripped on to her gown.

The wetness was like tears, but she could not cry. She felt a pain in her chest that was almost physical. She rushed the champagne into her mouth, and spluttered as the bubbles exploded in her nose. Her head and her heart were aching.

She sat on the couch as the darkness deepened, watching the coffin.

When she stood up, the champagne glass fell from her fingers, and rolled on the carpet. She crushed it with the long thin heel of her shoe. She remained for a while at the darkening window, looking down sixty floors to the Avenue of the Americas.

Ruth picked up the evening bag which lay on the sofa and opened it. It contained a money clip with a wad of dollars, her comb, a handkerchief, a makeup compact, and a small tooled leather case.

She opened the leather case and moved the ball of her thumb gently across a tiny engraved plate inside which read *To Ruth with love from H.* Then after looking for a moment at the elegant gold-plated manicure set, she removed a pair of scissors, needle-pointed, of fine surgical steel.

Ruth walked slowly through to the bedroom with the scissors. She drew the curtains and switched all the lamps on. She sat on the bed to compose herself. Then she turned, threw back the covers, slipped off her shoes, and lay down.

She didn't know how long she lay there, hours, looking at the ceiling, looking at nothing, and was finally unwilling to glance at her watch for the pain it would cause her.

She held one wrist in front of her while she ran a sharp point of the scissors shallowly across the flesh, watched the skin part, and a thin stream of blood begin to flow. Then she suddenly balled her fingers around the handles of the scissors, and gashed the wrist deeply.

It wasn't as painful as she expected. More surprising. A flood of blood pumped on to her chest, and splashed in her face.

She changed hands with the scissors, ignoring the flow, and slit the other wrist.

Now, both her wrists felt numb rather than hurt, and her blood ran warmly down her arms and soaked into her dress and formed strange patterns on the pristine white sheets.

She turned on her side, and drew back the covers on the other side of the king-size bed. Then she rolled over embracing the pillows on that side of the bed with a moan of desperation.

Chapter 57

Hayden sat in Gerstein's office, and looked out at the traffic hissing through the rain on 21st Street, sending up a fine moisture-laden mist of diesel fumes.

Gerstein was late and came into the room shedding water from his raincoat. He had a damp sheaf of papers in one hand. He had put out a national alert for Heidi Stoller with a watch on all airports and shipping lines.

"Bad news, I'm afraid, Mike. The NY boys didn't pick up Heidi. She's gone. Apartment empty. Her office doesn't exist. She sold out. We've talked to some of her ex staff. She was popular, paid well, and they have no beef. They say they know nothing of the company indulging in illegal information gathering or hacking. But they would say that."

Hayden was getting more concerned every day that the track to Mariette was getting colder.

"Anything on the killer?"

"A few sightings of the van, which can't really be verified. None of the sightings suggest any specific place like Broadway 9."

"Our only hope is that the killer may return to kill Haffner," Hayden said. "We stake him out like a goat."

Gerstein and Hayden were silently contemplating the brick walls they were up against when an agent called from the doorway, "More action from New York, boss. Ruth Charlton killed herself in a suite at the Hilton."

Gerstein scanned the transcript he had been handed, hungrily. "Jeez, some bizarre story about a dinner at which she was the only guest, and a blood-stained bed. But before she died, she recovered consciousness and her voice was recorded. Here take a look—"

Hayden read the script quickly: *I waited for you ... you lied to me ... you should have told me there was somebody else ... you couldn't have got away if I had wanted to keep you here, not with all your beloved baggage ... I don't want to hurt you, but I don't want to lose you—*

He had a glimpse of the depth of crazy passion Ruth had for

Heidi. "*Not with all your baggage*—what does that mean? Sounds like a threat."

"Well, in a kamikaze kind of way she could have stopped Heidi Stoller by calling us," Gerstein said.

"I guess that's what Charlton means. But why the reference to baggage? Emotional baggage? That wouldn't be a hindrance to escaping to another place, another country. Could it be actual physical baggage? Stoller seems to have gotten rid of her possessions. Suppose she was taking with her copies of the material she had bought from her informants?"

"It wouldn't be bulky. Could probably all be stored on few disks," Gerstein said.

★ ★ ★

Hayden was with Gerstein at the field office, when a call came in from the agent they had left at the secure house with Haffner: *We've got company.*

"How the fuck did the killer get on to this address?" Hayden asked as they were running for the cars.

"We'll check out who knew. There's a goddam leak somewhere," Gerstein said.

Hayden was thinking Karen Bridges, apart from Gerstein himself.

Hayden piled into his rental Mercedes, and followed Gerstein's FBI Ford, which also contained another pair of agents, and drove flat out to Frommer Park, where Haffner had been placed in a modernised apartment on the top floor of what used to be a run-down tenement building. The premises had been provided by Wayman, part of his company's executive accommodation.

The cars drew up outside the apartment building. It was built in the early part of the 20th century. Hayden followed Gerstein into a lobby with a checkered stone floor, a grey granite staircase, and high rococo plaster ceilings, all restored to their original condition.

Gerstein began to speak to the porter, when a curious mounting scream echoed around them.

There was a rush of wind, and the solid fleshy thunk of a soft and heavy object falling from a height.

At the foot of the stairwell was a crumpled body.

It was a man, on his back, with an arm and a leg bent beneath him as though they were the limbs of a doll. A stain of blood spread slowly on the pale marble beneath his head, and a rivulet ran from one nostril.

It wasn't Haffner.

The porter and the FBI men and Hayden were stilled for a moment.

A woman who had just entered the foyer with a shopping bag was quicker than any of them to approach the body. The man's eyes were half open, and his hawkish face relaxed. The porter hit the button on his phone for the ambulance.

"I think he's dead," the woman said.

"Ed Keenan," Gerstein said, naming one of his agents.

Hayden and two agents jumped into the modern elevator fitted out of sight behind the stairwell, and shot toward the tenth level top floor.

When Hayden came out of the elevator, there were only two doors, and the door of Haffner's apartment, number 101, was open. The passage was empty, except for a discarded loafer shoe lying on its side.

He ran through the open door and heard a moaning from a bedroom. He went in. An FBI agent was nursing a shoulder wound on the bed.

"I'm OK," the agent said, pointing to the closet. "So's Haffner. He's in there."

"The perp?"

"I winged the bastard. Fire escape."

Where was the fire escape? The agent on the bed was soaked in blood and nearly unconscious. The apartment was empty apart from a few signs of Haffner's transitory occupation, his jacket over a chair, a half-drunk cup of coffee on the dining room table.

Hayden rushed through to the kitchen and found the emergency exit. It was already ajar. He stepped out on to the metal rungs of the fire escape. He had a view down ten floors, but obstructed by the zigzag of steel ladders as the steps descended.

A thick-shouldered figure was moving down from the second level in blue denim overalls with a baseball cap.

Hayden began to descend. It was without thought, another Charge of the Light Brigade, like Broadway 9. His throat was swollen more with anxiety than effort. He could hardly breathe. His feet clattered and slipped, and his legs jarred painfully as he took the steps three and four at a time, missing some, stumbling, only supporting himself by tearing the skin off his palms on the rusted handrails.

By the time he hit the ground, falling on all fours in the mud with the trashcans, the killer had disappeared around the corner of the building.

There was a parking lot around the corner, and Hayden came at a run, but not knowing in which direction to go.

He could see at least three clean-cut young FBI men moving around amongst the vehicles, vainly trying to locate the killer. There was no blue van. Hardly any vehicles moved. The killer must be here, but he had vanished.

Then there was a shout from one of the men, muffled at the same time by the crisp snap of a handgun.

A car snarled, and swerved out of the lot a hundred yards away, leaving the agent prone on the ground.

★ ★ ★

Hayden in the Mercedes, and the other agents in their cars, vroomed out of the parking lot after the attacker's dented silver Toyota Corolla.

Hayden picked up the Toyota after three blocks by sheer luck, and kept it in sight way ahead.

Annoyed at being ill-equipped, Hayden had prepared himself for the kind of encounter he thought might come up—more in hope than with any conviction that it was necessary. He carried in the car a very sharp switchblade knife, a Colt Double Eagle 45 with a five-inch barrel and adjustable sights, a pair of night fieldglasses, and a pair of cuffs. And a pair of black Reebocks.

★ ★ ★

Hayden had the sense that the driver of the Toyota was heading back to the Adirondacks. He followed the Toyota at long distance on the straights, for three and a half hours, losing it occasionally, and then picking it up again, until he had to stop for gas on Interstate 87.

He didn't push too hard when he had filled the tank, and was back on the highway, because he figured the Toyota would stop too, and he'd overshoot.

He was tooling along at forty-five, thinking he had lost contact, when the Toyota came past him in the Glen Falls area.

Hayden planned to stay on the tail until he found the vicinity where the attacker went to ground. Then call Gerstein to search the area.

Hayden followed the attacker to Blue Ridge and then lost him around Cheney Pond. He tried to call Gerstein on his cellphone, but there was interference on the line.

He had a choice: go back to a gas station and make the call, or keep looking around.

He calculated there was plenty of time. The man would either be hunkered down for a few days, or at the very least until dawn—hours away. He idled the car slowly along the Ridge past the Indian Creek intersection.

There were a few cabins in off the road. He checked the entrances looking for parked vehicles. He found the Toyota a quarter of a mile away, up a short track, under a log shelter.

The man's cabin had to be somewhere near. He tried Gerstein again on the cellphone and got an earful of static.

Hayden decided to have a look. He put on the trainers, slipped the gun in the side pocket of his suit, stowed the knife, glasses, and cuffs in other pockets, and stepped out into the light, bitterly cold rain.

For a while Hayden staggered around in the dark and wet, sliding down banks, barking his shins on rocks, kicking over trashcans and disturbing dogs.

Where he could, he watched windows from a distance with the night glasses. Finally, near Newcomb Lake, when he was near giving up, he thought he had found the cabin.

He could see the silver bullet head moving about inside, the powerful swaying shoulders, under a naked light bulb. And Hayden had a painful glimpse of a girl he thought was Mariette, her head bowed like a nun.

Hayden knew then that he was going in there to take the man, and get Mariette.

Hayden moved closer. He expected a dog, and a bull terrier on a long lead came roaring at him out of the darkness. He closed with the dog, offered his forearm to it, felt the teeth bury in his flesh.

With his free hand, he swept the switchblade across the dog's throat, sunk the knife deep as the blood gushed in a warm stream down his legs. Then he thrust the blade to the hilt in one of the dog's eyes. The animal made a mewling noise as it collapsed, its jaws opening to release his arm reluctantly at the very last.

Hayden was standing still, smelling of blood and dog shit. The warm body across his feet. He changed his position, moving to the side of the cabin, by the front door.

The man opened the door of the cabin, and stood quietly on the porch, out of the light. He called the dog. Then he scooped up the chain which was fastened near to the door, and reeled it in.

The carcass of the dog, shining with blood, was dragged into the pool of light from the door. The man took a moment to assess what might have killed the animal, and dropped the chain.

"Stand still, man," Hayden said.

He touched the killer's small flat ear with the barrel of the Colt. It wasn't Hayden's choice of a moment to hold the man. It was the moment he had to take.

The man was rock still. He moved his shoulders slightly, said nothing. Hayden could smell the weed. The man was probably high.

"We're going inside. Turn round slowly. Feel the barrel close to your neck. Don't let me blow a big hole in your head."

The man shrugged and chuckled. "Whyn't you take me down. Squeeze, son. Squeeze."

It wasn't solely the dope. There was a coldness about the man. He seemed not to care. And Hayden realised that meant the man wouldn't hesitate to strike when he was ready. His left arm hung at his side, and Hayden could see a stained bandage wrapped around his bicep, protruding below the sleeve of his T-shirt. Hayden pushed the barrel of the Colt closer to the man's ear.

"I want you alive. You've got a big tab to pay. Especially for the girl."

"The girl? Whatsa problem? She loves me," he guffawed.

Hayden, rigid with fury, could have blown the killer's ear through his skull then, but a small voice inside him said, *Wait a minute. You can't let the words of a madman fire you.*

They eased into the cabin. Hayden kept the end of the barrel a couple of inches from the man's skull. It may have looked undignified as gun toting goes, but it was effective. The man spotted the uncertainty too.

"Yar an amateur, ain't you, son?" he said with fearless contempt.

Mariette was lying on the couch, her eyes half open, one delicate arm and hand trailing on the floor, her greasy hair across her half open eyes.

"She juiced," the man said.

"You can't pay enough for this," Hayden said, more to himself, than the killer.

"Whatzamatter? You the boyfriend? You wanna know what's been happenin' to your baby? Well, now you know she's been gettin' a helluva fine rocketing."

"If you say any more I'm going to kill you," Hayden said coldly.

"Whyn't you let me have that bullet you're achin' to let go, and then go fuck her yourself?"

Mariette let out a distracting cry.

The man chose that instant to move, while the words were scoring red trails in Hayden's mind, and Mariette's agony was in the air. Hayden squeezed the trigger in a surge of loathing, but the deafening shot ripped into the wall.

The man spun to face Hayden with a kind of rough amusement on his red face. He hit Hayden with his fist. It was like a fast moving rock, and Hayden fell, his vision in a grey haze.

★ ★ ★

Through the mist, Mariette saw him come in the door of the cabin, as she had seen the cold woman in the fur hat, but she knew he was different, he had come for her, and she knew him from a long time ago, Mike Hayden. She had been a prisoner for years, almost a lifetime. He was holding a gun on the killer now … it was happening like it was on an old black and white TV set she was watching, cloudy and grainy, and so far away she couldn't reach out and touch … she would be saved, and she cried out at the thought …

Chapter 58

When Hayden's head cleared, the man was on top of him, his knee across Hayden's throat. He seemed to be built of metal.

"Stay still while I fix you, motherfucker," the man said as he reached for a coil of thick nylon rope.

He trussed Hayden's wrists and ankles quickly, but awkwardly with his wounded arm, and left him panting on his side like a roped steer. Hayden was aware that the man was moving around briskly now, making preparations, although he never spoke.

After about five minutes, he said "Get on," to Mariette, and she went meekly out of the door, while the man untied Hayden's ankles, jerked him to his feet, and pushed him out of the door.

They were walking up a track beside the cabin, Mariette leading with a torch, then Hayden, and the man hanging on to Hayden's rope. They walked for twenty minutes through the trees, with the man cursing and urging hurry. Mariette put one tired leg in front of another, and never looked back or spoke.

They came to a clearing beside a two-strand wire boundary fence. In the clearing, under a tarpaulin, which the man stripped away, was a new five tonner Volvo diesel with plain grey sides, double doors at the rear and a built-in goods hoist. Hayden could make out a well-made track leading up beside the fence line.

The man jerked his chin at the cab door, and Mariette climbed in with the leather bag.

"You ain't gettin' in. In fact you ain't ridin' at all," he said to Hayden with a dry laugh.

Hayden's throat constricted. He thought the time had come for him to cross over. He frantically looked around for some way to save himself, but there was none. He was tightly tied at the end of a length of rope, held by a man whose weight and physical strength outmatched his own.

The man told him to get down in the mud. Hayden only dropped to his knees when the man raised his fist. He kicked Hayden over on to his side. Trussed like a turkey, there was no way to fight back.

Looping the rope around Hayden's ankles to hobble him, the killer changed the binding, strapping Hayden's arms to his sides. He was feeling pain from the gunshot, and his teeth were gritted. Then the man freed the hobble. He paid out about twenty or thirty feet of rope, and tied the end to an iron on the hoist at the rear of the truck, as Hayden climbed to his feet.

"You're goin' to get some runnin' practice, pardner."

"Why're you doing this?" Hayden said unable to keep the horror of anticipation out of his voice.

"I don't work with bullets mostly," he said, his voice calm and throaty. "I'm goin' to rough you up into good red meat on the mill road, and then feed you to a herd of pigs I know down near the highway. Goddam pigs eat anythin'. Nobody much'll recognise you then."

He swung into the cab of the truck with a vicious grin, and turned the engine over. With its cold valves clattering, the Volvo pulled away in low gear.

Hayden coughed through the smoke, felt his lead tighten, and began to move with the vehicle. He struggled in the bonds, trying to free his left hand. One mistake the killer had made in his dope haze was to fail to search Hayden. The bloody flick-knife was still in his trouser pocket.

In a few yards Hayden was pacing, and in a few more running, staggering occasionally as the truck changed gear and speed on the climb. When the road, which was compacted and metalled for forestry trailers, straightened, and the Volvo accelerated, Hayden lost his footing, and crashed over.

He tried to keep the binding around his arms and lower body as the cushion between his flesh, and the gravel which tore past him like a rasp. But the potholes in the road jogged him from one position to another. The small stones scraped his ears and cheeks, scoring and drawing blood.

The man put on more speed and adjusted his rear-view mirror to get a better view. Hayden had a flash of him sitting back in the cab, watching with half an eye as he drove, and a sadistic smile, shouting something to celebrate the success of his idea.

The tortured ropes were looser now, punished by the gravel, and Hayden, taking care to keep to the right of the road, out of vision of the rear-view mirror, had slid his hand into his trouser pocket and grasped the flick-knife.

Now the mill track seemed to be battering and burning Hayden at the same time, although he felt no actual pain, only explosions like mines in his head which became blacker, and blacker, wiping out his consciousness of the road beneath him.

He slashed at the bonds wildly, first cutting one, then feeling the rest come loose, and snake away from him. He was flung on to his face on the road.

The truck had come to a steeper slope, and changed to crawler gear, spewing out gravel as it tried to gain traction.

Hayden dragged his aching body to his feet, and ran after the truck.

★ ★ ★

Mariette could see the man stumbling and falling behind the truck as they climbed the hill, like a doll towed along by a careless child.

She took a towel from the bag beside her and unwrapped it. The world became clear and sharp when she was handling the contents of the towel. She picked up the hypodermic syringe, and inserted the needle into the rubber nozzle of the phial of heroin solution.

The man looked at her approvingly. "Go ahead," he said.

She tied the rubber tube tightly around her right arm until the veins, with their lines of small scabby sores, stood out. She brought the needle of the loaded syringe near a bulging vein. It was a precious moment. Before the needle entered she could anticipate the rush of ecstasy, feel the sunlit beauty of it, the freedom of turning slowly in space, the perfection, feel all her rasping pain dissolve …

She was sitting away from the man, working on her blind side in relation to him. But he was glancing at her face, when his mind wasn't on the road, urging her on, getting a rush himself from hers … but he couldn't see the tip of the needle touching the bruised skin, couldn't know the agony she suffered as she drew the needle away from the vein, leaving it pulsing, crying out, untouched. Taking the needle away was like tearing her flesh.

"Ah,ah,ah,ah," she sighed, her mouth falling open, as she rewrapped the loaded hypodermic in the towel. He was in pain from his arm, but he grinned.

"Good one, hey?"

★ ★ ★

Hayden ran furiously, and caught up with the truck as it moaned up the logging road. For about a minute he had a foothold on the rear step, and clung to the handles of the rear door, to get his wind back.

The choices were stark: Hang on here until the killer reached the pig farm, and take his chances then. Or tackle him now, try to stop the truck, a man in the driving seat with only one strong arm.

For Hayden, it wasn't a rational choice. It was a case of act now while he still had the strength.

He dropped off the back of the truck, and sprinted up the left hand side of the vehicle. The driver saw him coming, a torn and bloodied, wild-eyed assailant.

Hayden was on the running board before the driver had a chance to close the window, reaching both hands inside the cab and around the man's powerful neck. The man's left arm was too weak to thrust Hayden away.

★ ★ ★

Mariette sat swaying in the cab of the Volvo as it crept up the hill. She didn't know how long she waited until she let her hand drop to the bag at her side, opened the towel that rested on top of the other contents, and closed her fingers around the barrel of the hypodermic needle ...

Then Mike Hayden appeared at the driver's door, shouting like a madman, reaching in to try to throttle him into submission.

She withdrew the hypodermic on the blind side of the driver, and as he fought Hayden, she transferred it to her left hand, holding it like a dagger, and when his head turned away from her, she raised her arm ...

★ ★ ★

Then, suddenly, the truck swerved violently into the clay bank on the right side, grinding against the earth. And just as suddenly roared, and veered across the road in the opposite direction, as Hayden and the killer wrestled.

The Volvo plunged down a bank, through a small growth of saplings. Hayden felt the young trees beating at him. And then the vehicle was sliding on a scree slope, the stones on the slope running with them as the truck, which slewed sideways, threw Hayden off, and overturned, cartwheeling down to crash on a rock beside the stream at the foot of the hill.

Hayden was face down on a bed of dirt and stones. His whole body was red hot. The stones beneath his eyes were coated with his blood.

He sat up painfully. He could see the rear of the truck, on its side, ahead of him.

It was unnaturally quiet. No sound came from the woods. None from the vehicle, except the ticking sound of hot metal cooling. He knew then that he had been there only a short time, although it seemed like hours.

The distant clouds were still. The moon shone on the slope where he lay, and through the trees where the truck rested, to dapple its greyness.

Hayden inspected himself with alarm. Blood flowed freely inside the threads of his trousers and jacket. His shoulders and hips and back were lacerated. But he was sure his bones were not broken.

He got slowly to his feet, and moved gingerly toward the truck on his torn shoes. He prayed that Mariette had survived. He had to climb laboriously up the chassis to get to the passenger door of the cab. Eventually he stood upright on the cab, opened the door, and drew it back. Mariette was strapped in her seat, her pale face expressionless.

Hayden reached out a hand to touch her wrist and felt a pulse.

And at the same time he was looking past her, at the maniac who had done this, also strapped in his seat. His eyes were half open, his face in a kind of rictus, and his paws clasping the air. His head was slumped sideways.

Beside the fire extinguisher clipped under the dash was a flashlight. Hayden removed the flashlight, switched it on, and examined the cab more closely.

Mariette was alive and stirring mutely.

At first Hayden thought the killer had had a fit, and been paralysed in a crazed moment. Then in the beam of light he saw that there was something protruding from the base of the man's skull.

Hayden looked more carefully in the shadows. It was the barrel of a hypodermic syringe.

Chapter 59

Hayden got a blanket from the paramedics, wrapped himself in it, and remained down the slope near the truck when they lifted Mariette out, and took her to hospital. He wanted to know what was in the back of the truck.

The FBI agents decided to look before the vehicle was hauled back up the slope. Hayden was groggy with shock, and even with the blanket, he felt he was freezing. If he didn't cooperate, the paramedics threatened to fill him with morphine and take him away by force. But he insisted on waiting.

When they opened the rear doors, the FBI agents found the back filled with packing cases marked *Cabot Properties, Johannesburg—company records and files.*

As Hayden was helped into the ambulance, he said to Al Gerstein, barely able to phrase the words: "Do you think that could be the baggage Ruth Charlton was talking about?"

★ ★ ★

Hayden was at Mariette's bedside when she came round, dressings all over his skinned body—well hidden by his shirt and trousers—and a raw face, with dressings on his nose and cheeks.

She was in a sunny room in the ward, her face still that pale, unlined mask. The sky was clear blue, and only the bare branches of the tree outside suggested how cold it was out there.

The doctors had told Hayden that the detoxification for heroin would take about a week, with a long period of treatment afterwards to eliminate her dependency, and a lot of counselling to get her to live with what she had been through. Apart from loss of weight, she was otherwise in satisfactory physical health.

For a few minutes they sat together without speaking. Hayden took her hand, kissed her lips very gently.

"I can't remember all of it, but I can remember some of it, Mike. A bad dream ... but I didn't forget my job, and I want to make a report ..."

Hayden protested that this could all wait, but the hospital psychologist had a different view. He took Hayden aside as he was leaving.

"She's been talking to me about this. I understand she's some kind of intelligence agent. You know, she was probably kept alive by the determination to do her job. You ought to listen to her now. Even if it's no use to you. Let her talk. It'll do her good."

★ ★ ★

Gerstein reluctantly agreed, and a day later they assembled around Mariette's bedside with a tape recorder.

Mariette was very professional, and made little of her own suffering as she told her story, from being picked up at the point of a knife, in the car park of her apartment house, to the desperation which led her to plunge a hypodermic syringe loaded with heroin into the base of Addis's brain.

She said she realised she was a toy to Addis, and if she didn't play along, he would kill her. In the first days, she was so sedated that she could not do anything, although she could often understand what was happening around her. She was waiting for her opportunity to get the wary Addis.

Addis boasted to her of his exploits—Bray, Leman, Delia Marris. His last mission was supposed to be driving the truck to Boston where the goods inside were to be shipped, but Heidi Stoller had appeared, and wanted Addis to deal with Haffner.

"Did you know what the goods were?" Hayden asked.

"I heard they were the hard copy, tapes and disks from WayCom's back-up store at Rochester. Addis was particularly amused by it. Apparently the store was robbed and burned, but officially it was a fire that destroyed everything, not a robbery. Those in the know were paid off," Mariette said.

Gerstein nodded: "The cargo in the truck has been identified by Karen Bridges. It's the back-up material, right enough."

Hayden was thinking that Al Gerstein's cursory FBI investigation had failed to discover this, and there had been a ready acceptance by Karen Bridges that all the back-up material had been burned. And there were a few other things about Karen, like the internal videos which didn't work at critical moments, her blast-them-to-hell attitude when they were in pursuit of Addis, the raid on Haffner at the Bowen, the blowing of Haffner's hideout.

Mariette positively identified Heidi Stoller as Addis's boss. When she had finished she was exhausted, but pleased.

But Hayden came away from the hospital with two names irritating his mind like sand in an oyster: Al Gerstein, and Karen Bridges.

★ ★ ★

Hayden was at the FBI operations room on 21st Street, watching and listening to the reports coming in on the search for Heidi Stoller.

He didn't seriously expect her to be picked up. He thought she was too clever, and the *most wanted* system for catching criminals was easy to walk through. There were a few flurries when possible sightings of Heidi at a railroad or port were made, but these were soon run to ground.

In Syracuse they could do nothing but watch and wait.

The duty agent came into the room, and said, "Here's something hopeful. A report from the Loudonville Aero Club, operating out of Albany County Airport. Seems a woman chartered an aircraft for Mexico City. Problems about the flight plan due to storms. Weather held up the takeoff. The woman wouldn't wait, and changed the flight plan to Hancock. She'll be airborne soon. All we have is a young woman. Not even a blonde."

"I bet she's dyed her hair," Hayden said.

"We'll have a squad at Hancock when she lands," Gerstein said, unimpressed.

Chapter 60

Olsen had worked hard, as his spin doctor insisted, on recreating a speaking terms relationship with his ex-wife and daughter.

The scene at the Milstein's, the family argument, might be misinterpreted, the PR man insisted. Some influential people might see Olsen as a man of bad temper, one who lets his words fly when the pressure is on.

Olsen could help to correct that impression by being seen to be friendly with both Diana and Sherry.

Olsen was a skilful actor. He bit back the gall in his throat, and astutely worked his softest and most apologetic telephone manner on Diana and Sherry over a period of days. They eventually agreed to accept his invitation to a house party at Springvale, an annual post-Thanksgiving party, when Olsen repaid the more generous hospitality he had received during the year, and courted people he wanted to influence.

It was no secret that Olsen was being pushed to enter the Senate, or that he was thought of as a future Presidential candidate. And on this occasion he was entertaining the people who were pledging their support in the forthcoming Senate race.

It was virtually accepted in this part of the State that if Olsen were to declare his candidacy, he would get the nomination and take the seat. The elderly present incumbent, who had already agreed to endorse Olsen, was exactly the same class and political colouring. The pair differed only in age—and perhaps beauty, because Olsen had that necessary modern quality of the politician, alpha male charisma.

The party took its usual form. Riding and clay pigeon shooting on the estate, or golf at the nearby High Trees Club on the Saturday, with bridge, poker and billiards at the house for those who found it too chilly out of doors. The day was followed by a lavish dinner and speeches at Springvale in the evening.

To Olsen's mind, the day had gone well. He had ridden a little on one of his thoroughbreds, and played nine holes—always choosing his company carefully, and making his points.

Now he sat at the head of the table in the dining room, under the sparkling chandeliers, sipping a dry white wine with his pâté foie gras. His guests were lined out before him, the men in tuxedos, and the women in shimmering gowns, until they faded into the shadows at the far end of the table.

It was a moment when he appreciated the adrenalin of influence. In this room were a number of the people, businessmen, generals, politicians, administrators, who controlled America. And they were paying homage to him.

Olsen had soon put behind him his disappointment about the Defense Committee hearing. He reconciled himself to Cerillo's advice. A battle lost, but the war would go on. Diana, looking particularly dazzling, was seated quite close. This he had arranged carefully. Sherry, too was seated near, with two of the younger men—there were not many young men. His first thought was that it was absurd that Sherry, a kid, should be present at all. But his PR adviser said it showed he was treating Sherry like an adult.

It took the butler a few seconds to get his master's attention, so enthralled was Olsen with the snatches of conversation, the jokes, the heady atmosphere of exquisite food smells and wine and women's perfume.

"There's somebody to see you, sir. I'm sorry, the person insists."

When Olsen finally took on the import of this message, he was incredulous. "I *can't* be interrupted," he blurted out of the corner of his mouth.

The butler wilted before the stare from the bloodshot, slightly prominent blue eyes. He marched out of the room.

"Damn fool!" Olsen laughed quietly, and then began to ease himself back into the interchanges going on before him, like retuning a radio.

But in hardly more than a minute, the butler reappeared with a note. "I'm dreadfully sorry to disturb you sir, but the person insisted."

Olsen found the intrusion unbelievable. His colour mounted. He snatched the note.

He became aware that Diana was looking at him, her stare fixed like a damned spy telescope. He pulled his glasses from an inside pocket, and put them on deliberately. The note was only a few neatly pencilled words. *You need to see me now. HS.*

The buzz and the aroma of the dinner began to subside in him like an outgoing tide, leaving stones and shingle and grating sand. He controlled his facial muscles.

His eyes flicked back to Diana. A small frown had appeared between her brows. She was reading his thoughts, the cow.

Olsen nodded gently to the butler, replaced his glasses slowly, and with a chill smile excused himself from the guests beside him.

In the anteroom, the butler told him the lady was waiting in the study. He strode through, entering the room and closing the door carefully behind him.

"What the hell have you come here for?" he snarled, as Heidi Stoller rose from a chair beside the walnut desk.

He had never seen her like this. She wore a black silk anorak and trousers and black Eccos on her feet. Her hair was tucked under a black baseball cap. She removed the dark shades she was wearing.

"Because if I phoned you, somebody would pick up the call. Believe me, this is the best way to communicate, Jed."

"Our business is over," Olsen said, trying to grapple with a turgid background of activity he had relegated to oblivion in his mind.

"Not quite. I want to use the cabin for a week, maybe two. The FBI are looking for me. Making it very hot. When I can, I'll slip away without bothering you."

"But I can't guarantee you'll be undisturbed up there!"

"It's your problem. Do it. I'll need food, blankets. You don't want me taken, do you?" Her voice was commanding, her question rhetorical.

Olsen paused to think what that might mean, his face now mottled blue-red. "What *happened*—"

"Ruth Charlton blew my cover. And the hardball I paid to fix Haffner, failed. He killed an FBI man by mistake. Haffner survived, and his testimony is still available, Jed, and in FBI hands."

"Jesus! But Haffner knows nothing positive from me about our operations," Olsen said, pouring a large Scotch out of the decanter on the table, into one of the crystal glasses ranged round it, his hand shaking slightly.

"Exactly. He's a storm you can probably weather."

"*Probably*, for fuck's sake!" Olsen spat, with visions of the shining monolith that was his life and career crumbling.

"Since you're not offering." Heidi Stoller helped herself to an equally large drink. "One good thing, Addis, the man I arranged to deal with Haffner, is dead. But a little mouse of an undercover agent has survived. She doesn't connect with you, but she can identify me."

Olsen was thinking that Heidi Stoller was a menace to him.

Without her, there would only be Haffner, a storm he could probably weather.

"OK. Get up to the cabin. I'll bring food and blankets, and try to keep others away. You might have to disappear into the woods if somebody comes ... What a fuck up!"

"Look at the bright side, Jed. You're nearly up there with Wayman in your research. We have to fold our tent now. That's the way it goes. Human error. Don't lose your nerve Mr President."

She even had a slight smile as Olsen let her out of a side door, into the darkness.

★ ★ ★

Hayden called Al Gerstein in his car about a couple of hours later. Gerstein was reluctant to talk, so Hayden knew he was on to something.

"You didn't actually arrest her at Hancock?"

"Didn't need to. We had her cold. Weren't entirely sure it was her. Disguised. Differently dressed, you know. We followed her. She hired a car and drove to Springvale."

"Olsen's place?"

"Yeah. Holed up at a vacant farm worker's cabin. Seems to have the entree."

"So now you know it's her?"

"Yeah. We'll move in and take her."

"What about Olsen?"

"Leave that to me. Listen, I got work to do. Your client will get the information he's entitled to when we can give it."

★ ★ ★

Before he returned to his guests, Olsen went into the bathroom to reassure himself about his appearance.

He was shocked at the image in the mirror, the purple sheen of his cheeks, the yellowness of his eyeballs. The skin seemed to have tightened on his forehead and jaw, and plunged into cavernous holes around his eyesockets. For a second he could see the skull, with staring dead eyes like marbles.

He washed his face in warm water, applied a skin conditioner and then a dab of cologne. He needed only to pat the waves in his hair with his fingertips, but even that luxurious growth looked dry and grey.

He fixed a smile, and walked in to the dining room to his seat. As he sat down apologising, he saw Diana watching him again, as if she could read his damned mind. She seemed to understand something was wrong.

At least Sherry was too busy with the men to notice. Those immediately near seemed oblivious. Senator Harbord, at his elbow, half dozed. The Senator's youngish and stupid wife on Olsen's left was giggling and untroubled.

While he re-engaged half-heartedly with the chatter, Olsen began to sum up the danger he was facing. The connection between him and Heidi Stoller was made if he harboured her on his estate. If she was caught alive, he would have no chance. It would be the end. He shuddered.

The thought of killing her came quickly through the bubbling of conversations. It was her life or his. While he was forking salad into his mouth, pretending to an appetite he did not have, he was thinking how to kill Heidi Stoller. It would be something he would have to do himself. Too late to engage help, and too dangerous. Shoot her, and bury her deep.

He wasn't sure he had the balls to do that, or if he should wait and chance that she would get away.

For Olsen, the dinner became a ritual of torment, as it dragged through the dessert and coffee to the brandy and liqueurs, and finally, speeches.

The loud voices and platitudes needled his ears. The rich food balled up in his stomach and made him feel like retching. And all the while his thoughts were on how to deal with Heidi Stoller.

When his own turn came to make a speech, the event of the evening, the informal acceptance speech for his candidature, the witty aphoristic script which he had carefully drafted and memorised went out of his mind.

At first he tried to follow the draft he had written, seizing on the phrases that came out of the mist to him—but they made nonsense, and he had the sense to thank his benefactors, and sit down. He did not even announce his candidature. The applause was mild, and there was a consciousness amongst those near him that he was either unwell or had had a little too much to drink.

Diane Wayman actually rose from her seat, came to him, and put her hand on his arm. "Jed, are you all right? Do you want to lie down?"

"Of course I'm fine, woman!" he groaned under his breath, pushing her arm away, and starting up from the chair.

Some nearer guests sensed the awkwardness of the moment, and looked at him.

In that second, Olsen saw two young men in dark business suits by the door at the far end of the room. They just stood there, looking at him. The butler approached Olsen, looking startled.

"Pardon me, sir. Could you step outside again? There are men here to see you," he muttered discreetly.

"Tell them to go away!" Olsen said sharply. "I'm entertaining, can't you see that—"

The butler spoke quietly but fiercely: "It's the FBI, sir. They have said unless you come outside, they will have to come in and get you." Diane Wayman had fallen back a step or two, but she had heard.

"For God's sake Jed, see what they want, please. Come and *get* you? What does that mean? What's happening? We can all wait, we're OK. Look, I'll come with you."

She attempted to take his arm again.

"You stay out of this," he slurred.

Olsen went unsteadily down the room while some of his puzzled guests looked on. One or two got up, and followed him offering help, and by the time they reached the anteroom, there were half a dozen worried people, including Diane Wayman, Sherry, and Byron Cerillo, gathered around Olsen.

Gerstein, lumpy, jaundiced, and grim in the night light, was obviously the leader of the younger men in dark suits. He looked uncertainly at Olsen's supporters, unsure whether to speak in front of them, or ask for privacy. Olsen swayed in front of him, eyes burning, and Gerstein knew there was no more time for palliatives.

He put it as delicately as he could.

"Mr Olsen, we have evidence linking you with espionage at WayCom Inc, and with the deaths of two of their executives, and another staff member. We have just arrested another person similarly involved, Heidi Stoller, on this property, and I'm going to have to ask you to come with me—"

"Oh, Jed!" Diana Wayman said disgustedly.

"Call your lawyer, Jed," Cerillo said.

The rest of the onlookers fell back in shock. Sherry, silent in confusion up to now, squealed, and flung herself forward against her father.

"Daddy, Daddy, how could you hate Vance so much! How *could* you?"

As Olsen unwrapped his daughter's arms from his shoulders without looking at her, he thought her touch wasn't the cuddling affection of a daughter, but more like the reserved compassion of a carer for a sick person. And he wasn't sick.

Olsen, stone-faced, excused himself to call his lawyer, and get his billfold and keys.

When one of the young agents made a move to follow him, Gerstein nodded his head at the man to signal privacy.

★ ★ ★

Once inside his study, Olsen moved purposefully. The desk lamp was on, throwing a white glow down on the table with its papers, and a soft green glow upwards over the shelves of books, to the corniced ceiling.

He extracted, from the open gun cabinet, his double-barrelled Burlington shotgun. Even now, as he grasped the stock, he could appreciate the balance between the twin blue steel barrels, and the butt with its chased silver inlay.

In the draw by the desk he kept a few spare cartridges, in case he ever had to deal with an intruder. He broke the stock, and pushed one red cylinder case with its shiny brass base into one of the twin chambers, snapping the chambers closed, and releasing the safety catch.

From the coat-stand by the door, he took a malacca walking stick with an angled handle like the letter L. He rested the butt of the Burlington on the cushion of his swivel chair, and positioned the handle of the stick loosely in the trigger guard. He had one hand around the end of the barrels, and one hand gently on the reverse end of the walking stick.

Olsen's movements had been unhesitating, and had taken hardly more than a minute. Now he stepped up to complete the sequence.

He was not a man who had given any thought to taking his own life. He had believed he could survive anything. He had never lost a second's sleep in spoiling or disposing of the lives of others. But now he was conscious that he had surely fallen from a great pinnacle, with a Senate seat and perhaps even the Presidency within his grasp, and he would go down and down into utter shame and disgrace.

It was worse than death.

He reached his mouth toward the cold barrels of the shotgun, tasted the oily bitterness, and pressed the stick against the trigger—

★ ★ ★

Gerstein hadn't slept for twenty-four hours, and he now looked more like a waxwork image than a human being. His face was dark and immobile as Hayden faced him across the desk in the field office.

"It's been a night of disasters," Gerstein said in a thick, clotted voice.

He toked heavily on a cigarette. He was recalling the Olsen guests who stood around in the anteroom, their eyes glazed, their bright talk evaporated, waiting for their host to speak to his lawyer, and make himself ready to go with the FBI. It was one of those anxious, timeless eternities.

Then they had heard the gunshot. Full and loud enough to put pressure on the ears. And reverberating, if that wasn't imagination.

Gerstein had been first in the door of the study, letting out the billow of acrid smoke, seeing the splash of Olsen's brains on the delicate cream wall, watching the chips of bone and flesh run down the wallpaper.

And the would-be-Senator himself collapsed on the floor, a mere memory in the elegant way he used to move his limbs. The face itself untouched, sincere looking.

"Will there be any sort of inquiry or complaint about your handling of the arrest?" Hayden asked.

"I doubt it. Olsen was due a certain amount of courtesy. He hadn't been charged."

"What about Stoller?"

"Trouble about that. Bad trouble. I may be sent to Moscow. I left her in custody of two junior agents. She was a hundred and twenty pound woman, for fuck's sake. Two big guys couldn't manage her! Shit. We shoulda had a woman with us. Maybe she'd a reminded us to look up Stoller's pussy."

Taking Heidi when they first staked out the cabin had been easy. Gerstein had a force of eight, apart from himself. They had followed Heidi from the airfield to the farmhouse, taken their positions, moved quietly in. And pounced. Copybook stuff.

"In the final rush, Stoller didn't even fire a weapon. She gave up. We cuffed her. Held her in the living room at the farmhouse, while I dealt with Olsen. It was too too fuckin' easy with us big men, and this frail woman."

Gerstein was thinking of his heavy-hearted return to the farmhouse after Olsen's death, the car lurching around on the farm roads in the dark. Getting out of the car at the cabin. Realising oddly that there was no movement from within the cabin. Going warily to the doorway and looking in.

Seeing one agent, Berg, pallid on the floor with blood flowing from his chest, and running across the bare wooden planks making a curving course like a river seen from an aircraft.

Unslinging their guns at the sight of him, and moving in. The house creaking, but quiet.

In the passage: the suited legs of an agent sticking out of the doorway of the lavatory. Shiny shoes edged with mud from the path.

Agent Burns was resting with his head against the john, his throat cut from ear to ear, his chest as red as a cardinal's. On the floor were the open cuffs.

Heidi Stoller had fled, moved into the darkness of the trees.

It had taken an hour to get dogs, but searching dense woods in the dark, with or without dogs was hopeless. When dawn came, all they could think of was a chopper, more dogs, and wider sweeps.

No luck. Only mud, spattered up to their elbows, and wet feet, and curses.

"How did she do it? Could you work it out?" Hayden asked.

"Berg told us enough. He'll survive. She persuaded Burns she had to have a shit. Yeah, a shit. Difficult to shit with cuffs on if you're fully dressed, unless you're not particular. Burns, the gentleman sucker, took her cuffs off, and stood outside the door," Gerstein said, shaking a heavy head.

"Yeah?" Hayden said. "If he'd pulled her pants down and held her over the john and wiped her ass afterwards, he'd have been accused of indecency."

"I guess so. One little woman inside the box. One big man outside. She came out with a smile of appreciation, and cut Burns' throat as she did. Berg said she came through to the living room silent as a cat, and was on his chest with the knife before he could move."

★ ★ ★

Hayden and Mariette were on his roof terrace at lunchtime. He had fixed tuna and cucumber sandwiches, and a glass of crisp Sauternes. Mariette was watching the grey clouds scudding over, and the whining airliners. She looked good. A little gaunt, but otherwise sparkling. Hayden thought she was very sexy, somehow older, but other than snuggle up to her on the couch after dinner in the evenings, he'd let her be.

Hayden brought Mariette back to his apartment for a few days each week from the time she was discharged from hospital. The rest of the time, she spent with her parents, being spoiled at their home in Rhode Island. Her psychologist was clear that discussing the case with her helped her to live with the past, and as a witness and an agent herself, she had a real urge to contribute.

Hayden had told her his thoughts. He now had what he needed to launch a billion dollar lawsuit against Fairford for exemplary damages. Wayman was a very satisfied client. From the point of view of this action, it was unsatisfactory that Heidi Stoller was at large, but not fatal. With Mariette and Haffner as the chief witnesses, a sufficient picture of what happened would emerge.

Hayden reckoned he had been wrong about Albert Gerstein. Gerstein took a favour from Olsen, the High Trees membership, and he was sometimes dilatory in the investigation, but that was about all. After all that had happened, Hayden had to credit him with being a loyal, if not very brilliant, FBI man.

But Hayden's suspicions about Karen Bridges were not allayed. He wondered if she was the inside contact. The sure-footed way Heidi Stoller had moved suggested inside knowledge.

Mariette was inclined to agree. "I feel there were probably other inside contacts, otherwise it wouldn't have worked as smoothly as it did, but I can't name anybody," she said. "Why don't you talk discreetly to Karen. See if she reacts."

"She's one armour-plated broad. I don't know I'd get very far."

"What else can you do?"

★ ★ ★

Karen and Hayden would have to do a lot of work together to get the case against Fairford into court, and he decided to accept Mariette's suggestion, and test his suspicions.

He had a meeting with Karen and others at WayCom to discuss preparations for the lawsuit. When he went into her office unannounced, he noticed she had a folder of airline tickets on her desk. She pushed them into a drawer when she saw him.

"Going away?" Hayden asked. He meant it as a pleasant conversational opening.

"Just a vacation," she said brusquely.

"Yeah. Good idea. I might hop down to the Caribbean myself for a week. Where are you off to?"

"Oh, Florida," she said hesitantly. "I want to rest and think a few things over."

Hayden thought she was alluding gloomily to their brief connection, using it to embarrass him, and he veered away.

He talked about the case, how it was working out. Then he

mentioned the thought he shared with Mariette, that there was an insider, or perhaps more than one.

Karen deliberated quite seriously about Heidi's other inside contacts for a moment. "I guess you're right. There probably are contacts we don't know that oiled the wheels."

"The internal video debacle, for example."

"I think that was a coincidence."

Hayden took this grudgingly.

"You think *I* did it?"

"It was your responsibility."

"Yes, it *was* my fucking responsibility," she glowered.

"And the way Leman's house was cleaned up—PCs and papers taken after his death."

"I'm not making an apology for recovering my employer's confidential property."

The big spur to Hayden's suspicions was the raid on the Rochester store which had been disguised as a fire. Hayden had Stella and Cathy Ong review all their information on that, and every time he came up with the conclusion that a really thorough examination of the debris—forensic tests—would have revealed that the debris wasn't genuine, and that the real records must have been removed.

If Gerstein failed here, Karen Bridges really failed too.

"The quick, glib acceptance that there had been a fire at Rochester, and nothing was missing," Hayden said.

"I made a mistake, you dope. Maybe I should have insisted on more tests, but what I had seemed conclusive. We weren't looking at a robbery, were we?"

Karen was seething, and whether it was the right moment or not, Hayden decided to take her over the edge.

"You could be the girlfriend couldn't you?" he said with a wry smile.

"What do you mean?" Karen's brow wrinkled.

"Heidi Stoller's girlfriend. The one Ruth Charlton was jealous of."

Karen's dour, steamy temper was suddenly replaced by a brightness, a liveliness, as though Hayden had dug his finger in her ribs.

She didn't speak, but her eyes widened, and her breasts rose. Then she giggled, trying to hold it back, her eyes fixed wonderingly on his. And she laughed, her eyes glistening, still fixed on him, and finally she crumpled up helplessly, gasping.

"Oh, Mike, you fool! You need a psychiatrist, shock treatment!"

She flung her arms around his neck. "You're seriously loony, you know?"

* * *

Back at the Bowen, Hayden called Al Gerstein and persuaded him to get Stella to find out where Karen was going. He had noticed from the cover of the ticket wallet that Karen was flying United.

Within a day, Gerstein rang and told him she had a first class ticket for Johannesburg. Not Florida.

"That's a single, Mike. She ain't coming back in the forseeable."

"This is important, Al. We can stop her."

"Too late. She's gone."

"Why the fuck didn't you get back to me sooner? A day to get info you could have produced in a couple of hours."

"One, because I don't work for you, counsellor. Two, because we couldn't stop Karen anyway."

"Don't give me that shit, Al. Karen is circumstantially involved in screwing up the investigation on at least a half a dozen points—"

The line was dead. Gerstein had cut off. Hayden made a face at the receiver and replaced it.

* * *

When Hayden arrived back in Washington, he took Mariette to dinner at Enrico's on K. She still picked at her food, but he was doing what he could to encourage her appetite with Maine crab, and cold gin and lime to help it down.

"You're not happy about the case are you?" she said.

"I've got a happy client, a big lawsuit which will be settled generously out of court, the psychopath Addis got his, Olsen capped himself—"

"That's a good score, Mike."

"Maybe." He described his meeting with Karen Bridges.

"Perhaps she's not involved. I mean, that reaction to being the girlfriend. But I suppose she could be a good actress."

"Why should she lie? Florida instead of Johannesburg, home of Zosmark," Hayden pressed.

"Right, with connections to Leman and Heidi Stoller. But Mike, people sometimes lie for all sorts of little personal reasons we don't know."

* * *

When Hayden got in to the office about ten on Monday morning, he found to his surprise that Cathy Ong wasn't in. She was usually there every morning by eight-thirty. He had a briefcase-full of instructions he wanted to give her. He got his secretary to chase Cathy on her cellphone, but it was turned off. Her answering machine at her apartment was turned off too.

Hayden was still troubled by the rough edges in the case, Karen's flight, Gerstein's tardiness. He had a sense that they had lifted a stone, revealed some of the crawling things, and then dropped it back.

He was worried that something bad could have happened to Cathy, and he sent one of the office's investigators over to her apartment. The PI called him back in an hour.

"Hey, Mike. Check out the address you gave me will you? The apartment's vacant. It's for letting. I called the agents. Tenant moved out yesterday. They're doing a cleanup today. Prospective tenants can view tomorrow."

Hayden had a let-down feeling, like one of those drops in an airliner making landing approach in bad weather.

He verified the address to the PI. There was no mistake. For letting! Christ! He got Cathy's CV and references on screen, and called Gerstein. "Al, can you get Stella to verify all this data?"

By three in the afternoon, Stella had confirmed that Cathy Ong was the brilliant student at Fordham that they all thought she was. Her references were genuine. But her parents, and the condo in San Diego, were a myth. And the pre Law School educational record showed that she was a graduate not of a Californian high school, as they had all assumed, but of the American School in Peking.

It began to come clear to Hayden, the uncanny prescience of Heidi Stoller and her allies.

He had a later call from Gerstein, faintly amused.

"It's a funny life, Mike. We did another trawl of the airlines. Cathy Ong flew to Mexico City yesterday, in her own name on a Chinese passport, first class by American Airlines, and onward to Shanghai."

"Thanks, Al. I guess if you want to eat noodles with Heidi Stoller, you can take a walk along the Bund."